MURDER ON THE MOUNT

MURDER ON THE MOUNT

A JACK PRESTER MYSTERY

SANDY DENGLER

MOODY PRESS
CHICAGO

ISBN: 0-8024-2178-4

1 3 5 7 9 10 8 6 4 2

Printed in the United States of America

Contents

1

Angels We Have
Heard on High

The last thing John Getz saw as he lay dying was the Bigfoot. It had to be nine feet high. In the light of the quarter moon it loomed as big as a house directly over him. Wide. So wide. And it stank. John's nostrils, his lungs, his throat and mouth were filling with foamy blood, and still he could smell its stench.

They stared at each other, frozen inside the moment. Then the Bigfoot, like a crazed gorilla, leaned down toward him. Its massive paws were coming at him. He raised his arm in a feeble attempt to protect himself. It was his final act.

* * *

Tony Bennett lost his heart in San Francisco. Jack Prester lost his stomach in Elbe, Washington.

It happened again seven miles up the road at the Ashford Market, which boasted restrooms on its marquee. He barely made it to the office of GSI, the concessioners serving Mount Rainier National Park, farther up the highway. Whatever the cause of this—to put it delicately—gastrointestinal distress, it was nailing him good.

He used the facilities at the Nisqually Entrance of Mount Rainier. At Longmire, fifteen minutes uphill from the entrance, he stumbled downstairs to the basement restrooms in the administration building. Finally, praying for respite, he sought out the chief ranger's secretary.

Slim as a pencil, Kerri Haskell was an older lady with altogether too much good cheer for Jack's wilted spirits. Her lean build and short-cropped salt-and-pepper hair kept her from looking like the motherly type. Too bad. Jack could use a mother right now.

He forced a smile. "Dr. John Prester. Investigator at large assigned to the John Getz murder. I'm supposed to pick up a key." Talk about being out of it—that's not at all what he wanted to say, or ought to say. It just came blurting out.

She fished in a side desk drawer. "Dr. Prester, you look like you're ready to die."

"An hour ago I was afraid I might. Now I'm afraid I won't."

She burst out laughing. "Oh, I hear you! The stomach flu's been going around. I had it myself a couple days ago. You have all the pity I can muster. Here. I'll help you set up. Come on."

Jack would take any help coming. Meekly, and feeling the need for a restroom once again, he followed her out into the December cold.

At one time, Longmire had been the only settlement in Mount Rainier National Park. It had always existed to serve the tourists. Perched at about twenty-seven hundred feet elevation on Mount Rainier's craggy flank, it still contained a lot of old buildings from the golden age of parks, the twenties and thirties—rough brown houses, a huge, blocky, log-and-riverstone administration building, the Longmire Inn, the natural history museum, a cramped little gas station. All these nestled beneath a dark, dense stand of Douglas firs and hemlocks.

Jack followed the secretary across the street to a row of clapboard apartment units that had to date from CCC days. Such residences tended to be drafty, impossible to heat, and always on the verge of being carried off by pack-rats. Right now he didn't care.

She opened the door to the second unit in the row, a small one-room apartment with the kitchenette, table, and chairs by the front door and the double bed by the back door. Jack headed for the bathroom. By the time he had checked out the plumbing, she had opened the curtains and turned up the thermostat.

"Where are your bags? I'll bring them in for you."

Jack flopped face down on the bed. The springs squawked in protest. "The backpack in the jump box." He closed his weary, burning eyes. What an end for a two-day marathon drive. *Bleh.*

Gruesomely effervescent, Ms. Haskell pressed on undaunted. "You have telephone service—your number's on the set. And here are keys. We gave you an M-1—it will get you into the admin building for the fax and copier, as well as the gates and everything." They clunked on the table. "And a radio. It's right there on the nightstand. You're 901. Are you listening?"

"I'm 901." He had seen the handy-talkie perched primly there in its charger, the charger's red light glowing, and it hadn't registered. Listening, yes. Perceiving, hardly.

"I'll bring over the incident reports and supplementals we have so far. And may I have your keys? I'll put your truck outside the front door here. You're in a no-parking zone."

Jack fumbled his keys and lay very still with his eyes shut. The door clicked open. The door clicked closed. The door clicked open.

"There's a huge black dog in the cab of your truck. Is he—you know—does he defend his turf?"

Jack didn't move. "Nah. He doesn't give a rip about my stuff. He only defends his stuff. He shows burglars where my silver's hidden; just stay out of his dog treats. His name's Maxx." He had better warn her, though. "He licks."

9

The door clicked closed.

A few minutes later it clicked open. One hundred fifteen pounds of rambunctious black Labrador retriever bounded across the room, thundering like a buffalo stampede.

Jack opened his eyes. A slurpy tongue slapped them shut. Jack shoved the mutt away. Contrary to established rules and protocol, Maxx hopped onto the bed. Jack felt too drained to object. The dog curled up against his hip and began to lick his own feet.

Guardedly, Ms. Haskell said, "When you told me he licked, I didn't realize you meant . . . you know . . . that much. He's certainly friendly."

"Grotesquely so."

"The body was discovered Saturday. Jerry called the Washington office Sunday, and this is only Tuesday. How did you get here so quickly all the way from Washington?"

So long as Jack didn't move a muscle, not a solitary muscle, the nausea and lower intestinal misery abated somewhat. "My boss, Hal Edmond, lives in DC. I came in from Kansas. Hutchinson. I figured if I live in the middle of the country I can reach any park in the contiguous US in two days."

"Well, you made it here fine, and you're about as far up in the Northwest as you can get without going to Canada."

Jack would not consider his condition fine by any means. His gut gurgled, mocking her words.

The door clicked open. Now Jack was going to have to resemble a human being. He lurched to sitting.

An energetic man on the late side of his thirties had entered. His blond moustache matched his blond hair. He was well-built and what women would call handsome, a great, golden teddy bear of a man. He wore the gray shirt and green jeans of the typical Park Service maintenance man.

Jack heaved himself to his feet and extended a hand. "Jack Prester." Actually, it was Dr. John Prester, with a

10

Ph.D. in criminal psychology, but he didn't normally mention that part.

The fellow shook with a hearty grip. "Darryl Grade, chief of maintenance. The superintendent thought I ought to come talk to you, but this seems like a bad time. You don't look very good."

"Either a bug that's going around or food poisoning. The jury's still out. Grade. You discovered the body."

"Not exactly."

Jack waved a hand toward the table by the front window. "Here. Sit down."

"You sure you want to talk now?" Grade crossed to the kitchen chairs and pulled one out for Jack. He settled himself in another one.

Ms. Haskell aimed herself toward the door. "You probably aren't interested in eating, but you ought to have some juice. I'll run up to my house and get you some. And they surely have ginger ale over at the Inn. I'll ask." The graying angel of mercy swept out the door.

Jack pocketed the admin building keys and sat down. What was it about Grade that annoyed him?

The teddy bear rumbled as he spoke. "I happened to be out with the road crew, doing some repair work up by Reflection Lake. Two hikers came out and said they'd found a body. We radioed for the rangers, and I went back in with the hikers to secure the scene until the rangers got there. It wasn't far from the road. A quarter mile. Less."

"'Secure the scene.' You used to be in law enforcement."

Grade grinned. "Better advancement and better pay in maintenance. Besides, I like to get out and work with my hands. I like to see something when I'm finished, like a stone wall or a new bridge. As a ranger I didn't have that feeling of accomplishment." The grin faded. "You sure you want to do this? Can I get you something?"

Grade's solicitous attitude really grated. It wasn't just the words he said but his whole demeanor. No doubt he

11

was only trying to be sensitive and helpful and all that Alan Alda stuff, but it came across somehow as unnaturally unctuous. At five eleven and a hundred sixty-five or seventy, with ordinary brown hair and ordinary brown eyes, Jack wasn't an especially imposing person. He deliberately dressed casually, usually jeans and a chambray shirt, in order to further the appearance of being Just an Average Guy. It got him farther in the long run than did coming on like gangbusters. Now, though, he almost regretted not cutting a sharper image for this fellow.

Sharper image? He was a vegetable. A wilted vegetable. A vegetable with a self-destructive alimentary canal. "Yeah, you're right." He tapped the pile of file folders. "Besides, I ought to do my homework first before I start asking questions. Maybe they'll be more intelligent questions. Let's get together tomorrow."

Grade nodded, grinning, and stood. He whipped out a little wirebound notebook and pencil and jotted down a number. He tore off the sheet and dropped it on the table. "Call me if you need something. Hope you feel better soon." He left.

Jack managed to remember to thank Ms. Haskell profusely when she brought the juice and ginger ale. He remembered to feed the dog because Maxx wouldn't let him forget. He called Hal and told him why he wouldn't be on the case yet for a day or two.

He didn't bother to undress. He peeled his running shoes off and crawled under the covers, clothes and all. The springs squeaked as Maxx illegally joined him, and he was too dead to care. Lying horizontal prevented the nausea from being active, but it didn't do much for the rest of it.

* * *

The voice of an angel on high burbled cheerily, "Poor Jack. You look terrible. Come on, Maxx. I'll let you out." Maxx's long line rustled.

That voice.

Jack forced his eyes open. "Ev?"

It was Evelyn Brant all right. The slim build, the per-petually tousled black hair in the flyaway Amelia Earhart style, the huge brown doe eyes. She was wearing dark blue woolen stirrup pants and a knockout cowl-neck sweater, bulky and blue with white snowflakes knitted in. She looked like an ad for a ski resort.

She put Maxx out the back door on his long line.

Cold air flooded across Jack's bed. He tucked in deeper. The last he'd noticed, it was night. Now orange sunlight bounced off a bush outside the window.

His confused mind mulled all this, floundering help-lessly like a cow in quicksand. Ev was trained as a budget analyst, and there was nothing about budgets in this case. She was a city girl, and they were well over seventy miles from the nearest McDonald's. She had no training as an investigator and no experience except for the two cases she and Jack had handled together. She worked for some other department in the Washington office, not Hal's.

He tried to force himself to alertness. Fat chance. "What are you doing here?"

"As soon as you hung up the phone last night, Hal called me. He wants someone on this case quickly, and so he asked me to help out. He faxed me all the info he gave you. I read it on the plane coming in."

"You live in Maryland."

"No problem. You know Hal. He loves to pull strings. He got me a red-eye and lined up a GSA car to be waiting for me at the airport. I arrived at SeaTac just before five this morning and was up here by eight."

"What time is it?"

"Oh, eight-thirty about."

Eight-thirty. Jack was accustomed to getting up at five or five-thirty. Come to think of it, he did get up at five this morning. Also at three and at two and at midnight and

13

at ten last night and at . . . He let his eyelids bruise each other slamming shut.

Her relentlessly cheery voice bounded onward. "Hal said that the longer a crime goes unsolved, the less chance that it will ever be cleared, so he wants us to get right on this. He says you want to close it quickly, but he didn't mention why."

"I fly to Hawaii the eighteenth to spend Christmas with my folks."

"I remember—you mentioned once that your dad is superintendent at Hawaii Volcanoes now. You're not dreaming of a white Christmas?"

"Absolutely not. My Lord was not born in a snowstorm."

Her voice paused. "That's cutting it kind of close, isn't it? This is December fifth."

Jack snorted. "Hal seems to think I can produce a third miracle in a row here. We cleared those cases in Death Valley and Acadia each within ten days. I told him I didn't want to assume that's always going to be the pattern, but he shrugged it off. Says I can cut out for the holidays if it comes to that."

She opened the back door. Maxx came bouncing in on the crest of another blast of cold air. His water dish rattled. "How much do you feed Maxx?"

"Scoopful."

He heard the front door click open. It clicked shut. He forgot to tell her the dog food and the scoop were in the big ammo box on the passenger side of the truck cab. Maxx the inveterate thief just loved to tear apart his dogfood bag and gorge. Jack kept the dry kibbles in a dogproof can now to forestall looting.

The door clicked. Maxx barked and romped in circles, his toenails ticking and sliding merrily on the linoleum. Moments later he slurped and snorted and smacked his lips. His dish skidded noisily about on the floor. He crossed the room to the bed, stuck his face in Jack's, and belched.

"I'm going to run over to the office," Ev called. "Kerri has some supplemental material she forgot to give you. Also, she lined up an interview with one of the hikers who found the body. I'll be back in an hour or two. Rest well."

The door clicked.

Something, somehow, had gone dreadfully awry here, and not just Jack's digestive system. Jack was spearheading this investigation. He was in charge. He was supposed to be taking care of his own stupid dog. Here he lay, virtually comatose, and Ev the neophyte investigator was covering all the bases. Capably too.

The springs grated noisily as Maxx hopped onto the bed and curled up at Jack's side. Jack planned to force the dog off the bed, get up, shave, and get cracking. But he dozed off instead, dreaming of Hawaiian steel guitars strumming vaguely defined Christmas carols.

2

Go Tell It
on the Mountain

J ack's legs slogged, as sturdy as toilet paper that's been left out in the rain. His arms like cooked noodles flopped at his sides. His lungs were threatening to take him to court if he didn't stop and sit down. And they were less than halfway.

Fifty feet ahead on the trail, Darryl Grade marched resolutely, stalwart and strong. Darryl was wearing sunglasses today, of all days. It was cloudy, gloomy. He needed them, he claimed. "Ever since I got measles when I was a kid, my pupils don't close down right," he said. "But I can see like a cat at night."

Right behind Darryl, Ev was keeping up very well, considering she was an urbanite who eschewed hiking. She exclaimed excitedly over the scenery, and the lovely lake they were passing, and this majestic country, and all the dark, mysterious, slender evergreen trees, and the stark nature of the rocky landscape, softened here and there by sloping meadows. She bounced and babbled, like Tinkerbell on amphetamines.

Just ahead of Jack, Jay Chambers walked as if he were touring a city park along a paved path. The varying pitch of the trail didn't make him lengthen or shorten stride. He simply strode, never scrambling, never lagging.

16

The weather wasn't doing Jack's mood any favors. A coarse mist that could almost be called rain kept everything clammy and cold. He was wearing a rain shell over his sheepskin-lined denim jacket, and still he felt cold. The brim of his Stetson tended to collect moisture and dump it on his shoulders when he turned his head. He hated cold, clammy, wet weather.

Even Maxx was wearing on Jack's nerves. The mutt knew better than to do it when he was on leash, but he stuffed his muzzle into every bush and grass clump anyway, snorting and snarfing, absolutely elated by this golden opportunity to explore vast new horizons. Maxx had never been up this way before to stick his beak into Northwest scenery.

Bringing up the rear, Chief Ranger Mike Sanchez strolled as casually as if they were shopping at the mall. Bulky and sturdy and strong, he wore his hair in a close crewcut that suggested he was once a Marine—or ought to have been. Kerri Haskell had mentioned in passing that Mike had made three ascents to the summit of Mount Rainier so far, and he'd been in the park only sixteen months.

Climbing two vertical miles through snow and ice was not Jack's idea of a cheery adventure. Doing it three times was just plain loony. ("Then Lou Whittaker, who heads up the guide service, is ready for the funny farm." Kerri had grinned. "He's been to the top well over two hundred times.")

So far, although Jack was now plodding up the shoulder of the mountain, he had still not even seen its top. Theoretically, upslope of Reflection Lake one enjoyed a splendid view of the summit with its snowfields and glaciers. But ever since they arrived, the peak had lain perpetually hidden behind a thick gray overcast. Jack had worked here for the concessioner during his teens, so he knew the mountain was out there somewhere, all 14,000 feet of it. Ev had never been here before, though. That meant she had never seen it at all.

17

The trail wound up beyond Reflection Lake through a meadow and into an open cluster of subalpine fir. The steep mountainside filled the sky before them, practically blocking their way, ascending into the curtain of cloud. Jack had forgotten how rugged, how close to vertical, this Cascade country was.

Darryl and Jay were not the least winded. They chatted amiably about favorite bow-hunting areas. Both sounded like avid bow-hunters. When Ev asked details, Darryl admitted to going out for deer during the archery-only season, and Jay had taken an elk. Killing an elk with bow and arrow is no small achievement.

"Here," Darryl announced. He stopped beside a stunted, twisted, lone fir tree. "The hikers found him right here." He pointed to a place about six feet to the side of the trail.

Maxx immediately got interested in the spot, and Jack called him off. Maxx delayed obeying, so Jack gave him a sharp yank with his leash. Reluctantly, the Wonder Dog came around and stood by his left knee.

Jack flopped down to sitting beside the place. Maybe no one would notice his rubber knees or shortness of breath. Maybe they'd think he simply wanted to examine the ground closely. Ev squatted beside him and tapped his shoulder. "What's wrong with Maxx? He's acting funny."

Maxx was sniffing a bit, then returning to Jack and standing near him a short while. Then he'd go off sniffing some more and almost immediately return with a worried, hangdog look about him.

Jack interpreted. "Probably a bear or mountain lion in the area. That's his 'It's bigger than I am' behavior."

"Really?" Her voice trembled a mite.

Big mistake. Jack had forgotten that Ev was a city lady, to whom bears and mountain lions belong only in zoos, if at all.

Darryl began a rambling explanation that bears and mountain lions often investigate an area with blood smell

18

in it, and there was nothing to be concerned about, *blah blah blah*. Sanchez described two recent lion sightings near Longmire and talked about the hundred-mile range they often prowl through.

But Jack's attention had turned to the loose forest duff beside him. As soon as he could get a word in edgewise of the natural history dissertation, he commented, "The medical reports say the victim bled copiously. There's hardly any blood here."

Sanchez hunkered down across from Jack. "The substrate got pretty much stirred around as we were taking the body out."

If the scene was destroyed that much, Jack couldn't destroy it further. With his fingers he dug down to bare ground around where Darryl indicated the body lay, probing, seeking. If John Getz bled heavily, he did it somewhere else.

Ev stood erect and brushed herself off.

Jack unsnapped the dog's lead. "Maxx. Find."

The dog buried his nose in the duff and snorted like a steam train gearing up to leave the station. He moved off a few feet, sniffing all the way, and stopped. His great anvil head turned to Jack. *Well? Are you coming or not?*

"What is he supposed to find?" Grade looked dubious.

Jack shrugged. "He'll tell us when he finds it."

Ev moved in beside Maxx. "Look. There's a drop of dried blood here—I think it's blood. Brown?"

By the time Jack crawled to his feet, Darryl and Sanchez were gathered tightly around her, congratulating her on her good eyesight. They didn't need him.

Maxx had moved on. By following Maxx's exact route closely, and thereby Maxx's nose, they found a couple more drops and blobs. They left the trail and bushwhacked through the tangled ground cover of a patch of woods, then out across an open meadow. The body had indeed been transported. Why? Why kill someone over-the-hill-

and-gone from the nearest trail—and the trail not much used this time of year anyway—and then haul the body to trailside nearly half a mile away?

Easy answer: to ensure the body be promptly found.

Next question: Why so far off the trail in the first place? What was Getz doing way out here where it's hard to get to? Was he compelled to come? Was the killing opportunistic?

No easy answer.

Sanchez and Grade—and probably Ev as well—didn't seem to notice Maxx's nervousness. The dog kept glancing behind, making certain his backup remained close at hand. That concerned Jack. Few things made Maxx nervous.

A strange odor, something like very stagnant water, hung in the air. Maybe rotting flesh. Something vile, at any rate, was stinking up the area.

Maxx stopped. He dug into the duff beside a gigantic cedar, backed away, and moved in beside Jack. Jack purred heartfelt phrases of praise and took this opportunity to promptly sit down again. His legs thanked him grudgingly, still bent out of shape by the long, hard climb up the slope. Maxx took this as an invitation to be scratched and shoved in against him. Jack rubbed Maxx's belly and head without thinking.

He interpreted again. "Maxx just told us that's where John Getz died."

"Oh, come on . . ." Grade growled. He pulled off his sunglasses.

But Ev was already kneeling where Maxx had dug. She stirred briefly through the duff, wrinkled her nose, and stood up. "Maxx, you're a marvelous dog! This is where he died, all right, Jack. At least, it's where he was attacked. The blood—" She exchanged mere speech for a twisted face, which said more eloquently than any words could, *A death scene that's been lying around for days is yucky.*

That would explain the stench.

And then Ev surprised Jack by quietly backing away

20

from the spot by exactly the route she had entered. Where had she learned that bit of procedure?

Sanchez nodded. "We'll get some people in to go over the place right. It's old, but they might find something."

Grade wandered over and sat down at the base of the giant cedar. He leaned back against it and rubbed his face. Sanchez asked him to come away, to stay farther away from the alleged crime site. Instantly he hopped to his feet and settled himself at the base of a smaller cedar near Jack.

Sanchez casually flopped into the duff beside Jack's running shoes. He stared at Jack without actually being impolite.

Jack stared at Sanchez similarly. "OK. So the killer entices, or happens upon, or forces Getz to this remote spot, stabs him repeatedly with a sharp piece of obsidian, lets him bleed awhile, and then hauls the body out to the trail and down toward Reflection Lake, a distance of about thirty miles."

Sanchez smirked. "More like a third of a mile, max."

Maxx's ears pricked up at the sound of his name.

"Third schmird," Jack snorted. "When you've just been so sick you'd have to get better to die, it's thirty, at least. Trust me on that."

Ev giggled and sat down not beside Jack but next to Grade. She sobered instantly. "The hikers didn't move him. I'm pretty sure of that. The girl I talked to—Elizabeth Munro—said they backed away immediately, and she stayed to keep an eye on the scene as the man ran down to the road crew to bring help. The man knew they'd have radio communication with the rangers. Her story flowed naturally, and their reasons for doing things sounded logical. Normal. I couldn't see any reason to think she changed something, you know?"

"Same impression I got when I talked to them." Sanchez crossed his legs and folded them up.

Jack nodded. "And the attacker used a piece of obsidian. Why a piece of obsidian? Is there any around here?"

"Sure." There went Grade instantly trying to be helpful again. "This mountain is an active volcano—the whole Cascade Range here is volcanic. There's obsidian all over, if you know where to look. Or if you're blasting trails out of the hillside."

"I mean right here. Within immediate reach for a spur-of-the-moment murder if you don't have your knife and gun handy."

"Mm." Grade studied Sanchez. "I don't know of any. Do you?" His eyes flicked over to Jack. "You're sure it was obsidian?"

Jack nodded. "The M.E. reported flecks and chips of obsidian left in the wounds—including, apparently, the tip of the blade that broke off."

Ev was frowning. "I still don't understand how they found that. I mean, you look at pictures of stone axes —and I saw one at the Smithsonian on a school trip years ago, all right? They're a lump. Blunt. They're stones. You can't see how they could cut butter, let alone chop wood. And how in the world can you cut a person so much he bleeds like that? Bludgeon him, OK. But not slice him. Not with a stone."

Jack shifted. His legs were getting stiff. Why does an illness of the intestinal tract leave your legs in dismal shape? There shouldn't be any connection, except that people with prodigious appetites are said to have hollow legs. That must be it. And here he'd always thought that was an old wives' tale.

"Obsidian is called volcanic glass. It's usually glossy black, sometimes even translucent. Real glass. In its finest form, it breaks and chips in a swirl pattern. You can build a remarkably keen edge on an obsidian blade, just by chipping at it. When we were kids, we'd make cave-man tools out of it—axes and knives and things. We could cut leather, slice cooked meat—do lots of things. And cut our fingers.

Our fingers were constantly wrapped in Band-Aids."

"But it's fragile," Grade added. "Obsidian tools break easily. They shatter, especially if you make them too thin. We used to play with them when I was a kid too." He grinned. "Complete with the Band-Aids."

Maxx fidgeted against Jack, standing up, lying down, sitting, lying down again, sitting up. Was a bear still in the area? Was a lion watching them from some perch? Jack caught himself scanning the trees overhead, although Maxx would certainly have told him by now if something were that close.

He thought about the soft X-ray that accompanied the medical report, with its white shadows of tiny stone chips inside the body. The man had been stabbed three times. One, a glancing blow on the arm, may have been the first such, or the last, made when he either turned to run or flung the arm up to defend himself. The other two were placed with surgical accuracy. One entered just below his ribs in the very front, angling slightly upward, to take out his xiphoid process and then his aorta. The other penetrated between two ribs and through a lung at such an angle as to pierce the heart. It had to be a very long, thin-bladed obsidian knife or spearhead to wedge between ribs that way without breaking them.

Ev pointed across to the gigantic tree. "What kind is that? It's magnificent."

"Cedar." With Ev, Grade sounded paternal, not motherly as he did with Jack. It was a strange difference, but somehow detectable. "In fact, it's a particular cedar. In the record books it's the Grandfather Cedar. Biggest one in Mount Rainier that we've found so far. Tallest and biggest around both."

She craned her head upward. "I can't imagine climbing that tree to measure it."

"You don't have to. You can measure it fairly simply by trigonometry. I'll show you how sometime."

An idea forced itself in among Jack's random

thoughts. He lurched to standing. "If I were committing your average, run-of-the-mill stabbing, I sure wouldn't use an obsidian knife, especially a long, thin one. Too easy to break it off, and then you're defenseless. Or at least you've lost your weapon. So why go to the trouble of fashioning a murder weapon that might give out on you when you need it most?"

Maxx stood pressed to his leg.

Sanchez sprang like a cat to his feet. Apparently he was under the mistaken impression that Jack was ready to start hiking again. He grinned. "About the only reason to take a risk like that would be so that your weapon isn't metal. Then it won't show up with a metal detector."

Jack was grinning too. "So if I throw it away afterwards, I can feel reasonably sure it'll stay lost forever. An effective weapon that literally melts right into the scenery. Why, I could even break it up into little pieces afterwards and scatter them. Maxx! Find."

The dog, still nervous, trotted off to cut a circle, his nose poking busily here and there.

Sanchez frowned. "How does he know what he's looking for?"

"He doesn't. Neither do we. We just see what he comes up with. He'll work a circle around us, and then a wider circle, and then a wider circle, until he finds something with human smell on it. Or anything with blood. If our cave man tossed the bloodied obsidian away anywhere around here, Maxx can tell us."

Go Tell It on the Mountain, Maxx.

But Maxx could not tell them. Actually, he did tell them the negative, that no one had thrown away a bloodied piece or pieces of volcanic glass. The weapon was not here. After an hour of searching, Maxx had deposited at Jack's feet two extremely old deer bones that rodents had gnawed on and a desiccated dead shrew, but nothing remotely forensic.

So they all went home.

24

3
Jingle Bells

This was not the Seattle Jack remembered from his youth. Three times as many vehicles crowded the freeways, and they all wanted to drive where he was driving. The traffic on northbound I-5 entering the city slowed to a crawl. More rubber than asphalt, his father used to say. Maxx curled up on the seat beside him and fell asleep, bored to unconsciousness by the lack of movement.

Half a dozen new skyscrapers he had never seen before stuck up out of the city center. Just north of the King-dome, a black glass tower with a gracefully curved east side looked brand new. It shone against the gray sky like polished obsidian.

Elizabeth Munro lived in the U District just north of East 45th, Kerri Haskell had explained. On a Seattle map she pointed out to Jack just how to reach Miss Munro's place by the easiest way. She did not mention these thousands of other cars who were obviously trying to get to Miss Munro's house also. And this was Saturday. What must the commute be like on a Monday morning?

The freeway swept him across the ship canal a hundred-and-some feet above the water and plunged him into the weird and bustling university district. He hoped he'd have some time today to prowl through the University of

Washington bookstore. The off-ramp dumped him out onto 45th, he turned right, then left onto 9th Avenue, and he was there. Kerri Haskell was an excellent directions-giver.

It was a little brown house, probably originally intended as a single-family dwelling but now inhabited by college kids. Shaggy and weedy, its lawn obviously had not been given an end-of-the-season trim, and the shrubbery out front needed pruning. The house perched on a five-foot embankment, small and quiet and forlorn amid a row of bigger houses. A high-rise apartment building towered on the corner uphill. If it tipped over to the south in an earthquake, Miss Munro's house and all the others on this street would be history.

Jack put Maxx in his cage in the back of the truck and climbed the steps to the front door. He pushed the doorbell button. He didn't hear anything, but door chimes were sometimes that way—*bing-bong* on the inside, inaudible on the outside. He waited a few minutes and tried again.

From down on the sidewalk, a girl's voice called, "Can I help you?"

Probably her blonde hair was natural, for her skin appeared almost pallid. Her blue eyes were set rather shallow in her face, giving her a fragile pre-Raphaelite uniqueness that her long nose and small, pointy chin amplified. She wasn't pretty, and yet she was. Her pale eyebrows seemed set in a more or less permanent frown, as if nothing in life were perfect.

She had a point. Nothing in life is.

"I'm looking for a Ms. Elizabeth Munro at this address."

"That's me." She came jogging up the steps with two environmentally correct canvas shopping bags full of groceries. Jack noticed she was wearing Birkenstocks and REI all-cotton sweats, the uniform of the Northwest activist. On the porch she set the bags down and looked at him with a "So? Justify yourself" frown.

As he introduced himself, he displayed his badge.

She never glanced at it. "Come on in, Mr. Preston. Sorry the house is a mess. It's Gretchen's turn to clean, and she hasn't gotten around to it yet." She dug keys out of her zippered nylon tummy-pack.

Jack picked up the grocery bags and waited.

She opened the door, turned to get her groceries, and stared at him. He couldn't tell if she was going to thank him because she was a lady at heart, or pop him one because she was liberated and she could carry her own groceries, thank you very much. He had run into both types.

Whatever her thoughts, she kept them to herself and marched inside. He followed, carrying the bags on back through a narrow hall to the kitchen. He set them on the floor beside the counter because there was no room on the counter itself, or on the table—or even on parts of the floor, for that matter.

He surreptitiously looked around. "How many live here?" From the clutter, it had to be fifteen or twenty.

"Three. Want some coffee?"

"I'd like that. Thanks. Can I take you out for coffee?"

"It's right here."

She didn't invite him to sit. He was hoping she would. Eventually, he let his manners lapse and pulled out a kitchen chair.

He picked up the stack of magazines on the chair and laid them on the floor and sat. "The rangers at Mount Rainier, and Evelyn Brant out of the Washington office, talked to you about the body you found on the mountain. I have a few questions too, if you don't mind."

"I was afraid that's what it was. I figured that's what it was, but I hoped you came to talk about the access proposal."

"What access proposal?"

She turned to him, and her frown deepened. "They didn't relay it to the Washington office? They were sup-

27

posed to. I told them to. Evelyn said she never heard of it either. Honestly! The proposal for wheelchair access that I submitted to them."

"That sort of thing goes to region, not Washington, for special funding."

"Oh, really. Well, the regional office downtown says it has to go to Washington." She had dumped a pot of water into one of those drip machines. Now she was grinding her own coffee beans. This might be a pretty good cup of coffee.

Jack pondered for a moment the various reasons Region might be putting Ms. Munro off by passing the buck. Handicapped access proposals were usually pretty cut-and-dried. He laid it aside for the moment. "You and a companion were hiking above Reflection Lake. Just a day trip?"

"Business."

"Oh?"

"The park claims that laying wheelchair access along the major route would diminish the wilderness experience for the other climbers. It's a point. The wilderness experience is what it's all about. So Jay and I were researching alternate routes."

"Hiking trails for wheelchair-bound visitors? I understand the park already has several and is planning more."

She looked at him as if he lacked the brains God gave a goose. "To the top."

His mind boggled. "To the top."

"Being physically challenged should not be a barrier to achieving the ultimate experience of reaching the summit."

Her tone of voice made Jack wonder how he could be so foolish as to ask for clarification.

"Now let me make sure I have this right. You are campaigning to get wheelchair access to the summit of a fourteen-thousand-foot-high mountain. You're talking about a wheelchair ramp that goes up almost nine thousand vertical feet. Roughly two miles straight up, we're talking about here."

28

"Why not? The physically challenged have the same needs and desires as anyone else. Denying them the same options that others enjoy is a violation of their civil rights."

"Have you ever been to the top yourself?"

"No. I don't have to. You see, that's not a dream of mine. But if it were, and if I were physically challenged, I should be able to do it, just like anyone else can. You see?"

Jack pursed his lips and pondered this a moment, weighing different ways to go. She surely had already heard anything he could say to her. Still, his was a word out of the Washington office, which she seemed to equate with some small-town, three-desk chamber of commerce, where everyone knew everything that was going on.

He would start with logic, though he had absolutely no confidence in logic at this point. "But not just anyone can reach the top."

"Exactly."

"I'm not talking about handicapped. It's not always an option for the able-bodied either. I've been there. I worked for the concessioner here two summers when I was eighteen and nineteen. It took me three attempts, and I was in excellent condition. The first attempt, the altitude got me, and I had to quit at Muir. The second time, we were turned back by bad weather. In fact, the third attempt almost failed. No one has a guarantee they'll make it."

"I've heard all that."

"Besides, there are stretches there that simply cannot be made wheelchair accessible. Across ice and snowfields, sun cups, a hundred things that can't be flattened or widened or changed."

The coffee smelled good.

"That's the standard Park Service line. I've heard it a hundred times, and it's baloney. If they can build a trail, they can make it accessible. Period."

This argument was not Jack's, and he was grateful. He would leave it to others to trade nonsense with her. "So you and Jay Chambers were exploring alternate routes. For the access route to the summit?"

"Exactly."

"When the two of you left the Reflection Lake parking area and went up the trail, the body wasn't there."

"But it was when we came back down an hour later. Right. And we didn't see or hear anyone. Some rangers already asked. And Evelyn. She asked that."

"When you two came upon the body, you stayed while Chambers continued out. How did Chambers know a road crew was down there? It's Sunday, and they were working downhill of the parking area, beyond Reflection Lake. You didn't pass them on your way to the Reflection Lake parking lot."

"I didn't ask."

"Ev's report says you never met the victim, John Getz."

"No." She pulled out two coffee mugs, a clean one off the shelf and one from the drainboard, which she washed out with a couple of perfunctory swirls. The coffee smelled wonderful. She poured the mugs three-fourths full, snatched a half-gallon carton out of the refrigerator, and topped them off with chocolate milk.

Jack found himself gaping again.

She handed him a mug. "Mocha. I always make mocha. Much better than plain old coffee, don't you agree?"

If he didn't, it was too late now. He smiled and accepted his mocha.

She removed a plastic drugstore bag full of shampoo and other mysterious potions from a second kitchen chair and sat down.

He asked one of the questions no one else had asked yet. "You didn't know John Getz. Did you know *of* him?"

"Sure. Everyone with any interest in advocacy knows *of* him."

"No one has been able to interview Jay Chambers at

any length—he left town the same afternoon the body was discovered. Did Mr. Chambers know of Getz, do you think?"

"He must have. He phoned him the day before."

"How do you know?" Jack lost interest in the mocha.

"He told me so. Jay did, I mean."

"You didn't mention this to anyone else who talked to you."

"No one asked. Nobody said, 'Did Jay call Getz?' I can't read minds." She gestured with her mug. "I forgot to ask—do you want whipped cream on it?"

"No, thank you. This is fine. Do you know why he called?"

"I didn't ask."

"What did Jay say, exactly?"

"Exactly? Let's see. I don't remember exactly. When we saw the body he said something like, 'Oh, my god—this is Getz! I just called him yesterday!' I forget exactly who his god is. Not one of your usual gods. He's a druid, you know."

"No. I didn't know. A druid."

"You know. White robes and hoods. Not Ku Klux Klan, of course. They wear robes and hoods too. Different hoods. He gets together at summer solstice and winter solstice—is solstice the word?—with other druids. And he celebrates Halloween like you wouldn't believe."

"I believe it." Jack was having some difficulty keeping this Alice-in-Wonderland interview on track. He felt like a person expecting *The 1812* Overture and hearing "Jingle Bells" instead.

"And May Day." Elizabeth rolled onward. "The first of May or so. Maypoles and the whole works. Mom used to send us out with little May baskets to set on people's porches, you know? With candy and flowers. Sneak up and set them on the porch and ring the bell and run. It was fun. But not maypoles."

"So you don't agree completely with Jay either."

"For a lot of things. Like hunting. I am absolutely

opposed to blood sport of any kind, and Jay goes bow-hunting. Duck hunting over at the Potholes. He spends weeks out hunting during the season. It's disgusting. It shouldn't even be called a sport. Legalized murder."

The hunting-equals-legalized-murder issue seemed to get her more worked up than did the illegal murder of her fellow environmental activist.

Jack studied his mocha mug a moment, analyzing the conversation thus far. "I'll bet your older brother made all A's in school."

The perpetual frown deepened. "How did you meet Benny? He's in Duluth! Are you from Duluth? You don't sound like it."

"Just a wild guess." Jack shifted topics before he accidentally let the word *ditzy* slip. "I have people I call friends whom I've never actually met—people I only talk to on the phone. Would Jay Chambers know Getz in that capacity, or were they actually face-to-face friends?"

"I don't think John Getz had many friends. People who agreed with him maybe. But not many did. He was a real dork, you know?"

"Explain, please."

She was all wound up now. "Jay says the mountain is sacred, that he can tell because he's a druid attuned to the life forces of the earth. And ley lines. You know about ley lines, don't you? Well, they all come together under Mount Rainier. So it's holy ground, so to speak."

"So to speak. Do you yourself—"

"So Jay is interested in as many people as possible coming to the mountain and getting renewed, you know?"

"How about John Getz? He was an enthusiastic environmental advocate and gadfly. Was he interested in your access plan?"

"No, just the opposite. That's why he's a dork. Was a dork, I should say. He wanted to pull out all the existing trails and make it inaccessible to everybody. That way, nobody would have an advantage everyone else didn't have too. I admit it would solve the lack-of-access problem, but then no one would be able to have a meaningful wilderness experience, and that would defeat the whole purpose, you know? He thought you ought to get rid of Sunrise and Paradise and all those places and make it all wilderness."

"What constitutes a meaningful wilderness experience?"

"Oh, you know. Where you can go hiking and not step in any horse poop."

Jack would have asked his next question, but his mind blanked out, trying to process this latest. Like tossing water into a computer keyboard, it messed up all his circuits.

From out on the curb came Maxx's sudden insistent barking. It was not the joyful baritone yip that Maxx sometimes gave a friend or even a friendly stranger.

Jack jumped up and ran for the living room. He almost tripped over a canister-type vacuum cleaner in the hallway. He yanked open the front door.

A man was trying to break into the driver's side door with a Slim Jim. He wheeled, stared at Jack bug-eyed, dropped the Slim Jim, and took off upstreet.

"Call the cops!" Jack bolted out onto the porch. He didn't bother with the cement steps up the embankment— he jumped off the bank directly to the sidewalk and threw open the door of Maxx's cage. "Maxx! Go get him!" The mutt was a Labrador retriever. Let him retrieve the perp. Maxx leaped out and bounded off. How the pooch loved this cop stuff!

Jack started running up the street after them, and he was surprised that the slight uphill slope winded him so quickly. He didn't have to go far, though. Growling like a lion taking possession of a slab of meat, Maxx had the fellow nose down on the sidewalk on this side of the high-rise apartment building. From his pocket Jack pulled his nylon porta-cuffs, the handcuffs that fit in a wallet, and bound the guy's wrists behind him.

The man looked small-time, a graying bum in need of a shave, wearing a dirty T-shirt under a dirty sport coat with one button missing. He looked just like the kind of fellow you'd picture if someone said "Seattle street person." The conventional wisdom required that Jack pat him down for weapons, but he could just see himself getting stuck on a needle in the guy's pocket. He'd let the arresting officer pat the guy down if they wanted him patted badly enough.

Jack called Maxx to heel and hauled the fellow to his feet.

The man was shorter than Jack first thought, maybe five-eight at most. "Gimme a break, huh?" he whined. "I been out of work."

"Panhandling's one thing. Taking it without asking is another. Next time, ask down at the mission instead of stealing."

"They preach at you."

"So do I." And, fully and succinctly, Jack explained the gospel to the fellow as they walked back to the car. He enjoyed that—it wasn't often he had the audience to hear exactly what he wanted to say, even if in this case it was, literally, a captive audience.

When they reached the truck, Jack glanced up at Ms. Munro on her porch. He called, "Cops coming?"

"Are they open weekends?"

Jack managed a nod.

"What's their number?"

4
Silent Night

A druid! I thought druids were people that used to hide behind rocks at Stonehenge or something. You sure she said *druid?*"

Ev stood at Jack's kitchen counter chopping tomatoes for the salad. They were on a Saturday night date, if you call staying home to swap information and write supplemental reports a date. Jack's social life was a veritable whirl.

Maxx lay stretched out on the floor, dead to the world. When he was hungry he was miserable, and he did his best to make everyone else miserable. Once he got his supper, life was complete. That's what people must refer to as a dog's life—binary simplicity.

"White robes and hoods and the works, she claims. I look forward to talking to him. I don't think I ever interviewed a druid before." Jack tore the lettuce into two salad bowls.

"Let me do that interview, all right? You'll get off onto religion and forget everything you're supposed to be asking him. You won't get anything at all from him."

"O ye of little faith."

"O ye of too much faith."

"Never too much faith. French or Thousand Island? You see, Ev, there are only two religions."

"What?" Her head snapped around. The shining fly-away hair followed belatedly.

Good. He'd captured her attention. When it came to discussing things religious, she had the attention span of a butterfly in a rose garden.

"Thousand Island."

He went into the fridge door for the salad dressing. "One is when you do something for your deity of choice in order to earn help or points, and the other is when God did something good for you that you don't deserve, and you accept that." He plopped Thousand Island on his own salad and handed her the bottle. "Buddhism, Islam, all of them —you do something to earn merit or win God's favor or both. Whatever god. Christianity is God giving everything for you first. See the difference?"

She sighed. "I suppose by now I should have known where this would be going. I do wish, Jack, you'd quit try-ing to stuff your religion down my throat."

"Not stuffing. Offering." He paused between the counter and the table, holding the salads. "I want you to have what I have, Ev. Eternal life and peace."

She wheeled on him. "Well, I don't want peace, all right?" Her voice was rising. "I had a peaceful childhood being the perfect little girl. And I had such a peaceful high school I didn't even have a boyfriend. Just lots of perfect report cards. And I had a terribly peaceful college earning degrees and proving myself. And I have a peaceful career as a budget analyst, just sitting there analyzing away. *I'm sick of peaceful!*"

Jack really ought to explain that that wasn't the kind of peace he meant, but this didn't seem to be the moment. He put down the salads and spread his hands, a gesture of conciliation. "May the adventures of Indiana Jones pale in comparison with yours."

She hesitated and almost smiled. "You don't under-stand how much I've loved these last few months as an investigator, Jack. You can't. I never ever had a real, gen-

36

uine adventure until Hal asked me to work with you. I never traveled out West, I never got into a dangerous situation. Nothing. It's . . . I . . ." She took a deep breath and sat down at the table. "I can't explain it."

"Sounds to me like you just did pretty well." He paused to bless the food, and she waited for him. At least he'd gotten that far with her. *Change the subject, Prester, and bring it back to God some other time.* "Where are you going for Christmas?"

She shrugged. "Probably stay right here, whether we clear the case or not. Especially if it snows down low here. I've never gotten to see snow much. Darryl and Kerri both say that this is an unusual year. Warm. They usually have snow here at Longmire by now, and especially up higher where the body was found."

She nibbled at her one-dish dinner and again almost smiled. "I didn't think canned chili with extra hamburger would be as good as it is. This Monterey Jack makes a nice difference. And I would never have imagined you can work tortilla chips into the day's main meal. You and your junk food." She wagged her head.

"The lazy cowboy's supper. Ah, but you should taste my spaghetti. I build the sauce from scratch. World class. Your family's not getting together this year?"

"Mom and Daddy are taking a cruise through the Panama Canal. In fact, they would have flown to Miami today. Bert will probably go to his wife's family's place. I think her folks get together."

"Your younger brother, Bert." Jack pondered the possible meanings behind her casual dismissal of a major holiday. "So how did your family celebrate Christmas when they were all together?"

"Oh, you know. The usual. Open presents. Go out to dinner somewhere."

He stared at her before he caught himself. "That's usual? No Christmas tree with lights that inexplicably go out after you have it all decorated? No big turkey dinner with all the friends and relatives and a couple stranded seasonal rangers? No luminarias for the little kids to burn their fingers lighting? No kids getting into a big snowball fight where one of them gets a bloody nose?"

She wrinkled her delicate nose, her familiar "Oh, gross" expression.

Jack grinned. "Hey. It's not Christmas without at least one bloody nose."

"Ho, ho, ho. What are loomin airias?"

"Lumi-nahrias." Jack rolled the R. "Hispanic idea, but it's spread way beyond the Southwest. It's a plain old Kraft paper bag with sand in the bottom and a candle in it."

"Sounds homey." Ev's tone of voice suggested that homey means hopelessly rural with the sophistication of hominy grits.

"San Antonio strings thousands of them out along their riverfront walk, and the effect is nothing short of stunning."

"And I take it your family is big on Christmas."

"Yeah, really big. It's when we all get together."

"Even the seasonals."

Jack kept forgetting Ev was not Park Service. "Temporaries—seasonals—who work off-season are usually older people without close family ties, or college kids who are too far away to get home to their families. Sort of orphans when holidays roll around. So you just about always end up with a couple extra people celebrating with you."

She shrugged. "Of course, if you have to cook for all those people, the kitchen's a mess, and you end up with so many dirty dishes. Not what I'd call a good way to celebrate a holiday."

"Yeah, I suppose. And I doubt the turkey's too thrilled with the idea either." Jack thought about this awhile. "Your family surely has some Christmas traditions. Like, do you open gifts on Christmas Eve or on Christmas morning?"

"Whatever's convenient."

He mulled the ramifications a few moments. "I know

what. Why don't you come along with me? I'll call the airline and see what I can do. Come on down to Hawaii with me and celebrate Christmas with my folks. No snow, but I can guarantee you a happy time."

"No, I can't. Thanks anyway. Your parents—you know."

"Mom takes extra guests in stride like a steeplechaser jumps a coffee table. That's something else about the Park Service. You never know who's gonna show up, especially if you live way out of town, and most do, so you're always prepared for company. She and Dad don't mind a bit. I promise."

"It's not that. She'll think I'm your girlfriend and get her hopes up."

Jack laughed. "That's silly. I've told them all about you. They already know you're a co-worker. You're a friend. It doesn't matter whether you're female."

"Of course it matters. They don't have any grandkids anymore, right?"

"Yeah."

"Then it matters. And I don't want to get anywhere near a matchmaking situation like that. Thanks anyway."

Matchmaking? Never in her life had Jack's mom pushed that kind of thing on him, although he had to admit she had absolutely adored Marcia and fawned all over Matthew. Still, he knew Mom better than Ev did, and matchmaking wasn't an issue. How should he—

Someone knocked forcefully on the door. Maxx leaped to life. His basso profundo bark filled the apartment and made the walls vibrate. Jack laid his napkin aside and answered it.

Darryl Grade stood there smiling that teddy bear smile. You kind of expected shoe-button eyes.

Jack pasted a friendly smile on his own face. "Come in! You're just in time for dinner. Humble vittles, but tasty. We even managed to incorporate junk food into the main meal of the day."

"Thanks." Grade shook his head. "I want to speak to Evelyn if I may."

"Ev?" Jack returned to his seat.

She hopped up and hastened to the door.

Jack should sit down and resume eating, but that didn't seem quite the thing to do. He was, after all, the host and master of this mansion. On the other hand, they had stepped outside into the clammy December darkness, and not only were they not including the host in their conversation, they were letting in a lot of cold air.

He took the opportunity to refill his glass of Pepsi from the two-liter on the sink.

Ev came bopping back in, operating on rocket fuel. She grabbed her jacket and purse off the bed. "Darryl wants me to go down to Ashford with him—he says the only proper introduction to this area is to hear the live band at the Clearcut. The Cold Cowboys. Sorry to run. There are all my notes in the envelope there. I'll be down at my cabin tomorrow so we can go over reports, OK?"

"Sure." He watched the door swing shut. Was Grade smirking? Hard to tell in the darkness, but Jack's mind's eye could see it clearly. The Cold Cowboys. Country western. Since when was Ev, the effusive fan of Tchaikovsky, Rachmaninov, and Rimsky-Korsakov, interested in country western?

He ate his dinner in silence. He marveled at this sudden, compelling silence. No conversation, no arguing or banter, not even Maxx snoring. When Ev was here the place seemed alive and noisy, even when they weren't actually saying anything. Now? Nothing.

He put Ev's half-a-serving in the fridge, not because he expected her to finish it, but because he couldn't bear to throw food away until it grew blue hair. He cleaned up, more or less, and spread his notes and files out across the table. He couldn't concentrate. He fought it for almost half an hour and gave up. But then, Ev had the right idea. Why work on Saturday night?

Because he wanted this case closed so he could get out of here, that's why. Ev didn't care. She didn't have family waiting for her in Hawaii. She wanted to see snow.

The snow had stayed away this long; let it keep staying away until he was done here. He hated shoveling his truck out, and scraping the windshield in the morning, and driving in the stuff. He'd been driving in snow since he was fifteen, but he hated it. And what he really dreaded on a snowy road was some turkey who had no idea how to maintain traction, coming at him sideways.

Snow. *Bah, humbug.*

He wasn't going to just sit around here and mope. He kicked his somnolent dog and grabbed his jacket off the hook. Maxx stretched, yawned, snarfed, and followed him out the door. Jack walked smartly into the street in front of his apartment—and stopped. Going out was one thing. Having an actual destination was another.

It wasn't raining, but with the heavy overcast and temperature hovering at thirty-five or forty, it might rain or even snow by morning. No traffic, no television or radios audible, no one talking, no dogs barking. No wind in the trees. By coming out here he had not left the silence behind. It had followed him. Now it perched at his shoulder in the dank darkness of the night.

On impulse he crossed to the admin building and let himself in. Easier said than done—the burglar alarm system was one of those weird, silent turn-this-key-and-then-that-key things that you were never quite sure you'd rendered inoperative.

He sat down in Kerri Haskell's little office and cranked up her computer. Maxx flopped down in a lazy wad beside the chair and began noisily licking various parts of his anatomy.

Were personnel records as easy to tap into here as they were at White Sands? Yep. Maybe even easier. A few false tries and Jack cracked the file.

SANCHEZ, MICHAEL. Probably Miguel at home. San-

41

chez spoke English with no trace of an accent, but his first park was Big Bend, and the second was LBJ Ranch, both in Texas. District Ranger at Mesa Verde and now here.

HASKELL, KERRI. Interesting. This was her first tour in the Park Service. Married to Jeff Haskell.

HASKELL, JEFFREY. Roads foreman, formerly at Wind Cave, Yosemite, and Indiana Dunes. He was out on the road crew working that Sunday when the body was found. Jack noted his house number in Longmire.

GRADE, DARRYL. And Jack's conscience jabbed him in the heart with an ice pick. He hadn't been giving Grade the slack the man needed and deserved. And Jack, of all men, ought to know what Darryl needed. Darryl Grade was a widower, just like Jack. Three years ago, about the same as Jack. Jack's dead wife was named Marcia; Grade's had been Margaret. No mention of kids. Jack's only child, a son, died in the mangled car along with Marcia. Did Grade lose a child?

He backed out of the file and turned off the monitor. He stared out the door at the dimly lighted hall awhile, beating down the memories and sadness that still plagued him every now and then.

He reached down absently and scratched the back of Maxx's head. "Come on, mutt. Let's go."

Maxx lurched to his feet and led the way out into the hall.

Would the Haskells be home tonight? Jack worked his way out of the admin building, hoping he was resetting all the right alarms. He motioned Maxx to heel and walked up the silent street beneath gloomy, black trees.

The Longmire residences looked as gloomy as the trees despite their cheery yellow lighted windows. Two-story frame houses many years old, they were painted the same dark brown nearly everything else in the Park Service was painted. The dense overstory of tree limbs kept grass from growing well, which left most of the yards bare. Cords and stacks of stovewood, kids' bikes, and picnic tables were scattered haphazardly among the homes and out-buildings.

Jack kept track of the house numbers, white numerals preceded by L, routed on wooden signs beside the doors. Here stood the Haskell residence on the corner.

And the silence fled.

Inside, the Haskells were arguing loudly. The pain and noise and friction seeped out into the cold, dark night.

Jack had a degree or two in psychology, and still he never knew quite how to approach these situations when he stumbled onto them. In an office setting, in a clinic setting, no problem. The folks there had come to him for counsel. Out here in the wilds of the real world, it was not so easy.

He motioned Maxx to sitting, stepped up onto the stoop, and rang the doorbell. Not one to leave something so important to the vagaries of electricity, he also rapped vigorously on the door. The cacophony inside ceased. Jack backed down off the stoop and stood waiting beside his dog.

Long moments later a tall, powerfully built man yanked the door open. In jeans and a dark, baggy sweat-shirt, he looked like someone who ought to be playing with the Dallas Cowboys. They could use the speed and muscle. "What?"

"Jeff Haskell? Jack Prester out of the Washington office. I'd like to talk to you a couple minutes about the Getz murder."

"Some other time."

Jack put an edge on his voice. "Now."

Haskell stared at him as the seconds ticked by.

Jack could see Kerri on the far side of the living room, a mix of fear and frustration on her face. But not anger. The only anger Jack saw was radiating from this man right here.

Haskell looked at the dog a moment and stepped out onto the stoop. He slammed the front door behind

him. The sallow light from a street lamp made his com-
plexion look gray. He was actually probably fairly swarthy
and sun-tanned.

"Thank you, Mr. Haskell." Jack softened and lowered
his voice, hoping to entice some of the silence back. "You
were on the road crew last Sunday up at Reflection Lake
when Getz was discovered."

"Yeah." Haskell stood there on the stoop, poised to
dart back inside. "I already answered all of Sanchez's
questions."

"I read his report. He didn't mention your tour at Yosemite. What was your position there?"

Haskell took one giant step and landed down off the
stoop in front of Jack's nose. He was at least six-two to
Jack's five-eleven. "What about Yosemite?"

"I was there seven years ago on special assignment
and fell in love with the place. Just curious."

"Valley District maintenance supervisor." Haskell's
anger had mellowed from fury to caution.

"At Yosemite you scheduled all the district's cyclic
maintenance and special projects?"

"Yeah." There was a hesitancy to his voice.

Jack had to play this just right. "That's a massive job,
as complex as the Yosemite Valley is. A dozen major irons
in the fire at once, all the time, and a lot of upgrading to
do. Has Grade put you in charge of scheduling here at
Mount Rainier?"

"No."

"Too bad. You certainly have the experience. So it
was Grade who scheduled Sunday work on the Stephens
Canyon Road last week?"

"Yeah, but he didn't have any choice. A rockslide
was partially blocking, and it took out some guardrail. If he
hadn't, I woulda."

Jack nodded. "And so you cleared the slide and repaired the guardrail."

"And stabilized the hill."

"The report didn't mention that."

"That's what took so long. There was still some loose stuff up there yet. We chained it and then went over it by hand." Haskell was relaxing by degrees as he talked about something obviously near and dear to him.

"Whose idea was that?"

Haskell scowled. "Mine."

"Checked the whole thing out foot by foot. That would take hours."

"Good thing we did. We found some big stuff that could be trouble."

"How often does that happen—that you work on Sunday?"

"Too often. And when it snows, every Sunday. That's when the tourists seem to think all the parking slots at Paradise oughta be clear."

Jack studied the dirt beyond Haskell's elbow. "Were you out on the hillside during the stabilization work?"

"Yeah."

"Good. I need your expert opinion. Think about this one for as long as you need to—can you recall any evidence, any little unusual thing, that might suggest to you how that landslide happened?"

"How does any rockslide happen? The ground is soaked and soft, a rock starts to slip, the mud gives way, and *boom*. Down it goes."

Jack kept his face relaxed, assumed a stance of waiting patiently, as if Haskell weren't done yet.

And the giant got caught up in the game. He stared beyond Jack for a few long moments. The anger had dissipated. He shook his head. "What you're asking is, did somebody start it deliberately. I can't think of anything I saw that you could point to. Somebody could have. But it could have happened naturally too."

"No footprints or anything like that."

"Footprints all over the place now, after we got through there. But I didn't see any where they shouldn't be.

45

No. Sorry if that ain't the answer you're looking for."

"I'm looking for an expert's observations, and that's exactly what I got. I couldn't be more pleased. Thank you."

"Is that all?"

Should he plunge in or not? Jack decided to plunge in. "No. One more thing. The fighting—you and your wife. Happen often?"

"None of your business!" And Haskell spiced it up with a few well-placed expletives. The anger flared instantly.

"It certainly is. I'm a commissioned peace officer required to investigate domestic disturbances. You two are disturbed."

"I didn't touch her, so butt out."

Jack could go a couple ways from here, but he couldn't see that Jeff Haskell was a man much given to either nuance or counsel. So he troweled it on thick. "I lost the only woman I ever loved to a car wreck, so I don't take it well when a guy has himself a perfectly good woman and doesn't treat her nicely. You won't do any better than Kerri, so you'd be wise to start appreciating her. I hear any little hint at all that you're still mistreating her, and I'm gonna be on you like ugly on a monkey."

"I ain't ever hit her."

"Abuse happens many more ways than just physical. If and when you decide you need some help, mention it. I'll do my best for you. I'm a qualified counselor. Good night. God bless you."

Jack turned away and headed back down the street, exceedingly grateful that he had big, hulking Maxx close at hand. He heard Haskell go back inside. He heard the door slam. He reversed himself then and hung around the shadows below the Haskell house, listening, until their lights went out.

The argument did not resume to mar the silent night.

5

O Tannenbaum!

Ley lines. Jack had heard about ley lines in the vague somewhere. Ley lines were supposed to be paths of exceptional energy within the earth. In theory they were spiritually active places, particularly where lines intersected. You built your shrines and temples and megalithic monstrosities such as Stonehenge along ley lines, that they might be embued with an extra dollop of power. Jack always assumed they were associated with distant and exotic places such as Glastonbury or mysterious trails crisscrossing some plateau high in the Andes. New Age somethings. But here? Mount Rainier? A volcano?

He pulled into the Reflection Lake lot and turned off the engine. Only one other vehicle was parked here, a brown-over-tan Jeep Cherokee at the far end. He sat in quiet reverie a few moments without knowing what he was thinking about, snapped out of it, and got out.

Maxx ought to go on leash, but Jack wanted the dog to be able to range out, perhaps to find things. What things? He had no idea. He didn't even know why he was coming back up here on a cloudy Sunday afternoon. He wanted to look at the area on his own, alone. That was the only excuse he could think of. He locked his door and motioned Maxx down out of the truck bed to join him.

They walked up the trail together, Maxx and he, in silence. The sky was still overcast, the air still heavy with moisture, just like the other time they were here. They walked around the lake and started up the hill.

Actually, he ought to get out and run awhile. It'd been ten days since he did any running. He was out of shape and slipping further out of shape every day. Get those muscles toned up! Play with that target heart rate!

Not today. Not yet.

At least today he could negotiate the steep trail without his legs turning to rubber. Maxx automatically left the path where everyone else had been leaving it lately. Between the Park Service folk and the on-loan forensics crew, it was getting so beaten down it had almost become a new trail, a highway blazed to the Grandfather Cedar. He followed Maxx cross-country over the steep hillside.

Maxx dropped back and moved in beside Jack's knee. Most uncharacteristically he stayed there as they walked out toward the death site. The Place. He carried his head and tail high. He wasn't missing a thing, and the fur on the nape of his neck stood up, all fluffed. Possibly—in fact, probably—they were entering the home range of a bear or mountain lion. A bobcat wouldn't do this to Maxx, and the dog certainly never grew uneasy about hoofed mammals such as deer or elk.

When they arrived at the murder site, Maxx didn't bother to check out the exact spot of the attack. That really disturbed Jack. The dog absolutely loved stinking messes, the stinkier the better. He seized any opportunity to roll on cowpats and gobble up unspeakable things before Jack could yell, "Drop it!" Here, with the foul odor of rotted blood still heavy in the air, Maxx paid no attention.

If Jack had hair on the nape of his neck, it would have prickled too. An ominous presence pervaded the place, a presence beyond the odor of rotted blood. He felt apprehensive. Edgy.

Maxx spun around to face the way they had just

come, barking furiously at the silent wilderness behind them. Jack wheeled and realized almost as an afterthought that his gun had leaped into his hands unbidden. Maxx growled from deep down in his throat.

"Don't shoot!" a man's voice called anxiously.

"Step on out here!" Jack kept his gun leveled anyway.

A short, spry man with a black beard loomed among the trees. He moved out into the open lea and stopped, his hands waving high. He looked like a hiker and dressed like a hiker and acted like a hiker upon whom a gun had just been drawn.

The man spread his hands wide. "Jay Chambers. I'm not armed."

Jack holstered his gun. "Sorry. Jack Prester, Mr. Chambers, with the Park Service. I've been hoping to talk to you. Didn't expect to find you out here though."

The man approached with quick, sure, swift steps. Very obviously he was a walker accustomed to traversing any terrain, a man at home in this steep and forbidding woodland. He extended a hand. "Sorry I startled you." He shook with a firm, even say aggressive, grip.

"I apologize for the gun." Jack realized he was more or less repeating himself, but it seemed the thing to say. The park radio hung from his belt in its leather carrier. Had this man been a threat, had Jack needed to call for help or for backup, how would he have directed rangers out here in time? Why did he bother carrying this stupid radio?

"No apology necessary." Chambers's bass voice rumbled almost subsonic. "Your caution is wise, considering what happened here."

"Oh? How do you know what happened here, Mr. Chambers?"

The man smiled. That is, Jack assumed it was a smile; the black beard moved around in a friendly manner. "I make it my business to know things about the park that

49

you don't hear in the naturalist's talks. Jack . . . sorry, I missed the last name."

"Prester."

"Prester. With the Park Service. I talked to Kerri Haskell this morning. She said you're in the area investigating Getz's death."

"And you left the area immediately after reporting the body."

"Not immediately. Soon after. I provided the investigating ranger with my statement, but I had to leave town on business for a few days." Chambers waved an arm at random. "Am I keeping you from something? Were you intending to go on? I don't want to hold you up."

"Not at all. Are you going on?"

"No." He looked around briefly. "I don't know if this is the time or place for you, but I'm happy to sit and talk if you wish."

"No better time or place. How about over there?" Jack pointed toward a rotting log fifty feet from the Grandfather Cedar.

"Fine." Chambers led the way.

Maxx, as nervous as ever, stayed close to Jack's side.

Chambers settled himself on the log as comfortably and casually as if it were an easy chair. "To be honest, there are better places. Just about any place would be better, in fact."

Jack sat down on the log beside him and leaned forward, his elbows propped on his knees. He felt a bit better sitting here. Perhaps his edginess was simply an aftereffect of the illness. "You've raised a couple points that interest me, Mr. Chambers. What is your version of what happened here, and why is this a worse place than elsewhere?"

"Are you familiar with druidism, Mr. Prester?"

"Only in the most general terms. I understand you are a druid."

"That's correct. It's a much maligned and misunderstood belief. That doesn't keep it from being valid, of course. Taking a vote on whether the Loch Ness monster exists, for instance, has no influence upon whether the beast actually does exist."

Jack studied the fellow's face. The man was staring at the ground, his mouth half opened, as if marshaling thoughts and words. Chambers was referring to an instance Jack had read about, years ago, where a number of scientists were polled about whether they believed the monster actually existed. If a majority said yes, it did. If they said no, it didn't. That was not exactly how it had been, but it was how the wire services and newspapers had picked up the story.

Chambers apparently had his words in order now. "The earth is not a dead glob of dirt spinning through space. It has a soul, a life, if you will. This is an inadequate explanation, but for lack of the right words let's say it possesses an invisible network of positive energy lines—"

"Ley lines."

Chambers beamed. "Ley lines! Where they meet and cross, the positive energy is understandably quite high. One of the quickest, easiest ways to find these sites of positive energy is simply to learn where people thousands of years ago worshiped—the places they considered sacred. They were well attuned to positive energy."

"More sensitive to the earth's subtleties then?"

"Very well put!" Chambers gestured to the south. "Mount Adams is a powerful site. The Indians still revere her. The Yakimas call her Pahto and consider her a goddess. And Mount Rainier here—Tahoma—is another." He pronounced the H in Tahoma as if he were clearing his throat.

Jack had asked his questions. He would for the moment assume Chambers was getting around to answering them. He shifted slightly on the log and listened. The log was damp through and through, and now the coarse mist was thickening into actual rain.

Maxx sat so close that the dog was pressed against his leg. Maxx was not licking his paws, or his private parts, or Jack, or any of the things he usually licked when he felt at ease.

Chambers continued, "There are also pockets of negative energy, places in which it seems as if all the positive energy is sucked away, leaving a deficit. This is such a place right here. That gun in your hand didn't surprise me a bit. You feel uncomfortable here. The place irritates, and you don't know why."

"Are you saying that's why whatever bad happened here happened here instead of somewhere else? Like out on the trail or closer to Reflection Lake?"

"You sound as if there were only one event. There have been several."

Jack studied him, watched the beard move. "For example."

"The Nisqually Indians tell about a monster named Tsiatko who lives in the mountains. He stays up in the inaccessible forests except in spring and summer, when the salmon are running, and he comes down to catch them. They feared him greatly because simply looking at him was fatal. Well, about a hundred years ago a half-Nisqually named Joe John decided a cache of gold coins (the white man's medium) and fetishes (the Indian's medium) existed high on the mountain here. He claimed he received this in a dream. So he began climbing, following the Nisqually River. Still obeying his dream, he left the river gorge and crossed to a pristine lake high on the flank of the mountain. He continued upward. At the base of an ancient cedar he met Tsiatko. He died immediately."

"He was alone?"

"Yes."

Jack felt the cold dampness of the log. "How does anyone know what happened, then?"

"His in-laws got worried and tracked him. They found the footprints of the monster beside his decomposing body.

52

Footprints twice the size of any human being's. From the description in the original narrative, I am certain the lake in question was Reflection Lake, and the cedar tree this very tree."

"Mm." Jack had been hoping for something a little more recent. In fact, he was hoping Chambers would let slip that he knew Getz had died here. It was not common knowledge.

Chambers rumbled on. "About twenty years ago, between Sunrise Point and Mystic Lake, two hikers crossed paths with an eight-foot bipedal mammal. Brown hair. It was headed this way around the mountain."

"Sunrise is over on the other side of the mountain."

"That's right! Less than twenty-four hours later, a child on this side of the mountain, less than a quarter mile from where we are right now, reported a Sasquatch. No one believed him. Apparently he was given to prevarication anyway. Wild tales."

Jack shrugged. "Easy explanation. Children are impressionable. He heard about the incident at Sunrise and got ideas."

"Possibly. Four years ago, a man out hiking with his dog lost his way, so he headed downhill, cross-country, figuring he'd end up somewhere in the Stephens Canyon drainage and hit a road sooner or later. He and his dog encountered a furry lump, hunched over in the weeds. They thought it was a bear. But the creature stood up and became an erect bipedal monster, an ape thing. The dog attacked it. It grabbed the dog and squeezed the life out of it with one hand. The man ran away downhill. He could hear the monster crashing in the brush behind him. He reached the road a hundred yards from the Reflection Lake parking area. Three cars refused to stop for him because the expression on his face was so wild. Insane man. Then a park pickup truck stopped and took him down to Longmire. He's still not right in the head."

Jack mulled this a moment. "So you're saying there's a monster afoot here."

"I'm citing the evidence. You see, the two hikers near Sunrise were also crossing a pocket of negative energy where they reported the beast. I went out there myself, to the very spot, to confirm it. The beast—Tsiatko—whoever or whatever it is—"

"Bigfoot?"

"Perhaps. The beast seems to gravitate to negative energy just as we humans feel best in positive energy."

"And never the twain shall meet. In answer to my question then, that's why this is a worse place than elsewhere. So why are you here today?" Jack twisted to face the man squarely.

"Two reasons. I saw you leave your truck and come this way."

"You drive a brown Cherokee."

"You're very observant. Yes. I saw you come this way and got curious. Besides, I was coming up here myself to measure the cedar there. It just might be a world-record holder."

"Mm." Jack thought about all this a moment and could not decide whether this fellow was a few bricks shy of a full load or whether he simply was an enthusiast of folk tales. "You're interested in trees."

"All druids are." The man was smiling within that luxuriant beard.

"Of course. How did you know the road crew was up here on a Sunday? Sunday's theoretically their day off, and you didn't reach or pass them before you and Ms. Munro parked here. You shouldn't have known they were there."

"I know everything going on in the park." Chambers seemed utterly comfortable. "I keep a radio monitor on the park frequency. You see, some years ago they planned to widen the road from the entrance to Longmire and in the process take out several hundred trees. Ancient trees. Trees with hundreds of years behind them and hundreds of years ahead of them yet. Public opinion was against it, but they seemed determined to go ahead with the widening. So unknown to the park, some friends and I started monitoring their radio. If they started to proceed with the project, we were prepared to nail them instantly with an injunction. Fortunately, cooler heads prevailed."

Jack could get into a rip-roaring argument here about meddlers doing more damage than good and about letting the Park Service take care of the land entrusted to it. He decided to back off for now. He changed the subject, just to be safe. "The man whose dog was killed. Do you remember his name?"

"Elroy Washington. He lives in National now."

"National. That's the area just west of Ashford, a few miles outside the park."

"Yes. You know, during the height of logging here, fifty years ago, National had a couple thousand people in it. Now it has less than a hundred."

"One of whom is Elroy Washington." The dampness from the rotting log was soaking into Jack's jeans. He stood up. "If I may, let me help you measure the tree."

Chambers stood. "Thank you. I can use the help. I was going to bring a friend, but I ended up coming alone. It's hard to do when you're alone."

"A friend. Elizabeth Munro?"

"Interesting young woman. I take it you've talked to her, from the questions you've been asking me."

"For an hour or so. Then she had to go to work." Jack needed a chisel to peel Maxx off his leg. He started for the Grandfather Cedar, with the dog again hard by his knee.

"She had to work today too."

"Sunday?"

"She works odd hours."

"Very. For a collection agency, did she say?"

From a small daypack, Chambers pulled a measuring tape. He handed the end to Jack. "She posts the collec-

55

tions made, prepares dun letters, and builds a list of telephone numbers for the callers to call next day. I would consider it unsavory work, but she sees the value in it, and it pays fairly well." He walked off around the Grandfather Cedar.

Jack called, "I know you don't measure around the base, but I forget how high up you go."

"About here." Chambers came around beside Jack and tugged the tape snug. "Approximate is all right. If it seems to be challenging the record, they'll send out their own crew to measure it exactly."

"Didn't the park already measure it?"

"I want to do it myself. Just a detail. I tend to obsess on details." Chambers whipped out a pocket notebook and started writing.

"This cedar is bigger around than some sports cars."

Chambers grinned. At least Jack thought he did. "Can you imagine this thing as the nation's Christmas tree? It would dwarf the White House. 'O tannenbaum,' indeed! Now. If you will hold this right here . . ." The bearded druid placed the end of his tape against the trunk.

Jack pinned it down.

Chambers walked away, stringing out the tape as he spoke. "I was, in fact, going to do this last week. But Liz asked me to help her, so I decided to forgo this. Two excuses to come up here instead of one—who can pass that up? Now will you bring your end of the tape to this point right here?"

Jack obeyed. Maxx stuck to his leg with SuperGlue. "Elroy Washington. I'd like to talk to him. Just for curiosity. It doesn't pertain to the Getz case or anything."

"No, you don't. He's not a nice man. Eerie Elroy didn't get his name because it's alliterative."

"And you say someone in a park vehicle picked him up along the road. Do you happen to know who?"

"Yes, I do. A friend of mine, a ranger named Darryl Grade."

56

6

There's a
Song in the Air

Wolves are not the only ravening beasts, nor are they limited to the forest. There are also news reporters.

Jack spent two hours of Monday morning being pressed in a press conference. He despised press conferences. "The public's need to know" was the phrase Hal used to dismiss Jack's whining and complaining about getting scheduled into this one.

"Why in heaven's name would the public want to know about John Getz? According to numerous sources he was a socially inept dork," Jack returned, and even though no one could give him a decent answer, he got to trade questions, answers, and irritated banter with a dozen members of the fourth estate anyway.

The conference itself was held in Tacoma, more than an hour and a half from Longmire, so the day was essentially shot by the time Jack got to town and got back. At the conference he tried to memorize faces. From the questions some of them were asking, he felt pretty certain that as soon as they hit a slow news bog they'd be out for live footage from the scene.

Sure enough, he wasn't back but an hour, and was walking from his apartment down to Longmire Inn for a cup of coffee, when the first of the news vans rolled by.

With KOOL emblazoned across its side and a satellite dish on its roof, it commanded interest if not respect from everyone who watched it pass. A little boy by the hiking center waved enthusiastically at them, a "Hey, mister! Take my picture!" gesture. No one in the van waved back.

Jack stepped into the Inn's dining room. He was known there by now. He made his own meals at the apartment, but one does not live by bread alone. There is also coffee and doughnuts.

The KOOL van was not the only such in the area. Two familiar faces from the conference this morning were eating lunch here. The instant they spotted him, both bobbed to their feet. He was ambushed. Jack mentally kicked himself that he had failed to check out the parking lot in back for press vehicles.

He recognized the younger of the two women as one of the lesser luminaries from the ABC news affiliate.

"Mr. Prester!" A manufactured blonde, the girl couldn't be more than twenty (or was Jack just getting old?). In her nattily tailored power jacket she trotted over and parked in front of him. "When the stringer from NBC asked you about the possibility of a Bigfoot, you very neatly skirted the issue."

Jack smiled broadly. "And I'm still skirting, ma'am. There's nothing to suggest something like that."

"A stone knife? Come on!"

"There's no record in the literature that Bigfoots—Bigfeet? What would the plural be, anyway?—that unknown things with huge extremities use tools or implements. Which is to assume such creatures exist, and that's a pretty ragged assumption. I'd much sooner suspect some neolithic back-to-nature freak who's not quite ready for the Early Iron Age. Or a primitive person. Or a really clumsy oaf who's always cutting himself on steel knives and doesn't want to leave his own blood at the scene. Blood typing and forensics and all that, you know."

58

"You're very clever. Answer one straight once. What are the chances that a Bigfoot exists?"

"Zip."

The young woman smirked. "They've been reported in this area. What are the chances that we have a Bigfoot situation here?"

"Double zip." Jack wished he could remember her name. His tirade would be so much more effective if he could address her by name. "Ma'am, I am an investigator. That means I'm going to exhaust the probabilities before I start spending any time on mere possibilities, particularly such a remote one. Is that straight enough?"

"Thank you. Do you see political implications in Getz's murder?"

"We discussed that at the conference earlier. In fact, I believe it was you who brought the topic up."

"That I did. You have a good memory—a lot of questions were coming at you."

Jack wanted to be done with this and get out of here. In fact, he'd even do without his coffee. But on the other hand . . . "Good memory, huh? I've forgotten your name."

"Norma Reid."

"That's right. Ms. Reid, you keep pressing those two points—a political connection and the Bigfoot angle. Would you like to help me? Help the investigation?"

"Sure! How?"

"Provide me with whatever you can in the way of leads. The political angle, for example. Why do you keep drumming on it? What do you know that can help me?"

"Reveal my sources?" She gave him a sour "Honestly, Mr. Prester!" scowl.

"I'm not expecting you to sing like a canary. Just get me pointed in the right direction. I'm a stranger here. No contacts, no connections. As a reporter, you have plenty."

She studied him for a count of ten. As she reached into her purse, she said, "I'm sorry, Mr. Prester. I'm not going to sing at all. No." She fumbled in her purse a moment. "Now that I've turned off the tape recorder, tell me, did you mean that?"

"Yes."

"About me being a reporter?"

"Aren't you?"

She smiled weakly. "A lot of people would say that the pretty faces who read the news on TV shouldn't try to call themselves reporters." She waved a hand. "Come join us, please. Sure, I'd like to help you. So would Annie, especially if it'll give us a scoop or angle."

"There is no free lunch." Jack followed her to their table.

The other woman of the pair wore tweed the way an Englishman wears a raincoat—sort of born into it. She was somewhere past fifty, somewhat beyond innocence, somehow above being conned or cajoled. Her steel gray eyes pounced on one from behind a strong, time-sculptured face. She reached out a hand for a shake. "Anne Somersby, *News Tribune.*" Her grip was firm.

"Local Tacoma columnist. Sort of the Paul Harvey of Pierce County." Jack sat down because both women reseated themselves.

"You know how to flatter a person. Thank you, Mr. Prester." Her voice flowed like contralto water. Radio trained.

Over by the kitchen door, the waitress caught his eye and raised her eyebrows hopefully. *The usual?*

Jack nodded and turned back to Ms. Somersby. "Ms. Reid here just offered to sing like an angel in return for a scoop, and claimed you'd join her in a duet. She even pretended to turn off her tape recorder, which is, no doubt, still running in order to catch every nuance of the music. I'm willing to buy. I need leads to follow, ideas to pursue, names to investigate. Anything you can offer will be remembered as a favor to be returned."

Ms. Reid looked somewhat abashed, but not enough that she admitted she was still recording.

The columnist smiled slightly. "I'm not looking for hard news. I'm looking for the overlooked story, the human interest material that casts a new light on the story."

"But you wouldn't mind being in ahead of the crowd."

"You're asking, would I mind being considered a prophet? I'm too vain to deny it. I'd love it. But not at the cost of sources."

"I understand."

The waitress arrived with his coffee and maple bar. They had good doughnuts here, even in the afternoon.

He waited until she left. "For starters, list for me the people and organizations you would consider prime suspects."

Those cold steel eyes locked onto his and held steady. "Foremost, the National Park Service, removing the thorn in their side before it festered worse. Secondly, timber concerns. They are many around here, and they are powerful. He opposed them. But even worse, he was drawing attention toward wholesale conservation of existing forests. They didn't want him continually bringing some new aspect of extreme conservative environmentalism to the public eye and ear."

"He was that powerful?"

"No, that noisy. It's not the people on the side of right or reason that win—or even the most powerful. It's the noisiest."

The blonde nodded sagely. "It's the squeaky wheel that gets the grease."

Jack nodded just as sagely. "It's also the first replaced. Didn't he have any friends?"

"The Forest Friends." The blonde finished her bran muffin, or whatever it was. "They're a group dedicated to preserving trees."

"He wasn't a card-carrying member. They weren't extreme enough for him." He could hear Anne Somersby's voice tighten. No doubt she loved to blot information up, but she sure didn't like giving information out. "He shared some goals, had some contact."

"Jay Chambers a member of the group?"

"Founded it."

"Would you consider Jay Chambers a suspect, were you a police officer?"

The blonde half smiled. "No one ever asked me a question like that before. I like it. If I were a police officer—which I very nearly was once, but then I went into journalism instead—I'd suspect the Park Service. John Getz was constantly writing letters, notifying media, holding press conferences, filing torts, initiating suits and complaints. He had quite an arsenal of tricks, all the standard ones with variations, and he used them all."

"What did he do for a living? There's no employer mentioned in any of the reports I read."

"Trust fund. No need to work like us common folk."

"The great faceless National Park Service as a bunch or specific persons therein?"

The blonde shrugged. "You Park Service people are like the military. You even wear military creases in your shirts. It doesn't matter who in the chain of command pulls the trigger, general or infantryman. Know what I mean?"

If Jack knew what she meant, which he did, he failed to say so because here came Ev hurrying in the doors at the far end of the dining room. He stood up as her line of sight came skating across the room toward them. She spotted them instantly and glided up to the table.

Jack introduced everyone around, and Anne Somersby invited Ev to join them. As they settled back into their chairs, Jack felt proud to be seen in public with Ev. It was not just that she looked good; she cut a smart figure, brisk and confident. Professional. Competent.

And here was the phenomenon that always amazed him. The women developed an almost instantaneous bond, a camaraderie. Without preliminary, they addressed each other on a first-name basis, smiled, skipped that whole sizing-up ritual of cautious circling that men tend to carry out. They laughed together, and Ev was not a laughing sort of person under normal circumstances.

Jack sat back and carefully avoided intruding. Ev would probably get much farther much faster with these two than he possibly could. He gave them five minutes before bringing it back to business. After all, they had invited him to sit here in order to conduct business. The waitress refilled his coffee cup unbidden.

Jack grimaced. "I hate to think the flat hat folk in gray, green, and cordovan are the only possible suspects. You said something about timber interests?"

"Talk to the people who put out a periodical called *Logger's World*. They can give you all the names and phone numbers associated with the timber industry."

"But you're not going to."

Anne shifted her shoulders, a gesture even less committal than a shrug. "I can, I suppose. And some other possibilities. For information only. Sources, not suspects, of course."

Jack smiled on the inside. He was getting a little music out of these two after all. "Of course. Look. I'm not greedy. I'm happy to give if I can get. Short of identifying the murderer in your presence and granting you an exclusive, which I'd love to do but am not quite up to at the moment, what can I do for you?" He looked from woman to woman.

Anne Somersby studied him intently, silently. Suddenly she snapped, "Turn off that stupid tape recorder, Norma. Set it out here where we can see it."

Ms. Reid reluctantly, begrudgingly, hauled her tape recorder out of her purse and plunked it on the table.

Anne reached out and flicked the switch. "There." She leaned back and returned to studying Jack. "John Getz kept a journal. An intimate journal, apparently. He planned eventually to edit it into a book. I would love to get my hands on a Xerox copy of that journal. The complete journal, no missing pages. I understand how law enforcement agencies would need the original if it contained any evidence—and it certainly would. But I want its content."

"A journal." Jack pursed his lips. "Any hints where to find it?"

"You're the detective." Anne shrugged. "You find it. Besides, you can cross the police tape. We can't."

Jack looked at Ev. She hadn't said a word. Surely she could add something to this discussion. She was a woman, these two were women—sisterhood and all that.

She asked, "Do you smoke, Anne?"

Suddenly Jack felt embarrassed to be seen in public with Ev. Of all the cockamamie non sequitur things to say . . .

But Anne apparently didn't consider it off-the-wall. She replied with a guarded "No."

Ev smiled. "Just wondered."

End of that little exchange.

Jack looked from face to face. "I'll see what I can do."

"And I'll develop a list of leads for you." Anne Somersby stood up, and Jack was startled to realize the woman couldn't be more than five four. Seated, she had seemed a giant.

They parted company then, Ev and Jack out the back door and the two reporters out the front because the ladies' room was on the way at the front of the building.

Jack paused beyond the doors. "Where you going?"

"Over to your place? I spent the day talking to a girl John Getz used to date, and a couple others like that. I didn't get much, but I'll write up what I have."

Jack nodded and headed down the walkway.

She trotted along at his side and bubbled. "At the Clearcut last evening, Darryl showed me the drink you just have to have."

"I need a drink?"

"It's called Black Dog Ale. There's a picture of a black Labrador retriever on the label. It's Maxx!"

"Now that really burns me. Here Maxx has been modeling behind my back, and he's not cutting me in on the proceeds. He makes more than I do, and I'm the one pays for his dog food."

She giggled. "He never told you about that ale account, huh?"

"Doesn't that beat all? What's this 'Do you smoke' stuff?"

"She had a little square something in the breast pocket of her jacket. Didn't you notice it? She doesn't use a hearing aid, so it's either a cigarette hard-pack or a recorder. If it's not a cigarette pack . . ."

"Gotcha. Clever." It grated on him that Ev the neophyte investigator would notice something like that and he had missed it.

Ev grimaced. "The reason I came looking for you—I figured since you weren't at the apartment you'd be over here—is because Hal just called. He's getting really anxious that we sew this up. That we get the case all sewed up, I mean."

"Only eight days and I'm supposed to be flying. *Mele Kalikimaka.*"

"What?"

"Merry Christmas, in Hawaiian. He can't be any more anxious than I am."

"I'm sure. But he did seem insistent. He didn't sound very impressed when I described what we have so far. He has a point—it isn't very much." She frowned. "Did you actually accomplish anything with those two? They weren't very helpful."

"Neither was I."

"Or the people I interviewed today. All they want to talk about is whether this business about spotted owls and all is good or bad, and something about ancient mermaids, and—"

"Murrelets?"

"That's it. Nothing really useful."

"The *Logger's World* angle is a good lead. I admit it isn't exactly the 'Hallelujah Chorus,' but there's a song in the air."

7
Good Christian Men, Rejoice

Breaking and entering being a criminal offense, good Christian men won't even think of it. Jack slipped his laminated driver's license into the narrow space between door and jamb. If you do it just right, and twist the knob just so, and aren't hampered by a deadbolt, you can open a locked door that way. The door of murder victim John Getz's apartment swung open, and Jack stepped inside, an official breaker and enterer.

Not only that, he was contributing to the delinquency of an innocent young woman. Ev stepped inside behind him.

She closed the door and flicked on the overhead light. "Oh, dear! What a . . ."

Jack could understand why words would fail her. This two-bedroom apartment had belonged to a man whose childhood experience must have consisted exclusively of Mom's saying, "Johnny, please clean up your room!"

John Getz, the police reports stated, lived alone. That was obvious. There was no room in here for a second person. He used the spare bedroom as his office. Fully equipped it was, with a computer and all the trimmings, enough file cabinets to handle the Congressional Record, a fax, a modem, a cordless phone, and a police radio with scanner. Whoever had gone through it during the preliminary investigation—feds probably—hadn't turned the scanner off. At random times it still squawked numbers and arcane messages as dispatchers sent public servants out on errands of mercy and mayhem.

Getz's bedroom walls were lined with metal shelves to hold reams and reams and reams of papers. The living/dining room was crammed with books. Crowded bookshelves covered the walls; unshelved books covered every available flat space.

Jack looked about more in dismay than in amazement. "I guess I'm not surprised. John Getz fitted the profile for all this. Loner. His whole life wrapped up in his environmental interests."

"It's a modest apartment, actually. He must have spent his money almost wholly on his crusading. Getting the word out. Saving the world."

"Would that more Christians were that single-minded about the gospel! Think what God could do. OK, Ev. You're John Getz. You're keeping a journal. Where do you keep it?"

"You can't be serious! You can't expect to find anything in this mess. All he had to do was slip it between two files. Coded label, of course, or no label at all. It would take a dozen people a month to sift through all this. Look at it!"

"No, I said, 'You're John Getz.' Think like he thought."

She wandered from room to room, her face hardened into a puzzled frown. Suddenly she softened, brightened. She walked over to Getz's ergonomically correct kneel-on-it chair, settled herself onto it, and turned on the computer.

Jack smiled. A man with all these electronic toys would not put his journal on paper. Jack considered himself fortunate to find the ON switch of the average electronic gizmo and never did bother figuring out how to program a VCR. Ev played computers the way Horowitz played the violin. Or was it the piano?

"Jack? Something's wrong! I mean, really, seriously wrong."

"The investigators who did the prelims probably messed something up because they didn't know what they were doing with that thing. Try fooling around with it. There might be a password thingamabob or something."

"No, I mean wrong." She ticked the keys some more and sat back, grim. "Someone reformatted the hard drive. Every single solitary thing on the hard drive is erased. Clear gone."

Jack leaned over and propped against the computer table, his chin practically on her shoulder. "You sure? That's not something that happens accidentally. You have to do it on purpose. Not even investigators are that clumsy or stupid."

He twisted a little so he could look at her, and she was studying him. She frowned. "Someone heard he was killed and hurried over here and did it before the cops . . . no." She shook her head. Her hair floated. "As soon as he was discovered, this place would be sealed off. Out of reach of a civilian. Is that right?"

"That's right. I'll check and make sure, but I think they taped it and went over it pretty soon."

"Therefore," she said slowly, "the murderer is responsible. The murderer knew Getz was dead—or would be—and slipped in and did this. Maybe even the morning of the day he died." Those Bambi eyes enlarged from pint to quart size. "Jack? We find out who was here just before he died, and we've found our murderer!"

"A cause for rejoicing, maybe." The thought tickled his breastbone. "Which would give us a good start, but no evidence. This isn't like the game of Clue, where you win if you're first to guess the culprit. There are two parts to this game—figuring out the killer and convincing a jury you were bright enough to get the right person."

"A jury would believe that. I mean, that whoever

69

came over here, say the morning of the murder, would be the one."

"And the murderer's attorney would come back with 'How about the person who had borrowed his bathrobe and was bringing it back? Or the fellow who dropped off something Getz asked for and left again because Getz wasn't home? Or the guy who just stopped in to say hello and went inside and left a note?' You need a solid chain of evidence linking the crime to the alleged criminal. No breaks, no gaps. See what I mean?"

She nodded dejectedly.

"Is there any way of retrieving what used to be on the disk?"

"Sometimes. In fact, I think there are people who specialize in restoring data. Hal would know. But I don't know if they can restore it when it's been reformatted." She began to stare at him again. "Backup. Getz surely backed up his most important stuff."

"Backup." Now it was Jack's turn to become deject-ed. He nodded toward at least two dozen of those plastic diskette file boxes, some big, some small, lined up on the shelf above the monitor. "Look at them all! The five-and-a-fourths hold plenty, and those little three-and-a-half high-densities hold huge amounts. The whole *Oxford Dictionary*. Maybe even the complete rules of croquet, but that's probably stretching it. And as you so neatly pointed out, he surely would code the label, or mislabel it completely. We'd have to read every one of these suckers!"

"Or . . . think like John Getz." She turned her atten-tion from Jack to the diskette file boxes. She looked at the dozens of software manuals stashed on the uppermost shelf.

Chewing her lip in that way of hers, she stood, pulled down the Spinrite binder, and slid its diskette out of its sleeve. "You understand about grandfathers, don't you?" She slipped the diskette back in.

"The original diskettes you receive when you buy a

program. I know you never use them. You copy them and use the copies."

"Right." She opened a ten-disk storage box labeled WP5.1 MASTERS and leafed through the disks. She removed the next to last one, identified by a printed factory label as PRINTERS DOT MATRIX.

She popped it into the machine and switched to the A-drive. It wouldn't read it. She settled into her chair. "I'm going to put the operating system and WordPerfect back on the hard drive, so we can use it. It will only take a couple minutes. Will that mess up the evidence somehow?"

"No. For you, easy. For me, days. Go for it." Jack crossed to the dead man's desk. He borrowed the dead man's pen and the dead man's paper and wrote up their finding—that the machine had been erased by reformatting—while it was still fresh in mind.

"Jack? Look."

He walked over to her, leaned by her ear, and looked. He stared. "How in the name of all that McDonald's puts on their Big Mac did you come up with that?"

She was scrolling page after page of diary entries, all dated and all keyed by an ALL CAPS string. "Like you said. 'Think like John Getz.' He was terribly sloppy here in the apartment, right? People who are pigs in real life are very often extremely orderly in their work or some other area of living. I saw it all the time in college and in the Washington office. So there had to be a logical order to his filing and hiding stuff."

Jack knew that. Jack was the psychologist.

She continued, "And Getz was a computer whiz. He loved technology. I mean, look at all these toys. The high-resolution color monitor, fax, two printers. If someone really wanted his journal, they'd read all his diskettes. But not his grandfathers. These are the factory diskettes with the original programs. You copy them and stick them away somewhere and forget them. You don't even think about reading the grandfathers."

"So he erased the WordPerfect factory-original diskette and put his journal backup on it instead. Where no one would ever think to look for it. Beautiful. But how did you find it?"

She sat back, beaming. "To avoid accidentally damaging information on your grandfather—your original—you put one of these write protect stickers on it. Then you can take information off it, but you can't inadvertently send any messages to it, like accidentally erasing it or something." She held up Diskette Number One of Getz's WordPerfect program and pointed to its lower right edge. Over the little notch in the side, a metallic sticker had been pressed.

Jack knew that. He rarely ever stuck one of those write protect stickers on anything he transferred to disk—nothing he transferred to a floppy was worth protecting.

Triumphantly she continued, "But he wouldn't put a sticker on a diskette he was constantly transferring information to, and a journal is daily entries, or nearly so. It would be clumsy and inconvenient. So I looked for any grandfather disk with an original factory label that did not have a write protect sticker. There it was."

There it was. Cause for rejoicing indeed. Not in a million years would Jack have come up with that. He would have begged his boss, Hal "Ebenezer Scrooge" Edmond, for money to hire half a dozen people for a couple weeks to read through this mess seeking needles in haystacks. Read through every single diskette. But not the original diskettes holding commercially prepared programs. And "I Suppose, Cratchit, You Want Christmas Off" Hal would have told him to find out what he needed some other way.

Ev had pulled it out of the hat in less than fifteen minutes.

She ticked the arrow-up key in rapid staccato. "There's an awful lot of stuff here, and I'm sure this is only the latest disk. So I'm starting a few pages up from the end here, right? This one's dated November first."

Jack read the screen from over her shoulder. "'Marriage is like flies on a screen door. The ones inside want out, and the ones outside want in.' Now there's an interesting philosophy for you. So he was a philosopher as well as a gadfly."

"I think you used the words 'socially inept.' And how! I assume you're not going to adopt his philosophy."

"Never make rash assumptions." He read on. "'How could Kerri marry into a situation like that? Oh, well. It's useful to me.'" Jack frowned. "Can you scroll back and find a prior reference to Kerri?"

"Easier is just search backwards." She leaned on the shift and hit the F2 key. "Do you think he means Kerri Haskell?"

"Not a whole lot of Kerris around who spell it that way. He seems to be a fairly careful speller too."

The screen jumped, and the cursor landed on *Kerri*. Ev scrolled up to the date, October 28, and scrolled back down to the reference.

It worked ha ha. My invention worked. Fiction. She knows it and I know it, but it's so true to life the world would believe it. And of course, so would Jeff. He is such an ignorant, arrogant, black-hearted, pompous donkey that I derive a great deal of pleasure in this. I only wish it were he instead of Kerri who held the position of power. I would make him squirm like the worm he is. Now that would be pleasure!

Ah, the power of fiction! If only I had known years ago how powerful fiction is, I could have done so much more, and quicker. A few lies well placed, and the world is yours. Hitler learned it early. I, after wasting years, understand it now.

Ev sat back and stared at the screen. "He's not just socially inept, Jack. He's a certified fruitcake."

"It isn't Christmas without fruitcake."

"When I'm in his apartment here on his machine reading his journal, he doesn't seem so dead—know what I mean? I have to remind myself he's a dead fruitcake."

"All fruitcakes are, from the moment they're baked. Did you ever try to eat one? Aunt Belle sent us one for Christmas maybe ten years ago. Mom sent it to a cousin in Springfield and got it back three years later from a niece in Arizona, so she sent it to Aunt Belle the next year. Aunt Belle was tickled pink. She never recognized it. She cut its odyssey short by eating it."

Ev giggled. "My mom got one too, from some shirt-tail relative. She was disgusted, so she sent it right back to him the next year. Same wrapping, same bow, everything."

"He get the hint?"

"Did he ever. He never sent a present again."

Jack wagged his head. "Your mom really does get into the spirit of Christmas."

They explored references to Kerri and found few others, save for cryptic notes about bugging her to respond to this letter or that. He must have been a royal pest. Next they searched for *Darryl* and *Grade.* On December first, John Getz wrote:

Personal relationships. How much better off we would all be without them. I cannot begin to imagine how much pain, frustration—yes, even crime—mankind could save simply by minimizing relationships to those necessary for survival. Grade constantly amazes me. Every time I think I know him, some new aspect of him crops up. In some ways, he is the quintessential renaissance man. In others, he is Hitler. You never know which face will turn toward you. Simply amazing!

Jeff Haskell was the brunt primarily of editorial comments.

What a boor. What a Neanderthal. That brainless oaf.

Jack perceived that Getz, like Elizabeth Munro, was staunchly antihunting.
Of Elizabeth Munro:

Jay called to talk to me about a girl who's causing problems. She's making unusual demands that could cause the park and the public as well to grow bored with our message. She's too extreme even for Jay, and that's going some. He wants to cajole her into diverting her interests elsewhere. I think that's a mistake, and I'll tell him so. At least he's wising up to the fact that I can give him the kind of advice he needs. He's certainly not getting it from his white-robed tree nuts. I have so much on him, I don't know why he bothers listening to them at all.

Of Jay himself:

I'll bring him around to my position or get him shunted aside. One or the other. This can't go on. He's messing me up.

Ev scrolled to the end. She whispered, "Look!"
Getz's final sentence of his final entry read,

I've got to shut Elroy up.

8

God Rest Ye
Merry, Gentlemen

A person's surroundings—his home, his car, his work area—will, one way or another, tell you who that person is. Everything Jack saw here proclaimed, "This guy is cuckoo."

He had just driven over a road so rutted a goat could break a leg, up through woods as dense as pudding, to a small log house clinging to the mountainside with little more than ground covers and creeping raspberry vines to hold it in place. Eerie Elroy Washington's domicile.

Jack never would have found it without Darryl Grade on the seat beside him, navigating. ("His place is a little hard to get to," said Darryl. "That's like saying King Kong is too big to fit in a Datsun," said Jack.)

Eerie Elroy's work area, if it could be called that, was a pile of cedar logs and spools, sawdust and chips beside the house. Elroy, obviously, created heroic-sized woodcarvings with an ax and chain saw. A dozen chunks of cedar logs, all hacked at with a chain saw and none completed, lay a-jumble among the chips. But even that chaotic mess did not define Eerie Elroy as well as did his vehicle.

Eerie Elroy drove a hearse.

Jack pulled his pickup in behind the hearse and took his time walking back to Maxx's cage. Darryl crawled out the other side. Jack let Maxx out and removed his collar. "Maxx, heel."

They got maybe seven steps before a shotgun blast from the house still further defined Eerie Elroy.

"Maxxdown!" Jack dived behind the hearse and yanked his own gun. "I thought you said he was a friend of yours."

"This is how he treats his friends. It's all yours. I'm not commissioned anymore."

"Mr. Washington?" Jack yelled. "Darryl and I want to talk to you."

"What about?"

"The death in the park a couple days ago. Up at Reflection—"

The shotgun went off again. So far, this interview wasn't proceeding all that well. Eerie Elroy was firing across Jack's bow, so to speak—he didn't seem actually to be peppering anything. But that made Jack no less hesitant about stepping out into the open.

He would try once more before they beat a graceful though hasty retreat. "Mr. Washington? Why did John Getz hate you so much?"

He half expected another load of buckshot. Instead he got "Did he say that?"

"He sure did. An entry in his journal. I have a print-out right here of everything he said about you."

"Fetch it in."

"OK, so maybe I look like my IQ and my golf score are running neck and neck. But I'm not that stupid." Jack paused a second, looking at Darryl without really seeing him. "Stand out on the porch with your shotgun at your feet, and we'll come on in." He whispered to Darryl, "You sure he lives alone?"

"Jack, who would want to live with Elroy Washington?"

"Right. And cruise downtown Elbe, population a hundred and eighty, in a hearse?"

When Eerie Elroy stepped out onto his porch and laid his shotgun down, Jack took the liberty of assuming some other shotgun was not pointed at him from inside. He pulled the two-page printout out of his shirt and held it aloft in his left hand. He had made no promises about his own weapon, and he kept none. He raised his right hand, his gun clearly visible, as he started for the house. "Maxx, heel."

Beside him, Darryl spread his hands wide, holding them clear. So this was how Eerie treated friends?

Eerie almost bolted, but the printout, like a magnet, drew his eyes and his attention.

Jack reached the porch and held out the paper, his arm stretched. Eerie stepped over his shotgun in order to reach out and grab the gossip. He stared at Jack's eyes. Jack stared back. Contact.

Eerie looked like the upholstery in his hearse—dark and gloomy and a little ragged. The plaid flannel shirt, the trailworn jeans, the wide red suspenders were what everyone around here wore. The steel-toe logging boots were a dime a dozen in these parts. The short, scraggly salt-and-pepper beard, the close-trimmed gray hair could belong to any logger over fifty-five. But those listless, watery gray eyes set deeply were one of a kind. From behind scratched glasses, Eerie Elroy viewed the world through a permanent film of moisture.

He watched Jack another moment, nodded to Darryl, and glanced down at the printout. Within moments he was engrossed. He read the second page as Jack waited. He looked up. "This is Getz's diary?"

"The parts that mention you, yes. Since November first." Jack risked holstering his gun in order to reach for a handshake. "John Prester. I'm investigating Getz's murder."

"Murder. You sure he was murdered."

"Certain."

"Not just scared to death."

"Real honest-to-goodness murdered."

"You two didn't come up here to give me this."

"I told you. We want to talk to you."

"'Bout the Bigfoot."

"About the murder."

"Same thing." Eerie studied Jack another few seconds. "Come on in, I guess." He nodded toward Maxx. "Him too."

"Thank you."

Before Eerie could reach down for his gun, Jack scooped it up, broke the breech open and pulled the two shells in the barrels by digging his fingernail under them. Obviously, the ejector didn't work. It smelled strongly of cordite. Jack handed it to him still open. Eerie didn't bother to snap it shut. He turned and walked inside, the shotgun slung loosely at his side.

Eerie's home inside looked like the rest of the place, except for one corner. The cabin interior was divided by an archway into two rooms, and a staircase at the far end led to a loft. In this kitchen-dining area stood a battered table, a couple of chairs, and a fairly modern-looking propane stove and fridge. The faucet on the sink under the window dripped. Sleeping quarters must be the loft, because the other room was a living room and office combination. The office was the exceptional area.

Eerie's small desk in the corner looked neat and orderly. On the two walls of that section of the living room, floor-to-ceiling bookcases—nothing more than roughhewn planks on cement blocks—were crammed full of books and binders. Every edge was lined up just so against the outside edge of the shelf. Every volume, large or small, stood ramrod straight. The few books taller than the cement-block spacers were neatly stacked flat on a shelf, largest on the bottom.

Jack realized his mind was off in a cloud puzzling over the strange inconsistency when Eerie repeated, probably for the third time, "Sit down." Jack pulled out a chair by the table and sat. Darryl sprawled at ease in a chair beside him.

Eerie laid the emptied shotgun on the table. "What do you want?"

"You know about Getz's death."

"Who don't? The day he was found it was all over town. All kinds of rumors floating around."

"I can imagine. I grew up in a rural area. You run your car into a ditch five miles out of town, and the news gets back before you do." Jack pointed to the printout in Elroy's hand. "Can you speculate on why Getz wanted to get rid of you?"

"You ever meet him? He was *weird,* man."

"That's not reason enough. I'm weird too, and I'm finding you fascinating. Why else?"

"Who knows, with him?" And Eerie essentially clammed up.

Jack tried a flanking maneuver. "Your office in there. That's part of what I find fascinating. If my office were that tidy I might actually be able to find something. Don't count on it ever happening, but 'if.'"

Eerie smiled sadly. "I don't read very well. Got so-so grades in school. Quit in the tenth grade to work in the woods. So I'm not good at using libraries and books and things. I have to keep it cleaned up there, or I can't find what I'm looking for. Even so it takes me awhile sometimes."

"Find stuff. You mean cross-referencing and rereading material."

"Yeah."

"Did you and John Getz ever exchange material—books or papers?"

"He wanted me to give him stuff sometimes, but I wouldn't. This here's my collection, and I don't part with any of it."

"Did he ever give you any books or papers?"

80

"Nah. Besides, I already have everything that there is in my—whatchacallit—my field of interest."

Jack took a stab in the dark. "Which is Bigfoot."

Eerie scowled darkly at the blond giant. "You told him."

Darryl shook his head. "No. We didn't discuss you much at all. I came along to help him find the place. You know how people get lost on these old logging roads."

Jack shrugged. "Easy guess. You quit work right after that incident when your dog was killed. You drew unemployment as long as you could, and now you make enough money to live on by creating chain-saw carvings. I saw your saw yard out beside the house there. You make various sizes of sculptures of bears—and of Bigfoot."

"You know what it was like when I came out of the woods with my story? My best friends, if you can call 'em that, laughed in my face. The newspaper wasn't interested. Not even the *Dispatch*. My friends, they said I hated that stupid dog anyway, so I got rid of him and this was my story. Some friends."

Jack fired another shot in the dark. "Did the Bigfoot kill Getz?"

"He could have."

"Hoffa could have. That's not what I'm asking. If all those books and papers around your desk are material on Bigfoot, you know as much about it as any man alive. Getz was stabbed to death. Is it likely a Bigfoot could have done it?"

Eerie looked from Jack to Darryl to Jack. "No."

"Why not?"

"Not likely. You said likely. The thing would've just grabbed Getz and squeezed. No need to use a knife. You shoulda seen the way the life just got squeezed out of my dog. Besides, there's no record of a Bigfoot ever threatening or killing a human being."

"Even when cornered?"

Eerie snarfed much the way Maxx snarfed. "You don't corner a tiger. A Bigfoot, either."

"A news reporter told me two days ago that a Bigfoot was reported in this area. That would be your report, right?"

Eerie stared at Jack a moment and leaped out of his chair. He chugged off through the archway into the other room.

Jack looked at Darryl, and Darryl looked at him. Should they wait politely or follow? Jack wanted a full look at the other room, so he stood up and followed, motioning Maxx silently to his side. Darryl heeled as well as Maxx ever did.

Sure enough, the living room was messy and unkempt save for that one corner. It had a nice picture window facing out onto a clearing that passed for a front yard.

Eerie pulled a worn two-inch ring binder off his shelf. He plunked it open on his desk and thumbed through. "There's lots of sightings in the Northwest. One at Spirit Lake, down by Mount St. Helens. Here." He flipped pages to a yellowed newsclip mounted on a sheet of lined notebook paper. "July 1970. Between Sunrise Point and Mystic Lake. Two hikers."

Darryl frowned. "For certain a Bigfoot, or just footprints?"

Eerie's finger, a wee bit shaky, traced the words as he read. "Eight-foot bipedal mammal with brown hair. Apelike face. Slightly bent at the waist and knees. Does that sound like a footprint? Or even a bear?"

"Not eight feet. Not around here."

Elroy flipped over a couple of pages and tapped another clipping with that pointing finger. "September 1990. Some mushroom hunters up on the slope behind National." He looked up at Jack. "You know where National is?"

"Right here, west of Ashford a mile. We're in it."

Eerie grunted. "I live here for a reason—what'd you say your name was?"

"Prester."

82

"Prester. The mushroom hunters found a line of footprints in the creekbed up behind here. Fifteen-inch footprints. That's less than a quarter mile from the door here."

"You want to find a Bigfoot, in other words. And what? Shoot it? Prove you aren't crazy?"

"That wouldn't prove that. They'd still say I'm crazy. But it'd prove I wasn't lying about the dog and all."

"You don't do a whole lot to dispel the myth. Why a hearse, for pete sake?"

Eerie grinned and shrugged. "Got a good deal on it. You know they never run them things right. Always poking along at fifteen or twenty miles an hour—no wonder they carbon up and run rough. This thing was really coughing, like it had tuberculosis, so I bought it cheap. Besides, the upholstery was torn inside. I rebuilt the engine—ground out the cylinders and everything. And she hums. Don't matter about the upholstery. I carry wood in it, and goats, and every other thing. Really roomy inside. Better'n a pickup truck for most hauling."

Jack grinned. "Smart, when you explain it. I still don't think I want one, though." He frowned. "Why didn't you just retrieve the dog's body?"

Darryl answered that one. "We went up there the next day to do just that. It wasn't around. We never did find it."

"Carried off by some predator?"

"That's what we think."

"Carried off by Bigfoot?"

Eerie nodded. "Could be. We assume they're vegetarian, but that might not be strictly true." He leafed rapidly through his notebook to an entry near the back. "Here's a sighting of a Bigfoot carrying a deer carcass. The experts —and I use the term loosely—claim a thing that size can't be pure carnivore, but apparently it's at least omnivore."

"Interesting." Jack twisted around to where he could read the newspaper clipping. "Do any sightings suggest a Bigfoot would carry or use a weapon, say, to bring a deer down?"

"Nope. No weapons that I found so far."

Jack stood erect. "So that still doesn't answer the first question. Why was Getz so down on you?"

"I don't know, and I don't care." Eerie flipped his ring binder shut and wandered over to the picture window. He stuffed both hands in his pockets and stared at his clearing.

Darryl headed off to settle into the far corner of the sofa.

Jack walked over to within six or seven feet of Elroy, careful to keep some space between them. "Why were you out behind Reflection Lake that day?"

"Hiking. I was hiking, like the report says."

"Loggers don't hike."

Eerie exploded unexpectedly with an expletive and a derisive guffaw. "Then what was I doing there?"

"Hunting for a Bigfoot."

"No!" Eerie wheeled to look at Jack. "I never believed in them until that happened. No, I wasn't looking for a Bigfoot. I wasn't looking for trouble."

Jack kept his voice smooth and even and soft and, he hoped, curious. "What were you really doing up there?"

"Looking at a tree."

"The Grandfather Cedar."

"Yeah. If you know all this, why are you asking me?"

"Because I don't know as much as it sounds like. Keep going."

He stared at Jack again with those watery eyes and turned back toward the window. "What's the most important thing in all the world to you?"

"Jesus Christ."

"I mean besides that."

"There isn't anything besides that. He has to be where you start and where you finish. What's the most important thing in the world to you?"

"Bigfoot. I guess because my friends laughed. Or maybe it goes deeper than that. When that thing rose up in

84

front of me . . . I can't describe it. It's taken over my whole life. It's consuming me. I can't rest for thinking about it. And I can't laugh anymore."

Jack waited.

Eerie stared off into space awhile, then continued. "That day—that day when my whole life changed—I was going up to check on the cedar. I wanted to see if Getz had cut it down like he threatened to."

"Whoa. Getz the superenvironmentalist wanted to cut down the tree?"

"You see, a couple months before, he came out from town and started hanging around the Clearcut."

"The tavern in Ashford."

"Right. Chumming up to the fellows that hang out there. I was one of them. None of us liked him. Didn't have anything to do with him really. Wouldn't let him in. Know what I mean?"

"He was allowed on the premises as much as he wanted, but never in the circle of friendship."

"'Zactly. So finally he sticks himself onto me. Not any more welcome than a leech, but there he was. He had a list of what he called key trees in the park. He wanted me to help him locate the cedar and some others and cut it down. He didn't have a saw because a bigshot environmentalist like him would never have a chain saw, right? Besides, you need a big machine—a Stihl or a Husky, for instance—and at least a four-foot bar before you can think about falling a tree that size. Not some rinkydink little yuppie McCulloch."

Jack owned a McCulloch with a twenty-inch bar. Suddenly he felt distinctly and uncomfortably yuppie. "He promised to pay you for this?"

"Yeah. Not bad, either."

"But why?"

"He wanted it to look like vandalism. Then he was going to use the hornet's nest it stirred up to say, 'Let's get everybody out of the park.' That's what he wanted, you know. Just seal off the park and let it sit there."

"Did you go along with it?"

"No, I didn't go along with it. Too many of my friends, their wives make money off the tourists. You know? Waitressing. That stuff. But I went up to look. Just look."

"And you came upon the Bigfoot up by the Grandfather Cedar. Where Getz was killed."

"No. Getz was killed over on the trail, down a lot closer to the lake. This Grandfather Cedar, it's way off the trail, up around the side of the hill. Darryl here can tell you. He was one of the first to find the body, you know." Eerie scowled at Darryl. "Didn't you tell him that?"

"We didn't have much time to talk, bouncing up your road."

Eerie smirked and let it by. Nothing on his face suggested to Jack that he didn't believe that.

Jack prodded, "And the very first were Jay Chambers and Elizabeth Munro. Do you know them?"

"I know Chambers pretty well."

"How well?"

"We go hunting now and then. Elk. Over to Potholes occasionally for ducks or chukar. I don't go for the bowhunting like he does, but regular season I go. He's a good hunting companion. Nuts in some ways, though." Eerie lost interest in the clearing. He strolled over and flopped down on his sofa, wagging his head. "They call me crazy. Know what Sammhain is?"

"I've heard the word, but I forget."

"You might as well call it Halloween. Same thing. Druids—Chambers is a druid, you know—they celebrate the wildest, wooliest three days you ever saw, the last of October. It's Halloween with a vengeance. All the usual Halloweening and some nasty stuff too. That's the chaos the world was formed out of, you see. Then they observe the first of November with rites and rituals and things, and that's the new order of things. Then that's their New Year, and they start another cycle of holidays. Observations."

86

"What? Chambers invited you along on this?" This business of standing up while Eerie was sitting down wasn't working. Darryl had the right idea. Stay eye level. Jack settled down on the nearest thing, a battered old armchair.

For the first time, Eerie began to act a little animated. "He said I'd make a good druid because I know so much about the woods, and I respect it. And he says I'm wise. I don't know about the wise, but he's right in a way. I do know my way around out here. And I do respect them. The trees. They were here centuries before I was, and they'll be here centuries after I'm gone. You gotta respect that."

"Any of the rites include ritual sacrifice?"

Eerie never batted an eye. "Chambers says that part of druidism is way overblown, the stories about sacrifices. I didn't see anything like that. That don't mean it doesn't happen. I just didn't see it." He looked over at Darryl. "You ever see any evidence like that?"

Darryl shook his head. "But like you say, that doesn't mean it doesn't exist."

"There are rituals, I'm sure, you wouldn't be permitted to observe unless you took up the practice." Jack sat forward, his elbows on his knees. "I see a lot of sadness in you. Do you think druidism might ease some of the sadness?"

"I dunno." Eerie's voice was soft, almost plaintive. "I doubt it. I'd mostly be doing it for the woods. The woods gave me a good living once. I owe it. But no. Nothing can heal the pain of your friends all turning on you like that." His eyes flitted away from Jack as another expletive burst out of him. "It happened! The thing is there! And they called me a liar." He tightened, hardened. "Anyway, the word got around what Getz was up to. Darryl here knew. I told him. Too many people knew, so I guess he gave up the idea. But I think it was still at the back of his mind, you know? A trick to use when all the other tricks fail. Later— when everyone's forgot about it."

Jack shifted back so he could settle into the chair

more snugly. "How can I help you? How can I help you ease the bitterness?" Maxx assumed they were staying and curled up in a casual, bulky ball at Jack's feet.

"You don't know me. It's no business of yours anyway."

"Sure it is. Remember what I said about Jesus? He's my CEO, if you will, since my Mac saw makes me a yuppie. He says when someone's hurting, I'm to do my best to help. True, I don't know you. I wouldn't be doing it for you so much as for Him."

"That's crazier'n Chambers."

"I'm guessing that BB—that's Before Bigfoot—you laughed a lot. You lived well and worked hard and enjoyed your friends. You didn't hide up here in the woods firing your shotgun whenever a stranger pulled into your yard. Or a friend." Jack nodded briefly toward Darryl. "I'd like to see you enjoy people again. Get a good night's sleep. And I'd like to see you merry again."

The misty eyes grew just plain wet. "No. No, it'd be nice, but some things you just can't ever bring back. And I expect happiness is one of them."

9

Bless the Beasts
and Children

Maxx was supposed to be Jack's Best Friend. You'd think that as Best Friend he would at least show Jack a little consideration. So why did the mutt so constantly embarrass him? Best friend? Beast friend.

As patches of fog drifted across the hillsides under the usual overcast, Jack and Ev walked down the Stephens Canyon road far enough to check out the new rock work and the newly stabilized hillside above it. Here is where Darryl and Haskell's crew were working when Jay Chambers came to them reporting Getz's body. Maxx expressed interest in the rock wall, but his attentions were of the crassest sort.

The road plastered itself to the steep hillside, more or less tacked in place by rock work on both sides. The canyon fell away to the left as one drove downhill; a hillside rose steeply on the right. Every land surface within sight sloped.

Jack turned Maxx loose with a "Find" and worked a circle up around the disturbed hillside. Ev was not a cross-country hiker. She struggled with brush, with rocks, with loose dirt. They crawled, eventually, to the top of the fresh scar. Jack paused there, mostly to catch his breath.

"I'm never going to get them clean." Ev stared glumly

at her white leather mall-walker shoes. Then she pointed. "This is where the slide started, right?"

Jack nodded. "It loosened some other rocks, so the road folk rolled them on down. Stabilized some loose dirt—see there? Packed that area down over there. They were stomping all over the place."

"To prevent another slide. I see."

"Also, perhaps, to prevent anyone from figuring out whether the slide occurred spontaneously or with a little help. Most of this ground is pretty soft. If your footprints are found up where the slide started, someone might get the idea you started some boulders rolling on purpose."

"Why would anyone . . ." Her Bambi eyes grew wider. "Oh. Of course! He causes the slide, then he knows the road crew will be handy for when the body is reported."

"Or he's on the road crew and wants a legitimate excuse to be up here."

"Who was here? Darryl. Haskell."

"Half a dozen others—I have a list—and maybe one of them with a motive we don't know about. Or not any of them, if the slide occurred spontaneously."

"There are never any easy answers, are there?" She fell in behind him as he headed off across the slope to explore the other side of the scar.

"Only in grade school, where the multiplication tables stay the same."

"They weren't easy. I did terrible in grade school numbers until we moved and a next door neighbor sort of turned me on to math because she loved it."

"Really? You're a budget analyst. She changed your whole life."

"Isn't it crazy? The things that make a profound difference are never the things you expect are going to."

Maxx woofed.

Jack cut across the ragged slope and met his mutt halfway. Maxx obediently dropped into Jack's hand a dusty, dirty wristwatch. It must have snagged on something, because it looked intact except for two bent and spread band links. It was still running. No initials or ID.

Jack praised Maxx affectionately and headed on down the hill. Maxx found nothing more. They got back in the truck, and Jack turned it uphill.

Back at the Reflection Lake parking lot, he showed Ev where Elizabeth thought the new wheelchair access route ought to begin just as soon as the Washington, D.C., office approved it—right there beside the parking lot barrier. They'd have to take out a section of the existing rock work, of course.

As he pointed to the place, Maxx sized it up by sniffing it over. Jack dragged him away. Enough is enough.

They headed up the trail behind the lake. Jack unleashed Maxx and waved an arm. "Maxx. Find." Maxx trotted blissfully off, unhampered by social niceties, sticking his nose into this bush and that.

The fog clumped itself into globs, totally obscuring one part of the hillside, erasing the tops of trees, then clearing away completely only a few feet farther on. It slipped in silently to wrap itself around them. Somewhere upslope, a Clark nutcracker scolded briefly.

Jack's ray of light in this bleak day was that he felt healthy again. He had gone out running this morning and hadn't done badly, considering it had been nearly two weeks. And he could negotiate this steep climb without looking like death in a teakettle. He was comfortably matching gaits with Ev the Health and Fitness Freak, and that pleased him.

Maxx ceased to be an embarrassment. He moved in close, heeling without being told to. His hulking body bumped Jack's leg every now and then. Jack pointed quietly to his dog. Ev looked at Maxx, at him. Now Ev was starting to act nervous.

"Maxx. Find."

The dog lurched forward reluctantly and took up the search again. The farther he ranged out, the more closely he watched Jack. Three hundred feet to the east of the trail, though, he lost interest in Jack. He pawed at the duff, buried his nose in it, pawed some more. He woofed in baritone and snarfed through sinuses that echoed like fifty-five gallon drums.

Jack moved in and knelt beside him. He had to shift the radio on his belt back a little way. Together they brushed the cumulus of several years' leaves, needles, and dirt from a small crumbling skeleton.

Ev pressed against Jack's side. "That's gross! What is it?"

Jack shoved Maxx back and groped through the duff. "Skull ought to be at this end, if it's still around here. Good dog, Maxx!" He paused to rub the bulky head. "You're a good dog!"

Ev squatted down beside the dog and took over the soft-soaping, cooing Maxx's praises as she vigorously scratched behind his ears. He ate it up as a child would cookie dough. He licked everything on Ev that his tongue could reach.

The skull was disarticulated, but it hadn't gone far. Jack found it maybe two feet away from the rest of the skeleton.

He held it up so that Ev could see the teeth. "The dentition is Canid—that is, dog. Either a coyote or a domestic dog, and it's pretty small for a coyote. But it's not a juvenile. See? The sutures in the skull here are fused." He pointed out the faint lines, barely discernible, where the various skull bones joined. "If this were a sub-adult coyote, the lines would be more distinct."

The tip of the right upper canine was broken off, and the animal in life had needed a toothbrush. The teeth were stained dark brown at the gum line and had started to deteriorate.

"So it's a dog. Eerie Elroy's?"

Jack groped and groveled in the duff some more. "I wish it had a collar. In fact, I wish I'd asked Elroy about a collar. Forgot to." He brushed away at the other end. The tail bones ended two-and-a-half vertebrae from the pelvis.

And then a funny feeling swept over him. His neck hairs bristled as his stomach did a little flip. For he had brushed away enough duff to view the remains clearly.

The ribs of this skeleton had been crushed.

Did Ev notice? He decided not to mention it, at least not yet. He stood and pulled the rolled topo map out of his back pocket. "You any good at sketching?"

"Not much. I can try." She stood up.

He handed her his notebook. "Just sort of draw what it looks like in place, before we move it."

"You're taking this—these bones—with us?"

"Yeah. We might want to do some lab analysis on them."

"It's a dog."

"Probably. I'll find the exact spot on the map." He unfolded it and carefully worked out their position relative to the bends of the trail. They were less than a hundred yards short of where John Getz had been found.

It took ten minutes to document it and bag it. Jack urged Maxx to seek for another few minutes, still hoping for a collar. The dog's search came up zip, so they continued on.

The fog backed away from them as they moved across the hill, then closed in again behind them. A little rusty-brown Douglas squirrel poured itself up a fir trunk and began its rapid, repetitive "Look who's coming!" chirps.

The chirps ceased suddenly as the squirrel disappeared somewhere in the upper story.

As they approached the Grandfather Tree, Maxx moved in tight beside Jack's leg. Jack didn't have the heart to chase him off. He felt uneasy too. The murder's musty odor lingered here.

Then Maxx wheeled so suddenly he almost knocked Jack's leg out from under him. He snarled practically subsonic at the rocky ledge beyond the tree.

Ev sucked in air and froze.

"Maxx. Down. Stay!" Jack muttered the command and backed it up with an underplayed hand signal. The last thing they needed was for Maxx to tangle with this . . .

Mountain lion. The amber beast lay low, bellied out on the rocks beyond the Grandfather Cedar, and stared at them unblinking.

"Jack?" Ev murmured.

"So far, so good." He wrapped his fingers around the revolver holstered at the small of his back, knowing full well that if the cat began to move, so terribly swift was it that he wouldn't have the least chance to get off a shot.

Maxx virtually vibrated at Jack's feet, watching, wanting to give chase, knowing he dare not, torn 'twixt fear and the thrill of pursuit that dogs find so delicious.

Jack purred a few words of encouragement, punctuating them with "Down."

For how many minutes did the world cease motion on its axis and hang suspended, free of time? Then, smooth as oil, the cat rose to its huge, loose paws and flowed up the hillside into heavy brush.

Ev was gripping Jack's arm so tightly that his fingertips tingled. "Oh, Jack!" She was still murmuring, despite that the cat had apparently gone. "That was the most beautiful animal I've ever seen. The way he was just there. It's amazing. He's so big, and he was right out in plain sight, and yet if it weren't for Maxx I never would have noticed him. And so graceful."

"I agree with every word." He dropped down and praised Maxx thoroughly, rubbing him in all his favorite spots. What was Jack feeling now? Plenty. His nerves were dancing, but for the longest time he couldn't sort it out. Relief, certainly. Had Maxx not been the wise though inveterate coward that he was, he'd be sliced up like a salad cucumber now. Relief—the cat showed no interest in them beyond simple curiosity. Disappointment. Raging, palpable disappointment. Jack realized only now how much he had been hoping there really was a Bigfoot.

Several hundred yards uphill, a brace of Steller jays set up a warning squawk.

Ev started one of those running narratives she sometimes launched. "So that's why Maxx has been so antsy. Darryl was telling me about some of the mountain lions he's seen. He collared and tagged some once, did you know that? Like you did with the moose that time—you told me once, remember? Darryl says the males especially can roam over a hundred miles of territory. The females stay closer to one area, especially if they're raising cubs. Was that a male or a female, could you tell?"

"Couldn't see. Probably a male. It was pretty large for a lady."

A quarter mile away, another flock of jays announced that a prowler was passing through their district.

"Have you ever seen one before? Of course. You must have." She giggled. "You know what, Jack? You know how I complain sometimes how boring my life has been, really, when you look at it objectively? And now . . . do you see what I've been saying? Ever since Hal started sending me out here, it's been one adventure after another. Do you realize how many people I work with in the budget office have ever seen a wild mountain lion? None of them! I've just about decided I'm not going back to the budget office. They can get me transferred to Hal's Pals. Or if not there, somewhere else. But I'm not going back to that. Not after this!"

Maxx had already thoroughly scoured the area several days ago. No sense asking him again to find. Jack led the way out around the hillside, just to see what was there. Maxx hugged his leg.

Ev was still babbling on about cats, parroting apparently Darryl's lengthy narratives. "Anyway," she concluded (or at least, Jack hoped she was concluding), "that's why there seem to be a lot more of them in the Northwest here, and why they're considering letting hunters take them again. Outside the park, of course. You can't hunt in a national park, right?"

"Right. All the animals in the park have inventory accession numbers on them. If you come across roadkill, be sure you send the accession number to headquarters."

"But how can they . . ." She stopped in midstride. "Now that is why I almost hate to talk to you, Jack Prester. I never know when you're serious and when you're making fun of me."

"Making fun, yes. Making fun of you, never!"

"Darryl doesn't do that to me. He's sweet and sensible, and he doesn't pull my leg."

"Glad to hear it. How thick are you and Darryl Grade, anyway?"

"And just what do you mean by that?"

Jack back-pedaled as fast as his legs would take him. "Just wondered. Making conversation, mostly."

"So talk about something else. It's none of your business."

"Yes, it is too. Rule number one—you don't date the suspects until the case is cleared. I don't—"

"Suspect?! Oh, get real! What about that floozy in Maine, huh? You certainly didn't hesitate to date her in the middle of a case!"

Jack threw up his hands and headed back toward the trail. "I'm sorry I spoke out of turn. I apologize."

"And you think that just takes care of it." Petulantly, she slogged through the duff. Her shoes were filling up with dirt. "I don't pry into your private life. Why do you think you can pry into mine?"

Jack didn't need his dog to embarrass him; he was doing just fine on his own. "No, I didn't mean it that way. I just wondered. Casually."

Jays were crabbing lustily almost half a mile away across the hillside.

"Oh, sure. You just wondered. Making conversation."

She dogged close to his elbow, no doubt a reaction to the known presence of mountain lions, while trying to keep her distance, a normal reaction to being totally torqued.

Jack weighed her tone of voice a moment and paused to twist around and stare at her. "You like him, don't you?"

She paused too and glanced almost guiltily at him. Then defiance overcame guilt. Her eyes snapped. "Yes, I like him. He's a charming man. He's a widower too, did you know that? He talks about her so tenderly. And guess what. If I want to date him, I'm going to date him. And that's that."

"OK, OK. You don't have to act like a child about it."

"A child! Look who's talking! You're jealous, aren't you! Honestly!" She forged ahead, her chin tipped high, and her nostrils flaring. She looked like a second-grader trying to win an argument with a first-grader by acting older.

Jack rolled his eyes heavenward as he picked up the pace.

Most unfortunately, she happened to turn and see him do it. She flayed him with an epithet usually employed by truck drivers, now that mule skinners were a thing of the past, and took off practically at a jog.

"Bless you too." *In fact, to quote Tiny Tim, "Bless us every one."*

10
Rudolph the Red-nosed Reindeer

Some years before the Soviet Union broke up, a news station in Odessa decided to try to pattern themselves more on Western newscasts. You know—an anchor, with different people covering weather and sports and local events. They felt that their current format of a guy sitting at a desk reading off news items was pretty boring."

Darryl Grade pulled his Pathfinder into the sloping, gravel parking lot of the Clearcut Tavern. It was early evening, but the sun had been down for two hours. Darryl didn't need his ever-present sunglasses.

Jack knew this joke. In fact, it wasn't even new. He'd heard it years ago.

Darryl yanked the parking brake and closed down. "So they hired a weatherman, Rudolph Sokov, not because he knew anything about meteorology, but because he was a faithful member of the Communist party. You don't want any imperialist weather out there, right?"

Behind the driver's side, Jack slid out of his seat into the cold, damp night air. This wasn't what you'd call a disastrous double date, at least not yet, but it sure was strange. Jack and Ev and Darryl Grade and Elizabeth Munro, of all people, were out to spend a carefree evening at "the place to be on Friday night" (Darryl's direct quote).

Maxx, being the only one without a date, was relegated to guarding the Pathfinder from nobody at all, because in Ashford, population a couple hundred maybe, you never bother to lock the car when you leave it.

Jack stopped long enough to roll down the passenger-side window for him. The mutt did like to survey the passing scene, perchance to sniff it. He couldn't do that very well if he was bottled up in a closed vehicle.

What irritated Jack most about this so-called date was the pairing. Ev and Darryl stuck close together, acting suspiciously like a couple on a date, and Elizabeth clung to Jack as if his arm were wrapped in flypaper. The arrangement unsettled him. And that was just as stupid as his embarrassment regarding the dog this afternoon. This was the job. They were all on the job, except perhaps Elizabeth, who wasn't on the ball, let alone the job.

Elizabeth obviously sensed the pause in Darryl's story. She commenced to talk nonstop, rocketing them into the Clearcut with verbal jet propulsion. "The ADA is very specific on the point, and because it's federal law, it's binding on the park. Equal access across the board. You realize what that means, don't you?" She didn't wait for an answer. "Equal access around the Wonderland Trail—up to the ice caves—everywhere."

"The ice caves aren't there anymore," Jack reminded her. "The glacier they were a part of has melted away."

Ev pointedly ignored Jack's comment. "I see. Carrying the park's policy to its logical conclusion."

"Oh, this isn't the conclusion. It's just the beginning! We have to get the physically challenged out on the snowshoe walks, and back country hikes, and all sorts of places yet."

Darryl glanced back at Jack.

Jack grimaced. "Feel free to jump in here anytime, Darryl."

"I've already told her our operating budget has a two-hundred-thousand shortfall this year. We can't even accomplish routine maintenance. Building her facilities is out of the question unless she can come up with private funding." Darryl pushed through the door into the large, stuffy room.

All around the walls, neon lights and plastic signs displayed the brand names of beer, just in case someone on the premises had never heard of them yet. A poster revealed that Tarzan's best pal is neither Jane nor a chimp but a six-foot-long beer bottle with legs—the wild man stood in a heroic posture on a windswept bluff with his arm wrapped around one. A cigarette vending machine glowed near the door. Stuffed animals and other toys, some of them electronic, gathered dust on a shelf up behind the bar. Jack figured out that they were prizes for the punch cards.

Strings of colored Christmas lights outlined the bar in here as they outlined the door and windows outside. They seemed harshly incongruous in this milieu—the birth of the Lord of the Galaxies as observed in a tavern.

Elizabeth was still rattling on as they slid into a dark, varnished wooden booth. "And I assured him I am fully aware that he's overstating it. Of course, if we expand the project to provide for the visually challenged, we could probably get some money out of the foundations, and if we—"

"Wait. Visually challenged?" Darryl was plastered so close to Ev you couldn't have slipped a credit card between them. "They couldn't see what they were doing, and they sure couldn't see the view. Why would the blind want to climb the mountain?"

"Because," quoth Elizabeth in sonorous tones, "it is there."

"There are a good many physical sensations in mountain climbing besides just the view," Ev defended.

Jack was getting increasingly irritated, and he couldn't figure out why. "Sure. But you can get the same physical sensations by standing inside a frozen-meat locker and turning a big fan on high. Wind chill. Frostbite. It'd help to run a marathon first—sheer exhaustion is a biggie."

Darryl laughed loosely and freely. He was on his turf here, you could tell. And he genuinely enjoyed the company. You could tell that too.

Elizabeth added, "You shouldn't refer to them as the 'blind.' That's demeaning."

Jack looked at her. "It's accurate. Doesn't accuracy count for anything?"

"The word 'blind' creates too many negative connotations. 'Visually challenged' is meaning-neutral. It doesn't carry all those ugly connotations."

"Go on with your story," Ev urged Darryl.

"Anyway, for weekend weather they hired a woman named Natasha Volsky." Darryl briefly flashed a wave to some friend across the room. "Unfortunately she was a Social Democrat, not a Commie, but they needed a pretty face, and she was about the best available. Turned out she was pretty good. Natasha's predictions were right on the button, a lot oftener than Rudolph's. It was embarrassing, kind of, that a Social Democrat was showing up a card-carrying Communist."

Jack was here in order to get acquainted with Eerie Elroy's ex-friends, either to interview them or set up some other time for an interview. Darryl was here in order to introduce Jack to said friends and to ease Jack into the local scene. Waving at people across the room was not going to accomplish that purpose. On the other hand, Jack didn't really want to be here doing this and meeting those people. Maybe that was the irritation. He was working at cross-purposes with himself.

Ev was here because Darryl invited her, and Elizabeth was here because Ev had invited *her*. Elizabeth had shown up in the park about noon, Kerri said. Elizabeth and Ev had been together ever since Jack and she got back from seeing the mountain lion. Whatever the two women talked about, they had established a solid rapport.

The story went on hold again as the barmaid, a slim girl in faded blue jeans, arrived to take their order.

"A pitcher of beer—" Darryl smirked at Jack "—and Prester here will have a Black Dog."

"Big or little?"

"Big, of course. You should see the size of his mutt. And nachos."

She smiled at Jack. "So you have a big black dog, huh?"

"Yeah, and I see so much of him I'm not really interested in seeing more on an ale label. How about Pepsi-no-ice instead?"

She glanced at Darryl, bobbed her head, and left.

The moment she left, Elizabeth announced, "I want to visit the ladies' room."

Her eyes and Ev's didn't even really meet before Ev said, "I will too."

Jack and Darryl let them out and sat back down.

Darryl jammed himself into the corner against the wall. "Now there's a phenomenon I've never been able to figure out. How women instantly and instinctively turn that into a social occasion. One goes, they all go. They need company? They travel in herds? What?"

Jack chuckled. The way these booth backs were slanted, wedging into the corner was really quite comfortable. He settled in and cocked a leg up. "I've never been able to decide whether it's synchronous biorhythms or a quirk of mob psychology. You've known Elizabeth for a while, haven't you?"

"I met her when she first started pushing this equal access for the handicapped project. The superintendent dumped her off on me, since I'm chief of maintenance and she's talking about building stuff. She was up here doing a survey of existing facilities and needs not met. Something like that. Dated her once or twice. Twice, I guess. Lunch at the Inn one day, and I took her to Seafair last August for a day. Nothing heavy."

"Survey. Where the wheelchair ramps go and where they don't—that kind of thing?"

"Right. My first impression of her was, I thought she was a real airhead. But her—"

"No, no, no, Darryl," Jack chided. "Not 'airhead.' That's demeaning though accurate. Negative connotations. 'Cerebro-atmospherically challenged.'"

Darryl laughed loudly enough to make elk five miles away raise their heads and look around. "But her final report was good. Really good. Comprehensive. I know she didn't have help with the survey, and she did a thorough, professional job. So she's not as brainless as she looks. And there are some other instances—things she said, for example—that make me believe that under that fluffy exterior she's one smart lady."

So date Elizabeth and leave Ev alone. Jack changed the subject before he started saying the wrong thing out loud. "Is anyone here in the room now someone I ought to talk to?"

Darryl shook his head. "Different crowd from Elroy's old buddies. They'll probably come around, though. They like the Cowboys. We ought to give it at least another hour."

Ev and Elizabeth came chattering and giggling their way back to the booth. Ev was a totally different person from the stern and apprehensive young woman Jack first met a few months ago. He marveled at the transformation. But maybe it wasn't a transformation at all. Probably this was the real Ev, and the woman he had first known was a woman cautiously crossing frightening and unfamiliar territory.

Jack straightened up as Elizabeth slipped onto the seat beside him. But Darryl stayed where he was, scrunched into the corner, and Ev slid in close to him.

The barmaid delivered their order, a pitcher and three glasses and Jack's giant Pepsi-no-ice. And here was a big bottle of ale. Obviously Darryl was a regular custom-

103

er—when he spoke, the barmaid listened. There on the label was a black Lab all right, a male. Big anvil head, dopey expression—pure Lab. A name plate on the dog's collar said "Chug."

Oh, well. Darryl had ordered it, and Darryl was buying. You can lead a horse to water, but you can't make him wash behind his ears, or however the saying went. Jack didn't have to drink it just because it was sitting there, so he stayed with his Pepsi and, except for checking out the label, ignored the Black Dog.

Over in the corner, five young men in cowboy duds were setting up sound equipment and adjusting mikes. In a brilliant flash of insight, Jack deduced that these were the Cold Cowboys.

Darryl lurched erect and poured. "One weekend, Natasha predicted snow for next Tuesday. But Rudolph came on Monday night and promised rain instead. Whaddayaknow, it rained buckets. And the station manager, a good Communist himself, called up Natasha and said, 'There, you see . . .'"

With a groan, Ev and Jack joined in the familiar punchline ". . . Rudolph the Red knows rain, dear."

Elizabeth didn't get it.

The women fell to talking about Zoo Lights in Tacoma.

For Jack, Darryl pointed across the room. "Now the giant blob over there at the end of the bar—see him? Talk about ethically challenged."

"What?" Elizabeth frowned.

"Ethically challenged. He's a crook. Elroy hates the guy. Hates the guy beside him too. The short man there. He does whatever you need doing, cut-rate. Anything from carpentry to poaching. Used to fall trees until the market died. That fellow's never held a steady job in all the years I've been here. Fried his brain on drugs. Can't keep a thought going for more than thirty seconds. When you try to talk to him he sounds real intellectually challenged."

Ev glared not at Darryl but at Jack, as if Jack were

somehow responsible for these simple, charming variations on Elizabeth's meaning-neutral theme. "Are all the
people in here loggers?"

"Just about, or they were once. Or loggers' wives."
Darryl nodded toward a booth of four women across the
room.

Jack surveyed the thirty or so people sitting about.
"Are we the only Park Service customers?"

Darryl nodded. "Park Service doesn't come in here
much. I sort of crossed over by joining the volunteer fire
department, but I'm not completely accepted. The Park
Service is conservation oriented, which paints it with the
same brush as the environmentalists."

Jack shrugged. "We *are* environmentalists."

"Right. That puts you on the other side of a wide,
wide chasm from the timber interests. Believe me, you are
persona non grata in here. Logging provides most of the
jobs in this area."

"Aren't there any middle-of-the-roaders?"

"Jay Chambers. Nobody listens to him."

The Cold Cowboys opened with a number with a
pounding beat. Ev glanced at Darryl. He bobbed his head,
and they scooted out of the booth to the dance floor—that
is, the small open spot between the bar and the booths.
Clearly, this wasn't the first time they had danced to the
thumping rhythms of the Cold Cowboys.

Jack looked at Elizabeth. "Obviously, Darryl's a good
dancer. Dance with me, and you'll walk out of here with
flat toes. I don't recommend it."

She giggled. "Did you and Darryl know each other a
long time?"

"Met ten days ago. Why?"

"You seem so comfortable with each other, like old
friends. And in the Park Service, I've noticed, it seems everyone knows everyone else from some other park."

"There's a lot of that, yeah."

"Ev says you lost your wife. So did Darryl, you know."

"So I heard. Under what circumstances, do you know?" Jack noticed that one of the rough-hewn types at the bar, a burly fellow sitting near Elroy's hated Blob and Short Man, was keeping an eye on Elizabeth. Did Elroy hate that guy too? And where were his erstwhile friends?

"She came home from town one day and walked in on a burglar in her house. He shot her with Darryl's gun. He was stealing it and just happened to have it, they think. It's very sad. He—Darryl—really loved his wife. He talks about her like she was a saint."

"They ever catch the burglar?"

"I don't remember exactly. Not then. A couple months later, I think."

Jack mulled two or three different ways to go from here. Unfortunately, he was a bit too slow with his next question, and Elizabeth jumped into the silent space with still another homily on handicapped access. Now she was talking about building all new dirt trails so you could pave the existing trails.

Darryl and Ev returned, none the worse for wear, as the Cold Cowboys launched into a lethargic, mournful paean to a lost love.

"Besides, I'm sure Darryl of all people knows," Elizabeth rolled on, "nothing is permanent. If you don't like something in one place, you just move it to another place. Isn't that right, Darryl?"

His mouth tightened down to a flat line.

Jack was glad to see there was a limit to Darryl's desire to talk about the physically challenged. Jack's tolerance was even less—he had reached his limit twenty minutes ago. But then, Darryl was refreshed, so to speak, having enjoyed that breather on the dance floor.

They hung around another half hour, but none of Elroy's friends showed up. Darryl and Elizabeth sampled the Black Dog and almost finished it between them. When the Cowboys broke between sets and Darryl asked, "Ready to go?" Jack wanted to jump up and down for joy. He'd been ready before they got here.

Ev and Elizabeth headed off for one more examination of the decor in the ladies' room.

Darryl stood and stretched. "Where shall I drop off you and your date?"

"So soon you forget. She's not my date. She's Ev's. Her car's parked by the library, isn't it?"

Darryl nodded.

"So drop us there. I'll send her home with a cheery wave and hike to my simple apartment. Probably walk Maxx a few minutes."

"Some hike. It's fifty feet from the library to your door. What? You're not going to invite her in for coffee?"

"And listen to still more of that? My ears are becoming functionally challenged."

Darryl laughed that jovial roar again. He decided he'd use the facilities before they left and walked off to the men's room. The women appeared from their mysterious sanctum and headed back. The Cold Cowboys started another set.

And Jack's comfortable little world suddenly disintegrated.

The disintegration started when the burly, rough-hewn type left his bar stool and approached Ev and Elizabeth on the far side of the room. Ev shook her head. He blocked their way.

No. Jack absolutely did not need this. No. With extreme reluctance he headed their way, desperately hoping that Ev would just go ahead and deck the guy and nip this situation in the bud. This was definitely not the Christmas spirit building.

Jack had trouble making himself heard above the racket the Cold Cowboys were creating. He called a cheery, "Shall we go, ladies?"

Old Burly lurched a little, definitely tipsy if not downright sodden. He turned to Jack and grinned inanely. His teeth needed brushing. "I don't like you."

"Peace and joy to you too." *Darryl, get out here! Now!* Jack looked at Ev and dipped his head ever so slightly toward the door.

Ev could have left, but Elizabeth's way was still blocked. Ev hesitated, uncertain.

Burly sneered. "You know, I just love spotted owls." He paused a beat. "Done in garlic and butter."

"I'm very happy for you. Ev?"

Burly obviously wasn't going to quietly step back and let Elizabeth move, and Elizabeth was either too numb or too mentally challenged to just firmly and politely step around him.

If Jack lost his gentlemanly demeanor and made a scene, the worst they would do would be to throw him out, and he was leaving anyway. Uncharitably, not the least in a warm and friendly Yuletide spirit, he lashed out with a foot and nailed the guy in the kneecap.

Burly's face assumed an expression of instantaneous pain and shock.

Bless her, Ev grabbed Elizabeth's arm and yanked the confused girl off toward the door.

Using the heel of his hand, Jack shoved Burly back with a blow to the throat just above where the two collar bones come together. That plus his blood alcohol level ought to put the creep down long enough for them to exit.

Too late Jack saw, in his peripheral vision, swift motion by the bar. Raising an arm to defend himself, he started to turn. The Blob exploded in his face. Jack flew backward as lights sprayed all around—some were stars from getting slammed in the face, some were cigarette machine, and overheads, and a few Christmas lights, and neon. He landed on his back on one of the tables, skidded along it, kept sliding off the other side into a chair. He heard the chair creak as it gave way, a ridiculously clear, slow-motion sensation. The chair dumped him out on the floor. He rolled.

Someone tugged at the holster at the small of his back. The one thing that terrifies peace officers most—that a felon will kill them with their own gun—was about to happen to him, and he was nowhere near conscious enough to prevent it.

His gun blasted. He was a dead man.

Then Ev's voice purred, solid and clear, pitched an octave below her usual speaking tone. "Someone grabs me from behind, and you have a bullet in your belly. Understand?"

Jack decided to raise his head and look around. Nothing happened.

Ev's voice was telling someone to open the door. Moments later she called, "Maxx! Come!"

In a heartbeat, toenails came clicking and galumphing past Jack's ear.

Did Jack's own Noble Canine Companion pause to lick him, or greet him, or even snigger a doggy "Oh! It's you there in a pile on the floor, you dork"?

No.

Ev ordered, "Maxx. Guard."

Maxx's basso profundo growl rumbled like an army tank in granny gear. Jack could tell from the direction of the growl that the dog was ignoring him.

The bartender called, "Sheriff's deputy will be here in five."

Jack lurched to sitting.

Ev stood in a perfect, yet graceful, braced stance, Jack's revolver cradled two-handed. She was positioned between him and the Blob, sheltering Jack from his nemesis. Maxx kept the Blob at bay, and Ev was calmly, coolly holding the rest of the room at gunpoint.

Jack lurched to his knees, to his feet. He glanced at his gun in Ev's hands as he steadied himself on the table. "Want me to take over?"

"Why?" The ice in her voice reminded him he had just impugned her liberated status. Some questions are better left rhetorical. He kept his mouth shut.

His face above his right bicuspid felt as if a horse had stepped on it and someone had stuffed a brick up his nose. It was bleeding.

Here came Darryl, thundering to the rescue a day late and a dollar short. He paused, looked around, and relaxed, grinning. "Look at all this holiday spirit!"

Jack grumbled, "Ho, ho, ho."

Ev glanced at Jack and quoted directly, "Hey. It's not Christmas without at least one bloody nose."

11

Ring the Bells

Jack was beginning to resent people shooting at him. True, it didn't happen often, but getting shot at is one of those things that wears in a hurry, like someone punctuating a joke by repeatedly jabbing you in the arm. Once is plenty. Maybe that's why he didn't really relish driving up to Eerie Elroy's place again.

Maxx didn't like it any better. He sat on the seat so close to Jack's right arm that he made shifting gears difficult. They lurched up into Eerie Elroy's wet and gloomy front yard.

Jack's foot barely touched the ground before the shotgun went off. OK, so probably—technically—Eerie wasn't shooting at him. Some distinction.

"Hey, Mr. Washington! Save your ammo—it's only me. Jack Prester. Shells are eight cents apiece, you know." He muttered, "Maxx. Come," and stepped out, still behind the partial cover of his truck door. He hated this. He hated this whole scene, start to finish. And he felt he was going to hate it worse before he was done.

Eerie stood in his open doorway with his shotgun cradled in the crook of an elbow. He seemed even more grizzled and unkempt than Jack remembered. Jack paused at the bottom of the stoop, awaiting an invitation in and rather wishing he wouldn't get one.

Elroy smirked. "Whudja do to your face? Where it's swelled up there beside your nose."

"Barroom brawl."

"Yeah, right." Elroy studied Jack's face a few moments and sobered. "What's wrong?"

Jack held one hand above the other. "Your dog was about this high and weighed twenty-five to thirty pounds. He had a docked tail this long and bad breath."

"Knew I shoulda blasted you when you got out of your truck." He sighed. "But I didn't, so come on in, I guess."

"Thanks." Jack followed the man inside. Eerie Elroy definitely sagged more than he did before. Jack flopped down in a kitchen chair and motioned Maxx to sit by his side.

Elroy sprawled out across from him. "Who were you talking to about my dog?"

"No one. We found the remains." Jack paused a beat. "A hundred yards downhill from where Getz was discovered."

It took Elroy a few moments to digest that. He shook his head. "Nope. Then it wasn't my dog. That's nowhere near where he was killed."

"Broken upper right canine tooth." Jack pressed his finger to his own upper right bicuspid.

Elroy's mouth worked. "He broke it catching rocks. You know how other dogs catch sticks in midair? Jump up and catch Frisbees and things? Throw him a rock, he'd do that." For the longest moment he stared at Jack. "The Bigfoot musta moved him. Musta carried him most of half a mile down the hill."

"You're sure?" Jack watched the man's face a second. "You're sure." He weighed the moment and decided to give this tormented man an item not even the newspapers had. "Getz didn't die where his body was found. He

112

died out around the hill by the Grandfather Cedar."

Elroy stared. The grizzly gray beard moved about as his mouth worked. He purred a vivid expletive. "Maybe they do use tools!"

The comment jolted him, and Jack realized how nearly he had dismissed Elroy as just a kook. This man focused everything he owned on one single obsession. Absolutely everything he thought or did related somehow to Bigfoot. Twisted as his mind might be, so long as it operated in reference to a mythical beast, he could offer clear thinking and valuable insights.

Jack leaned an elbow on the table. "Why would a Bigfoot, or anyone else, move the dog's body or Getz's?"

Eerie accepted the question in all seriousness. "I'm wondering about that very thing. There's no definite evidence on whether they're territorial. Like, maybe he'd move the bodies out of his territory or something."

"What's their habitat?"

"Old growth with glades—open areas. Not wood margins as such, but open places. I think only one sighting was in an area that had been logged over. It'd been replanted maybe five years—trees stood this high maybe." He held his flat hand four feet off the floor.

"You checked, I presume."

"You bet I did. I've stood in exactly the spot of every sighting that's ever been made, including all the ones in California."

Jack pondered that and tried to figure how any of this could be of help. He didn't see that he was getting anywhere at all, so he changed the subject, he hoped. "You say you knew Getz. What did he think about Bigfoot?"

"Ridicule, same as everyone else. Maybe stronger than everyone else. He was a 'scientist,' you know. Scientists don't believe in that hooey." The way Eerie sneered as he said the word *scientist*, it was obvious that science and science alone was responsible for war, famine, pestilence, hangnails, and an occasional hole in the ozone layer.

"I saw a mountain lion up behind Reflection Lake yesterday. They're not uncommon in the park, I assume."

"They're around. Increasing, I'd say. It used to be, when I first worked in the woods, I wouldn't see one but every couple years or so. Now I see a couple a year."

"Do they compete with Bigfoot or prey on him?"

"He's nine feet high, Prester. Nobody preys on him." He sat quiet a moment. "How'd the dog die?"

"So far, cause of death unknown. But some of the ribs are broken."

"Aha!" Eerie leaped triumphant to his feet. "How do I get my dog back? I want to bury him."

"Your ridiculing friends claim you hated the dog."

"I want the bones! They prove my story."

"They're filed and documented as evidence. Maybe someday, but not right now."

"Evidence of what?" Eerie sat down again.

Jack shrugged. The guy had a splendid point. Evidence of what indeed. "They're bones of a dog. An exotic. Non-native. Maybe evidence to convict the owner of dumping rubbish in the park or having a dog off a leash. By the way, was there a collar on him? We couldn't find a collar or rabies tag or anything."

"I kept him on a choke chain whenever we were in the parking lot or someplace like that. Left him run free in the woods. So sue me."

"That makes me feel a little better. At least we didn't miss finding something crucial."

"So the ribs were broke!" Eerie purred the words as if they were "I can't believe I just won the Washington Lottery." He studied Jack. "You didn't have to come up here to tell me that."

"No, but I figured you'd like to know."

Eerie Elroy hopped again to his feet and jogged off into his living room. Through the archway, Jack watched him rummage through one of his desk drawers. Elroy found what looked from here like a folded topographic map. He found another, looked at them both, and dropped one on the desk. He unfolded the other as he returned to the table.

He spread the map out, but not flat. So much junk, from half-empty jelly jars to old magazines, was stacked and stored on the table that a postcard would have a hard time lying flat. Jack stood up to look at the map better.

"Show me exactly, can you?" Elroy handed him a pencil.

Jack had already worked out the exact spot on the topo map he had used to document the find. It took him but a moment to mark a tiny X on Elroy's map.

Elroy took the pencil. "And Jay said he found Getz right there." He poked the exact spot. He leaned over the map, both fists on the table, and studied it.

Jack watched his face. "That ring any bells? What's the significance?"

"You know how Mount St. Helens blew her top off and left a caldera, a bowl shape instead of a pointy peak? So did Mount Rainier. The top is dished in."

"Right."

"But if you sort of draw in lines where the top used to be, they'd come to a peak right there." He pointed to a small X penciled into the white part of the map, the summit.

"Then you could draw almost a straight line from the peak down through Getz's location to the dog's location."

"Not 'almost.' It *is* a straight line."

Jack frowned. If you continued that imaginary straight line beyond the dog's location, it almost exactly passed through the spot where the road crew repaired the rock-slide that day. In fact, if you moved the line less than a quarter inch, it would dissect the new rock work. "Interesting. What are these lines and X's?" He pointed to penciled markings that looked like trails, most of them following contour lines. Elroy had studded X's and O's here and there along the network of pencil lines, perhaps half a dozen altogether.

"That's the ski-and-saddle trail they're putting in. The solid line's finished. The dash lines up there are proposed." His pointing finger skated about the map, the visual of his audio-visual explanation. "These X's are hostels that are built. The O's are proposed."

"What's the squiggly marks there?"

"The trees Getz wanted cut down. I told you about that, didn't I?"

Jack nodded.

"He had their locations all written out, but I do better with a map in front of me, so I drew them in."

Jack saw the squiggly mark, rather like a turtle outline, marking the Grandfather Cedar. He sat down again and watched Elroy deftly fold his map. "Ski-and-saddle trails. Something new?"

Elroy nodded. "Horsemen in summer and cross-country skiers in winter, with hostels about half a day apart. You stay in the little hostels overnight, and you can ski or ride without having to carry all your camp gear." He tossed his map on the table by Jack's elbow and sat down.

Jack sat also. The chair creaked. "You sound like you're not too sure it's a good idea."

"There's already a network of private trails just like that outside the park, in the Elbe Hills. The park don't need more trails, even if they're paying attention to minimum impact. It's experimental. If folks use them a lot, they'll get serious about putting them on forest land too."

"I would assume Getz was adamantly against more trails in the park."

"Right. And Jay's all for it. He says this new trail system will help people develop a better communion with the earth. He just loves them Mount Tahoma Trails."

Jack studied the folded map a moment without really seeing it. "If I bring a topo map by, may I copy your marks there?"

"Sure."

Jack had learned something, it seemed, but he

116

couldn't for the life of him tell what. Maybe he could ring some more bells. "Getz's private papers." That sounded better somehow than "Getz's personal journal." "He mentioned a Barney now and then. For instance, 'Saw Barney today.' But he never mentioned what he and Barney talked about or what Barney's full name would be. My colleague in this investigation has been trying to learn of anyone named Barney who might have dealings with Getz, and can't find a thing. Do you know of anyone like that? Nickname maybe."

"Barney." Elroy pondered a coffee stain on the worn oilcloth table cover. He mulled the question for a couple of minutes, and Jack could see nothing about his demeanor to suggest he was withholding information or feeling nervous about the question in any way. He wagged his head. "Nope. There was a Barney's up on the junction of 161 and the Eatonville cutoff, north of Eatonville. It burned down. Just stood there all burnt out and boarded up for years. Then someone bought it and tore down the gutted shell and built a gas station. It's a BP station now. It's still called Barney's, but Getz wouldn't know that, I don't think, being from out of town."

"It has nothing to do with an actual Barney."

Eerie shook his head. "I have no idea whatever happened to Barney. Likely in Florida, retired with his insurance money. I don't know."

Jack probably could ask a few more things, if only he could think of something to ask about. Eerie Elroy still seemed open to conversation. But why wear out your welcome? He did that last night at the Clearcut, and as a direct result Ev blew a hole in their ceiling with his .38. He stood up.

Elroy stood too. He picked up the map and handed it to Jack. "Take this along."

"You said you didn't like to swap material with Getz. I don't want to take your map here—you might need it."

Elroy shook his head. "I got others. You don't even

117

need to return it. I appreciate you coming by to tell me about my dog."

"Thank you." Jack slapped his leg as he headed for the door, motioning Maxx to heel. The dog took his ruddy time, standing, stretching mightily, pausing to lick Jack's hand.

Elroy saw him to the door of his truck and thoughtfully left his shotgun behind. A shotgun greeting coming in is bad enough. A twenty-one gun salute going out would really frazzle Jack's nerves.

He motioned Maxx into the cab, slid in beside him, and torched the motor off. He sat there a moment with the door open. "You seem tired or something. Like someone let the air out of your tires. Anything wrong?"

"No. Nothing wrong."

Jack bobbed his head, an acceptance. "Thank you again."

They good-byed in general terms, and Jack started his truck down the tortuous track toward a decent road and Longmire.

At the park entrance he stopped by Ev's digs, a little brown cabin behind the ranger station. She wasn't there. He lifted the big rock to the left of the door stoop. As per their standard arrangement, she had left him a note.

"Gone to town. Ask Kerri about Zoo Lights. EB"

OK, so it was Saturday, and in theory you only work a five-day week. But this case simply wasn't happening, and they were never going to get anywhere if she didn't buckle down and put forth some extra effort. The least she could do was work a Saturday or two to sew this up.

Back at the apartment Jack called his boss, Hal— Hal was working on Saturday, and Hal wasn't even being spurred on by a ticket to Hawaii. Hal had as much as promised that Jack could cut out for the holiday if need be. Well, Jack was going to need to.

Two minutes into the conversation, he could tell that the promise was broken.

Hal sniveled, he threatened, he cajoled, he pleaded. Maxx didn't beg this hard when the doggy-treat box was open.

Jack found himself promising to try the first thing Monday morning to get his ticket changed to the twenty-fourth.

He hung up the phone, vaguely disgusted with the whole world. *Mele Kalikimaka* to you too, Hal Edmond.

12

Mary Had a Baby

Of all the space-age phenomena that have so profoundly altered life—supersonic planes, CAT scans and MRIs, call waiting, cellular phones—Jack appreciated Burger King's breakfast croissants most. Not only are they cheaper than the Concorde and cellulars, they are a lot easier to find, and, unlike CAT scans, you don't have to be sick to enjoy them. Jack mulled this and other arcane concepts as he sat in a Burger King booth in Puyallup munching a sausage croissant with egg.

In fact, he was having a terrible time simply pronouncing *Puyallup.* Pyu-AL-ip. Pyew-AAL-up.

From a list of several churches Kerri Haskell had suggested, Jack had chosen one on South Hill near Puyallup, more or less at random. He felt the Lord had blessed his choice: it was a friendly little church, warm and close, with a fine pastor. By getting up hours before the crack of dawn, he attended the earlier of their two services and was back out on the street by nine fifteen. He would meet Jeff and Kerri Haskell at the Boathouse in Point Defiance Park at five. That gave him opportunity to ruin the balance of the day by working.

He bussed his debris, left the tray on top of the trash

container, and walked out into a bright and cheerful morning.

In his cage that had replaced the tailgate of Jack's truck, Maxx yelped and turned a few wheelies in place. His tail flailed exuberantly. From long experience, Jack knew better than to interpret all that as love. Not when Jack had sausage on his breath. He let Maxx out and opened the driver's side door for him. The mutt bounded up into the cab.

Kerri had given Jack a sketchy map to the Pierce County Sheriff's Office. It took him more than half an hour to find it and only five minutes to locate a parking slot on the street. He worked his way through three different gatekeepers and finally reached the inner sanctum.

The Pierce County Sheriff's Office was almost as cheerful as the day. They had adequate room to move around, and the place was about as nicely appointed as a place like that can be—which isn't exactly the lobby of the Sheraton.

"You want Sergeant Means," a lady at the horseshoe counter declared and ushered him into a back room.

"Sergeant Means? Dr. John Prester with the National Park Service." Her duty faithfully discharged, she returned to her information desk.

Sgt. Sargent Means shook hands in the firm, friendly way of a man at peace with the world. Such men do not occur often in law enforcement organizations. He was cheerful too. Five feet eight or nine, he had a round, pudgy, well-creased face and enough of a paunch that he could have been a jolly friar in some distant, prior era. He even had a little bald spot at the back of his head, an incipient tonsure. With a happy flourish, he offered Jack a seat beside his desk.

Amid all these shades-of-green uniforms, Jack felt somewhat out of place in his faded denim and chambray shirt. "About three years ago, a ranger's wife walked in on a burglary in progress and was shot and killed. Grade. Margaret Grade."

Sergeant Means stared at Jack a moment, open-mouthed. He smiled. "I remember that one. Up in Ashford. National. Around there."

"That's the one."

"But she wasn't shot. She was stabbed. They never found the blade, though. It was probably about three or four inches long, so it could've been a pocket knife. Do you believe in luck, Dr. Prester?"

"When all else fails, though I prefer to call it by its real name, divine providence."

The sergeant's laughter bellowed. Yes, indeed, he'd make a fine jolly friar. "Divine providence. That's what I call it too. So you're a Christian. So am I." He nodded his head in an unusual way, as if it had been tipped off balance and was bobbing back to stability. "The murder was never cleared, but we're pretty sure we know who did it. We nailed him cold on another burglary in the area about two months later."

"Convicted?"

The sergeant's head bobbed loosely again in that interesting way. "Let's see—let me make sure I've got it." He licked his lips a moment in studious thought. "Plea bargain, as I recall. Avoided a jury trial. Besides, we had him cold."

"Breaking and entering or burglary?"

"Burglary. The owner of the house was away all that week. An alert neighbor noticed an upstairs light come on, then go off. Since it wouldn't be the owner, it was probably a burglar. Several houses up there had been hit in the prior six months or so. When the deputy surprised him, the kid had a pile of stuff stacked on the living room floor."

"Same as the Grade job."

"Just the same. And he was walking out the front door with plastic grocery bags full of silverware and jewelry."

"I see." Jack mulled all this. "But no evidence to tie

him to the Grade murder of several months before."

"Right. Except for some similarity in the burglary modus. He did eighteen months in juvenile corrections. He was paroled, he stayed clean for a while, and that's where your luck comes in. Your divine providence."

"How so? He just got dirty again?"

"Exactly. We stuffed him back into Remann last night. The paperwork came across my desk an hour ago."

"Which, translated loosely, means he just got in trouble again and is in your juvenile detention center?"

"You got it."

"I'd like to talk to him."

Sergeant Means lurched forward in his chair and stretched to reach the receiver of his AT&T Merlin. He punched an autodial button and sat back, mashing the receiver to his ear with one broad, ham-sized shoulder. Historically, friars were not particularly noted for efficiency. Maybe Sergeant Means wouldn't be a good friar after all— he was much too efficient for his own good. He set up an appointment for Jack with the culprit in question, pledged to buy two raffle tickets to something from the voice on the other end of the phone, and handled some bit of business regarding a Dorothy, all in the space of about ninety seconds.

He stretched again to hang up his phone. "The kid swears to this day he's not a murderer. He's in detention now because of complicity in an armed assault, so draw your own conclusions."

"Is the report available?"

"I'll dig it out and fax it to you. The boy and his uncle got into some sort of altercation. Drinking. He and the uncle both brandished guns. He claims it's the uncle's gun, but of course that doesn't let him off the hook."

Jack grunted. "Regarding the burglary, I would assume the boy's lawyer plea-bargained because he was afraid even a slight taint of murder would prejudice the jury. Get the kid out of there with as light a sentence as possible."

123

That nod again. "The arresting deputy did a fine job on that one. He arrived with his lights doused, set up his camcorder on his vehicle's hood, and filmed the whole sequence, the headlights coming on just as the kid was walking out the door with the goods, and the bust. He's been a plainclothes investigator for two years now, and we still call him Cecil B. DeMille."

The friar sat forward again. "I don't know what you hope to find when you talk to the boy."

"I don't either. The rangers did a good preliminary investigation on Getz, but they have neither the time nor manpower to dig into peripheral things."

"How can the Grade murder be tied to the Getz murder? Is there something we missed?"

Jack smiled. "Rest easy. The connection is that Darryl Grade, the first victim's husband, was one of the first on the scene of the second victim's discovery." He would not add that he was also looking into Darryl's sorrow because Getz's journal implied some sort of blackmail. He refused to seriously entertain the foolish notion that were Ev not interested in Darryl romantically, he would not have bothered with any of this.

The friar smiled suddenly. "Know how to get there? Out 16 toward the bridge."

"I can get exact directions from the desk officer." Jack sifted thoughts a few moments. "Juvenile. Tried as an adult?"

"No. He seemed to do pretty well under the strict discipline of summer camp. He even started to catch up scholastically. But then he got out, and I don't know what happened to him over the last few years."

"Parents?"

"Foster. Ward of the county. No, wait. The uncle, I believe. A ward, but in the care of the uncle."

Jack stood up. "Did you ever meet the boy yourself?"

Sergeant Means stood up also. "No. I know him only by the paperwork that crosses my desk. A mug shot, not a real face. He's fifteen now and has en—"

"Fifteen! That would make him twelve when he went down for burglary."

The friar lost his cheery smile. His rumpled face melted into sadness. "And his accomplice was seventeen. Prester, they get younger every year."

"Yeah," Jack replied softly. "My doctoral dissertation was on communicating with murderers aged ten and under. But they mostly . . ." He sighed. "Yeah."

They said good-bye and asked God's blessing on each other. Jack found his way out of this rats' maze and back down to his truck and Maxx.

More cars than exist in all New Mexico were out on the streets and highways of Tacoma this morning, and it was Sunday. What must it be like, say, 8:00 A.M. on a weekday?

Jack fumbled his way to Remann Hall, but it turned out to be fortuitous fumbling. He missed the turnoff and caught sight of the Tacoma Narrows Bridge. On impulse he drove across it just to drive across it.

Hundreds of feet above the Sound, it arched in graceful splendor, suspended upon cables big enough to anchor clouds. Far below, sheets of miniature sparkling ripples hemmed by ragged lines told him the tide was turning against the wind. He pulled off onto a side road on the west shore and came back eastbound. A sharp crosswind tugged at his wheel. He relished this brief and airy respite from reality, soaring so high.

Fifteen-year-old boy. Jack understood most of the defenses troubled kids that age erect. On impulse, he leashed up Maxx and took the dog along into the detention center.

When he entered Remann Hall, the sunshine stayed behind. This institution was just as depressing as any other juvenile detention center. Broken hopes and lost promises littered the waxed linoleum floors. Jack hated these places, and for years, preparing his doctorate, he had worked in them.

So well had Sergeant Means paved the way that Jack

was ushered almost immediately into a low-security contact room. It was small and drab, but someone had hung curtains at the barred window. Besides the table and two chairs with which all such rooms are dressed, a long brown sofa hugged one wall.

Jack spent the few minutes waiting for the boy by squatting on the floor and scratching Maxx behind the ears. Jack even cooed a couple of pleasantries, fondly hoping to keep the mutt's fickle affection until dog food time.

The door opened, and a uniformed guard motioned the boy into the room. The guard nodded briefly to Jack and closed the door behind him.

Jack stood up and extended a hand. "Jack Prester. You're Ernest Mulrose?"

Small for his age, Ernest Mulrose stood maybe five five at most. If he weighed a hundred thirty, that was fifteen pounds more than Jack would guess. He was fair complexioned, getting pimples, and only now starting to lose the towheaded look of childhood. He wore one of those goofy haircuts where you shave it in a straight line all around the bottom of your head and leave a thick, floppy mop on top. His head looked like a thatched hut in Pago Pago.

The kid spent a second or two staring at Jack's hands, apparently making decisions, and decided against shaking. He stuffed both hands in his pockets.

Jack grinned. "That puts you in the same class as a senator I met in Washington, D.C., last month. The senator refused to shake hands with me too."

Ernest's eyes crackled. "Maybe you're using the wrong deodorant."

"Or maybe I was helping with an investigation into her Park Service connections. That'll do it too. Sit down." Jack waved an arm toward the sofa.

The kid stood there.

Jack lowered his voice, tightened it a little. "It's not a suggestion."

Obviously it was not Jack's authority but Maxx's to which Ernest bowed. He looked at the dog and sat down, scrunching himself as tightly into the corner of the sofa as a body can be wedged.

Jack pressed himself into the other corner. "Ever see a Bigfoot?" He motioned Maxx to come sit by his leg. Maxx plopped his bottom down obediently.

The question caught the kid totally off guard. He frowned. "No. Never looked."

"Mountain lion?"

"No."

Jack sat and watched him, as if expecting more of an answer.

The silence got to Ernest in a hurry. "Almost did once," he drawled. "There was a lion hanging around National for a while. Chicken showed me his tracks once, in some sand by the river, but I never saw him."

"Chicken. Now there's a name. They called me Doofus in high school, but Chicken's worse. Who's Chicken?"

"Friend."

Jack knew that perfectly well already. He'd read the sheriff's report on the burglary that had been this boy's downfall. The seventeen-year-old partner's nickname was Chicken. "What's he doing now, you know?"

"Three to five at Walla Walla."

"Ever hear of a guy named Eerie Elroy?"

Apparently Ernest had not been expecting any of this. He paused, hesitant. "Real nut case up behind National."

"Ever try to burglarize his place?"

"Don't do that anymore."

"Years ago. Back when you were in the business. Or did you and Chicken steer clear away from nuts and morons?"

127

"He wasn't nuts then. Hung around the Clearcut a lot, but he wasn't crazy."

"Really." Jack wagged his head. "Well, he shot at me twice so far, but then I'm from out of town. He probably treats the locals better."

Maxx relaxed from alert sitting to half-lying, curled around, and began licking his hind toes.

Curiosity got the better of Ernest. He asked the classic question. "What'd you do to your face there?"

"Speaking of locals, I tangled with some at the Clearcut. Bar fight. There was no real harm done, except the bullet hole in their ceiling. It's going to be hard to spackle, way up there in the rafters."

Ernest almost smiled. "Your dog fight too?"

"He saved me." *So did Ev, but I'd better not mention that. It's not macho.*

"How much does he weigh?"

"About the same as you. He's big enough he doesn't have to fight much. He snarls, and that usually does the trick."

"Teach him to do stuff?"

"Yeah, some stuff. Catching Frisbees is his favorite thing. And he's police trained. Maxx." Jack snapped his fingers. "Go." He pointed to the far corner of the room.

The dog hopped up and walked over to the corner. He turned, ready for the next command.

"Down."

Maxx flopped to his belly, watching, his leathern ears pricked.

Jack pointed to Ernest. "Maxx. Go to Cheese."

The dog lurched to his feet and walked over to Ernest.

"Sit."

He sat.

Ernest was staring at Jack. "How'd you know I'm Cheese?"

"Your rap sheet. Maxx. Dead dog."

Maxx dropped heavily onto his side, stretched his

head out and opened his mouth. The white teeth glittered against his dark lips.

"Good dog, Maxx. Come."

Maxx hopped up and jogged over to Jack.

Jack dug out a treat for him and rubbed his chest. "Sit."

Maxx plopped down, but his tail wagged on.

Ernest watched rapt, quite clearly impressed. "His name is Maxx, huh?"

"Actually, it's Hall's Maximian Luxembourg, according to his registration papers. Maximum Licks and Burps."

And the smile broke through onto Ernest's face.

Jack smiled too. "You'll appreciate the name better the first time he belches in your face. I think he saves up stomach gas for when he gets near enough."

"I had a dog when I was little. He wasn't fancy like this one, but he was OK."

Jack waited.

"He could really catch a Frisbee. He could jump up higher than your head and catch it while it's sailing along. My uncle said I oughta enter him in contests and win some money, but I never did."

"You had it when you were little. I assume you don't have it anymore?"

"Mom moved, and we couldn't take him along, and I don't know what happened to him." Ernest shrugged helplessly. "Guess he went to a good home, you know? Mom said he did."

"My mom's name is Elizabeth. Liz. What's your mom's name?"

"Mary." Ernest waited nervously a few moments until the silence got to him. "Mary Mulrose. She's Irish, she says. When I was a baby she called me the leprechaun. That's a little Irish dwarf sort of person." More silence. More fidgeting. Ernest went on. "She really cried when they took me down for burglary, but Harry just said it served me right and wouldn't let her talk to me."

"Peach of a guy. Who's Harry?"

"Her boyfriend. He's a jerk. Prime time jerk."

"That's why you're with your uncle now? You couldn't get along with Harry?"

"Yeah. Is that on my rap sheet too?"

"No, I just sort of guessed it. Easy guess. It happens to more guys than you can believe. Happens all the time. And it's not their fault."

"Mom never shoulda took up with him. I told her he's no good. She said I was just jealous."

"She should have listened to you. Now you're both hurting. Everybody's hurting except good old Harry, who thinks he knows everything."

Ernest purred a choice expletive in total agreement with Jack's analysis.

Jack brought the conversation finally to his point. "Did your mom cry when they tried to hang that murder on you, or did she kind of believe maybe you did it?"

"Sure she cried." Ernest looked fleetingly at Jack's face. Then his eyes darted away to Maxx, to the wall, to anything except the harsh reality. "I guess she did. Harry wouldn't let her near me to talk to me anymore, but she called me up once when I was in here. When Harry didn't know about it. I guess she cried. She didn't say."

"You and she were living in or near Ashford then?"

"Eatonville."

"Eatonville's only twenty miles or so from Ashford. Chicken had a driver's license, so you could get around, right?"

"Suspended, but yeah. And he had a car."

"OK. You didn't do it. The murder, I mean. Who did? Chicken?"

Ernest clammed up. His mouth tightened down to a thin, hard line. Jack had just asked the wrong question. He had momentarily forgotten how loyal a fifteen-year-old can be.

He shifted back to a warmer topic. "Your mom ever

130

talk about her dreams for you? What she wished you'd be when you grew up?"

Warily, balancing his egocentric hunger to talk about himself against the possibility he might let something slip, Ernest waffled awhile with "I don't knows" and shrugs and reluctant "Well, uhs." Then, the egocentrism winning out, he pulled the bung and let the memories flow. "When I was a baby, she said, I was always trying to fix things. I'd tip something over, I'd try to set it back up. I took an alarm clock apart when I was about six. First grade. One of those wind-up alarm clocks."

"Bet you didn't fix that." Jack grinned.

So did Ernest. "You shoulda seen it. I can still remember it. A million pieces. She thought I ought to be a doctor. Then after she started seeing my grades, she thought maybe I'd be a good auto mechanic. She said that right up till Harry came along."

"And Harry isn't very good mechanically—not nearly as good as you are—so he ridiculed you out of jealousy. You're better than he is, and he can't stand that."

"You talk to Mom? Did you talk to my mom?"

"No. Never met your mom. Or Harry either. I told you, it's easy to guess. You fit the pattern. Rather, Harry fits the pattern. Like you said, a real jerk. How about your uncle? Does he think you'd be a good mechanic?"

"He never said. I didn't ask him."

Jack shifted topics, keeping Ernest off balance, with a question no one as yet had asked him. "Ever meet a man named John Getz?"

"Yeah. Mousy little guy? Sort of a creep?"

Jack's breastbone did a little thump. "Sounds right. Where did you meet him?"

"My uncle knows him. He wants my uncle to do some work for him."

"What? Cut down some trees?"

"He never said what. My uncle doesn't talk to me much."

"I'd like to meet your uncle sometime. Hey, if you're good at auto mechanics, I want to ask you something." Jack launched into a description of a ping in the engine that he took care of two months ago.

Ernest Cheese Mulrose listened to a description of the symptoms, accurately diagnosed the problem, and explained what's involved in repairing a sticking valve lifter. Jack needed this kid! For the next time weird noises emanated from beneath his truck's hood, he needed this kid.

Jack weighed what more he might gain, skirted around the edges of the Grade murder some more, and decided that Ernest's uncle played it so close that Ernest didn't know much more about Getz. The strange connection between Getz and this neophyte burglar intrigued him.

Eventually he stood up. He motioned Maxx to heel. The dog sat down by his left knee. "I guess that's all. I mean it when I say it was a pleasure talking to you, Cheese. And thanks for the info on my engine problem." He extended his hand.

This time, without hesitation, Ernest shook hands.

Jack rapped on the door.

The guard opened it and looked at Ernest. "Your uncle has come to bail you out. He's out front."

A look of relief washed across Ernest's face. He glanced at Jack. "You must live right. You want to talk to my uncle—here he is."

"I try." Jack followed the boy down the hall. "That doesn't mean I always succeed, but I try."

A swarthy man with a four-day growth of beard and the whipsaw-lean build of a basketball player lounged at the information counter. He stood erect as Jack and Ernest approached.

Ernest knew two adults who did not know each other. Grabbing this rare chance to be a man, he stepped up to his uncle. "Jack Preston. This is my Uncle Barney."

13
When Lights Are Lit on Christmas Eve

Amazing power lies in the official badge of the law enforcement officer. It takes you through closed doors; it gets you into the hallways and back rooms of a million places the general public cannot tread; it empowers you to make arrests; it lets you get stuck with a lunch check for $38.67.

Treating Ernest and his uncle to lunch, for that $38 and some (plus a $6.00 tip), Jack learned that: (1) Barney thought it terribly cute that Jack got his face bunged up in the Clearcut; in fact, it gave him Brownie points with this joker he could never have earned otherwise; (2) Getz had made contact with the uncle only once, about three months ago; (3) they could not come to agreement on a price for illegally falling selected trees inside the park boundary; (4) the blustering and virile Uncle Barney dismissed Getz as an extremist geek who probably walked a little light in his loafers; and (5) Ernest consumed approximately two times his weight in food each day, most of it at free lunches.

The incident report for which Ernest had been so fortuitously incarcerated in Remann Hall had probably rolled off the fax at Longmire by now. Fat lot of help it did Jack down here in Tacoma.

He sat back as the waitress whisked away the little black tray bearing the bill and his credit card. "A Sgt.

Means is sending me the paperwork on that fracas last night—the one that got you in trouble." He looked at Ernest. "But I'd rather hear about it from you two."

Barney studied Jack closely. "You sure you're a cop?"

"I'm a ranger. For present purposes, that's the same thing. Federally commissioned. Want to see my badge again?"

"Not particularly." Barney twisted his face up into what would pass as a leer. "Nothing to say. It got blown all out of proportion. Some dudes wanted to sell us some crack, and we didn't care to buy. They came on us heavy, so we came on them heavier."

"So why didn't the cops bust them as well when they took you two down?"

"They run faster, I guess."

"Too bad. Ernest here's been keeping his nose clean. I'm sorry to see him in trouble again. If Getz comes up with a better offer, do you think you might take it?"

The sneer turned into a wicked grin. "Of course not, Mr. Park Ranger. Fall trees in the park? Not me. I'm a law-abiding citizen."

"I'm sure you are, at least off and on."

Throughout this interview, punctuated as it were by drinking and chewing, Jack had referred to Getz as if he were still alive, a half dozen different ways. Not once did Barney or Ernest make a slip to suggest they knew otherwise, nor did they act at all nervous or apprehensive discussing the murder victim.

Jack tried another bunny trail. "Has Getz approached you recently about hitting an Ashford local named Elroy Washington?"

Barney hardened like ice cubes in the freezer. He rumbled, "No," but what Jack really watched was Ernest's startled expression.

The boy's face said yes.

Jack pressed the point. "I know for certain he feels the need to shut Elroy up. It certainly wouldn't be hard.

There's that screwball up there on the mountain, all alone, isolated. You drive up to the door, empty your nine mil at the harmless though unnerving shotgun blast that always greets visitors, and drive away. *Bang bang,* it's done. Literally. The neighbors won't even call the cops because they hear gunfire up there all the time. How much was his initial offer?"

Barney wagged his head. "You watch too much TV. They don't do that for real."

"Sure they do. And since Elroy is still alive and well in his mountain fastness, it's obvious that you refused to do it. You're off the hook, and the illegality is all on Getz's side of the fence. Not yours. How much did Getz offer?"

"Five hundred."

"Interesting. So Getz is not only a fluffbrain, he's a cheapskate."

Barney laughed, and even the dour and cautious Ernest grinned.

The waitress returned with Jack's credit card. He paused to add in the tip and sign the ticket. She trotted off, and he slipped his card back in his wallet. "Let's take it in the other direction. Who asked you to do Getz?"

Neither Barney nor, more tellingly, his nephew seemed nervous or put off in the least.

Barney grunted. "Nobody. Who'd want to spend money dousing that little dork?"

"Somebody did."

Still at ease, Barney shrugged. "Nobody asked me to."

"He was stabbed to death two weeks ago. Two weeks ago today, in fact."

Again, Barney and Ernest reacted with the facial expressions and body language one might expect.

Barney smirked. "If that's so, you been asking a lot of stupid questions."

Not really. You've been answering with far more than just words. "It's been all over the papers. There was a

135

press conference. How did you manage to keep from hearing about it?"

"We been out of the state."

"You'd just about have to be." Jack sat forward, an overture to actually standing up. "You know what I'm working on. If either of you hears anything, keep in mind that I pay for information."

They walked outside, Ernest greeted Maxx, Maxx returned the kindness by slobbering all over his face and belching, they shook hands, and Jack climbed into his truck.

He delayed pulling away until he saw Barney and Ernest drive off in Barney's huge, dinosaurian Chevy Impala. He eagerly wanted to touch base with Ev, but he had no idea how to reach her. He wanted to leave for Hawaii. He wanted to be back at Longmire working on his notes. There had to be nuggets of gold in all this ore he'd shoveled up.

Restless and irritable and unable to say why, he found Point Defiance Park and stashed his truck in the Boathouse parking lot. He put Maxx on a longline and took the dog and his pad and pencil down to the shore. While Maxx explored the strange and exotic smells of the rather alarmingly polluted bay, Jack wrote up his notes from the interviews thus far today. If he didn't record that sort of thing right away, he usually lost parts of it.

Night fell at 4:30 in the afternoon, reminding him how far north he was. Jeff and Kerri arrived at the parking lot at 5:05.

This might not be the fun evening Jack had first anticipated. Kerri climbed out of their car tense as a banjo string. They'd been fighting again. He could tell. Neither she nor Jeff bothered to try to put on a happy face.

Jack paused but a moment. His evening was as much at stake as theirs. "Good to see you both! Come over here with me a moment, will you, please?"

Jeff's sullen frown melted to a confused look. Kerri

probably had a notion what was coming. She eyed Jack warily and Jeff even more warily.

Jack walked over to the low stone-and-cement wall on the edge of the lot. "Have a seat." He plopped down. From his incarceration in the cab, Maxx woofed a "What about me?"

"We have reservations in there." Jeff didn't seem in the mood to sit.

"Good. Good. This Zoo Lights exhibit that they set up every Christmas season is pretty good, huh?"

Kerri nodded uncertainly.

"And the food at the Boathouse is good."

"What are you getting at?" Jeff extended to Jack the trust a chipmunk would give a hawk.

Jack weighed his options. He could step back and let the matter ride, or he could jump in the middle of this and probably make them both enemies instantly. Was Kerri's happiness worth the risk? Yeah. He cut straight to the chase. "You've already invested an hour and a half in what could be a lovely evening. You have to invest another hour and a half to get home. Then there's the four hours or so in between. Now you two can continue to grate on each other all night. If you do, you'll both feel ugly and disappointed and cheated out of a nice time and bitter. Probably trapped too. Besides, you'll feel terrible about spilling your venom in front of a virtual stranger. That's me.

"Or—" he paused "—you can make this the first day of healing. Turn it around starting now."

"It won't turn around. It's too late." Kerri glowered at Jeff.

Jeff glowered at Jack. "Stay out of what's not your business, Prester."

"It is, in fact, the business I'm in, by training and licensing. This investigation stuff is only what I get paid for. However—" he stood up "—I'm not going to force it on you. Since I'm your guest, I do ask that you lay the tomahawks and howitzers aside for the balance of the eve-

137

ning. This is my first night out in two weeks. I don't want it spoiled by a running fight that's none of my business, as you call it. It's not easy for chronic fighters. You've heard 'Take it one day at a time.' It's a good way to start, to break the pattern of fighting. Put the hurt on hold temporarily, and let's all enjoy a breather from the mayhem."

He knew that chronic fighters not only enjoy fighting, in a strange, masochistic way, but they also usually turn on anyone who tries to put a stop to it.

But not tonight. Kerri broke the awkward silence by clapping her hands together. "Sounds good to me. I'm hungry. Let's eat."

Jack glanced over his shoulder at Maxx as they trooped inside. The dog, resigned to abandonment, disappeared below window level, no doubt to sleep his blues away.

They got a table by the windows that extended out over the water. The view was not only picturesque, with all the shore and boat lights and dancing reflections on the water, but fun. This was a major shipping channel. Barges, tugs, and even a container ship were plowing around out there.

The other patrons' plates looked so good that Jack ventured to try the seafood. He was a ranch boy unaccustomed to victuals that once sported fins instead of hair, or at least feathers, but he liked the combination plate just fine.

It was too bad Ev couldn't be here enjoying this. It would probably not only please her—she seemed to like this sort of thing—but it would offer a ring of familiarity. Her father was a Navy man; she grew up along the water.

Jack could see why Kerri had suggested the Boathouse. It hugged the shore of Point Defiance with the zoo not half a mile from its door. They didn't bother moving the vehicles. They walked up a densely wooded path to the zoo gate.

Because Maxx was persona non grata in the zoo,

Jack left him behind to sleep off his second disappointment in a row.

Jack was amazed at the long lines of Tacomans waiting to flock inside and see, essentially, a collection of colored lights. Jack, Jeff, and Kerri queued up with the rest of Pierce County and were inside in less than fifteen minutes.

"Hey! I just crossed that bridge!" Jack pointed to the first display they came to. The Tacoma Narrows Bridge was sketched across the lawn in gorgeous detail, outlined in nothing but thousands of tiny lights. Headlights and taillights streamed along its road surface.

Kerri grinned at him. "You ain't seen nothing yet."

They walked on through the darkness.

Uncle Barney claimed he met Getz only once. But the journal mentioned at least three such occasions just since 1 November, and for sheer accuracy Jack would take Getz's records, written for no one's eyes but his own, over Barney's word any day. Therefore, what was Barney covering up? Jack's cogitations were interfering with the pleasure of the evening.

Was Getz one of these people who rode a thin line between fantasy and reality, shifting from one side to the other and treating both alike? With his journal, Getz could possibly have been building a whole fantasy life with only occasional intrusions of reality, even down to the invention of imaginary persons. It wouldn't be the first time. How much weight ought Jack attach to that journal?

They passed a low building. To the left on the roof, a goose sketched out of appropriately colored Christmas lights appeared. Its wings were out, setting, as if it were coming in to alight on a pond. That picture faded. Twenty feet to its right, another view of the goose flashed on. In this one, the wings were set lower and the feet were braced out ready to land. That picture faded as a third flared on to the right. In this sequence of half a dozen vignettes, the goose soared down along the top of the low building and alighted beside a gaggle of other geese outlined in lights on a small lawn.

On another stretch of lawn, a kangaroo created with an outline of lights flashed into brightness. That figure faded as the figure of a hopping kangaroo flashed on ahead of it. As that faded, a leaping kangaroo came on. With the series of flashing figures, the artist presented a perfect illusion of a kangaroo bounding across the grass. As the final figure settled to a halt, a baby 'roo hopped out of its pouch. Delightful.

What if the journal itself was a plant? Someone scrubbed Getz's hard drive. Could that person have cleverly hidden a fictitious journal, knowing Somersby or other news reporters, if not the cops, would leave no stone unturned until they found it? If so, the only possible reason would be to serve a hidden agenda. That would mean carefully studying the whole journal, who-knows-how-many pages, and not just this last diskette. Even then you might not spot the real intent.

And all that was based on the assumption that the journal was a major factor in the murder. It might not be. It could be peripheral or nonsignificant altogether.

Jack had not yet even tackled the logger angle. Ev, apparently, had made contact with the good folks at *Logger's World*, but to the best of Jack's knowledge it had not progressed beyond that. Who were the activists in the Ashford area?

"Jack!" Ev stood in front of him, gaping. Another four feet and they would have bumped into each other. Beside her, Darryl grinned. Jeff and Kerri and Darryl greeted each other effusively. Ev and Jack stared at each other.

Jack snapped out of it first and babbled a greeting. What he really wanted to say was "I found Barney, and do I have a lot to tell you!" He couldn't here, in front of these others, and that made him all the more restless. He wanted Ev's input into this puzzle.

Most of all, he wanted Ev to know that he had found

the Barney she had been seeking. He wanted to reveal to her the curious link between Barney and Getz—and even Darryl. He was proud of what he'd found, no matter that he had stumbled upon it purely by happenstance.

"Oh, look." Ev nodded up toward the dark, dark trees beyond them.

The outline of a perching eagle appeared high in the tree. As its lights went out, the next outlined bird flashed on lower down, swooping. The next, very close to the ground, hit slashing, sparkling "water." The next carried a big fish upward, and the final sat up in a tree on a nest of lights, with two eaglet heads limned in it.

Jack stood watching as the sequence cycled through a couple of times, marveling at the artwork in the vignettes created with nothing save tiny colored lights, and at the perfect timing from vignette to vignette.

Ev commented along the same lines, but she was talking to Darryl, not Jack.

Jeff and Kerri had been doing very well so far, especially for chronic fighters. Jack watched their interactions from a professional viewpoint, so to speak, and saw a lot of potential there for healing and growth. They really did care about each other. They tried especially hard to put on happy faces for Darryl and Ev. As a result, this evening was indeed passing pleasantly for them. Kerri laughed a lot, and even the sullen Jeff brightened.

Ev bubbled, and Darryl smiled, solicitous as ever.

Thoughts about the journal, and Barney, and Ernest, and Elroy, and similar loose ends kept churning, but other thoughts insinuated themselves into the mess as well. Ev's note said she went to town Saturday. Apparently she went with Darryl. Here she was Sunday night with Darryl. Late Saturday evening, when Jack was working on reports and called her for any information she had picked up on a Barney, she was not home to answer her phone. Did she spend the whole weekend down here in Tacoma?

With Darryl?

He yearned to know, and he was too scared of the possible answer to ask.

The five of them hung together for the balance of the tour, wandering through darkness from display to display. Jack would have missed some of the little charmers, tucked into hard-to-notice corners, had others not pointed them out, and he spotted a few the others missed. Finding the displays became as much a game as admiring them.

Afterward, Kerri and Jeff led the way a couple of blocks from the zoo to one of those sandwich shops with lots of pink-and-white striped appointments.

"The coffee is good, the espresso is excellent, and their ice cream is matchless," Kerri promised.

All five merrymakers entered the shop and squeezed into a booth.

Could Jack trust Barney's testimony at all? Barney lied about the number of contacts between Getz and himself. He no doubt lied about other things. Which things? All things? Some things? Maybe finding Barney wasn't such a magnificent coup after all. Probably—

"Wake up!" Ev, to his left, poked his arm. "You better order the caffeinated coffee. You have to drive home."

Jack twisted to look at her. "I was thinking of letting Maxx drive and just curling up on the seat to sleep. He's not real good at intersections—he likes to chase cars, so the cross traffic gets him all excited—but he can handle anything outside of town." What he saw in Ev's face was ebullience, and he'd never ever seen that before. She was so happy right now that she glowed. It couldn't all be the light show at the zoo.

Kerri on his right was laughing. "Don't you ever take anything seriously?"

"I take lots of things seriously." He let his eyes linger on Ev's face as he added, "I take friendships seriously."

Jeff chuckled, which for him was a big step forward. "Kerri should talk about taking things seriously. Did you know she was Ms. Mount Rainier in the Elbe parade?"

Darryl laughed, and Kerri laughed harder. Obviously this was an insider joke.

Jack grinned at her. "And I can't envision a lovelier Ms. Mount Rainier. Elbe has a hundred and fifty people if you include the dogs and horses, and it takes a hundred and forty-nine to make a parade. How do they decide who will be the spectator? Draw straws?"

Darryl was grinning so wide he could bite a bus. "The Annual Elbe International Third of July Parade. It's the best Third of July parade in the nation."

Ev giggled. "Third of July? Aren't they missing a day?"

"Everyone else has a Fourth of July parade. Even Eatonville has a Fourth of July parade. So everyone else is somewhere else on the Fourth, you see? By having it on the third, Elbe catches everyone while they're still in the area."

Ev pondered this convoluted nonreasoning for only a moment. "Yes, but *international?*"

Jeff rumbled, "The first year they had it, they stopped traffic at both ends of town so the parade could go down Route 7."

"I'm not surprised," Jack interrupted. "It's the only street they have."

"The first car stopped on the east end of town was a Canadian vacationer. He asked, 'Can I join in?' and they said, 'Sure.' So he slipped his station wagon into the parade and drove the whole parade route. Clear around the block. When he got out to 7 again, he went on his way west."

Kerri finished Jeff's thought. "There he was in his station wagon crammed full of camping gear, and his wife and kids. They rolled down the windows and waved to all the folks. They had a wonderful time. And that's why it's international."

Jack nodded. Of course.

Kerri bubbled on. "The parade's a hoot. Nobody gets paid, nobody invites outsiders. It's the kids with their bikes

143

all fancied up with crepe paper, and all the kids who have horses. Someone drives the big red fire pumper. The only float, usually, is a flatbed trailer with the people who work in the Scaleshed burger place."

"And Ms. Mount Rainier." Jack was smiling too. "Don't forget Ms. Mount Rainier."

"Never." Kerri's eyes sparkled. "Sitting on the back of a little MG sports car, waving with everyone else."

Darryl was still grinning. "Homegrown. Everyone has a great time. That's the real purpose of a parade."

Ev bobbed her head. "The real American spirit."

The waitress had been standing there several minutes, waiting for a break, listening just as attentively as was Ev. She took orders all around, and Jack practically had to engage Kerri in fisticuffs to be allowed to order a plain coffee instead of the espresso that she insisted he ought to have. Two bucks for a cup of coffee? Hardly.

The talk shifted to skiing. Darryl preferred downhill. Ev wanted to learn. Kerri and Jeff used to go cross-country all the time, especially before they were married.

Jack left the yarn-telling to others and kept his war stories to himself, although he had some hairy ones, especially the time he and Ernie Morales had skied the unmaintained ledge trail from Glacier Point to the Yosemite Valley floor. Plastered against the side of a three-thousand foot cliff, that trail wasn't even fit for hiking.

Conversation paused.

Jack looked at Jeff. "Those ski-and-saddle hostels they're playing around with up in the park? How are they stocked? Private funds?"

"Some. Mostly donations. For instance, they asked merchants to donate remaindered stocks." He looked at Kerri. "Can you remember any specifics?" It was the first time that night that he actually asked her something.

She pursed her lips. "All those blankets from the linen outlet that was going out of business. No, not out of business. Moving to a new location. And some of the hostel supplies were purchased at a big discount."

"Oh, yeah." Jeff picked it up. "There's a big Korean market here in town. They found an extremely good deal on candles. So they donated part of the cost, which was low to start with, and a sportsmen's group picked up the rest. That kind of thing." He gestured with spread hands. "All different ways. Wangle. Finagle. Buy if you have to, but buy cheap. The locals here have a poor record of co-operating, unless it's the school. The school gets excellent support. But the ski-and-saddle hostels seem to be getting some support."

"Not a hundred percent." Kerri watched her approaching espresso mug with hungry eyes. A great fluff of whipped cream rode on its surface.

"No. In fact, some backlash." Jeff beamed at the humongous chocolate sundae the waitress set before him.

"John Getz?" Jack eyed his war-canoe-sized banana split with some trepidation. This was a late hour to be on-loading that much sugar. He was going to be wired till Tuesday.

"Especially John Getz." Kerri paused from sipping around the edges of her tub of caffeine. "Jack, I'm sorry to say this, but I'm not the least bit sad that John Getz got it. You cannot imagine what a pain he was. Two and three times a week, in my office demanding this information or that. Sometimes he'd even have a court order. And then he'd use whatever he got to file a tort claim or something. And if he didn't get what he thought he should have, he filed a complaint because it wasn't provided to him. He sometimes took up half my day. Really! He was such a . . ."

Apparently she decided that describing him was not appropriate in polite company. She settled back to sipping her drink.

As soon as the check arrived and they divvied it up, Jack excused himself, bade them all a fond good night, and headed back toward the mountain. He had put his finger on one source of his irritation, and leaving that source helped, if only a little.

He was the fifth wheel on a one-horse shay. Ev and Darryl obviously were a twosome. That twosome really bothered him too, which was ridiculous. Ev was happy. Ev was his coworker. He should be happy.

Jeff and Kerri, the other two wheels, had warmed up to each other considerably as the evening progressed. Nice as that was, it left Jack with Maxx.

Whee.

Bah, humbug.

14

Bring a Torch,
Jeanette, Isabella

The perfect spaghetti sauce starts with a pound of ground beef and four strips of bacon, chopped. Fry the lot but do not overcook. Jack listened to the sizzle and adjusted the burner again. He wasn't used to cooking with electricity, being basically a propane person.

Chop a whole onion, a green pepper, and a handful of fresh mushrooms. Add some chopped green Anaheim chilies if you have them (he did, but they were canned). Scramble all that into the meat without draining any of the grease. Dump in two fifteen-ounce cans of tomato sauce. Let it simmer on low until the flavors marry, adding the herbs and spices—lots of garlic, plus parsley, basil, oregano, and thyme—as it cooks. Not only is the sauce absolutely delectable served over spaghetti or angelhair, it makes the whole house smell good.

Jack was finishing up the chop-the-vegetables stage as Ev knocked at his door. Maxx answered with thunderous barking, his automatic reaction to any knock or doorbell. Jack yelled, "Come in!" because he was in the middle of dumping mushrooms into the sauce and couldn't answer the door like a proper gentleman.

She entered with her laptop and a smile. It was raining out there hard enough to drown frogs. She tipped back the hood of her rain slicker as she closed the door.

"Hello, Maxx!" She rubbed his head and chest. He squirmed with ecstasy and licked everything within three feet of his tongue. "That's enough, Maxx." She stood erect and peeled out of her slicker. "It smells great. Maxx, lie down."

"Maxx! *Down!* Thank you. It's about to smell even greater, as I add the herbs. How was your day?"

"Excellent. How was yours?"

Jack pushed an "Aah" through his nose. "Do you know you can't get parcel service out here without paying a body part? I ended up down in Ashford at the post office, mailing stuff priority. Very nice postal person."

"What stuff?"

"My Christmas gifts for the family. I managed to move my flight up to six A.M. on the twenty-fourth. It's a lousy time, but it was the only open seat left to Hawaii. This way I don't have to juggle all that stuff—don't have to check any baggage. Just grab my ditty bag and run for the plane. I can wear my cousin's clothes when I get there. Or buy a pair of loud shorts and a Hawaiian shirt and really wow you all when I get back."

"Oh." She sounded subdued, not at all wowed by the vision. "What about Maxx?"

"He stays with Jeff and Kerri unless we arrest them for murder first."

"Are you actually worried we might do that?"

"What? Me worry? Never."

The power dipped, browning out the overhead light. The light flared back to brightness. The power dipped again. The third time it dipped, it just kept going, plunging the apartment into blackness.

Ev sucked in air audibly. She murmured, "Maybe worrying isn't such a bad idea. Oh, well. We can eat salad."

"No problem. Let me borrow your slicker." Jack flicked his Bic for enough light to find her wet raincoat. "Have a seat. I'll be right back. Maxx, stay."

He stepped outside from utter blackness into utter blackness. No street lights, no overheads, no lights in windows, no headlights on the road. The rain came so thick and heavy that Peter would have had less trouble walking on it than on the Sea of Galilee.

Jack dug behind the backseat of his truck for his camping stuff. One by one, the windows of the houses in the residence loop began to glow orange as people lit lanterns and candles.

He carried in the first load. He'd give Ev some light first. She seemed uncomfortable in the darkness. He hummed a Christmas carol as he set his stuff on the counter.

She giggled in the blackness. "I know that song. The title is 'Bring a Torch, Jeanette, Isabella.' It's French. Very appropriate." Her voice dropped to something soft and tentative. "This is your camping stuff, right? We're sort of camping out."

"Camping in. Right." He hung her slicker on the back of a chair he happened to have bumped into. "Coleman stove and lantern. Later I'll bring in my sleeping bag, since it will probably get cool in here overnight. Then—"

"How long will the power be out?"

"In your national park? You never know. An hour minimum, four days maximum. I'd guess a tree came down on the line. The blinks would be it bobbing—which means we'll probably have the power back in a couple hours." He pumped up the tank of the lantern and flicked his handy Bic.

She watched the lantern flare from rinkydink yellow light to high-intensity blue. "You don't smoke, do you?"

"No, but that doesn't preclude me from carrying a butane lighter, does it? It's a lot easier than matches, especially when your pocket gets wet." He pumped up the stove and got his sauce cooking again with less than five minutes lost. He had forgotten how noisy these stoves are when you've got them going full blast inside four walls.

Behind him, Ev's laptop made beeping sounds. "For-

149

tunately," she said, "my battery's juiced up. I'm good for at least an hour and a half. By then we should have electricity back, don't you think?"

"Surely so." *Probably not.* He laid in the garlic lavishly—fresh garlic, not the freeze-dried stuff.

"I went through all the records I could find regarding that Barney you came up with. His last name is Hall. No permanent address. I'd call him a vagrant, but he works for various loggers off and on."

"On now?"

"Off. His last job. Are you ready for this?" She sounded as smug as the G-man who just found Jimmy Hoffa. "Was for Jay Chambers."

"Do tell!"

"Apparently Mr. Chambers needed some carpentry work done on his home near Ashford somewhere, and he hired Barney Hall to do it. Mr. Hall does odd jobs."

"Very odd at times. I can't imagine poor old Ernest was a burglar all by himself at twelve. Or even with Chicken's help."

"You think Barney might be behind that?"

"Possibly."

"And therefore behind Margaret Grade's murder?"

"Not out of the question."

She sounded thoughtful. "Do you suppose Darryl knows about him? It didn't seem like he knew the name when he heard it."

"You're discussing the case with Darryl Grade? Ev, you oughta know better! He's a suspect! You say nothing about nothing to Darryl Grade or Kerri or anyone."

"Darryl is not a suspect, but no! I'm not that stupid, Jack Prester! I'm disappointed you'd think such a thing."

"That's how it sounded. Why should he hear Barney Hall's name at all?"

"I asked him if he knew the name when I was getting everyone's alibi all over again. Their alibi for when Getz was killed."

150

"Mike Sanchez did that. There's a report—"

"Yes, but we've uncovered all this new stuff, so I thought I'd tackle it again. Fresh, so to speak. I asked all the people the same questions, and 'Do you know or have you ever heard of Barney Hall?' was one of them."

That's what Jack probably would have thought of, were he not buying lunches for felons, the aforenamed Hall not the least of them. Why did it irritate him mildly that she'd come up with it on her own? He returned his attentions to the spaghetti sauce, adding herbs.

"How do you want these alibis written up?"

"Same as your other reports, with the subheads."

"Good." Her laptop keyboard clicked. "Here's Kerri's. She was off that day. She's off Sundays, and she says she was in town at her sister's. Her brother-in-law works for Boeing. So I called the sister. The sister can't remember exactly. She hemmed and hawed in such a way that I suspect she doesn't know what's going on, but she doesn't want to get Kerri in a bind either."

"Good obs." Jack started the water for the spaghetti. It would take a while to reach boiling with this gutless old Coleman. His mom claimed the new ones were a lot better, but he was used to this petulant, even say maniacal, old beast and not of a mind to upgrade. "Which means that Kerri essentially has no alibi unless she gins one up with her sister."

"It sounds that way. I asked the sister if anyone had called her before, double-checking. You know, Mike Sanchez, for instance, though I didn't mention his name. And she said no."

"Mike took her word for it, in other words."

"You once told me rule number one is always to take nobody's word for anything. Do you realize you've quoted about six different 'Rule Number Ones' since I've known you? Like not dating the suspects. Things like that."

"OK, so I get the numbers mixed up, but I know all the rules. What does Jeff say?"

"I had trouble reaching him. It's snowing at Paradise, so he was out on the road. Jack? Can we go up into the snow? I'd love to."

"Won't Darryl take you?" *Bite your tongue, Prester.* Jack found his package of spaghetti in the cupboard.

"He said he would but he's busy. Jeff claims that Kerri was home sick with the flu that day. The gutbuster stuff, like you had. That doesn't mean, I think, that Kerri was lying about visiting her sister. You know how when you're sick you sort of lose track of time?"

"And the tides, and who's on top in the NBA, and whether you got dressed this morning, and any number of other things one usually keeps track of. Yeah."

"I think that's the case with her. She didn't seem like she was lying. She seemed genuinely uncertain, not sure."

"And Jeff was with the road crew."

"Not the whole time. This is interesting. He went down the hill to get some stuff he forgot."

"During the time Getz died?"

"Stretching it a little, but yes. And they weren't paying close attention to the time on that rockslide job."

"Darryl Grade?"

"Supervising the job. The new rock work and the stabilization. And also supervising some plowing at Paradise. They were opening up some extra spaces in the parking lot."

"Driving back and forth between the projects."

"No. Apparently he talked to the people at Paradise by radio. He sort of floated between the two projects in Stephens Canyon, he said."

Jack turned to her. "Then, Ev, he's a suspect. The workmen at none of the sites were really keeping tabs on him. Was he up here? Down there? In his truck on the radio? They wouldn't know."

"He didn't have time. Getz was half a mile off the trail. Think how long it took us to walk back to the spot." And then, quite clearly, she dismissed Jack's objection as invalid. She returned to studying her computer screen. "Now the Jay Chambers and Elizabeth Munro situation is interesting. I think you ought to talk to Elizabeth again."

Was she working on the case, or was she trying to get Jack interested in Elizabeth so that she wouldn't be the only one with a romantic involvement? And why did Jack constantly think up these suspicions?

She continued unabated. "Elizabeth apparently dropped her sunglasses somewhere up the trail and was very tired by then. She's not a very good hiker, I'm guessing. Jay went back up the trail alone to find them for her."

"Chivalry is not dead."

"Apparently not. He was gone quite a while according to her, just a brief time according to him. Regardless which of them is actually right, there is that gap, you see."

Jack nodded. He put the dry spaghetti into his almost-boiling water and pumped up the stove tank again. Its harsh, sputtering hiss roared louder.

"Jack? I've been thinking about Jay Chambers. You know, if he found out John Getz wanted to cut down those fine old trees, do you think he'd be worried enough and enraged enough that he'd kill him?"

"Possibility. Not a probability. I think he's strongly pacifist."

"Oh, come on! Druids participate in human sacrifices." And her voice faded to a whimper. "Jack? Do you suppose?"

"I'll talk to him about ritual a little. Find out, sideways if possible, whether a stone knife is involved. I expect he'll play that pretty close to the chest, talking about rituals and procedures to the uninitiated." His brittle spaghetti was starting to soften and bend. "But Eerie Elroy is more knowledgeable. I might get it through him."

"You're not going to be too disappointed if you don't make it to Hawaii, are you?"

"Bitterly so." He stirred his spaghetti.

"But it's not till the twenty-fourth. Is that what you said?"

"Right. I called Hal this afternoon, and I didn't ask him. I told him. I'm compromising by chopping six days off my holiday. He can bend a little too."

"He called me this morning, you know. He said he couldn't reach you—"

"I spent three hours on the phone with Sergeant Means and some others, getting the paper verification for what we found out this weekend."

"He said your phone was busy. He asked what we had so far and had me fax him a bunch of stuff. I told him a lot of it is just preliminary, but he wanted it anyway. To prove we were moving forward, he said. Prove to whom, Jack? Why is he so anxious with this one? He wasn't that way before. Is there some problem with funding or something?"

"I don't know."

"If it is about funding or something else important, there's a definite possibility you'll have to stay here, you know. He was talking that way."

"We'll see." *I'm going.* Jack didn't want to think about that. He shifted his full attention to the sauce. It didn't really bubble; it just looked as if it wanted to. Good. He stirred carefully.

Ev was saying something about duty first, but he didn't listen. Then she was saying something about setting up a meeting with Jay Chambers and some others, getting them all together.

Jack grabbed a spoon and tasted his sauce. "Not enough thyme." He reached for the spice can.

"Of course there is. We're not on a tight, demanding schedule." Ev sighed heavily. "Now look, Jack. You're just going to have to come to grips with the idea that maybe you're not going to get out of here exactly when you want to. A lot de—"

"Will you please quit dwelling on the subject of Hawaii?"

"I wasn't dwelling on it! You're the one keeps bringing it up."

"Me?! I didn't mention it." Why was he fighting with her? He didn't want to argue with her. He didn't want to argue with anyone. Stuff Hal's telephone receiver down his throat maybe, but not argue with Ev.

"Not directly. By implication."

The spaghetti needed about five more minutes. If he could somehow add the heat of his anger to the Coleman stove, he could have the stuff cooked by now. He wasn't asking so much—Christmas with his family and then back to work. What's a few days more or less? This project could stretch out for months, the way it was going.

Coldly, she continued, "Mike Sanchez seemed pleased that I asked him for his alibi. He thinks it shows we're being thorough."

"We are. You are."

Her laptop clicked. "He gave me his ticket stubs and some cash register receipts with the date and time printed on them. He took his family into Seattle to the ballet and did some shopping."

"Ballet." Mike Sanchez? The man who climbs Mount Rainier just for fun?

"Seattle has a wonderful version of the *Nutcracker,* he says, with sets by Maurice Sendak. Some engineers at Boeing built the growing Christmas tree so that it unfolds and actually grows."

Jack knew the name *Maurice Sendak.* He must have read *Where the Wild Things Are* aloud a hundred times with his little Matthew curled up in his lap. And when Matthew started to read at five, just months before he died, he could pick out nearly half the words. Jack could not picture the weird imagination of Maurice Sendak meshing with the classical ballet of Tchaikovsky.

Matthew. His son. Gone.

155

Marcia. His wife. Gone.

Marcia loved his spaghetti. So did Matthew.

Ev was rolling inexorably onward. "Mike's only contact with John Getz, he says, was arresting the man a few times for either disrupting traffic during some protest or other, or distributing propaganda illegally in the park. Jack? You're not listening to me."

"Yes, I am. Maurice Sendak did the sets for the *Nutcracker*."

Her voice sounded like Jack's fifth grade teacher, Miss Lambay, whom they called Miss Lamprey. "Jack, what is the matter with you? You're not paying attention. That's not like you."

He tried a strand of spaghetti. "Time to eat. Clear the table, please. Or since you're Navy oriented, clear the decks."

She lifted her laptop as he set out placemats, flatware, napkins, and the tossed salads. He heard it beep. She closed it down while he fancied up the table—two of those stubby white kitchen candles he kept with his camping stuff and a bowl of silk flowers he picked up when he bought the groceries. Very elegant and high-brow for a country boy. He handed her the Bic to light the candles and set the Coleman lantern on the counter.

He drained the spaghetti as he listed the drinks available. She chose tropical punch. Maxx detected the serving of food, awoke, and stretched. Jack ordered him back down. He poured drinks, set out the plates piled high with spaghetti and aromatic sauce, put the can of grated Parmesan on the table, and sat down.

Someone knocked.

Maxx barked.

Jack snarled. "If that's Darryl, he can't have you." He got up and answered the door.

The rain had abated to nothing more than a coarse mist, but the let-up must have occurred only recently. For here stood Eerie Elroy Washington in the gloom, looking like a drowned rat.

"Prester, I wanna talk to you. I think someone's trying to kill me."

15

It Came upon the Midnight Clear

Maxx belched. He sat on the broad, velvet-upholstered bench seat of a genuine hearse, eagerly enjoying the ride.

To Maxx's right, Eerie Elroy belched. "That was the best spaghetti I've had in a while. You sure that cute little number didn't help you cook it?" He stretched his legs out as he sat at ease on the passenger side.

Jack, the couth one to Maxx's left, didn't belch. "That cute little number thinks cooking is serving a scoop of ice cream with your Sara Lee cake, and she's the first to admit it. Not that she'd ever serve Sara Lees. She's into health food."

He had never driven a hearse before, though he'd operated aid vans a lot, as well as an occasional farm tractor. This was fun, in a way. It handled like a tank, and you had to remember how far your vehicle extended out behind you, a stretch limo for that final ride. The hood looked as big as a soccer field.

"Oh. One of them. So's Jay Chambers."

"And Elizabeth Munro, I suppose."

"I suppose."

Eerie seemed fairly relaxed, finally. Eerie Elroy in an agitated state was not a pleasant person to be around. For one thing, when he was truly upset, he got the hiccups. For another, he swore a lot more.

"I feel pretty good now. Sitting down to that meal helped a lot. I can drive now. And let's put this dog in the back. It's cramped up here with him."

"Not on your life. Or more accurately, on mine. I assume we're both being up front here. You emerge out of the storm with this wild, hairy tale about being run off the road, and ask me to come down to your place. Frankly, I don't trust you. I prefer to keep the wheel. And Maxx is added insurance."

"Still, it's cramped."

"True. At least he doesn't smell yet. Wait'll he gets wet."

"He won't. It's clearing off pretty fast."

Jack negotiated the curves below Longmire with one hand, courtesy of power steering. This monster held the road remarkably better than he would have thought. Black forest lined the black road on both sides, blanketing the night with the gloomiest of gloom. At least the rain had stopped.

"I still don't understand why you came clear up to Longmire to knock on my door. Why not just call 911 and get the sheriff's deputy?"

"I don't trust them."

"You don't trust me."

"That's true." Eerie eyed him. "But I trust them a lot less. You can do an accident report. And I might need it to get my money out of the insurance company for repairs. You saw my side there. All bashed in."

"County's supposed to investigate."

"I don't want them coming around."

Jack grunted. "I can believe it. Not the way you fire guns so casually. The less cops the better."

"Not casually." Eerie smiled slightly. "Never casually."

"OK. Frequently."

Eerie chuckled.

Maxx snarfed.

"Describe in detail what happened. You just sort of sketched it out roughly when we were talking at dinner."

"That's 'cause I didn't think you wanted to talk business with dinner. I was driving east toward the park, east of Ashford, and this big Silverado comes up behind me and flashes its lights. I slowed up to let it past. The lights pulled out around me, and all of a sudden they're veering into me. I hit the brakes and veered back at them. What the hey—I was driving as much steel as they were. It surprised them. Then they came at me more direct, so to speak, and I had to hit the ditch. Hit the power pole too, but I didn't mean to do that."

"Knock the lines down?"

"Not there. Knocked the pole to slanting, and the pole to the west of it got pulled to a slant too. The lines probably broke behind that one. I notice there weren't any lights from there on up the hill."

"And they drove on."

"Nope, they stopped. So I opened up with my .44, right at them. Then they drove on."

"Eastbound, toward the park?"

Eerie nodded. "That doesn't mean they came up into the park. There's plenty of other places to go. Even to Packwood down the Skate Creek Road, or Yakima."

"Or Chicago or New York City, depending how much gas they have in the tank. So who pulled you out of the ditch?"

"A guy I pulled out of the ditch drunk once, before the fire department got there. He owed me. I may not call them friends anymore, but that don't mean they don't owe me."

Jack pondered the story but a moment. "You fired at them, and they took off. Did you shoot to kill?"

"Tried to."

"I don't understand why they would pause. Surely by now everyone knows your calling card is a load of buckshot. If I were the one who ran you off the road, why would I stop then, knowing full well I'm going to get shot at?"

"It's something to ask them sometime." Eerie didn't seem the least bit defensive, as people who invent stories usually do if challenged.

"You said Silverado. You sure it wasn't a Chevy Impala?"

"Why'd you ask that?"

"'Cause I want to know."

"No, it wasn't. But I saw one recently. Where did I see it?"

The extreme darkness was opening up ahead as they approached the clearing at Kautz Creek.

Jack prodded Eerie's memory. "Chambers's front yard."

"Yeah! How'd you know? Jay says you've never been to his place."

"The guy who did some carpentry work for him drives one." Jack always found the Kautz Creek area interesting. Here, decades ago, a mud flow from the Kautz glacier inundated the stream channel. Hundreds of trees died standing in place, choked to death from the waist down by mud. Fifty years, more or less, and new trees were just now starting to grow back.

"You really get into an investigation. I bet Jay didn't mention the carpentry work."

"Why wouldn't he?"

Eerie shrugged. "I just betcha, that's all."

Jack pulled as far aside as possible on the narrow road and stopped the hearse. "Now look. You obviously figure you're going to get a fair shake from me, or you wouldn't have asked me to do this. Well, you're right. You will. But when I ask a question, it's because the honest answer has some significance. Neither one of us has time to get devious here."

Eerie mulled that a moment. "Jay is doing some

161

work in a clearing near his house—for ceremonial purposes. A sacred circle."

"What? Sort of a wooden Stonehenge?" Jack pulled out on the road and started down the hill again, over the Kautz Creek bridge.

"You might call it that. Line up some poles to orient with the sun at solstice and equinox. The arrangement here would be a whole lot different from the arrangement in Europe. Well, maybe not a whole lot, but—*that's him!*" Eerie pointed wildly at a large vehicle approaching, its right headlight out.

As the big, bouncing baby bus passed by, Jack could hear it accelerating. He grabbed the emergency and pulled a moonshiner's turn with a great deal of caution. That was a maneuver for dry pavement and certainly not something a hearse does every day.

The hearse swapped ends and did a wiggling little fishtail as Jack gunned it. Maxx slammed against Eerie and just about tossed him off the seat.

Eerie sat wide-eyed, gripping the dash. "Whoozie! I saw that on TV, but I never been in one!"

"I imagine it's even harder to do with a logging truck." Jack floored it.

Eerie cackled like a laying hen with twin eggs.

They whipped back up the deserted road a lot faster than they had come down.

"Know why they came up this way?" Eerie had to yell as the motor noise mounted. "They didn't think I'd head up into the park. I bet they thought I'd run the other way —or run home. And I sure bet they weren't expecting to get spotted."

"But why the time lag?" Jack was yelling too. "It's been almost two hours since they ran you off the road."

Eerie had no answer for that, but then he probably wasn't listening. He seemed caught up like a ten-year-old in the squealing tires, the dizzying ride.

Maxx slammed into Jack, and he regretted now not

relegating the dog to the back as Eerie had suggested.

Jack was starting to feel a bit of motion sickness despite that he was driving.

Eerie yelled, "Whoozie!" a dozen more times at least. Once would have been plenty.

They roared past the signs announcing Longmire and suggesting they reduce speed to twenty miles per hour. Jack saw no headlights or taillights ahead. The bus lot was closed off. The road continuing up to Paradise was closed, and the bar across it appeared intact.

Jack cruised the Longmire Inn parking lot. "Watch for movement, not just headlights."

Should he stop for the park radio at the apartment? Whom would he call? Sanchez directly, or whoever was on duty? Was anyone out and about? How long would it take them to respond? In fact, was anyone on dispatch this late? He had no idea.

He turned up through the maintenance area and did a quickie around the back. Nothing. He looped behind the residences. Nothing. "There's a possibility the guy lives up here and might have had a garage door open and waiting to drive into—an escape hatch."

"You mean like in the maintenance area? One of those truck bays?"

"Yeah. If he did, we lost him." There was a reason not to use the radio. If the perp was homegrown he might have a radio tuned to the park frequency—and Jay Chambers actually boasted that he did—which would blunt the element of surprise if Jack caught up to the guy. Let him think it was only Eerie—which was bad enough.

He cranked a hard left and just barely pulled the hearse around the corner onto the back road. They headed up the steep and winding road toward the community building. As they crossed the big wooden bridge over the creek, Jack noticed that the sky was clearing and brightening.

163

On the far side of the bridge he stopped. "What do you see in the dirt?"

Eerie popped his seat belt and leaped out. By the light of the headlight he put his nose down close to check the road. Jack rolled his window down all the way and moved his .38 from the holster at the small of his back to his belt in front. Caught up in the tension, Maxx bobbed his hind legs on the seat and woofed at nothing in particular.

Eerie hopped in. "Someone just came up this way. Fresh."

"Good!" Jack drove up to the parking area in front of the community building and stopped. "Where'd they go from here?"

The road Y-ed, embracing the abandoned Longmire campground in its arms. One arm angled off to the left, and the other pressed on through the trees straight ahead.

Eerie got out and studied the dirt. He pointed straight ahead and took off at a fast walk. Jack followed with the hearse crawling at walking speed.

He wanted to set Maxx to the trail. It was fresh enough, the night damp enough, that even Maxx's blunt nose ought to be able to follow it. But he didn't want Maxx to get too far ahead, and he didn't have the longline with him. Caught up in the thrill of the chase, Maxx would be excited enough to tackle a Silverado. He'd lose.

Rusting firebox grates stood here and there among the dark trees. The picnic areas and campsites partially cleared along the way left little gaps among the trees overhead. Echoes of summer revelry from bygone days lingered among the leaves and debris of decades of neglect.

The sky peeked through now and then, and Jack glimpsed a gibbous moon rising. At least on this part of the mountain, the night was now clear.

Wild and wet, the forest stood utterly silent, save for the thrum of the nearly idling motor and the measured whisper of Eerie jogging through the duff ahead.

Jack remembered that this one-lane road provided a back way down to the Forest Service's Skate Creek Road. A gate with dual locks—Park Service and Forest Service—closed it off not far ahead. The iron pipe was probably too sturdy for even a Silverado to crash through. Either the driver had a key to the gate and would escape into Lewis County, or he would come roaring back this way any moment now.

And Jack had decided against pausing long enough to get the radio? Stupid move.

He stopped. He hesitated a moment only, then parked the hearse at a broad angle, totally blocking the road. The trees close on either side would prevent the Silverado from getting around the vehicle. It would have to come through, if it came at all, and the hearse was heavy enough to discourage that sort of nonsense. Jack killed the motor, but he left the parking lights on to alert the Silverado that the black behemoth was sitting there wedgewise in the road.

Gun in hand and Maxx on the short leash, Jack did a double-quick jog to catch up to Eerie.

"Think they got through there?" Eerie asked.

"Could have." He listened, but watched Maxx. The dog heard and saw whatever could be heard or seen long before Jack could.

With the headlights gone, his eyes adjusted quickly to the extreme gloom. They began picking up details. The darkness opened a bit into a clearing where Maintenance stored pipe and cement slabs. The wet duff of winter *squitched* beneath their feet.

Eerie was carrying a .44 big enough to hunt elephants. Jack didn't ask him to put it away. Not now, not with his neck hairs and Maxx's bristling. Hang it, why did he neglect that radio?! Maxx woofed at the road ahead and tugged at the leash.

The driver of the Silverado did not have a key to the gate. He sat noiselessly in the darkness up ahead, all lights doused, waiting, a brooding, sinister blob of steel and menace. Suddenly Jack didn't doubt in the least Eerie's tale about being run off the road.

"There!" Eerie whispered hoarsely.

"Move out around that way, and I'll come around to this side." Jack grabbed Eerie's arm. "And you don't fire that gun, you hear? I don't want to be anywhere near bullets flying."

"Straight up—put the fear of God in him maybe. But not head level. I ain't stupid, Prester."

"No, but you get excited easy."

Eerie chortled and headed off through the trees to swing around the Silverado's passenger side.

The Silverado realized he was spotted, for here he came, and roaring. The cyclopian headlight flared to life. It washed across the trees and pointed itself straight at Jack and Maxx. Jack yelled and leveled his gun at windshield level, two feet above the light. He couldn't see.

The Silverado slowed and for a lovely moment Jack thought they had him. An arm extended out the open driver's side window and reached high, a gesture of surrender.

But suddenly the driver gunned it. The vehicle shot forward. Even if Jack destroyed the driver this instant, the Silverado wouldn't stop in time to miss him. It became a blinding blur of brightness. Jack dropped the leash and fired at the windshield as he dived wildly for a tree. Maxx yelped.

Jack's purchase in the wet forest floor gave way. He slipped, dropped to a knee, regained his feet.

Something—the headlight maybe—caught him in the thigh and flung him. At the same instant something else slammed his arms so violently they smacked back against his face. Something else struck him viciously in the back. Now he was leaning against a tree. His legs poured out from under him, and he slid gracelessly down the trunk to sitting. He couldn't see well. He couldn't think.

Dazed past caring, he watched without comprehend-

166

ing as the Silverado roared on down the road. Its brake-lights flamed brilliant red. With a mighty *fwhupp* it slammed into the hind fender and wheel of the hearse. Sparks flew and danced on the wet blackness. Glass shattered. Then the Silverado's roar picked up again.

The red lights disappeared beyond the trees.

16

Ya Viene la Vieja

From somewhere in the distant chambers of his childhood memories, Jack vaguely recalled the "Li'l Abner" comic strip, and in it a character who walked around with a perpetual raincloud above his head. Everyone else had nearly constant sunshine; but this guy lived in permanent rain. Lugubrious and melancholy, the fellow depicted Jack to a T.

Lying in a hospital in downtown Tacoma didn't do a thing to bolster his spirits. The city was experiencing what one nurse called "an inversion layer." That meant that the upper-elevation outlying districts all had sunshine, because they lay above this sheet of gray overcast. Tacoma lay beneath it. Apparently Jack could be enjoying some rare sunshine right now if only he were up at Longmire, or even Ashford.

He ached all over, some parts more than others. He stretched out on a hospital bed hard enough to teach cement a thing or two and watched dismal grayness out the window. The sun was up, probably, somewhere. That meant it was now nine in the morning or a little later.

A cheery intern in scrub greens came waltzing in, his freckly face aglow with health and youth. He looked like Doogie Howser with a burr cut. The last thing Jack wanted was some kid working on him.

The intern grinned. "I don't know how you did it. Get run over by a truck and not a thing broken. Your X-rays are clean, your BP's stable. Everything's copacetic. You're released. Your girlfriend is signing you out now."

"Are you sure? When I was checked in here, I didn't have a girlfriend." That was the first time in years Jack had heard the word *copacetic.*

"She was certainly acting concerned for a casual acquaintance."

"A constant surprise, that girl." Jack lurched to sitting. He ought to thank God for the good news that no bones were broken. He felt as if every bone in his body were broken. He tried to get dressed without tipping over and managed, but not gracefully. He noticed that these were clean clothes, not the wet and filthy outfit he'd worn in here. And yet, here was the tear in one sleeve from when he collided with the tree, or whatever it was he collided with before he hit the tree. He followed the intern out and down the hall.

In a little waiting alcove lined with chairs and sofas, a Christmas tree glittered. Most of the ornaments were construction paper and homemade, probably donated by patients and staff. The canned music wafting through the halls was Christmas carols. The current selection caught Jack's ear. *Ya Viene la Vieja*—"Here Comes the Old Woman." He used to sing it every year in New Mexico as the kids went door-to-door in the traditional posada, and hardly at all since he left home. But then, posadas were not an ordinary part of the Hutchinson, Kansas, holiday experience, nor probably of Seattle, for that matter.

At the nurses' station, Ev leaned on the counter talking to an older man in scrubs. She turned and watched Jack approach, and she was grinning, a full bore, genuine, uncontrolled grin. It was nearly the first time he'd ever seen that on her. He remembered a day when he could not so much as draw a smile from her.

He settled against the counter at her side as every joint in his skeleton griped. *Ya viene el viejo*—here comes the rickety old man. "Sources inform me you're my girl-friend."

"Really. That's news to me. Did you have breakfast?"

"A little, around seven, I think. I wasn't much in the mood. You?"

She nodded. The dark hair floated. "It's ten thirty. You want to go home, I suppose."

He had misjudged the time by over an hour. His internal clock was way off. "What do you want to do?" He watched her closely for nonverbals.

She dipped her head ambiguously. "That's up to you. How do you feel?"

"Like I was taken apart and put back together by a crew of blind elves who couldn't read the assembly in-structions. I can lie on the bed in that apartment and hurt all over, or I can hurt all over while we go up to Seattle and talk to Elizabeth Munro. *Cum see cum sah,* as they say in the French. We're less than an hour from there."

"Sure you're up to it?"

"Unless you have something better in mind, let's go."

Ev led the way to the main lobby and the doors. She apparently realized she was walking too fast for him and slowed somewhat. In an electric blue sweater and pale blue stirrup pants, she turned heads all the way across the lobby. "Mike Sanchez wants your statement. He has El-roy's." Her voice paused. They pushed out into bleak over-cast. "And Jeff Haskell is still in jail until Kerri can arrange bail."

Jack stopped in midstride. "Why Jeff?"

"It was his GMC. What do you call it—Silverado."

"No alibi?"

"Other than Kerri swearing that he was in bed."

"Stranger and stranger."

The hospital parking lot was not a good place to stand and cogitate. A car came tooling in right at him. It stopped in time, as outside he stood rooted in place and inside his whole body leaped. It took a moment for him to notice the light bar across its roof. He really was sluggish of brain today, not to mention gunshy about approaching vehicles.

Mike Sanchez climbed out of the white sedan bearing all the pretty PARK RANGER decals. "What are you doing out of bed? Morning, Evelyn."

Jack walked around to where he was no longer in the traffic pattern. "What are you doing under an inversion layer?"

Mike chuckled. "Looking for you. I want your story of last night's festivities."

"I'll fill you in if you'll fill me in. Too early for brunch?"

"Not at all. I know just the place."

Jack let the two of them work out details. He crawled into the backseat of Mike's patrol vehicle and vegetated as Mike and Ev chattered up front and they drove through streets. What streets? Who cares?

They parked in the lot of Aunt Somebody's; Jack didn't catch the name on the free-standing sign out front. Inside they were seated immediately at a corner booth in back.

The menu didn't say "Plain food at good prices," but it might as well have. Jack had been intending to eat lightly. He ended up ordering a full lunch—soup, salad, and sandwich.

Mike sat back and toyed with his mug of coffee. He set a microcassette recorder on the table between them. There is no free lunch. Let the business begin. "Evelyn says Elroy stopped by your apartment to get you to write up an incident in which he was forced off the road deliberately. You fed him dinner first, had a cup of coffee, then headed out the door. What did the two of you talk about in the car? I mean hearse."

Jack had to work a minute to recall the topics, let alone words. He laid it out.

Their soup and salad arrived.

Mike nodded. "Would you say Elroy identified the passing Silverado a little too quickly and easily, or not? Was it distinctive?"

"Distinctive. Especially with one headlight out. I didn't detect anything false."

Another nod. Mike was a world-class interviewer. He asked one little question after another, each designed to elicit a whole barrelful of information. They ended up eventually at the point where the Silverado bashed the hearse, and Jack could start asking questions.

The sandwich was good, the soup excellent, the salad—well, salad.

"I've worked out that the fender hit me and threw me into the sideview mirror, which I subsequently found in my lap. That flipped me around and into the tree backwards, which was a blessing, because if I'd gone into the tree frontwards my face would be concave and bark shaped now. The Silverado plowed into Elroy's hearse, shoved its back end aside, and kept going. At some time thereafter, Elroy more or less hauled me back out the road—on foot because the hearse wouldn't move—where you met us. One of your rangers—Clarissa?—gave me a ride into town to get checked out. What did I miss?"

"Most of the fun." Was Mike smirking? "I saw headlights going up the hill behind Longmire and knew they weren't supposed to be there, so I suited up and went out to investigate. I figured I'd find some teenagers necking in the campground or something. Had my window down, so even inside the car with the motor running, I heard the collision. The Silverado was driving on a rim—one front tire was ripped clear off it—from hitting the hearse. You put out the other headlight when he hit you, I'd guess, because it came at me dark.

"It rammed my patrol vehicle side on and knocked it five feet into the trees—me in it yet, of course. I got on the radio to Clarissa. She was waiting for it down by the bridge, but it stopped in front of the community building. We converged on it, she and I. When we reached it, it was empty. Whoever drove it had escaped clean."

"And you're assuming Jeff drove it."

"Yes, but we can't place him behind the wheel or even outside his house, so we'll have to let him go. He claims it was stolen. No sign it was hotwired."

"No key in the ignition."

"Not when we found it, no."

Jack grunted and finished his sandwich. He sipped his cola and sat back to think. Except that he couldn't think, at least not clearly. He looked at Ev. "And you came into town this morning to bail me out of purgatory there. Thank you."

"I came in last night."

"Oh. Then you did my laundry for me. He gestured toward his shirt front. "Thanks."

"You're welcome. It was something I could do. I felt so much like I had to do something, you know what I mean?" Her huge, dark eyes darkened further. "I was scared. You were cuckoo last night, Jack. When you'd talk, it didn't make sense."

"You say that all the time about me."

"I mean, this was for real. Not nonsense. Nothing seemed to connect right inside your head. You still aren't normal, but you're so much better."

"Thank you, I think." He asked Mike, "Anything left of the hearse?"

"Those buggies have an awful lot of heavy steel in them. He'll get a nice return for the scrap."

"That's too bad. It was fun to drive. It'd execute a moonshiner's turn like nobody's business."

Mike gawked at him a bit open-mouthed.

"What's that?" Ev asked.

"You're driving in one direction and flip the back end around so that you're driving in the other direction—a hundred-and-eighty-degree rotation. A really good driver can pull off a turn like that in the middle of a one-lane bridge and never crease a fender."

She frowned and glanced at Mike for signals, perhaps doubting Jack's veracity. "But not in a hearse."

Mike smiled. "Not in a hearse on a bridge. They're wider than bridges." He returned his attention to Jack. "The Silverado looks like it got caught in a gang war. The windshield is perforated with five holes, and there are seven in its right side, window and door. Large caliber. Elroy?"

"Three in the windshield are mine, the rest his. Elroy carried a six-shooter," Jack calculated, "so he—"

"I know. I lifted it off him. No firearms in the park."

"Do me a favor, please, and give it back to him, will you? Use hot pursuit for an excuse or something. If someone really is trying to do him in, he needs the protection. It may have saved him if someone actually did run him off the road."

Jack did some mental counting. "Since there are more than six in the van—something the size of a Silverado is a little hard to miss, you know—he must have unloaded his gun on them at the site of the initial incident and reloaded before he came to my apartment. That would be consistent behavior for him. Funny. I don't remember hearing a gun go off when that van came at us, not even my own."

"Frantic moments do strange things." Mike asked a few more questions, but he seemed essentially finished.

Jack was prepared to accept the check, but Mike grabbed it, and Jack ached too much all over to fight bodily. He returned to vegetating in the rear seat of Mike's rig while Sanchez drove back to the hospital the long way, showing Ev Union Station and some other points of interest. He dropped them off at Ev's GSA car and with waves and adieus drove away, toward sunshine and the park.

"This is sick." Jack hauled the seat belt down as Ev slipped into the driver's side of her car. "The sun finally shines on the mountain, and we drive fifty miles seeking an overcast."

She smiled and pulled to the stop sign at the end of the parking lot. "Which way do I go? Doesn't it get overcast in Kansas?"

Jack pointed left. "Down to Pacific and onto I-5 north. I suppose it does, but I wouldn't know. I've been on the road more than I've been home so far. So have you. Do you remember what your house looks like?"

She smiled again—a record number of smiles today, from a woman who was almost perpetually serious. "Vaguely. When I won that job in the Park Service finance office, I didn't have the slightest notion about what national parks really are. Oh, sure, you hear about Yellowstone, and you see these big magazine pictures of the Grand Canyon. But it didn't really register. Here I was working for the National Park Service, and I had never been in a national park."

"Oh, come on! Your dad's retired Navy. Not even Cape Hatteras? Or Statue of Liberty or Arizona Memorial— that's Pearl Harbor—or somewhere else nautical?"

"A couple weeks ago I got a register of all the parks and went down through it just to see if maybe I had. Until Hal Edmond asked me to take these assignments, I had never once visited one. Not one. And then Death Valley . . . and I was hooked." She took the sweeping curve up onto I-5, and they were on their way Seattleward.

"Washington Monument. Lincoln Memorial. They're Park Service."

"They're in DC. I work in DC. I don't tour in DC. And neither does anyone else who works in DC."

Jack pondered all this awhile and tried to imagine an American who had never visited a national park. OK, so he was third generation Park Service and therefore biased.

175

When as a child he visited Grandmother's house he didn't go over the river and through the woods but to Craters of the Moon National Monument. Place names such as Tuzigoot and Lehman Cave were as familiar to him as Minneapolis or Cleveland. Still . . . And now imagine an American who actually works for the Park Service who never visited . . .

His mind boggled, or maybe it was just the medications they probably pumped into him last night even though he asked them not to. Or maybe they honored his wishes and didn't, and they should have. His nerves were frazzled even yet by the memory of that blinding headlight coming at him, and the wet and slippery road beneath his feet.

Elizabeth Munro was not home, nor were her roommates. At a pay phone on 45th, Jack called her workplace, and she gave him directions to reach it. He folded up his body, stuffed it back into Ev's car, and guided her to a little storefront in a shopping plaza below the university district.

ALCOTT COLLECTION AGENCY

The sign above the door gave Jack the distinct feeling they were walking into a snake pit. Elizabeth, at a desk by the window, saw them come in. She stood up as Jack and Ev approached her.

"Here." She smiled somewhat, presumably a greeting. "Let me introduce you to my employer. Mr. Alcott?" She presented a short balding man, who did not look nearly as sleazy as the owner of a collection agency ought to look, and made introductions all around. Jack tried to shake hands without acting as stiff as a frozen trout. He didn't quite succeed.

Ev put on her businesswoman persona, crisp and efficient and firm—and sober. She totally lost the easy smile. Apparently she felt as uncomfortable in here as Jack did, and he didn't even owe anything.

Jack nodded toward Elizabeth. "Ms. Munro has been extremely helpful in providing us information regarding

176

the murder at Mount Rainier. We're indebted to her."

"I've read about it. The papers played it up with a big spread. And of course we're following with special interest since our own Liz here had such a prominent part, finding the body and all. About two weeks ago? An environmentalist, wasn't he?" The barely hidden sneer in Mr. Alcott's voice suggested that he put environmentalists in the same class as child pornographers.

"Of the first water, yes, indeed."

Mr. Alcott nodded his shiny head. "Tell you what, Liz. Since these good people probably want to talk to you, why don't you take a long lunch? We'll see you back here at, say, three, when the dailies start coming in, all right?"

"Thank you, Mr. Alcott."

As Elizabeth returned to her desk for coat and purse, Jack and Ev went through the proper motions of saying polite good-byes. Jack thanked Mr. Alcott profusely for the temporary use of his employee. They stepped from the collection agency office out into dull overcast. By comparison the gray sky seemed downright jolly.

Ev put it right up front. "Liz, I'd have a terribly hard time working there. How do you do it?"

Jack climbed in the backseat of the GSA car to give the women the front. His left side and leg flexed when he insisted they do so, but they sure hated to.

"Now, see? That's a misconception, just as there are so many misconceptions about persons who are challenged." Liz slammed her door and hauled her seat-belt rig down. "Dentists serve a valuable function, but no one likes the profession. You hate to go into a dentist's office even though it's good for you. The same with car dealers, or realtors. There is an air of distrust. Of distaste. Do you like Mexican?"

Jack was going to say, "We've eaten," but when Ev said, "Yes, we do," he realized his answer would have been wrong. They were taking Elizabeth to lunch.

Elizabeth waved a hand in a wild and meaningless

point. "Go out around that way. There's a nice restaurant on the other side of the mall."

Ev interpreted the meaningless gesture instantly and clearly and drove off. Jack would still be sitting there trying to figure out where to go.

Elizabeth was off and running on what was obviously another crusade: Appreciate Bill Collectors. "It's the same with our agency. We serve an extremely important function, even though no one likes us. Ask any business person. If money does not come in in a timely manner, you can't pay your bills in a timely manner. The vast majority of debtors are chronic debtors. Eighty percent of the people we dun for one company we've dunned for other companies. These people are essentially seeking a free ride at the expense of everyone else, accepting goods and services without paying for them. We're not taking money for our clients—businesses—that does not rightfully belong to the clients for goods and services rendered."

The argument sounded absolutely logical and convincing, and Jack still didn't like the thought of bill collectors. He dreaded walking back into that office, should he have to, just as much as ever. Did solid arguments about environmental concerns, or abortion, or capital punishment, or whatever, fall on similarly deaf ears? Was Elizabeth—or anyone else—getting anywhere at all with her preaching?

The place was called *El Toro Rojo,* "The Red Bull." Elizabeth insisted on pronouncing the J as in Joe. If Ev knew it was supposed to be Roe Hoe, she kept her mouth shut.

How were they going to do this? He was full from a lunch just eaten. So was Ev, surely; she was a light eater anyway. Yet they were going to feast Elizabeth. They settled into a booth.

Elizabeth ordered a combination.

Ev smiled at the waiter, a gentleman of actual Mexican descent. His accent sounded Sonoran or thereabouts.

178

"I'll have a side of tortillas only. I'm on a diet."

Well, there went one good idea. It would sound fishy if he claimed to be on a diet also—not that it had occurred to him. Then brilliance struck. He shifted into Spanish, asking the waiter, "I just ate lunch an hour ago. What looks like a full meal but doesn't take up any room?"

The waitperson grinned. In Spanish he replied, "I'll ask the cook to fluff up a light salad so it looks like a lot."

"Muchas gracias, y un mil flores para su mujer."

Chuckling, the waiter scooped up the menus and glided away.

By the same quirk of fate that if you learn a new word you can count on hearing it again within a day or two, the sound system in this restaurant was also playing Christmas carols. And the selection of the moment was also *Ya Viene la Vieja.*

Already Ev and Elizabeth were discussing the relative merits of various dieting practices. What startled Jack and gave him pause was how Elizabeth accepted Ev's ploy instantly and completely, as if it were the most natural thing in the world for a slim person to go on a weight-loss diet. These two women were so thin already that when they touched their toes they looked like paper clips. Why should they be concerned at all with dieting, let alone appear so knowledgeable?

Then the subject turned to that little fracas in the Clearcut, the one that led directly to the bullet hole in the ceiling.

Elizabeth asked Ev, "You learned how to handle firearms in police training, right?"

"No, from my father. He's military. I've been around guns all my life. He loves them. And he's very good with them."

"You're talking side arms." Jack frowned. "He's Navy. Isn't his weapon of choice a deck cannon or something?"

Ev ignored him. "In this day and age, Liz, you really

179

ought to consider taking some training. Carry pepper if nothing else. Especially here in town."

Elizabeth shook her head. "I'm sorry. I'm adamantly opposed to weapons of any kind. I think they should all be banned across the board."

Jack raised his voice a bit to avoid being ignored this time. "How about Jay Chambers? You apparently know him pretty well. What's his position regarding weapons?"

"He's strongly against gun control. We've discussed it more than once. But I can never convince him that he'll continue to appear hypocritical until he reverses his position. I mean, how does it look when a so-called environmentalist has a house full of all kinds of weapons. Honestly."

"Oh? What is his weapon of choice?"

"He and his buddies will go hunting with anything. Guns. Bow and arrow. And knives—he's an expert on all kinds of knives."

Ev wrinkled her nose. "He hunts animals with a knife?"

"No, he collects knives. From all over the world. And he's an expert on anything to do with Celts. Druids and Celts. It's logical, I guess. But you can see how it looks."

Her tone of voice told Jack that he was a donkey if he didn't see how it looked. Actually, he didn't. So what?

Ev puckered her eyebrows at him, a cryptic expression. "Are knives a part of his religious exercises? His druidism?" With her eyes she was probably warning Jack that she would handle the religious aspect of this, lest he get into it too enthusiastically.

"I don't know. I do know they have special blades for cutting mistletoe down out of trees and things like that. Very old-fashioned knives. Sort of like sickles."

Jack would have to study up on druidism a little more thoroughly. For one thing, he suddenly wanted very much to find out whether the practice existed, in more or less its present form, back in the late stone age.

When obsidian was the raw material for knives.

17

While Shepherds Watched Their Flocks by Night

In the quiet of a warm summer night, a clan of sheepherders sat around on a hillside, talking idly of mundane things. They were, in essence, doing nothing at all, and yet they were indispensable to the sheep in their care, the only protection the sheep had. And they knew it, for they took their work seriously. Crickets chirped in stately cadence. Peace. Routine. Boredom.

Without warning the skies overhead flared from starlit darkness into vivid brilliance, searing the sheepmen's eyes like a hundred instant suns. Angels appeared then, to make the announcement for which the world had been created. The moment the phenomenon faded, those experienced, responsible sheepherders left their flocks in the hands of Almighty God and ran off to see for themselves what the angels told about.

"Now there are some interesting ramifications to that." Jack settled to a comfortable seat with his back against a stump. He shifted the radio on his belt so that it didn't poke him in the side—he'd learned a thing or two about keeping a radio handy from that episode with the Silverado —and opened up the rucksack. It was past two o'clock, he hadn't eaten since breakfast, and he was hungry enough to eat snakes. Almost. "Tuna salad or ham on rye?"

"The ham sounds good, if you don't want it." Elizabeth Munro perched herself primly on the stump and zipped open her blue down parka. She waved her hand about in that same aimless way she had shown Ev which direction to drive. "You see? This matchless wilderness experience should be available to all, regardless of their challenges."

"Which do you have the most of?" Jay Chambers seated himself cozily among the leaves and trailside grass.

"There's three of each. That way we don't have to squabble over them." Jack dug out the two-liter of Pepsi.

Actually, "matchless" was not a bad word for this, not at all. As you walked uphill, the rugged shoulder of Mount Rainier rose steeply toward Paradise and treeline. Already the forest had loosened up; trees were spaced in dark clumps rather than a solid blanket. The open meadows between were covered with thick stands of mountain blueberries, tall spindly grasses, and the brown and scratchy skeletons of last summer's flowers. Great, crumbling blocks of exposed bedrock studded the slope, bedecking the mountainside with a host of little vertical cliffs and a few not-so-little ones.

As you walked downhill, wave after wave of dark foothills extended toward the horizon whenever the trees opened enough to permit a view. Here the trail tunneled through dark firs, and there it arched out across pleasant, undulant leas.

They sat now, the three of them, at the top margin of just such a meadow, beside a mat of dying bracken fern.

Ostensibly, Jack had invited Jay and Elizabeth up here on the mountain to get a better handle on their story about the day of John Getz's death. In truth, the area intrigued him. Besides, Jay knew as much about the mountain as any man alive. Jack could learn something from this druid.

Maxx had been off sticking his nose in bushes out toward the end of his longline. The ham and tuna brought him bouncing back like a ball on a rubber band. Jack os-

182

tracized him again with a hand signal. Dejected yet hopeful, he flopped down on his belly near Jay's foot.

"Ham." Jay accepted a sandwich from Jack and peeled away the layers of Saran wrap. "What ramifications?"

Jack passed a ham sandwich up to Elizabeth and kept the third for himself. "Well, for one thing, during those days shepherds were about the lowest scum in society. They were considered so despicable their testimony wouldn't be accepted in courts of law. They smelled bad and swore constantly. When the shepherds hit town, you locked up your wife and daughter." Jack looked up at Elizabeth. "So why would God announce His Son's birth to uncouth jerks like that first? Especially when He never bothered telling any of those clean-cut Mr. Nice Guy priests and Pharisees at all?"

She frowned, her mouth full of ham and Swiss cheese. "I don't know."

"Neither do I. But I do know David sang, 'The Lord is my shepherd,' and Jesus said, 'I am the good shepherd.' Jesus has always identified with the common people, the ones that get dirty and maybe a little smelly working. The sheepherders and fishermen and bureaucrats—Matthew the tax man, for instance. And by extension, I like to think, rangers." Jack paused. "And bill collectors." He took a bite. Good sandwich, if he did say so himself, having built them this morning.

Jay smiled, and the way he smiled you knew he knew the answer before he asked the question. "If this is the birth of Jesus, why did you set the scene in summer?"

Jack smiled too. Jay had slipped smoothly into the groove where Jack wanted him. "You know and I know He was probably born in summer, because sheepherders don't stay out in the hills with their flocks during winter, especially not December. The church established December twenty-fifth as the anniversary of His birth so it would parallel holidays on calendars already in place."

"Druid calendars." Jay poured himself a tin cup of Pepsi.

"Or proto-druid, at least. And wicca."

"You've been reading up."

"Yes, I have. They influenced Roman calendars, I assume."

"Profoundly." Jay paused to swallow his mouthful. "Legend has it—but not the very oldest legends, actually—that Atlantis sank into the ocean just as practitioners of black magic and white respectively were coming to blows. A rare few who escaped the cataclysm of Atlantis perpetuate that antagonism. Black magicians practice certain forms of wicca—"

"What the Christian church labels witches in the classic sense."

"Precisely. And the Atlantean practitioners of white magic are the Celts and druids, influenced by certain modifications from the East which occurred about the same time."

"Do you believe that?"

"I am not as well versed in early lore as are many. I can't say. I don't know." Jay twisted his beard into a sad sort of smile. "Which would mean, ultimately, that the roots of that infamous matter at Salem—the witchcraft trials—extend back two thousand years before Christ."

"As does the calendar which both druids and wicca observe, is that right?"

"That's right. And bearing on your original question, their calendar probably formed the framework for the Greco-Roman calendar. Although all calendars based on solar seasons will necessarily be very similar." Jay glanced at Elizabeth.

Jack looked up. She wasn't paying a shred of attention, it appeared. John Getz died on December 2. Jack asked one of his two biggies: "Winter solstice is hard upon us. Are there any observances, or perhaps preliminary observances to the solstice, that fall in the first week of the month?"

"No."

"A friend of mine in the Los Angeles County Sheriff's Department claims there are eleven covens of witches in his area, and every coven requires blood sacrifice on each of the eight prime holidays. That's eighty-eight animals a year killed. Or humans."

Jay murmured quietly, "Thirteen covens there. A hundred and four sacrifices."

They had Elizabeth's undivided attention.

Jack poured himself some Pepsi. "Blood drawn fresh for the observance, or can you . . . let's see . . . how can I say this? Store it up?"

"Freeze some for use later? No. Freshly drawn. If no fresh blood is available, they might use menstrual blood." Jay no doubt saw where Jack was going. "But that's that one branch of wicca. Black arts. Satanism. Not druidism. We share the same calendar. That's all. And I dare say that Christian observance parallels druid observance a lot more closely than does wicca."

Elizabeth was scowling. "What? Are you saying Christians are pagans?"

"Not at all." Jay's tone of voice purred, soothing. "Remember when the two of us were talking about Halloween? And I described a little of the druid observance to you?"

"Wild!"

"In important respects, yes. Literally. The Sammhain we celebrate is very similar to Halloween and falls on the same day. Eggs and rabbits figure prominently in spring observances for both systems. Evergreens at Christmas, and mistletoe and candles. All druid. Call it cross-fertilization. A sharing of custom."

"What sacrifices do modern druids observe?" There was Jack's other biggie. And he framed it as a do-you-still-

185

beat-your-wife question so that Jay would have to answer thoroughly.

Jay obviously had heard that question before. "The only written records we have of the original druids of Britain are the Romans'. The Gauls, the French and British—that is, the Celts which the Romans crossed swords with—had no written records. Theirs was strictly an oral tradition. The Romans were bitter enemies of the Celts, and their views were obviously jaundiced. They vividly chronicled atrocities and barbarities. Human sacrifice."

"Wicker men." Jack recalled a line cut in one of the books in the South Hill branch of the Pierce County Library. It depicted a two-story human figure made of wicker and poles and stuffed with living animals and human beings, ready to be set afire.

"And wicker men. Druidism is not like that now. And considering the dubious value of the chronicle of a culture written by an enemy of that culture, it almost certainly never was."

Jack brushed the bread crumbs off his fingers. "So if I'm hearing you right, John Getz could not be a sacrificial victim of either wicca or druidism or any other ism, despite the curious detail of an obsidian blade in his heart."

"To the best of my knowledge, no."

"Do you have any medical training, Jay?"

"Homeopathy. The wholeness of the body which leads to health. I'm pretty good with herbals."

"Anatomy?"

"It helps to know where the liver is if you're going to diagnose it."

Usually, Jack's Stetson, sheepskin-lined denim jacket, and jeans were sufficient to protect him from cold. Few places feel colder than the high plains of New Mexico when the north wind howls, with nothing between you and Canada but four strands of barbed wire and half of that blown down. At home he got by just fine with this much protection, and perhaps leather chaps if he was riding.

Here, sitting on the damp flank of Mount Rainier, he felt intensely to-the-bone cold, and the temperature was not nearly as low.

He stood up, apple in hand. "One of the reasons I asked you two to go hiking here today was to retrace your footsteps of December second, when you discovered the body." He'd better get moving if he wanted to warm up.

Elizabeth scowled. "I thought you wanted to look at the new trail we're proposing, as the first step in our access project."

We. Our. So she was including Jay in her plan. Jack glanced at him. He was up and brushing himself off. If he objected to being included in this hairy scheme, he made no mention.

"That too." Jack smiled. "Two birds with innumerable stones, as lousy a shot as I am." He hauled in Maxx's longline and brought his dog to heel. "Elizabeth, you discovered your sunglasses were missing. You were here?"

"Up that way a little farther, I think. Jay?"

He nodded. "By those firs." He led the way up the trail, accepting a proffered apple as he passed Jack. He walked a hundred yards to a pleasant glade, a wide, grassy gap in the brooding forest. The ground covers were all brown now except for a shiny-leaved woody plant about a foot high. Jack used to work here—he used to know all the plants—but he couldn't think of the name for this one.

"This is the place." Elizabeth stepped aside and stood beside a bank. "I sat down here and enhanced my wilderness experience while Jay went back up the trail."

"And remained here until he returned."

"It's a hard trail to walk. I was tired."

"And you want wheelchair invalids to climb it." Jack probably shouldn't have said that, especially in the tone of voice he used, but it popped out.

"'Invalid' is a defeatist term. It carries the same bad connotations as 'handicapped.'" Elizabeth looked angry, and probably for good reason.

Jack wasn't being very nice. But he wasn't going to apologize for using accurate language. He nodded. "Jay? I'd like to go on up to where you recovered the glasses. Elizabeth, do you want to go along or stay?"

She never hesitated. "Stay. I've been up there. Jay, you'll show him what we plan, won't you? Especially the switchbacks by the quartz seam."

Jay nodded.

She sat down.

Jack followed Chambers as the sprightly fellow took off at a much faster gait than they had used when Elizabeth was with them. Jack wished desperately that the lady had come along. He wasn't going to be able to maintain this pace too long, and his whole body screamed at him for making it flex so fast. Getting run over by a vehicle the size of a Silverado certainly does ruin an otherwise lovely wilderness experience.

Lackadaisically, Maxx jogged along beside, his tail half wagging, tossed about as his hind legs moved. Then the tail tightened up, the pace firmed. He moved in closer to Jack as his warm leather ears perked up.

Jack seized on the chance to pause. "Jay? For one thing, I could use a breather. For another, Maxx here says there's something or someone in the area."

Jay stopped and turned. He did not appear the least respiratorily challenged—no huffing and puffing despite the steep gradient. He frowned at the ground a few moments and shook his head. "I didn't see anything the last time we were here. Squirrels and chipmunks, of course. You don't mean that sort of thing. Nothing that would interest him."

Jack watched his dog. Whatever Maxx detected was bigger than a bathtubful of squirrels. He nodded, and Jay moved on again uphill. Bless him, the bushy-faced druid slowed significantly.

Maxx woofed and tugged happily at his leash. Jack looked off where Maxx was looking. "Jay?" He pointed.

On an open slope a quarter mile away, a dozen snow-white mountain goats browsed casually, nibbling here, taking a step or two, nibbling there. About the size of sheep, they looked somewhat like sheep and acted a lot like sheep.

Jack pulled his binoculars out of his pocket for a closer look as Jay returned and stood beside him. "Three billies, five nannies, and young-of-the-year." He handed the glasses off to Jay.

Chambers watched the goats a few moments, and the beard widened into a happy, contented smile. "Amazing creatures."

"As are all creatures, but them especially." Answering the call of the season, these goats no doubt had moved from the rocky high country down into the trees to avoid the extremes of snow and storm. The extremes of snow and storm had not yet arrived, though.

He owns the cattle on a thousand hills, Mount Rainier not excepted. In the Hebrew lexicon, "cattle" generally included sheep and goats unless specified otherwise. Probably camels too. He certainly owned and shepherded this flock of goats.

They watched them a few more moments and continued up.

"Here is where her glasses fell." Jay pointed to the trail at his feet. "They slipped out of a loop on her belt." They were out in another glade, a few yards short of plunging back into a tunnel beneath trees.

Jack turned to look behind him. The cloud cover was breaking somewhat. It might even clear a little. "You came directly here and directly back." It had taken them sixteen minutes to climb to this point. That would be fourteen minutes, subtracting the two minutes they spent watching the mountain goats. Fourteen minutes up, twelve minutes back—faster downhill. Almost half an hour.

Jay nodded. He smiled. "You really don't have anything to do with trail proposals, do you?"

189

"Not a thing. No influence, no input. Elizabeth keeps thinking I do, probably because I'm out of the Washington office, but I can't help you."

Jay sat down on a nearby boulder. "Then there's no need to continue up and show you the switchbacks."

"Not really." Jack settled on the turf beside the boulder, grateful for the rest. "You come up here a lot?"

Jay nodded.

"What do you see different over the last few years?"

"Higher concentration of wildlife, especially goats and elk. More deer. The glaciers are retreating."

"Do ley lines influence glaciers?"

Jay studied him. "Interesting question. Your tone of voice suggests it was sincere."

"So? Do they?"

"I studied that very thing for some years. The best I can tell, no. They do not. But the question is open. Why do you ask?"

"I'm trying to figure out where ley lines go up here, since I'm not attuned to sensing them. I'm assuming you won't bother to lie to me about the indications of ley lines, and where they go, such as glacial activity or something."

"You think I lied to you in other regards? When?"

"I know you did, on our first meeting. You said you know everything that goes on in the park. I think that statement, while not precisely true, is as near truth as a civilian can come. A non-park employee, that is. Then you explained in detail how monstrous beings—Bigfoot, for want of a better term—follow negative energy."

Jay Chambers watched him with crackling eyes. The beard had melted to a frown configuration.

Jack gave the leash a tug and brought his peripatetic dog back to his side. "That's the untruth. I'm not going to comment either way on whether I think ley lines actually exist. Whether they do or not is beside the point. All the literature claims that a tree the size of the Grandfather Cedar would not grow so large in a pocket of negative energy.

Rather, big trees or animals or anything indicate an area of great positive energy. You know that. And you claim an Indian encountered a Tsiatko there, apparently a Bigfoot, placing the monster at the Grandfather Cedar. What else are you lying about, Jay?"

The druid sat loosely, patiently, his elbows leaning on his knees and his hands at ease. There was no hostility or defensiveness about him—in fact, not even any tension. Either the man possessed immense control of his nonverbal signals—something that usually is impossible—or he was by nature extremely pacifist. "I underestimated you."

"A lot of people underestimate folks who dress like cowboys. That's why I wear a Stetson."

Jay laughed suddenly. The sun broke through the gray sky, not brightly and completely, as it would in New Mexico, but enough to cast a definite shadow. "Catch them unawares. Good strategy. As you caught me. You're right. I lied about that, because I don't want word to spread that Bigfoot can be found along ley lines. That a Bigfoot— if they exist at all, of course—gravitates toward positive energy. Not even a hint. If the wrong people heard that, ugly repercussions could result, for the park and for a Bigfoot if such exists. You were bound to be watched and quoted by the media, because of the high-profile nature of John Getz's murder. I—"

"I ended up at a press conference about Getz the very next morning."

"My point. Law officers often complain that the media muddy up some track they don't want muddied. Trial by press and all that. You would be no different. I was afraid you might toss them another bone. Give them something juicy and sensational to send them down some other track and keep them out from underfoot, if you will. Bigfoot would be perfect for that."

"They came up with Bigfoot; I didn't. The bone is already thrown, or they dug it out themselves." Jay underestimated Jack? Jack had underestimated Chambers far worse, if Chambers's explanation be true. "So you were afraid I'd toss out a red herring, as the mystery enthusiasts say."

"Except it wouldn't be red; it would be true. So I lied. If you quoted me at all, indirectly or whatever, you would give them false information. Anyone privy to ley lines and positive energy would look elsewhere if they chose to look."

"That's a pretty hairy excuse, Jay. Hard to swallow."

"As you wish." He still showed no tension whatever. "With growing environmental concerns, there is a growing interest in the spiritual nature of the earth itself and of the life forms that carpet it."

"A growth in druidism?"

"As a part of the trend, yes. I'm torn, Jack. I want more people to come here, where energy is high and they have the best chance to connect well with the earth that is quite literally their mother. Once they make that connection, they'll work harder to protect and preserve her, as well as grow in health themselves."

"Speaking holistically."

"Yes. But I want to protect the creatures that live here too. And sometimes the two desires are strongly at odds with each other."

Jack nodded. "The Park Service has the same problem. We're committed to preserving the parks for people to enjoy. But there's too many people in some of the parks. The parks are damaged by too many feet. How much of that mandate is preserve and how much is people?"

"Exactly."

"How did Getz fit in, if at all? He was at odds with you, right?"

"His extremism was at odds. His goals and mine were identical. Save the environment. Preserve the wilderness. Husband the dwindling resources. We had different views on how best to accomplish that."

Jack sat quietly.

A few long moments of silence prodded Chambers into continuing. "People are bipolar, Jack. Pick the battleground, and you'll find two sides only. No gray middle area. Yes or no. Intensely pro-life or intensely pro-choice. Creation or evolution. Gun control, for example. Elizabeth wants me to support her desire to take every BB gun away from every kid, and Elroy Washington thinks no closet is complete without a machine gun. They both vilify me because I'm middle ground."

"I hear you collect weapons."

"Knives and Celtic weapons. It's a hobby. And crossbows. I have a genuine crossbow from the Cromwellian era. My prized possession."

"Getz—was he into weapons or gun control?"

"I never debated the matter with him." Jay sobered. "I feared that Getz was so fanatic in his demands that he would create a backlash and shove public opinion to the opposite pole."

"To exploiting instead of husbanding."

Jay nodded. "It's a dark night for earth right now. We're on the brink of total environmental collapse. She's been pushed past the ability to heal herself. I don't think she can take another swing of the pendulum to thoughtless exploitation. Getz was a menace in that regard."

"Enough of a menace to be removed?"

"You're asking in essence if I removed him. I did not."

"I've caught you in other lies. How do I know that's true?"

"You don't." Jay said it simply, with no hint of rancor.

"So you set yourself up as shepherd of earth's flock. Interesting." Jack smiled suddenly. "Not to call you crude or anything. Shepherds shower and shave now, I understand."

"I like that. Shepherd of earth's flock. I and all who value the earth. Who value the environment." Chambers was grinning too. "John Muir himself once worked as a shepherd, did you know that? It was his first real taste of the Sierras. I'm in good company."

Jack hauled himself to his feet and tugged Maxx's leash. Time to go home. Getz's death could be directly related to his position as an environmentalist, or it could be totally unrelated. Now all Jack had to figure out was, did the shepherd die for the sake of the flock?

18

O Little Town
of Bethlehem

As Jack and Jay headed down the trail, God's goats were still visible. They browsed in green pastures, and two of them even lay down. With his binoculars, Jack watched one billy extend a leg forward and crank its head down to scratch an itch on its knee. He passed the glasses to Jay.

Chambers watched for a moment and looked at the binoculars themselves for another moment. "These are good glasses."

"Got them at K-Mart, sixty dollars. Eight-twenty is an adequate size for times like now, and they fit nicely in my pocket. I take them everywhere. For hardcore birdwatching I have a pair of ten-fifties the size of a coffee table, and a spotting scope for waterfowl and shorebirds."

Jay handed the glasses back. "Do you need me for anything else?"

"No. I appreciate your help here, and your information."

"Then I think I'll go wander over that way."

"It's going to be dark soon." Jack practically bit his tongue. Stupid thing to say. This man of the earth and nature knew that.

Jay smiled. "The moon is in its last quarter, and the sky is partially clearing. I'll wait until midnight or so and

195

get back just fine. Plenty of light then." He was far more forgiving of Jack's veiled implication that he wasn't smart enough to know what time it was than a liberated woman would be.

Jack nodded. Was shaking hands appropriate here? Must be, because they did so. Soundlessly the druid slipped away through the thick ground cover of the open hillside. Jack saw him fade into trees down slope. He was gone.

Jack envied that kind of woodsmanship, to be able to move through this dense growth so quietly and comfortably. He brought Maxx to heel and continued down the hill.

Here came Elizabeth up the trail, panting. She stopped when she saw him, looking grateful for the breather. She peered around, stretching to see behind him. "Where's Jay?"

"Took off cross-country. I doubt it's the first time. He wants to commune with some goats, I think. He's their shepherd, after a fashion. He and John Muir."

"I didn't quite understand all that. About shepherds." She fell in beside him, heeling as close to his right side as Maxx was heeling to his left. On a sidewalk or a broader trail—especially on a paved trail wide enough for the physically-challenged and their wheelchairs—it would have been a lovely arrangement. On this narrow one-groove track she kept bumping into the holstered handy-talkie on his belt, and there was no place better to hang it. Besides, if some trailside tree wasn't wiping Maxx off Jack's left leg, it was peeling Elizabeth off his right arm. Still she stuck there, latched onto his elbow with SuperGlue.

"Nothing to worry about. It's all very alpine and Heidi-ish. Just think of Jay as Peter the Goatherd."

"I want to show you another route we have in mind, while we're up here."

"Elizabeth." How should he state this in terms she would understand? "There are literally hundreds of government workers in the Park Service's Washington office. Hundreds and hundreds. I am but one, and I don't even work there. My boss does. I just get my orders from there. There really isn't any way I can help you. The improvements you want are not handled by the division I work for."

"Maybe not, but you can explain it to them, at least. Down here at this junction, we'll go right."

They went right. It was easier somehow to just go along than to protest further. Besides, this exercise was bound to loosen him up. Sitting around, the option his body begged for, would make him stiffer than ever.

She took him out around the side of the slope perhaps a quarter mile over a trail that hadn't been maintained in years. At one point, a fallen tree still blocked it. They had to climb over. Maxx skinned underneath.

Moments later they topped out on a rocky ridge with a splendid view off across the rolling foothills.

"There!" she crowed triumphantly. "Now isn't this a better route for hikers? Develop this trail for them, and rebuild the main trail for the physically challenged. Everyone profits from a rich wilderness experience."

Jack nodded sagely. Maxx bumped against his leg turning around to watch the way they had come. "It's open here."

"Yes. Isn't it."

Jack pointed around them with much the same vaguely general gesture Elizabeth used so often. "Park policy, as you know, consists of letting nature take its course. When a tree falls, it lies there. Period."

"I know. If you're referring to that tree that fell across the trail, they'd remove that one."

"Right. Cut with a chainsaw through the part that's blocking the way and let the rest of the tree remain. No problem. But. You notice this view is so great because a lot of trees have blown down in this area."

"Well, yes, quite a few. But they're not blocking the way."

"So many downed trees suggests high winds and unstable soil. Possibly even avalanche hazard. It's not a safe place to put a trail, which is probably why this one's abandoned."

She scowled as her dream went *poof,* temporarily at least. "You don't know that."

"It's an assumption. The people who prepare your environmental impact statement will verify it or nullify it. I'm just warning you what's probably coming."

She twisted around and studied him a moment. Wisps of blonde hair flittered around her cheeks. It was breezy here even when the air was still elsewhere. "You are so pessimistic."

"There are no pessimists; there are only us realists. Shall we start back?"

"I suppose."

She showed no inclination to let go of his elbow as they walked, so he let Maxx off his leash. At least now they'd be two-wide instead of three-wide. Even so, Maxx stuck so close that Jack bumped into the mutt's backside a couple times, until the dog's brain finally registered that if he stayed three feet ahead, he wouldn't get kicked.

"You and Jay talking about human sacrifice." She was breathing heavily going downhill, she was so out of shape. "Did you have to do that at lunch?"

"I'm sorry if we upset you."

"It made me nervous. I felt so uncomfortable I had to come up the trail and find you. That's why I met you part way up there. Besides, I wanted to show you this side trail."

He crawled stiffly over the log. With a whooshing rustle, Maxx slid underneath, plowing leaves. Jack held Elizabeth's arm as she wormed clumsily over.

"It's spooky, that's all. It made me feel spooky." She paused to brush bark chips off her clothes. "I felt creepy all the while I was sitting there waiting for you."

"Understandable."

They finally broke back out onto the main trail. Narrow as it was, at least it was maintained. What Jack wanted most of all was a hot meal, a warm shower, and a long night's sleep. What he faced was more than half a mile of trail with a blonde attached to him like a barnacle.

Which, when you thought about it, wasn't altogether bad.

Maxx acted edgier. Jack leashed him back up. He didn't want the dog taking off after a mega-cat or bear. Most of all, he didn't want Maxx drawing Elizabeth's attention to a mountain lion as he had with Jack and Ev. That would probably be a bit too rich a wilderness experience for the urban Elizabeth.

"Maybe we shouldn't have taken the time to go back there." She spoke in hushed tones to match the fading light of late day. "It's going to be dark before we get back, isn't it?"

"Probably." The trees pressed close around and above, preventing any movement whatever of the sullen air. The unique musty smell of damp, moldering duff hung heavy. What was the temperature? Thirty-five? Around that. He watched her a moment. "Interesting. You want everyone to have a rich wilderness experience, and yet you detest wilderness."

"I never said that!"

"Not in words."

She glanced at him guiltily.

He smiled to allay her guilt feelings, if that's what they were. "You know 'O Little Town of Bethlehem?'"

She nodded.

"'Town' by our standards is overstating it. It was a cluster of hovels. Most towns were back then. There were a few cosmopolitan cities—Rome, Alexandria, Antioch, Jerusalem—but nearly everyone lived in villages or out on the land."

"Then why did they call it O little town of Bethlehem, if it wasn't even civilized?"

"They didn't. That is, the contemporaries of Mary

and Joseph didn't. Songwriters eighteen hundred years removed from the fact did. Anyway, the point I'm making is that man's natural environment is not cities. It's hamlets. Small clan groupings. When you're pitching wilderness experience, you're getting people back to their roots, whether you yourself can feel those roots or not. That's good."

"I read somewhere that the best size for a town is fifty families. That that's how people feel most comfortable. I don't believe that a bit."

Jack smiled and let the matter slide. This city-conditioned girl certainly wouldn't think O little town of Ashford was civilization either.

And then she brought up the ultimate mark of civilization. "There isn't any restroom nearby, is there, until we get back to the parking lot?"

"There isn't any there either. Closest one is Narada Falls. And below that, Cougar Rock campground."

She looked up at him with panic in her baby blues. "But I need one before then!"

"Three hundred and seventy-eight square miles of trees, and you need a restroom?" For shame! He shouldn't have said that. It was petty. A cheap shot. And it just sort of blurted out. "Sorry. Here." He disengaged her from his arm the way you peel a used Band-Aid off a hairy place. "I'll wait down the trail for you."

"You want to leave me alone? It's almost dark." She glanced about nervously at all this wilderness.

To be honest, he felt a little tense too, but a lot of that was weariness. For him that discussion about human sacrifice had been academic, not Stephen King-ish.

"Consider the cloak of darkness a cloak of modesty. Jay won't be coming down behind you. He's on that other slope."

She hesitated and nodded.

He took off down the trail, walking quickly until he was beyond eye and ear of her. In just that moment of standing around, his left hip had started to stiffen up. What was he going to feel like when he woke up tomorrow morning?

Maxx stopped and growled and turned around, ears and nose pointed back toward Elizabeth.

"That's voyeurism, Maxx."

The brush uphill rattled. Elizabeth? It shouldn't be; a lady doesn't make a pit stop that quickly. Not Jay; he didn't brush bushes when he moved. Certainly not a mountain lion. They're silent in their passage. A bear?

Barking wildly, Maxx lunged forward. He yanked the leash out of Jack's hand and churned up the trail at an instant dead run.

Jack lurched from park directly into third gear, his stiff left side screaming at him. He yelled, "Come!" at Maxx. The dog paid no attention, but at least Elizabeth would know Jack was approaching.

Somewhere up ahead and off to the left, Elizabeth screamed. Now what was that fool dog up to? Jack prayed it was nothing more than a cold nose or a quick tongue. She screamed again as Maxx whooped half a yelp—the bark was choked off mid-yelp.

Almost without thinking, Jack fired his gun straight up even as he prayed. He left the trail and crashed through the brush and spindly young saplings, making plenty of noise. He fired again. Surely a bear or lion would exit as he approached—neither appreciates that much commotion.

Other feet stomped off through the forest ahead of him, charging away across the hillside.

"Elizabeth! Maxx!"

There was Maxx, ten feet away, a black form in the darkness. His hulking body lay in a fern thicket as if tossed there. Whimpering, the dog rolled from his side to his belly.

Elizabeth was curled up in a sort of seated position, leaning on one arm. She whimpered and began to sniffle.

A thin cloud of white downfeathers floated around

her and settled lightly on the dark forest floor. Her parka was ripped under her left arm. The sleeve was torn too, and Jack realized even in the half light that he was looking at blood.

He holstered his gun in his back pocket and gripped her shoulders in his hands. "Elizabeth? It's me. Jack. Hear me?" He tipped her face up to his. Nobody home.

Then she sort of snapped back to life. The vacant stare melted into terror. She latched onto him as if she were falling out of an airplane and he were her only hope. "Jack . . ." A red stain marked his jacket where her arm brushed his.

A few times in his career Jack had been forced into a triage situation, where he must judge which of several needy patients requires attention first. This was the first time he had to choose between his dog and a person. Both were breathing. The person was bleeding. The dog was not. He turned his back on Man's Best Friend to attend Elizabeth. But then, he would have anyway.

It took him a moment to extricate himself from her frantic grip. He cooed soothing words and couldn't tell what he said. He unzipped her parka and peeled it back off her shoulders.

She began to weep lustily, a good sign. Maxx came stumbling over and flopped down beside Jack's right knee, another good sign. He paused long enough to briefly rub the dog's head, an "I know you're there, Old Top" gesture.

The blood came from a ragged cut on her left arm and a slash across her ribs on the left side. He shrugged out of his own jacket and pulled off his chambray shirt. Rolled rapidly into a rat-tail, it made a satisfactory cravat to bind up the gash in her side. He knotted the sleeves together firmly. "What kind of socks are you wearing?"

"What?" *Sob. Sniffle.*

"What kind of socks?"

Sob. "Wool knee-highs." *Sniff.*

No good. Wool didn't make good bandaging. He

202

yanked his T-shirt and with his pocket knife ripped it into broad strips. "I don't have anything to bandage your arm with. This will do." The cut was long. His folded handkerchief was barely big enough to serve as a dressing. It didn't seem to go very deep, though, and the lips closed down when he applied some pressure. The bleeding eased. He wrapped it snugly.

With her bleeding controlled, the emergency eased. He yanked the radio and keyed it. Over the space of about five minutes, as Elizabeth sniffled and clung, Jack reached Clarissa, the seasonal ranger, and got help headed this way. It took awhile to explain where they were. Not even Elizabeth—in fact, especially not Elizabeth—could explain exactly what had happened.

Now what? Elizabeth by now had somewhat unclung. She sat, still sobbing in shuddering gulps, with her legs folded beneath her. He pinched her fingernail beneath his thumb. When he lifted his thumb away the color came back almost immediately, though he had to hold her hand in front of his nose to make sure, so dark had it become. Her circulation was in good shape.

He turned to his dog.

Maxx looked up with baleful eyes. *I failed the challenge. I let the perp get away.*

Jack rubbed the dog all over, in part checking for injury, in part reassuring and socializing. *You failed nothing, Old Man. You did fine. We're buddies. Friends forever.* Jack scratched him behind his ears. He purred praises as he removed the leash and pocketed it. When he stood up, Maxx stood up.

He pulled his jacket back on. "Can you stand?"

Elizabeth nodded and climbed to her feet, pretty shaky. "What are we going to do? What am I going to do?"

He helped her back on with her parka. White down floated, ghostly, in the gloom. "Just relax, and I'll take you to the truck. You know how Clark Gable carried Vivian

203

Leigh up that curving staircase in *Gone with the Wind?*" He tucked his gun in his belt up front.

Her eyes wide, she nodded.

"Well, that's not how I'm going to carry you. I'm not strong enough, and we have nearly a mile to go. But you can ride piggyback." He turned away from her. "Hop on."

Like riding a bicycle or ice skating, riding piggyback is something a person just sort of knows forever. She hitched herself up onto his hips. He locked her legs in place in the crooks of his arms, gripping his wrists in front of his belt buckle. "Maxx. Let's go."

The dog led the way out toward the trail, crashing in the duff and old leaves and ground cover. Jack had been listening all along to the silence surrounding them. With this noise he would probably not be able to hear a stalker at all.

They broke out onto the trail and headed downhill. Jack's running shoes slipped now and then in the wet leaves. The added weight threw him off kilter somewhat. His arms started to feel tired and strained. Within five minutes they ached. Soon they began to turn the air blue, telling him what they thought of his cockamamie notion of carrying a full-grown woman that far.

He stopped and let her slide to her feet. "Let's rest."

She sat down on the trail. "Jack? Maxx saved my life."

Jack sat too. "Now that we can view it from a little distance, tell me what happened." He was so tired, wearied past thinking about, and the day was far from over.

"I don't know. I can't . . . I don't know where to start. It was all so horrible. My side hurts."

"You'll hurt all over, probably, tomorrow. Start with when I walked away. What next?"

"I sort of picked my way into the woods a little way. Just—"

Something rattled a tree overhead. She sucked in air.

"An owl. It's OK. Go on with your story."

"I hate this country!" She took a deep breath. "There was this crashing sound right behind me. I don't know who it was. He was big and very dark. He just blew up in my face and swung his arms at me. Then your dog jumped on him. I heard gunshots, but I didn't think he had a gun. I don't know. It's all confusing. Oh, Jack! I'm so frightened! I'm so scared! Who was it? Why me?"

"We'll find out. The gunshots were mine, trying to scare him off."

"Did you see him?"

"No." Who was big enough and strong enough to knock Maxx for a loop? "And you didn't see his face."

"No. I don't know what he looked like." She stood up because Jack stood up. "I'm sorry."

"No apology necesssary." He stooped slightly, she climbed aboard, and away they went.

He had to stop twice more along the way to let his beleaguered arms rest. It was probably going on 6:00 P.M. when they arrived back at his truck.

Clarissa Craig's white prowl pickup and Mike Sanchez's white prowl car sat beside Jack's truck with their lights flashing in gaudy colors, ruining the darkness of the night.

Elizabeth instantly and obviously brightened. She literally sighed with relief. Headlights and Mars bars aren't civilization, but they're apparently the next best thing.

Mike's car trunk gaped open. He and Clarissa seemingly were just suiting up to head out on the trail to meet them. He grinned as Jack came stumbling down to the cars and let Elizabeth slide off. "That saves us some hassle. Thanks."

"Don't mention it." Jack sagged against Mike's fender as Elizabeth sat down in the dirt.

Instantly Clarissa was kneeling at her side with a blood pressure cuff, getting vitals.

"My car." Elizabeth looked at her white Toyota parked

beyond Jack's rig. "How am I going to get my car down the hill?"

"You're not. We'll bring it down." Mike turned to Jack. "No make on the assailant?"

"Not a bit. Roads blocked?"

Mike nodded. "But not well." He gave Elizabeth a hand to her feet, and Clarissa helped.

They put her in Clarissa's pickup. Clarissa hopped in, and they drove off down the hill. Somewhere between here and civilization an ambulance was headed this way to take over the care of Elizabeth Munro.

Bedraggled beyond description, Maxx did not look like a dog who wanted to jump up into a truck. Jack picked him up bodily and stuffed him in the driver's side door. The dog turned around three times and flopped down on the seat, totally knackered.

Mike nodded toward the far end of the lot. "Whose vehicle? It looks familiar."

"Jay Chambers. He plans to come out after moonrise. We're talking about one A.M. or so, I think."

Mike grimaced. "The guy's a certified loony. He's also the only person on the mountain here besides us. Think that's enough cause to arrest him?"

"I'm not certain he's the perp. The assailant made a lot of noise thrashing around in the woods. Jay sounds like a mouse on a cottonball when he moves. It was getting dark, but there was still enough light—I don't think Jay would be that noisy. Or clumsy."

"Unless he's trying to hide the fact that he's Jay Chambers, woodsman."

"True." Jack stared at nothing awhile. He felt tense and edgy again. And angry. Or maybe furious. Yes, definitely furious. That yay-hoo had kicked his dog. "I suppose you want me to hang around."

"Clarissa's coming back up as soon as she meets the ambulance. I can tell you don't want to wait around here."

"Why would Jay be so stupid as to attack Elizabeth when we all know he's here?"

"Because it's so stupid we wouldn't suspect him of doing it. We'd assume he's smarter than that."

Sounded logical. Jack's fury was the only thing keeping him awake.

Mike poked him. "Head on down the hill. I'll call if I need something."

Jack was going to come back with "By then it'll be too late," but he didn't want to talk Mike out of releasing him. To sit out here in the cold darkness for hours awaiting Jay Chambers was not an appealing prospect. He nodded. "I'll go fill Ev in. She'll want to know. She and Elizabeth are friends."

He crawled into the truck. Maxx was sound asleep. He backed out and drove down the serpentine road to Longmire.

19
Deck the Hall

Jack pulled up to the battered curb in front of his apartment at Longmire. The light was on in there. Now what? He poked the somnolent Lab beside him. Maxx lurched to his feet and stood spraddle-legged on the truck seat.

Jack walked around to the other side and lifted his dog out onto the ground. Maxx wandered stiffly away to take care of business. Moments later he came wandering stiffly back. Jack opened the door for him.

Ev sat at Jack's table, the ghastly light of her laptop display bouncing its blue onto her face. She looked at Maxx, looked at Jack. "You said you'd be back hours ago."

"That's the tone of voice my mother used to use when she said exactly that same thing. We've been engaged in an overly rich wilderness experience. What's up?"

Maxx flopped in the middle of the floor, stretched out, and sighed. His soft palate vibrated, making him sound almost like a horse's baritone sneeze.

"Hal called. He's really worried that we're not getting anywhere."

"So am I." Jack shrugged out of his jacket. There was that streak of Elizabeth's blood across the sleeve.

Ev watched Maxx at repose on the floor. "I thought his dog food was here. When did he eat?"

"He didn't yet."

"Then what's wrong with him? He's not begging for dinner."

"A person unknown attacked Elizabeth out on the trail—cut her up but not badly. Clarissa's taking her down to meet the ambulance, and Mike is waiting for our only suspect, Jay Chambers, to come down off the hill. Film at eleven." Jack poured dog food into Maxx's dish.

Maxx's ears tweaked. Casually, wearily, the mutt rolled to his belly. *Jack, Maxx saved my life.* He carried the dish over and stuck it under Maxx's nose, so the hero wouldn't have to get up to eat.

Ev was gawking. "I'm not exactly a great judge of people, but I'd never suspect Jay. Is she all right? Are you sure?"

"Not sure, of course, but not worried either. Her color was good when she got into Clarissa's truck, and she was alert."

"I'll go down to her then. Did Maxx chase the attacker?"

"The attacker knocked him silly."

"He stopped *Maxx?*"

Jack grinned wickedly. "Some loon knocks me across the room at the Clearcut, and you don't think twice. Let him slow Maxx up a little, and you're shocked."

"That's right. You were asking for it. I'll bet poor Maxx wasn't." She considered a moment. "I don't know if this is important, but it might be. Half an hour ago, about —maybe a little longer—a red pickup truck with plywood sides on the bed—do you know what I mean?—went roaring by as I was walking up here from the Inn. Really in a hurry to get down the hill."

He frowned. "The gate was closed when I came down the hill, but not locked. Hm." He could stretch out on the bed and rest his complaining body, or he could go chasing wild geese. "I'll call you from Ashford."

"Jack?"

He ought to take Maxx along, but he couldn't bear to disturb the beast. "I'll try to get back before curfew, Mother."

He climbed back into the truck and headed on down the hill through the glum and cloying night.

A red pickup with plywood-bed sides. Were it on its way to what passed for civilization—Tacoma or somewhere—it had almost an hour's head start. He'd never catch it. But if it were local, someone here would know whose it was. He drove down to the Gateway just outside the entrance. Closed for the day. He continued on to Ashford.

The options in Ashford consisted of a grocery store and the Clearcut Tavern. The grocery store pumped gas, which means they'd be more likely to know the truck, but the Clearcut came a third of a mile before the grocery did. He pulled in there first to inquire.

And there it was, parked in a corner of the Clearcut's lot. Pickup, wood sides. It wasn't exactly red, but the pole light in the parking lot did weird things to colors. Jack sat looking at it a moment, as his motor idled. So there it was. Amazing. *Thank You, Lord.*

Whether or not this rig signified in the business with Elizabeth, it may well have seen something. Jack swung his truck around and backed it up against the red pickup. With its nose against a low block wall and its tail against his back bumper, the suspect vehicle wouldn't be going anywhere. He spent a brief moment to check it out. A CB antenna stuck up out of its fender. The ubiquitous rear-window gun rack carried not a rifle but a compound hunting bow. The truck hood was still warm.

Jack walked inside.

He looked about for familiar faces and saw two. The Blob sat at the counter on the same bar stool he was sitting on before. It probably had his name engraved in bronze. Maybe even gold. The other familiar face perched on a stool down at the far end, entertaining a young lady of dubious appearance draped at his side. With a faint smile

Jack marched directly to the far end of the bar and settled on a stool beside Barney Hall.

"Why, Barney! Good to see you."

Barney smiled wanly. Obviously, accepting lunch from a park person was OK in town. Out here, even being recognized by a park person wasn't all that hot. The young lady looked at Barney oddly.

"Need your help, Barney." Jack leaned in close. "I want to find out who drives that red pickup out in the lot—the one with the plywood sides and the compound bow in the window and the chainsaw in back."

Barney started to mumble something.

The young lady stared at Barney. "That's your truck he's talking about, George."

Jack raised his eyebrows. "George?"

"Nickname," Barney mumbled.

"Of course. George is a natural variant of Barney. I wasn't thinking. Where's your Impala?"

"In the shop." Barney looked downright sullen.

Jack felt distinctly unwelcome. "Barney, where have you been this evening—say, from three on?"

"None of your business."

"We've been through all this before. Official inquiry. I'm not making small talk."

"Around. Running errands and stuff."

"Up in the park."

Barney tried to look detached, casual. He looked cornered. "Couple of them."

"You were really lead-footing it out of the park there, weren't you? The posted speed's twenty in Longmire."

"Going a little fast maybe. Not real fast. Had to hurry to get down here on time."

Jack was going to say something about a hot date, but the girl beyond Barney was glaring at him suspiciously. "I got here early and was surprised you showed up early. Were you going to meet someone else first, before me? Huh, George? What's going on here?"

"Nothing! I . . ." Barney looked uncertain about where to take this, as a truck driver might feel a bit confused about where to take a runaway rig.

Jack pushed harder. "I notice that your bootlaces there have a salal leaf stuck in them. See? Where you've been running through the woods. Not to mention the duff and dead needles and such down under the laces, on the boot tongues. We'd better go outside and talk to the sheriff's deputy. Come on."

The young woman who would have been Barney's date on a less star-crossed evening slid off her stool. "I don't know what you think you're pulling over on me, but I don't need this. My last boyfriend's still in the slammer, and I'm not tying in with you." She snatched her clutch purse off the bar.

Jack could hear the Blob moving in closer behind him. He slipped around behind Barney so that he could keep an eye on them all. He was not in a mood to make nice to the Blob, or to Barney, or to anyone else. Someone had tried to hurt a pretty, even if ditzy, young woman, perhaps to kill her. Someone had kicked his dog. He glared at the Blob. "This guy's going down on suspicion of assault. Wanna go along?"

"Assault!" Barney exploded in a cloud of invective.

The Blob glared back at Jack and at Barney and backed up. He sat down again on his personal stool to watch, scowling.

"Ma'am? Federal officer. How long have you been with Barney/George here this evening?"

"About fifteen minutes." She stared at the luckless ex-logger. "The final fifteen minutes of our relationship. I'm not his alibi. I'm not nobody's alibi."

Away she went.

Quite likely Barney/George lost a lot of money at poker, for his face and body told the world every thought his mind was thinking. Jack could see him tense up, could see his weight shift. Barney almost certainly carried a knife, and it most probably still had some of Elizabeth Munro's blood on it. Any fair forensics lab could negate or confirm that.

And suddenly Jack found himself out of patience. These last few days had asked too much of him. He was supposed to be in Hawaii basking in warmth, not stumbling around in forty-degree rain, not on the flank of a wet volcano chasing Silverados and other attackers, not in a hospital ward in Tacoma, not carrying an injured woman off the mountain single-handedly, not in this dive confronting this particular lowlife.

Come on, Barney. As that oft-quoted philosopher of modern Western culture, Dirty Harry, once said, "Make my day."

Barney came on. This uncle of a feckless, underage burglar swung around on the stool, his elbow headed for Jack's Adam's apple. Jack whipped his foot up, catching Barney in the backs of his knees. He kept his leg moving upward, hoisted both Barney's feet off the floor, tipped him backward. The combined effect of the stool's rotation with Barney's own movement pinwheeled the man off his perch and slammed him into the bar. As he rebounded off the padded mahogany edge, Jack pasted him, hard.

Barney dropped to the floor and stayed there.

Jack pointed to the bartender. "Call 911 and ask them to dispatch a sheriff's deputy. And tell your bouncer there not to bother."

The bartender and bouncer looked at each other. The bouncer backed off.

The bartender picked up the phone. "That other little business and now this—you aren't doing a lot for our Christmas spirit in here, pal."

"Sure I am." Jack whipped out his porta-cuffs. "I just decked the Hall."

20
Joy to the World

How can so much that happened here leave so little trace?" Jack stood beside the patch of ferns that had been mashed flat last night by the weight of a flying hundred-fifteen-pound black Lab. "No clear tracks. No scent trail. No physical evidence. No nothing."

Said black Lab sat by Jack's knee, watching. At Jack's other side, Darryl Grade stood with his hands in his pockets, trying to stay out of the way of the forensics team from Tacoma. Mike Sanchez leaned casually against a nearby tree with arms folded.

Jack had put Maxx first on the scene this morning before the forensics crew arrived. He wanted Maxx to be able to sniff out a trail if possible before the scent got bollixed by the smells of chemicals and other people. As Jack and Darryl watched, the dog dug his nose into the duff, snorted and snarfed, woofed once or twice, and otherwise got into his work. Nothing. He would follow some trace or other a few feet, then come bounding back to Jack and Darryl, his tail wagging.

Occasionally, Jack would slip him a treat. "If there's nothing clear for him to find here, there's nothing clear. But heaven knows he's trying."

And then Mike Sanchez arrived, directing the forensics crew in, and Maxx was relegated to Jack's side as the professionals took over.

The professionals weren't finding much more. They took lots of samples and photographs and videotape. They answered Jack's numerous technical questions with unflagging patience and good cheer. This forensics crew, two women and a man, played with fascinating tools and gadgets Jack had never heard of. They set little white numbered markers all around, seemingly marking nothing. This spot was a bit of latent blood. That was a broken twig. Little things. Periods at ends of sentences, letters, rarely a whole word, that when assembled and analyzed might tell some sort of story.

The duff was churned up from the scuffle. Rain during the night had washed away all visible signs of Elizabeth's blood, although the forensics folk were able to find enough latent stuff to get a good sample. Jack had to admire their thoroughness.

With tweezers, one of the women—Elaine—picked up a soggy little bit of gray. "There's a lot of this around. Any preliminary guess what it is?"

Jack smiled. "Ever hear of a Bean Goose?"

Darryl nodded. "European species, isn't it? Waterfowl."

"Well, this is an L. L. Bean goose. It's a downfeather from Elizabeth's slashed parka after the rain got through with it."

Darryl socked him in the arm.

Bummer. Jack's arms still felt stiff from hauling Elizabeth down the hill last night. Of course, macho pride prevented his mentioning that.

Elaine tucked her tweezers into her tool kit, conferred with her fellow experts, and declared their job about done. Mike led the herd out to the trail and down the hill. Jack and Maxx fell in behind, single file. Darryl rode pickup—the guy last in line on the horseback trail ride, who picks up the combs and bathing suits and sunglasses and

215

all the other stuff the other riders inadvertently lose along the way.

Back at the parking lot, the crew bade the rangers adieu and disappeared down the hill in their van. Darryl bade Jack and Mike adieu and headed up the hill to plow snow at Paradise.

Jack looked at Mike. "Think Barney's softened up enough?"

"Let's give it a shot."

Mike had ridden up here in the forensics van. He would go down the hill with Jack.

Jack let Maxx up into his cage and climbed into the cab of the pickup. Here was an aspect of the job he had not anticipated when he accepted it, but he should have. How much do you engage the park personnel in the investigation when they are technically suspects and perhaps even prime suspects? Sure, there are some areas clearly black or white. But what about the vast gray in-between? For instance, how intimately should Darryl or Mike be included, if at all, and how does one discourage them from involvement without engendering their suspicions, perhaps to put them on their guard? A park employee first and foremost could alter or destroy evidence were his/her suspicions aroused.

Unencumbered by weighty thoughts, Maxx curled up and slept. He was still one tired dog. The question of whether to include Mike Sanchez died, because he didn't say much at all on the ride down to the administration building at Longmire.

Unlike Yosemite National Park, for instance, Mount Rainier does not have a jail on the premises. Miscreants are trotted eighty to a hundred miles to facilities in Tacoma, other locations in Pierce County, or even farther. Jack did not want to drive all over western Washington herding prisoners and suspects. With Mike Sanchez's permission he had managed to con Clarissa into hauling Barney about for him. With a shrug, Clarissa philosophized, "It all pays

the same," and chauffeured Barney into county holding facilities overnight, then back out here to the park. Jay they
released on his own recognizance.

Uncle Barney "George" Hall did not appreciate being transported long distances. He did not consider Jack's
opinion of him as a suspect valid. He did not think he
should have been held overnight without the opportunity
to post bond. He did not think he had rightfully earned the
speeding ticket Mike slapped on him. It wasn't that he
could be called wholly innocent of speeding. It was simply
that the road was deserted, and there was no reason not to
go a little faster than posted. Now if tourists were around,
that would be a different story.

Mike Sanchez, Jack, and Barney sat down in a small,
cramped basement room of the Longmire administration
building. The only wall covering was paint over the foun-
dation block, the only adornment a calendar above a dusty
file cabinet. It was a calendar featuring park areas, and the
park photo for December just happened to be Hawaii Volcanoes. *Mele Kalikimaka.*

Barney sat on a pinched, straight-backed folding chair,
aired these and other protests, and fretted. Mike sat back
in the corner in an old-fashioned mission style wooden
armchair, his legs stretched out, his fingers casually laced
across his belt buckle. Jack sprawled out similarly in a
cozy, worn old office chair he'd found. He tipped it back to
a comfortable angle.

He smiled at Barney munificently. "How's your job
with Jay Chambers coming? About done?"

"Yeah."

"What's left to do?"

Barney eyed him suspiciously. "I cut the logs and
stacked them on site. He says he'll set them where he
wants them."

"Did he say anything about wanting it finished by
December twenty-first?"

Barney frowned. "Yeah, but it's not gonna happen.

217

Probably gonna be till next summer likely. I cut the wood, but he needs some other stuff."

Jack shifted in his chair. He was getting stiff already, and this interview was less than five minutes old.

Mike picked up the thread. "What were you doing in the woods, Barney?"

"I wasn't in the woods."

"Yes, you were. Your shoes are still damp. Jack mentioned the duff packed down in their tongues."

"I do logging."

"In the park?"

"Other side, outside the park by Chinook Pass. I had a date in Ashford, so I cut through the park. When I came through last night, I thought it was later than it was. I was in a hurry. Everybody gets in a hurry now and then." Barney tried to look contrite. An actor he was not. "Hey, it's Christmas, right? You don't want to write tickets and stuff. Joy to the world."

Mike snorted. "Joy to the world, sure. I get the distinct impression that your driver's license won't take too many more speeding tickets. How many points have you accumulated anyway?"

Barney shrugged. "If I could help you out, I would. You know that."

Mike engaged Barney in a fast give-and-take then, leading him on, expertly getting him to fire answers out quickly before he could think about them. It was a competent job all around. Mike didn't need Jack for this. Jack simply sat back and listened.

Helpful attitude or not, Barney chafed still more at being cited for speeding. He remained unshaken in his conviction that obedience to the law should be a matter of convenience, not necessity. He carried no knife of any kind when Jack took him down. He insisted that was normal for him—that he was not in the habit of carrying a blade of any kind. That had to make him the only logger in western Washington without a pocketknife.

218

He stuck to his story, though, and no matter how hard Mike pressed him, he didn't let anything slip. No doors to other lines of inquiry opened themselves. Jack pondered the ugly prospect that anything Mike and he dug up here would probably be inadmissible anyway, since Barney had no lawyer present.

They worked on Barney a couple hours and came away essentially empty-handed. If Barney were in on Elizabeth's attack, he was extraordinarily canny in covering up. But then, sneaky-petes such as burglars are usually quite good at lying.

With barely masked reluctance, they let the joker go, the speeding citation intact. Joy to the world.

Jack settled into Mike's office and got on the FTS line, then, the federal government's this-is-strictly-for-business phone service. He dug out the doctor who had treated Elizabeth Munro's lacerations. Dr. Morgan apparently was too busy making money to help a humble police investigator right away—it took Jack half an hour to make personal contact with her.

He introduced himself and got right to business. "Dr. Morgan, did Ms. Munro have much dirt in her wounds?"

"She sure did, no thanks to you."

"Doctor . . ."

"She spent quite a lot of time explaining how you and that other fellow dragged her all over the wilderness. When you're wallowing out in the dirt fifty miles from the nearest clean floor, of course the wound will be full of trash."

They dragged Elizabeth? The non-hiker who spent so much time sitting at trailside? Jack grimaced. "Trash. Humus and stuff from the forest floor. Any other kind of dirt?"

"Such as what?"

"Stone chips. Gravel."

"Gravel. Yes. As I recall."

Jack nodded, a gesture strictly for himself, since he was alone in the room. "Did you save them?"

"You mean for evidence? No. There weren't any bits big enough to save. I irrigated the area to clean it thoroughly. Frankly, it never occurred to me to save the irrigant."

"Did you notice if any chips or bits were obsidian?"

"What's obsidian? Isn't that a kind of stone?"

"Dark, shiny stone."

"When it's wet it's all dark and shiny."

Jack abandoned the conversation, thanked her, and let her go back to her money-making. He cradled the phone and stared at nothing beyond the wall awhile. He fooled himself into thinking he was marshaling his thoughts, planning the next move. What he was really doing was spacing out.

He stood up, stretched stiffly, and walked out into the little receptionist's office between the chief ranger's office here and the chief naturalist's across the hall.

Kerri Haskell paused, her hands hovering above her computer keyboard, and smiled winningly. "Did anyone mention to you about the Christmas party tonight?"

Jack shook his head.

She bobbed hers. "Six at the community building. Potluck. I'm bringing the lutefisk."

"*Lutefisk!* And here I always thought Christmas parties were festive occasions with good food."

"Oh, you've heard of lutefisk."

"Raw fish drenched in noxious chemicals."

Kerri folded her hands in her lap and sat back grinning. "My maiden name was Lundven. I grew up with the stuff, but still I almost agree with you. Most foods, you hear a comment like 'Oh, that's good.' Or 'Delicious!' But lutefisk? The biggest rave review I ever heard was 'It's all right.'"

"So you're a Viking."

"You got that right! My father used to put on a helmet with horns every Christmas and blow a trumpet. When he presided over the festivities, he presided!"

Jack quoted one of his favorite bumper stickers, seen in Minnesota: "'When lutefisk is outlawed, only outlaws will have lutefisk.'"

Laughing, Kerri came back with "I never met a lutefisk I didn't like."

"How about, 'Lutefisk doesn't kill people. People kill people.'"

Kerri raised a hand in a gesture of mysticism. "Visualize . . . lutefisk." Her eyes sparkled.

That pleased Jack immensely. She so often looked sad.

She continued, "If you want Santa to distribute a gift to someone, slip it into the big bag by the men's room. There's always plenty of food, so don't worry about having to contribute. You'll bring Evelyn, won't you?"

"Sure. Thanks."

Jack wished her a good afternoon and wandered back to his apartment. It was just about time to go down to the Inn for a doughnut. Maxx lay flaked out in the middle of the floor, cleverly positioned so as to be in Jack's way whether he wanted to hang up his jacket, go to the bathroom, or lie down on the bed.

He didn't know which of those things to do first and was contemplating his options when the phone rang. That he could reach without stepping over the dog. He flopped into a straight-backed chair beside the table and picked it up. "Good afternoon."

"And good afternoon to you. This is Anne Somersby. I don't know if you remember me."

"Columnist extraordinaire, Tacoma *News Tribune*. I certainly do. What can I do for you?" Jack watched Maxx's paws paddle as the eyes flickered; the mutt was dreaming again.

"I want your help to find a winter solstice observance. You know—druid ceremonies."

"Why me?"

"You seem to have gotten close to that sort of thing

221

in the course of your investigation. I've tried several avenues, including Jay Chambers, and the doors keep slamming in my face."

"Why are you interested now? That stuff's been around for three thousand years. Nobody paid attention. Suddenly it pops up in every conversation."

Ms. Somersby cackled. "It may have been around three thousand years, but I haven't, regardless what you might suspect. Sidebars to articles on the investigation. I want to observe, take notes."

"That's tomorrow night, right?"

"Right."

Someone knocked. Maxx jerked, woofed, and curled around to lying on his belly.

"Just a moment." Jack covered the receiver by pressing it against his thigh and without too much of a stretch reached over and opened the door. As Ev entered, he put the receiver back to his ear. "If you get a good lead, Ms. Somersby, or any lead at all, pursue it. If you're still stymied tomorrow, show up at my apartment here around four, and we'll go hunting. Sound all right?"

"Sounds great." She offered some parting pleasantry, extended best wishes from her cohort Norma Reid, and hung up.

Jack cradled the phone. "You brought dinner."

Ev had set a covered casserole on the table along with her laptop. She dropped into the chair. "That's for tonight. There's a potluck up at the community building. Darryl invited us."

"So did Kerri, about five minutes ago. What's in the casserole?"

"Mystery food. You'll just have to wait. Our paperwork is way behind again, and Hal wants the latest. I was thinking we might do that now, and I'll fax it to him so he has it tomorrow morning."

Jack stepped over the dog and walked to the bedstand to get his file folders. "Why the bur under his saddle?"

"What?"

"Why is he so nervous? Antsy-prancy? He's never been like this, not even when we were assembling the stuff for the grand jury in the Gibbs case." He stepped back over the dog and sat down at the table. "What can I get you? Coffee? Tea? Pop? Tortilla chips?"

"Nothing right now, thanks." She seemed tense, hesitant.

He watched her a few seconds as she nervously popped her machine open and plugged its charger into the wall socket by the table. "What else?"

She flicked her eyes up to him and let them flick away again. "Nothing." She brooded in the silence a moment. Suddenly she sat back and looked right at him. "Hal asked me to do him a big favor. More than a favor, actually. And he didn't just ask. He begged. He wants me to talk you into staying on and working through your Christmas holiday."

Jack felt anger rise so fast that his face turned hot. He kept his voice relaxed and even. "That, Ev, is between Hal and me. You don't have to feel some obligation to get involved. It's not your problem."

"Yes, I do, because he asked me to. So I will."

Jack didn't have to ponder the situation long at all. "You will because you think you don't dare say no to Hal. He's the one who makes the Hal's Pals assignments, and you desperately want in on that, to get out of your stuffy old budget office. To stay in his good graces, you'll do any little favor he asks of you. And if that means putting the pressure on me, you'll put the pressure on me. Thanks, co-worker. Thanks plenty."

"That's not so!" She glared at him. Her face tightened; her lower lip quivered.

Jack knew what was coming, and he hated it.

She clamped her hand over her mouth, but it did nothing to keep her weeping at bay. Her crying jag boiled up and over and past her defenses. Those huge brown Bambi eyes overflowed.

He probably ought to apologize, but he wouldn't. He was too furious. They were supposed to be a team, working toward a common goal, and she was undercutting him. He was anxious to close this case, and she was dragging her feet. It suited her purposes to stay here over the holiday—DC almost never knew a white Christmas. *Teamwork. Yeah, right.*

Jack stomped out into the clammy cold of late afternoon and rummaged under his truck seat. He found the box of tissues, carried it inside, and plopped it unceremoniously on the table by her laptop. Distracted past efficiency, he sat down and thumbed ineffectually through his file of unprocessed notes.

He didn't bother to look up as she blew lustily. The sobs abated. She blew a couple more times and began sullenly to punch her keyboard. He expected a thank you for going to the trouble of finding her some tissue. When thanks were not forthcoming he fumed even worse.

They worked in virtual silence, punctuated only by the tersest of necessary exchanges. Not the least of his ire stemmed from the fact that the more he worked at this, the more he realized that so far they had nothing to work on. No solid facts, no fingers strongly pointing, no nothing.

Without asking, Ev put the casserole in the oven to heat up.

It eventually, mercifully, approached 6:00 P.M. She closed down, he folded up his work, Maxx stretched and shook. Jack informed Maxx he was staying home. The dog conveniently refrained from comprehending plain English, and Jack knew good and well that the pooch understood English as well as he himself did. The dog's tail arched up expectantly when they put their jackets on, then sagged as Jack and Ev walked out the door without him.

They walked through somber darkness up the street, headed for the back road behind Longmire. Ev carried the hot casserole, wrapped in bath towels, on the crook of her arm. It smelled like a cheese dish or escalloped something.

Jack was going to have to somehow drive himself out of his dark mood. Who wants to cast a pall on a Christmas party? Good old Scrooge. Joy to the world. Uh-huh.

Not only did he not know how he'd do that, he didn't really want to. He could see his holiday melting away, slipping through his fingers, and he was mad at the world. Hal had no reason or right to do this to him. The question now before him was, how far dare he go in defying Hal's wishes?

Ev let fly a peculiar, gurgling cry of shock and horror. The casserole dropped with a towel-muffled crash. She froze in midstep, staring straight ahead.

Ten feet in front of them, darker against the darkness, bigger than life and twice as ugly, loomed a great ape.

21

Faith of Our Fathers

A few things in life, like an unexpected slap in the face or the shocking realization that you are falling out of an airplane, are sure to draw a startled response, and the sudden appearance of a huge black ape is bound to be one of them.

Jack gaped transfixed for unmeasured time.

The ape stood before them, motionless, and stared back.

Jack finally recovered the presence of mind to go for his gun.

Kerri Haskell's muffled voice yelled, "Don't shoot! Please don't shoot!"

Jack swung his revolver skyward. The voice had come from the ape.

The ape reached up with both hands and literally ripped its head off. Kerri Haskell's terrified face floated in the blackness above the black ape shoulders, as if disembodied.

Ev sucked in a barrel of night air. "Kerri . . . why . . . how . . ."

Kerri looked near tears. "I'm so sorry, Ev, Jack. I totally forgot that you two didn't know about this, or I would have been more careful. I was partway up the hill when I remembered I didn't bring the candy canes, and I was coming back to get them."

Jack's heart slowed to a mere two hundred or so beats per minute. "Halloween maybe, but a gorilla costume at a Christmas party?" He holstered his gun, somewhat ashamed that he'd drawn it.

Kerri's voice dropped closer to a normal pitch. "It's my shtick, I guess you'd say. I do it at most of the park parties during the year, if kids come. Especially going-away parties. The kids never get tired of it, and I try to think up some new little trick each time. Like tonight, the gorilla will wear a Santa hat and give away candy canes." She came forward to stand directly before them.

Ev cried, "Oh, of course! Ms. Mount Rainier! You and Jeff were laughing about Ms. Mount Rainier in the Elbe parade. It was an in joke, right? You're wearing the gorilla suit when you're Ms. Mount Rainier."

"That's right! Waving to the folks just like a beauty queen, only in this gorilla suit." Kerri finally relaxed enough to smile. "I really am sorry I frightened you. Let me run get the candy canes, and I'll walk on up with you." She hurried off toward her house, her full-head mask still in hand.

Jack dropped to one knee and gathered up the casserole, still wrapped in its insulating towels. Sticky, steamy hot juice had completely soaked them, and he could feel the broken glass grate on itself inside the limp terry lump. These were his only towels. What was he going to dry off with from now until he next did laundry?

At arm's length he toted the mess back to the apartment and left it by the front door. He'd take care of it later. He rejoined Ev. So did Kerri. Together they climbed the hill toward the wooden trestle bridge. He carried Kerri's burden, three plastic grocery bags of candy canes, and hoped that an act or two of chivalry would put him in a better mood. Being scared witless by a gorilla certainly wasn't conducive to good cheer.

Kerri wagged her head. "That's the closest I've ever

227

been to getting shot. And by a marvelous person too."

"Not too marvelous, had I blown you away."

She giggled. "True. Do you realize what you did, though? You got Jeff and me thinking about what we used to have, and how much we still care, and we're going to take off in a new direction. We're going to start working on our problems instead of just yelling at each other."

"Rekindling the romance?"

"That too." Her voice hardened. "I realize it was our Silverado that ran over you, but Mike's actions really hurt me. I can see where he had to question us about it, of course. But *arrest* Jeff? Jack, he knew better than that! I'll never forgive him for that. When Jeff and I swore we were both home in bed . . . I mean . . ."

"Rekindling the romance."

"Yes. Mike said a policeman can't afford to take the suspect's word for anything, but he had no reason to think we'd lie. I mean . . . Anyway, when he did that, it brought us closer together. It's strange."

"The two of you united against the world."

"You know, I think you're right. That's just how it feels."

They walked in damp quiet up a road last asphalted so long ago that it lay gray and crunchy-crumbly in the darkness.

"Kerri?" Jack asked. "Ever loan your gorilla suit there out to anyone?"

"Rarely. I try not to. You breathe and sweat in this thing for a while and it's not very sanitary." They were walking up the last stretch before they came to the community building. She pulled her mask back on.

Kerri had her shtick down very well. She waddled apelike into the community building, practically dragging her knuckles. Kids laughed.

Jack and Ev stepped in through the big double doors. The building consisted of one great room with varnished paneling and a hardwood floor. Giant log beams, their

228

joints trussed with great iron plates, formed pillars at measured intervals along the walls and laced back and forth across the ceiling. On the far wall stood the doors to restrooms and a tiny kitchen.

The room was set up classic potluck style, with tables strung out in long rows and cold steel folding chairs lining them on both sides. The gorilla leaped up onto a table and sat down, legs folded tightly. Kerry was as flexible as a carpenter's rule. She plucked some grapes off a fruit plate and flung them at a couple of the teenagers. The kids squealed delightedly.

Jack acted as Santa Ape's helper then, opening the boxes of candy canes and handing them to her one by one. He would have guessed that manipulating those big rubber ape-hand gloves would be like playing a piano in a catcher's mitt. His guess was wrong—she enjoyed almost perfect dexterity. She could pluck a grape or handle a candy cane two-fingered.

She completed her act. All the kids now had candy canes. She bounded off the table onto a folding chair. It tipped backward, and Ev yelped in surprise and fear. The ape rode the chair down and rolled a somersault as it hit the floor. Obviously, she'd done that little move before. With a final hoot and a wave, the ape exited through the double doors.

The mothers ran their kids through the line first, loading their plates, and sent them off to eat. The adults formed into a loose, ragged caterpillar queue.

Jack stepped into the line, and Ev fell in directly behind him. He looked all around. "You said Darryl invited us. He isn't here yet."

"I noticed. Neither is Jeff Haskell."

Kerri showed up about ten minutes later, her hair somewhat disheveled, her appearance otherwise normal. She laughed and talked at the back of the line with some other park wives.

This potluck business was rather new to Ev. She apparently had never indulged in potlucks much before consorting with Hal's Pals. The white lie she told Elizabeth Munro about being on a diet didn't jibe with the heap of morsels stacked on her paper plate. Just a nibble of each menu item becomes a feast when there are thirty entrées crowded onto the table. She chatted and laughed and licked the juice from her plate off her fingers.

The difference between the old dour Ev and this current cheery Ev would strike Jack harder than it hit anyone else here, because they had just met her. He knew her when.

They sat on those cold, uncomfortable steel chairs across from Kerri, the chief naturalist, and the museum curator/librarian.

Darryl Grade and Jeff Haskell arrived late, well after Jack had made quite a dent in his dinner. They complained about the rain here and the snow at Paradise. Clearly, they had just come off roadwork.

His plate loaded with enough goodies to fill a bathtub, Darryl plopped into the chair across from Ev even though the place to her left was available. So Jeff took that one.

Darryl greeted everyone more or less generically and dug in. He grinned. "What a night. We're not supposed to, but I used the snowplow to pull out some jerk who slid into the ditch just below the dorm. Paradise is slicker'n Vaseline on linoleum."

"Snowing at Stevens Canyon?" Jack asked. He wondered if a winter's blanket of snow would deaden the ugly smell at the murder site.

"No, and that's surprising. It's really late this year for the snowline to be up so high. Just below Paradise. In fact, we've been leaving the Stevens Canyon Road open. The snow isn't anywhere near that low yet."

"Interesting. But that didn't keep some common-sense-challenged yay-hoo from going in the ditch."

"He was dispositionally challenged too." Darryl finished a mouthful of potato salad. "Really torqued, as if it was the park's fault that there's curves in the mountain road."

Jack stared wide-eyed. "Isn't it?"

Ev giggled, something Ev hardly ever did.

Darryl was off and running now. "He was also—let's see—sartorially challenged. He wore jeans and a T-shirt and Birkenstocks, and that was about all. So I asked him, 'Don't you ever wear winter clothes when you go up into the snow?' And he said, 'Why? My car has a heater.' So help me he said that."

Ev wagged her head. "Until your car goes in the ditch."

Jack grunted. "Was he chemically challenged?"

"I don't think so, or I would have left him for the rangers. I'd guess he was just careless—I mean, care-challenged. Which left his car positionally challenged."

Jack glanced at Kerri. The strange, almost guilty-looking expression on her face defied reading. She glanced at him and looked even guiltier as she returned her attention quickly to her plate.

He laid down his fork. "Kerri? Say."

She shrugged. "Your politically correct stuff is fun. Amusing. I like it."

"But."

"But." She hesitated the longest time. Her voice, usually on the husky side anyway, nearly rumbled. "We're brand new grandparents, Jeff and I—our first grandchild was born eight months ago."

"Congratulations!"

"Thank you. Not that we had a lot to do with it, except eagerly anticipate." Kerri smiled sadly. "She's a Down syndrome baby. Trisomy. A genetic accident that happens once in eight hundred births. Everything she faces in life—things that are easy and ordinary for everyone else—is going to be a difficult challenge for her. Everything. 'Challenge' is a cute word, except for her, and it . . ." The husky voice ceased.

Jack looked at Darryl, and Darryl looked at Jack. What do you say?

Apologies didn't seem the appropriate response, though Jack and Darryl both offered them. Kerri apologized too, unnecessarily, for putting a damper on things. Then Ev sent the conversation off along more comfortable roads by asking some very good questions about Down syndrome.

Kerri got instantly caught up in the flow, explaining what she'd learned about it and how to best stimulate Down kids and help them grow. She knew more about the latest findings than Jack did, and it was his field more or less.

He surreptitiously observed Jeff. Here was a major cause of stress on the Haskell marriage, a genetically imperfect grandchild. Jeff wasn't dealing with it well. Jack could see it in his tense silence that bordered on hostility. His anger and frustration at life was going to have to vent somewhere. Or had it already? He was a volatile sort. Just how dangerous a man did this situation make out of him?

Then the conversation shifted to hiking and skiing. Kerri and Jeff, both inveterate outdoors sportsmen, were hiking when they met, Kerri said. They went cross-country skiing a lot in the winter, Jeff said. Ev, who had done neither to speak of, pumped them both for information on what it was like.

Jack lost track of the conversation. He already knew what hiking was like (walking until you're absolutely bushed over trails a million feet have trodden before you, so that you can make a smoky fire out in the middle of nowhere and eat lousy food with grit in it), and what cross-country skiing was like (struggling up hills, falling a lot, getting incredibly cold snow down your collar and up your cuffs, becoming wetter than you can imagine—wetter and wetter, with numb fingers—and eventually growing so tired you envy downhill skiers, all of whom have an ambulance

232

waiting at the bottom of their run, just in case). His mind drifted to other things.

So the Stevens Canyon Road was still open, making Ohanapecosh easily accessible. He mulled possible locations for a druid ceremony, assuming Jay Chambers's ring of poles was not completed yet. If Somersby showed up tomorrow afternoon, he knew a few places to try.

Somersby called the next day too, just after noon.

All day Ev had remained strangely cool and aloof. She and Jack faxed Hal a ton of stuff, most of it meaningless. When Darryl got off work early, thanks to a long night in the saddle plowing roads, he stopped by and invited her to dinner. In a trice, she abandoned Jack and went off.

When Somersby showed up, therefore, Jack was ready to flee himself. Ev's foot-dragging, her disregard for speed and efficiency in this case, irked him.

Anne Somersby waved her hand toward her little Datsun. "Who wants to drive?"

"That car? Neither of us." Jack waved toward his truck.

"Mine has a phone."

"Mine has a cage for Maxx. He's not a buddy you want in your backseat, not with that light gray upholstery. He sheds."

"You win." Somersby hopped up into the passenger side.

"Maxx. Saddle up."

The dog leaped into his cage, and Jack hooked the door shut. He climbed in. "I tried to reach Jay Chambers and got his answering machine. For starters, I was thinking we might go visit a druid-in-training who probably knows where the ceremonies will be held tonight. Don't let his marked tendency to fire shotguns at guests put you off."

"Oh? I think I've changed my mind about which car to take. The one with the phone. Wouldn't a phone call, telling him we're coming, pave the way?"

"It certainly would, if only he had a phone to answer."

Somersby was obviously deeper into this case than she let on, so Jack whiled away the time driving to Eerie Elroy's by asking seemingly innocuous questions. She knew about as much about Getz as Jack did, but not more. He kept quiet for the moment about the journal.

Eerie wasn't home. The silence told Jack that, even before he knocked on the door. In a way, he was immensely relieved. Much as he liked old Eerie, he felt constantly on edge when he was around the guy. Probably that shotgun blasting away didn't help a lot.

Somersby gaped at the ragged yard, the half-carved sculptures of bears and Bigfoot in the work area, all the junk, the hideous road they'd just driven over. "And he tops all this off with a shotgun?"

"Yeah. And wait till you hear about the hearse." Jack climbed back into the truck and turned it around. They headed down the hill toward civilization.

"Now what?"

"I'm thinking we might try the Grove of the Patriarchs." That would be a good place for a solstice fete if Uncle Barney was correct about Jay's ring of wooden poles being as yet unfinished.

A cathedral-like stand of massive, amazingly ancient trees, the Grove would sing like a choir to someone as forest-conscious as a druid. The Grove was the biggest such thing around and, unlike most years, still easily accessible for winter solstice. Unless the group had some regular place they absolutely had to go to year after year, this was the place to come. Get it while you can.

Jack had already checked the records at the admin building. No one had applied for a special-use permit for the Grove or anyplace else in the park, or signed up for a group campsite anywhere. So he was driving all over the mountain on speculation.

And then, for all practical purposes, the speculation became certainty. Up ahead a quarter mile, a hearse cruised the road to Paradise. Jack adjusted his speed to match.

"You mentioned a hearse." Somersby pointed. "That one?"

"With a rumpled right rear end, I'll bet. He wouldn't have had time to get the bodywork done on it, but I'm glad to see it's back in running order."

"He was involved in a hearse wreck? Was he firing his shotgun and not watching where he was going?"

"All of the above." Jack told the tale as he paced Eerie, keeping visual contact until they entered the park and the curves got too tight for that. He closed the distance as they approached Longmire and watched Eerie continue up the hill. It was dark now, but the hearse was an easy mark. Its right taillight was out.

Eerie turned aside onto the Stevens Canyon Road. With a glorious feeling of triumph, Jack followed him all the way to the Grove of the Patriarchs and pulled into the parking lot behind him. He parked half a dozen slots away from the hearse. Maybe fifteen other cars were here.

"You're brilliant." Somersby pointed out her side window. Eerie was slipping into a white robe as he walked from the parking lot light into the utter darkness of the forest trail.

Jack in turn pointed out his window. "The brown Cherokee parked over there is Jay Chambers's rig." He kept his voice low despite that they were still sitting inside the truck with the windows closed.

"Wish I could have latched onto some night-vision specs. They go to the reporters covering hard news on the Hilltop, not us fluff columnists."

"Your bitterness shows."

Somersby snorted. "Every now and then."

Another car pulled in and parked near the trailhead. Jack waited until they were out and on the trail before he slid out his side and locked the door. The overpaid overhead. You would think the whole purpose of bosses would be to support the legmen, the field personnel. Help them out. Obviously Somersby wasn't getting any assistance from her editor, and Hal was doing his level best to keep Jack out of Hawaii. Why couldn't bosses aid instead of undercut?

Jack put Maxx on the longline and headed for the trail, with Somersby hard by his side. The wet forest closed around them instantly. Shades of green by day had become shades of black. Environmentalists claimed this was genuine temperate rain forest, this southeast corner of the park. Rain forest brings to mind jungle. Jack felt swallowed.

"Wait." He stopped, so Somersby stopped. "The tape recorder in your breast pocket there."

"What?"

"You heard me. I'd prefer you not record anything. Invasion of privacy, whatever you want to call it."

"All right. You take it." She pulled out a gizmo the size of a pack of Virginia Slims and handed it to him. He stuck it in his jacket pocket, and they continued on.

Jack brought Maxx in closely to heel, depending upon the Lab's ears, eyes, and nose to tell them what was happening. Maxx tensed and growled. Ghostly white forms glided among the trees up ahead, men and perhaps women in cowled white robes. Eerie, and everyone else robed as well, had left the trail.

Jack moved off the track too. He stopped then and listened, following by ear rather than eye. Maxx vibrated by his leg, uneasy and perhaps even unnerved by the spooky nature of the whole surreal scene.

Then a lovely singing arose from among the ancient trees and their robed consorts, an Irish sort of tune, and lilting. Jack recognized it. Ash Grove—that was the name of the melody. Some hummed and some sang as a voice chanted over the music. They were gathered in a small glade ahead, forming a pallid circle.

Jack felt the strongest urge to join the song. He loved that Ash Grove tune. He couldn't remember all the words without a hymnal, and he couldn't make out the singers' words, but snatches came to mind. At one time or another, he had sung at least three different sets of words to the old Welsh folk melody, and they all meshed together now in his memory.

The Master has come, and He calls us to follow the track of the footprints He leaves on our way.... We love Him, we seek Him, we long to be near Him and rest in the light of His beautiful land ... at the close of the day.... The Master has called us in life's early morning, with spirits ... ta ta tata ta ... on the sod. We turn from the world ... ta ta ta, ta ta tata ... to cast in our lot with the people of God.

From beside him, Somersby sucked in her breath as fire flared up amid the celebrants, instantly and grandly, as if by magic. The dancing yellow light, vivid in the forest gloom, splayed across the cowls and robes and solemn faces. They ought to start moving closer, if Somersby was going to get any good material.

A thump on his back threw Jack against a tree. He wheeled and slouched against the smooth tree trunk, his breath knocked into the next ZIP code. His dog ought to be defending him. The stupid mutt just stood there, confused. Maxx's tail began to flail back and forth. This was A Friend. No need to bark announcing the approach of A Friend.

Darryl Grade loomed in the darkness. The enforcer.

"Mr. Grade." Somersby spoke, bless her, and that was good, because Jack didn't have any breath to speak with. "I didn't know you were involved in this."

"Just helping them out. Prevent unwanted attention. Throw out reporters. That kind of thing."

Jack rasped, "You can't. Public land."

"They have a special use permit."

"Not on file."

"I may have forgotten to file it. I'll do it tomorrow."

"After the fact." Jack's back between his shoulder blades ached and moaned and cursed his stupid dog, who

237

didn't know a friend from an assailant. He lurched erect, away from the tree.

"That's right, after the fact." Darryl nodded. "So no one knows about it till it's over. Derails the curious."

"I'm surprised you noticed us," Somersby said. "There were quite a few people walking back here."

Jack was finally getting his breath back. "Old measles problem. Darryl wears sunglasses during the day, but he sees like a cat at night. Right?"

Was Darryl smiling in the darkness? "Heavy memory."

"Even heavier badge. I can pull rank on you."

"But you won't." Darryl kept his voice low. "Jack, you don't want to mess up their observance just the same as you wouldn't want someone barging in and disrupting a church service."

"My God welcomes everyone."

"So did the modern druids until the hecklers and gawkers got so bad they closed the rites. It's nothing personal, believe me, but they've been burned too often. You're not going any closer."

Somersby sniffed. "You know, Grade, I used to work the entertainment beat for the LA *Times.* I'd visit film locations—TV and movies. The minute they close the set, you can be certain there's trouble. I can't help feeling that way about this. If nothing clandestine is going on, why the stringent security?"

"That's exactly the point." Darryl moved in closer, to lower his voice further. "People take this for a sideshow—something to get a kick out of or laugh at. And this isn't something that deserves to be written up for a segment of *Entertainment Tonight.*"

Somersby let fly with an expletive. "Don't give me that. They televise Christmas mass and broadcast the St. Mark's compline service. I want to know what's going on here. The Klan?"

Jack knew better than that, and he had a pretty good idea that Somersby knew better than that, but it was a great little shaker-upper. Obviously, she was baiting Darryl, trying to get him exercised enough to say, "OK, OK, go see for yourself." And that meant she was one sharp, experienced reporter.

Darryl bristled. "It's a religion, four thousand years old at least. The faith of our fathers."

"No, Darryl," Jack countered quietly. "The faith of our Father who art in heaven is infinitely more than this."

"In heaven? So where was He when Margaret died?" Darryl shook his head grimly. "No. You're not getting any closer—I don't care how much your badge weighs. I'll take the flak tomorrow if I have to. But no."

Somersby shot a sharp, bitter look at Jack. Clearly she was expecting him to bull a way in for her.

He weighed the situation from every angle that came to mind on short notice. He didn't have much of an element of surprise if he were to explode in Darryl's face. Darryl was ready for him. And Darryl was police trained, just as Jack was. This was more, though, than just logistics and military tactics. Much more.

He kept an eye on Darryl, but it was Somersby he addressed. "This is a friend, Anne. Under certain circumstances, I'd fight him if I had to. But this isn't one of those circumstances. He holds strong convictions about the situation here, and I don't. At least, mine aren't strong enough to violate our friendship. We found the place; you're here. We'll hang around as long as you like, and you can interview whomever you wish after the fact. Anything more than that you're going to have to arrange on your own."

The scowl on her face told the world that Anne Somersby was not the least pleased. She was probably hoping that if she scowled hard enough he'd relent.

Darryl visibly softened and relaxed. "Thank you, Jack."

22

We Three Kings

The main trouble with mountain goats is that they persist in living on mountains. Up very high. Virtually inaccessible.

Jack had Maxx on his longline because the last thing he needed was for the mutt to go romping off across an open slope chasing mountain goats. He didn't particularly mind the romping part—hulking Maxx needed all the exercise he could get—but chasing wild mountain goats in your national park is greatly frowned upon and a thing to be discouraged.

Ev sprinted along at Jack's heels, every bit as nimble and eager as Maxx. "Jack? Do mountain goats usually stay in one area? I mean, if you and Jay saw them up here, does that mean we'll probably see them too?"

"They have a home range, but it's vast. You gotta remember their pasture is mostly rock. So it's iffy. But we'll see." He led the way up the trail above Reflection Lake. They had passed the place where Getz's corpse was discovered. They had passed the place where you turn aside to work your way out to the Grandfather Cedar. They had passed the area where Elizabeth was attacked. They climbed still, seeking mountain goats.

Jack stopped in an open lea. "Here's where Jay left

the trail that day." Less than four days ago. It seemed like weeks. He pointed off across the open slope where once God's sheep/goats had grazed.

Ev swung up her binoculars and glassed the slope. "I don't see anything." She was carrying a pair of big ten-fifties from the ranger cache. Her small, delicate hands barely wrapped around the barrels. Her fingers barely reached the seesaw focus.

"Let's wander out that way." Today Jack couldn't simply force his way through the underbrush the way he usually did when heading off cross-country. Ev wasn't used to leaving asphalt. So he picked his way carefully, avoiding the worst of the slings and arrows of outrageous wilderness. He threaded between rank bushes and stepped carefully across loose rock. You had to hand it to the high plains and deserts of New Mexico. Unlike conditions in this sheer mountain fastness, the footing there was generally solid, the terrain fairly level. Easy going—except, of course, for an occasional rattlesnake.

Maxx struggled mightily, doing as much mileage straight up and down as forward, trying to leapfrog through the tangle of undergrowth.

They wound around a shallow drainage and out the other side, angling upward across the mountain flank. They stumbled through a patch of thick, musty forest and came out into another meadow. Maxx lost his happy-go-lucky cheer and grew increasingly edgy.

Jack stopped because Ev had stopped. She stood with the steep slope to her back, scanning the mountainside below them with her glasses. He was going to comment that she wasn't likely to see any goats down there, but it struck him that she probably wasn't looking for goats.

She was admiring. Slowly she lowered the glasses and gazed with the naked eye at the jumbled, orderly chaos below. Rapt, she stared down at jagged crags, patches of ragged trees, open meadows studded with stones and rocky outcrops and the dead brown grass of last summer.

She had been waiting for Jack at his apartment when he returned from church in Elbe this morning. She claimed that she wanted to see the mountain goats he mentioned in his report covering the attack on Elizabeth. That at least told him that she was reading the reports. Still, she seemed loath to work on Sunday (although she hadn't done much on Saturday either—the dating scene sure eats up one's time, and Darryl's lieu days were Saturday and Sunday) so here they were, seeking goats on a Sunday afternoon two days before Christmas.

The weather could be a lot nicer if it tried. A damp overcast hung as usual, obscuring the mountain above them and hiding the Tatoosh range across the way. A stiff breeze was picking up. It didn't look quite thick enough up there to produce snow or rain, but the day felt blustery and cold. Raw dampness cut through Jack's sheepskin-lined denim jacket and threadbare jeans.

She glanced over at him, lowered her head, and began picking her way toward him, her eyes on the ground. She really was no outdoorsman, at least not yet. Even relatively level going gave her a rough time. It wasn't all Ev, though. Repeated freezing and thawing had loosened the earth beneath their feet, making footing treacherous in spots. Rocks that you'd think were set solidly wiggled and slid when she stepped on them.

Up higher, where winter gripped far longer and more firmly, Jack was careful never to leave the trail at all. Even a few casual footfalls could damage the fragile subalpine meadows for decades. In fact, the park had a big Meadow Stomper campaign going. Its badge was a picture of a hiking boot with a red "Don't do it!" circle and slash through it. Keeping people on the established trails was one way to protect the open meadows. Another was replanting native vegetation in the damaged places and social trails. The park was doing both up around Paradise.

Once she caught up to him, he continued out and

around. If goats ranged this area, they would probably stay up in the crags beyond here at this time of day.

Maxx stopped, so quickly that Jack bumped into him. The dog woofed.

Jack pointed. Ev cooed as a pair of Pacific blacktail deer bolted out across a talus slope. They bounded spring-loaded, flying, and disappeared in a clump of subalpine firs beyond. Maxx whimpered and vibrated, his ears pricked, his natural doggy instinct to chase anything that moved held at bay by the leash.

Jack pondered the angle of the deer's flight and vaguely waved an arm toward the mountainside hard at their left. "Glass that area. They weren't running away from us. They were worried about something upslope there." He brought up his own pocket binoculars, scanning the slope. His eight-twenties had a far smaller field of vision than did her ten-fifties, but he was more accustomed to using binoculars than she.

"There!" They both said it at once.

A mountain lion padded at a steady walk along the flat top of an outcrop. Casually, it kept an eye on Jack and Ev and the dog as it worked its way across the hillside.

"Oh, Jack!" she whispered.

"King of the hill!" Jack watched the tawny beauty, the fluid grace, as enthralled as she.

"Do you suppose it's the same one we saw before?"

"Possibly. We're probably three quarters of a mile above the Grandfather Cedar right now. Maybe a little less. That would fall easily within its home range."

She watched until it disappeared beyond a rocky, jutting head. "Jack? Can we go see its tracks? Do you think it left some tracks?"

"Sure. Let's go check it out." He led off again, climbing the steep, loose hillside. Maxx bounded beside them. Moving straight up became impossible, so steeply did the slope slant now. Jack angled somewhat, switchbacking. He could reach straight out ahead of him and touch dirt.

Huffing and puffing, Ev struggled behind him. "I didn't . . . think . . . it would . . . would be this hard."

Jack scrambled up onto the outcrop where the lion had passed and stood erect at last. The slope was just as steep here, but a faint game trail traversed the hillside, tracing a nearly level line. It was that track the lion was following.

By usual Labrador retriever standards, Maxx's nose was a dud. For some reason, when it came to following a scent trail he was definitely smell-disabled. He bristled and fussed now, but he didn't seem interested in tracking the lion. Jack ordered him to lie down, and he did so without hesitating or objecting.

Jack squatted and pointed. "Those two deer were following this trail. Walking. See?" Sharply pointed little hoof tracks showed up every now and then in the dirt.

Ev squatted beside him, pressed so closely that their legs touched. "How do you know they were walking?"

"The distance between them, the way they cut into the ground. Do you see the lion's track?" He could feel her moving slightly as she breathed. A funny feeling, that.

"No." She sucked in air. "Yes. Right there." She had very good eyes. She hopped to her feet and started along the trail around the slopeside, studying the ground. "Here's where they started to run! Their feet dug in." She crouched low and actually followed a few feet on hands and knees. "I see!"

Maxx woofed again.

Jack snapped erect. "One o'clock up the slope a quarter mile!" He swung his glasses up on a pair of mountain goats. That mountain lion in its own way might be king of the hill, but these goats were king of the mountain. They reigned over an icy, rocky fastness other hoofed mammals couldn't get near. Sole monarchs of the vertical.

The goats headed off around the mountainside away from them. Impulsively Ev followed after them, staying on that faint trail, watching, keeping up with them. Jack stood

244

still. He and Maxx could do Ev no good; he and especially his dog would make the goats travel faster, if anything. Let Ev enjoy her wilderness experience. Maybe she could get a little closer to the crag kings. At least she could watch them a little longer.

Jack squatted down and rubbed Maxx's chest and neck and skull and back, all the places that dogs enjoy. He rubbed the spot down low that made Maxx's hind leg rise unbidden and wildly scratch air.

It seemed to be getting colder, and it was certainly getting darker. Nightfall arrived at 4:30 in the afternoon, and the sun refused to return until nearly 8:00 the next morning. That was another point in favor of New Mexico— winter days not nearly so short nor winter nights so long. Maxx thrust his muzzle in Jack's face and belched lustily.

In the distance around the hill, Ev screamed. Her voice pierced the cold gloom like a factory whistle. Jack's legs were churning even before he had leaped fully to his feet. She screamed again.

The lion. It had to be that mountain lion. It would have kept track of the interlopers in its territory—lions know about everything within their range, including intrusive human beings. It must have doubled back and startled her. Jack prayed to God that all the lion was doing was startling her.

He followed this faint trail at a dead run. Maxx galumphed ahead, bounding. Suddenly Maxx stopped cold and turned sideways to furiously bark at something downslope. Jack barreled into him with both legs.

The dog yiped, and Jack yiped. Where Maxx would end up was anybody's guess, but Jack was going over the side, and he couldn't catch himself. He plunged downhill headfirst.

His shoulder gouged into loose duff, and he somersaulted. He slammed into a tree. It stopped his top half, but the bottom half was still flying downslope. He spiraled away from the tree before he could arrest his slide.

245

He grabbed at thin air. He spread his arms and legs, trying to self-arrest. He went into free-fall for what felt like a mile or two before he made contact with terra firma again, slamming down a steep, loose talus slope.

He didn't actually black out, but everything went a-jumble. Sticks and branches poked him. Rocks and trees pummeled him.

He stopped.

So did the world, but only for a moment.

The rocks broken loose by his fall came tumbling down behind him, a dozen of them, crashing into the brush that had caught and held him. One struck his ear. Others came to rest against his side and hip.

He was lying on his back, tangled in low bushes growing in loose talus, and his whole body moaned. He had trouble breathing, but part of that was the stench. He seemed to have landed in a musty, no-longer-used sewer or leach field. But that couldn't be. Not out here in the middle of nowhere.

He raised his head, an experiment designed to confirm that he was still alive, and made an astounding discovery.

Bigfoot exists.

Forget the skepticism, the controversy, the exploitation. Forget the endless hypotheses about whether they ever lived. Here it was, for real, and he had just tumbled into its lap, almost literally.

It had to be nine feet high. It loomed as big as a house directly over him. Wide. So wide. And it stank.

They stared at each other, frozen inside the moment. Then the Bigfoot like a crazed gorilla leaned down, its massive paws coming at him.

An instant ago, Jack could not move. He moved now, snapping erect to sitting, flinging his arms up to protect himself from the monster. He twisted and rolled away, but the ground no longer sloped. He had reached the bottom of his downhill slide. He flipped up and around onto his knees. He didn't dare turn his back on the thing until he could gain his feet and run. With snapping black eyes the creature stared at him as it shoved aside a toppled tree that had wedged at an angle among the saplings.

Once he had seen a zoo gorilla pick up a truck tire and nonchalantly fold it in half. This beast had that kind of strength, and against it he was virtually defenseless.

He grabbed for his .38 at the small of his back, but his fall had skewed it. He had to grope, to find where it had slid along his belt. By the time he could yank it out and aim it, the beast had wheeled away. A brown-bear form rose out of the salal just beyond the beast. The Bigfoot reached down and grabbed at the bear creature as it began a lumbering run away from Jack. With a mighty heave, it hauled up the brown blob and kept going. It was leading a young one away by one arm, gripping its wrist, dragging it along.

The sight paralyzed Jack. So utterly human, to lead a child by the hand to safety. So utterly terrifying, the size and power of that thing. So utterly impossible to comprehend, this whole incredible incident.

A Bigfoot.

And young.

And . . .

Ev!

Where was Ev? Nearly a quarter mile away, probably, upslope. Part of that slope was vertical and thus for all practical purposes unclimbable. Jack remembered free-falling part way. He was going to be twenty minutes just getting back to where he started.

"Jack?" Her voice was distant, and straight up.

He yelled, "Here!" On second thought, he added, "Stay there! Stay!"

Stones and brush rattled uphill. Something was coming down the steep slope toward him. He managed to lurch to his feet and swing around to meet this new threat. Did Mom and baby have a dad on the scene?

It was Maxx, struggling to stay upright as he followed Jack's scent down the near-vertical slope. The dog was skidding out of control. He was taking seriously Jack's admonition to stay, but he couldn't stop.

Jack struggled out onto the loose talus slope, turned, and sat heavily, his heels dug in. He tried to spot where the hulking beast could have gone. It was impossible to think a creature that size could hide on this slope. It was too open, with too many meadows, too many avalanche chutes.

The thing was gone. It had never been. It was a figment of Eerie Elroy's imagination, gone horribly awry.

Maxx slid right on by, crashed into the same bush Jack had landed in, and stood up shakily.

Jack rescinded his "Stay" order. "Maxx, come."

Ev called out again, almost directly upslope.

Jack responded, spacing his words, telling her to stay there, promising to come.

Maxx clambered up through the loose talus and crawled into Jack's lap to avoid sliding back down. His right front foot was bleeding where he had literally ripped out a claw.

Jack wrapped it with his handkerchief and administered lots of sympathy and love. He searched once more for some sight of a nine-feet-tall, dark, skulking form. Nothing.

Battered and worn, he and his dog began the arduous climb back to Ev, and that faint little game trail, and sanity.

23

I'm Dreaming of a White Christmas

If thoughts could kill, Hal Edmond was in little pieces. Sliced like sushi. Dragged by a herd of stampeding buffalo. Forced to listen to six-year-olds sing the "Star Spangled Banner." Tied to the railroad tracks as the freight train came roaring.

And Jack was handling the throttle of the locomotive.

He sat asprawl in his wooden chair, as rain beat down outside his apartment window, and glared at the telephone on his table. He was within an ace of picking up the receiver, punching in Hal Edmond's number, and saying, "I quit."

Two words. That's all it would take.

Hal was so adamant that Jack was going to stay on the job, stick it out, go to Hawaii some other time. Hal was so anxious to see the case cleared. Let Hal scramble to find someone else to fill Jack's position—and see how fast his case cleared if someone new had to come in.

Two words.

The only reason Jack didn't speak them was that— the other 364 days of the year—he loved this job.

No, there were two reasons. There was the creature. He could not conceivably walk away from this now that he'd seen the creature. He could see why something like that would tip Eerie Elroy right off the scale. The beast dominated Jack's thoughts and teased his credulity. Its form, its smell, its movements haunted him.

And yet, maybe it didn't. Falling off a mountain does nothing beneficial for one's mental processes. Jack was a trained psychologist. He knew better than most people about the strange and devious tricks the mind plays with itself. He understood somewhat the sheer power that suggestion can yield.

He had seen Eerie's agitation, had listened to Eerie's sales pitch, so to speak. That would be sufficient seed to sow. The whole thing quite possibly was a false construct of his mind, a figment of imagination arising out of the same source from which dreams and nightmares spring.

And so he sat and stewed, and thought about that apparition at the bottom of the talus slope, and dreamed of Hawaii with his family even as his worst nightmare loomed in his immediate future—a white Christmas.

Very immediate. This was the twenty-fourth.

Ev's white GSA car pulled up to the battered railroad tie that formed the curb out front. She clunked into it, battering it a little more. She glanced at his window and saw him as she climbed out. He gave her a half-hearted wave.

She rode in on a blast of cold, clammy air. Hawaii's clammy air was not cold. "I'm going up to see the snow. Want to come along?"

Good old Maxx, supposedly his best friend, greeted Ev with the kind of enthusiasm he normally reserved for people bearing treats, and she never gave him goodies. She rubbed him a moment, submitting to his exuberant licking, then pushed him away.

"No, I think I'll do something new and novel and work on the case. I'm still browsing Getz's journal disks." Jack gestured toward the notebook computer humming away in front of him. "If you get tired of playing, feel free to join me."

She scowled. "I logged fifty-five hours last week, Dr. Prester. I don't owe Hal anything. And it's Christmas Eve."

"Don't I know it. I'm supposed to be on an airplane right now. Enjoy the snow."

"You're trying to make me feel guilty. Well, it's not working." She hesitated a moment. "Anyway, it's not working very well." The scowl came back to her pretty face and intensified, narrowing those huge brown eyes almost to slits. She sat down in the other chair. "Jack, I'm worried about you."

"You needn't be."

"Ever since you fell down that slope you haven't been yourself. You're dark. Brooding. That's not like you. I think you should go down into town and get checked out."

"Ev, I'm a trained emergency medical technician. I know the signs of head injury, and I don't have them. Trust me on that."

"No, I don't trust you on that! You don't realize the change. Jack, you're as creepy as Eerie Elroy, the way you sit around brooding. That's what it is. Brooding."

"I'm not brooding. I'm thinking. And if we all did a little more of that, this case might be cleared by now."

She glared at him for long, uncomfortable moments. She hopped to her feet suddenly. "You, Jack Prester, are a run in the pantyhose of my life. Merry Christmas."

"Mele Kalikimaka," he answered, but she was already headed out the door. She got back into her little white car and popped the clutch backing it out into the street. Actually, the car didn't have a clutch, but she made it jump all the same. She roared away.

Maxx curled up in the middle of the floor and instantly zonked out.

A run in the pantyhose of my life. He had never suspected a poetic streak in her.

Brooding, huh? *Ev, if you only knew.* But she wasn't going to know. No one was.

Three minutes later, here came Darryl Grade across

the street from the admin building. Jack did not want to make merry, or entertain guests, or even answer the door. Darryl came marching right to his apartment anyway.

Jack rapped on the window and waved.

Darryl accepted that as an adequate invitation and stepped inside without knocking. He grinned and took the chair that Jack proffered with a wave of the hand. Maxx, sound asleep but a moment before, leaped up and went wild with enthusiastic greetings, licking and nudging. Jack called him away. Enough is enough.

"Wet enough to drown fish out there." Darryl pulled a big bottle of Black Dog ale out from under his coat and plunked it on the table. A red Christmas bow graced its neck, shoved only slightly askew. *"Mele Kalikimaka."*

Jack smiled. "Thanks. So Ev told you."

"Yeah. Frankly, I think you're nuts. Christmas in Hawaii? I was a ranger at Haleakala for two years and got out of there the minute I could."

"My family's gathered there."

"Oh. That's different." Darryl stared at nothing a few moments.

Jack didn't feel enough like talking to start a conversation.

Darryl sounded half asleep when he spoke again. "I don't have what you'd call family anymore. My brothers are kind of scattered all over. And my parents stay to themselves. No invitations, no travel. They think all the holiday fuss and celebration's foolish. Stupid."

"I do lots of stupid things." Like playing silly board games with the cousins' kids, and trying to convince his dad of the wisdom of buying a pickup truck, and maybe eating too much on Christmas Day, and . . .

"So do I." Darryl chuckled. "I try to counter them with smart things. The bad with the good." He smiled at Jack. "That's what they call 'well balanced.' Hey. What I came by mostly to do was thank you for not causing trouble down at the Grove of the Patriarchs last Friday. You could have. You could've won too. I appreciate that you didn't."

"You're welcome. How thick are you with Jay Chambers and his tree huggers?"

"With his druids, not very. Sympathize, but not a part of it. I was serving as bouncer as a favor to him. With his environmental group, not at all. I don't agree with a lot of what they say. Even if I did, I probably still wouldn't join."

"They don't celebrate Christmas, do they?"

"The Christian druids do. Most of them don't. I'm not very close to any of the bunch." Darryl dipped his head and grinned boyishly. "See? Right back to where we started. No close people to spend Christmas with."

Jack pondered this a moment, and the open invitation Marcia's parents extended him to come to Australia. "How about your in-laws?"

"Margaret's parents? They're in Connecticut. They seem to have more or less forgotten me. No cards or anything." He looked grim.

"Are you working tomorrow?" Jack hated this dismal conversation, but he couldn't think of anything cheerful to discuss.

"Yeah. I'll probably be plowing at Paradise most of the day. It's really snowing up there. That way Len can stay home with his kids. Parents ought to be able to do that on Christmas. It oughta be written in somewhere."

"I agree. I was out of town on a special assignment one year. In November, when I accepted it, Marcia and I both figured it wouldn't matter that year—after all, Matthew was only two. Come Christmas Day, it mattered." Jack's heart went thud all over again.

Darryl hung around a few minutes more, they talked about nothing significant, Jack thanked him again for his gift of Black Dog, and the chief of maintenance wandered absently out the door.

Jack had known for years, ever since his psych courses in college, that people hit their lowest ebb over the holidays. Suicides and passive-suicidal acts skyrocket. While Marcia and Matthew graced his life, he never did understand how that could be. He understood now.

Ah, well. Back to John Getz's demented ramblings.

> November 23—I find myself losing track of the line between fact and fiction. I've used inspired invention so frequently, it blurs into reality at times and I don't remember what is truth and what is false accusation. Fancy.

> Not that it matters. One works quite as well as the other. In fact, the fancy sometimes works better, as in Kerri's case. And the hard evidence in hand, like Darryl, is particularly valuable to me as a reminder that "This is FACT." Incidentally, I found the perfect place for it. At the feet of Old Grandpa. Isn't that ironic? Ha ha.

How long did Jack go through the motions of actually reading and analyzing this weirdness? Not long. He was seriously considering just closing down and taking a nap when a horn blasted outside his door.

Darryl, in a dump truck with a blade mounted on the front, was parked in the middle of the road. He leaned on the horn again as he cranked down his window. He waved an arm frantically. *Come!*

Jack grabbed his coat and ran outside, slamming the door behind him.

"Hurry!" Darryl yelled. "Don't take time to send him back—just bring him along."

Jack was around to the passenger side of the truck before he realized who Darryl was talking about. Maxx, eager Maxx, was right at his heels. The mutt had slipped out the door in the split second before it closed.

Jack yanked the passenger door open. "Saddle up!"

Maxx leaped up inside, and Jack climbed in beside him. He slammed the door and shoved Maxx off the seat onto the passenger side floor. "You stay down there, you dork. Stay!" He fumbled his seat belt. "What's up?"

The truck lurched forward. "Len's plowing between here and Paradise. He just called in a two-car accident on the radio. Beyond Glacier Bridge. I think one of them is Ev."

What were Jack's last words to her as she left? Sarcasm. Bitterness. Invective. She had wished him a merry Christmas. He threw it back at her.

His prayers sailed heavenward in a violent, confused package of begging and pleading. They flew on wings of remorse for his curtness, his ugliness. The Bible promised that the Holy Spirit would sort it out and channel it properly, and Jack was depending on that. He couldn't think.

Maxx started to climb up onto the seat—Maxx had a tendency to motion sickness anyway, and riding down there couldn't be much fun for him—but Jack shoved him roughly back to the floor. He snapped, "Lie down! Stay!" so viciously that Maxx melted into a humble, frightened black pile.

They were doing thirty-five around tight curves in a dump truck with chains on over clear pavement. The vibration shook Jack's teeth, made his eyeballs rattle in their sockets, and ripped his kidneys off their mounts. But he wasn't about to suggest that Darryl go any slower.

Once in a while he could glimpse the responding ranger vehicle on the road up ahead, its roof-mounted light bar flashing red, white, and blue. In a race on clear pavement, this dump truck didn't stand a chance against the cruiser. But should the road turn slick ahead, Jack's money was on the truck.

Turn slick it did. White Christmas? Bah, humbug! They hit snow well this side of the Christine Falls hairpin. The rain turned into a thick, swirling, swarm of huge flakes. The windshield wipers couldn't keep up. Even before the truck reached the graceful, sweeping expanse of Glacier Bridge, two inches had accumulated on the road.

Darryl set his blade at a sharp pitch and lowered it as they approached Christine Falls, that he might plow as he went, but he didn't slow down. Snow flew like buckshot off the side of the blade.

The white ranger cruiser up ahead fishtailed on the bridge and pulled off to the side just beyond, lights still flashing. The dump truck blazed on by, and the car fell in behind. Jack saw Mike Sanchez at the wheel. Probably that was Clarissa beside him.

The Nisqually River, nothing more than a meager creek this close to its source, dashed beneath Glacier Bridge and on down its narrow canyon, bounding over the smooth river rocks and slipping between them. To the left, the snout of Nisqually Glacier peeked around the bend of the canyon. To the right, the world fell away in a deeply notched V. The road snaked up the far side of the V at a steep slant, climbing toward the crest along a bare, open avalanche chute.

Near the top of that long, straight stretch, Ev's two-car accident had become a five-car pileup. Jack could see a white car hanging precariously off the shoulder, and he knew it was hers. His prayers intensified and became even more muddled.

Darryl slowed and rearranged his plow blade. Up ahead, a red Toyota sat sideways in the road, blocking their way. Carefully, casually, Darryl engaged the Toyota and shoved it neatly aside against the inside shoulder.

"That *is* Ev!" Jack rolled his window down, but he didn't have to point. Her GSA car had tangled with the rock work that theoretically protects motorists from the sheer drop hard beside the road. The wall lay in chunks, more or less destroyed beneath her car. Her front wheels hung out over nothing at all. A million feet almost directly below, the river bubbled along the floor of the canyon.

Darryl stopped the truck just short of the nasty scene. Fluffy snow tumbled down all around them. Cars sat criss-cross and wedgewise all over the place. Another vehicle, a blue minivan, was coming down the road sideways. The driver must have hit his brakes just a little too hard. It *fwumped* casually, lazily, into the red Toyota.

From the roadside, a visitor yelled up to Jack, waving his arm toward Ev's car. "We told her to stay in it and sit still. Any little jiggle can tip it off balance. It's ready to go over the side any moment!"

Darryl snorted. "That car's not going anywhere. He's overreacting. But let's make sure." He fiddled with his controls. He ran his blade into the air as high as it would go. "It's close. Am I gonna clear?"

Jack leaped out. Maxx took that opportunity to jump up onto the seat. Jack stood close to Ev's car and crouched low, watching as Darryl maneuvered the blade over the back end of the car. He glanced inside momentarily, expecting to see her terrified face. There was her face, but she wasn't terrified, and that startled him. She looked . . . she looked . . . trusting. Relieved and trusting. That was it.

With a heavy, metallic *clang,* Darryl lowered the plow blade onto the trunk of the car and kept on lowering. Metal screeched on metal. The blade crushed the trunk.

The moment the car's rear end squashed solidly into the pavement, Jack braced a knee against the rock work and yanked open the passenger door. It took all his muscle—the door was sprung on its hinges, and its lower edge grated harshly against the stone.

Ev tumbled into his arms as a couple dozen onlookers cheered and clapped. "I knew you'd come! I knew you'd both come!" She might be excited and no longer worried, but she clung to him desperately.

On the uphill side, yet another vehicle slid into the blue van and red Toyota. Mike's cruiser disappeared around the bend at the far end of the straightaway, on his way to cut off the downhill traffic.

Ev was babbling, venting nervous energy. "Do you know, I was hanging there—I looked out the windshield and couldn't see anything! No ground out there, no anything! Clear off the edge."

From inside the cab Maxx woofed hopefully. "You wouldn't want to forget me, would you?"

Darryl appeared at their side.

Jack smiled and nodded toward the GSA car. "Your rock work's really taking a beating this winter."

"Isn't it, though!" Gently Darryl tilted Ev's head, examining the lump and bruise above her left eyebrow. "How'd you get there, anyway?"

"That gray car." She gestured vaguely. "I was driving up the hill, doing all right, I thought, and here he comes down the road toward me, and he's turning around. I mean, turning like unscrewing a lid. Full circles, two or three of them—sliding down the road in a spiral. There was nowhere to get away from him. He just spiraled right into me. Then I started turning around in circles too. I couldn't help myself."

Jack grimaced. "Ready to believe me when I say a white Christmas leaves a lot to be desired?"

"But it's so beautiful!" She pushed away from him and held a hand palm out, to catch snowflakes. "Look!" They fluttered all around her face, her injured face. They caught in her flyaway hair, white against the black, and lingered there a moment before they silently disappeared. Once in a while, one would perch on her eyelashes. Jack had never specifically noticed before how long and thick her eyelashes were.

Someone's car *whupped* into the far side of the dump truck.

A white Christmas?
Dream on.

24

What Child Is This?

In New Mexico, when the snow quits the sun comes out and the temperature drops to ten. With the wind chill factor, minus twenty. In Hawaii, the temp drops to eighty; wind chill factor seventy-nine. Here on the flank of Mount Rainier, the snow and rain had stopped, and the temperature remained exactly the same. Probably about thirty-five. Wind chill factor not much, with the protection of all these trees.

Lunch—a can of soup and sandwiches—was past. Ev seemed fairly chipper and not even particularly stiff. Of course, tomorrow was another day. Now she stood at the window in Jack's apartment staring at the gray outside.

"Darryl offered to take me up to Paradise this afternoon, but I suppose he has to plow."

"That pileup put them all behind, but they should be caught up soon. It's quit snowing. Nine cars, not to mention the snowplow fender. Enough paperwork to fill a hot-air balloon. Lovely weather."

She glanced at his face, and her own hardened. "Look, so you don't like snow. That doesn't mean that's automatically the right attitude and everyone else is wrong. It means you're in the minority, is what it means. You have this hideous attitude that whatever you think is the right thing to think and anyone else's opinion is wrong."

"That's not true. I—"

"It most certainly is, and I'm sick of it."

Jack drew air in through his nose. "Go get in the truck. I'll take you up to wallow in snow if you like."

Her voice dripped acid. "I certainly wouldn't want to put you out."

"Do you want to go or don't you?"

She glared at him for a count of ten. "Yes, I do. And I just decided I'm not going to lose the chance just because you're acting like a two-year-old. Thank you. Let's go." She picked up her parka from the chair and glided out in a huff.

The snow was probably deep enough up there by now that Maxx would have a hard time navigating through it. Jack could take him along to flounder miserably for a couple of hours, or he could let him sleep in the warm apartment. "Maxx. Stay." He walked out and shut the door behind him.

The road crew had swung the uphill gate closed across the road to keep tourists from driving up to Paradise. The downhill side was still open so that tourists could leave Paradise. Jack was not a tourist. He drove out around the red-and-white striped barrier and headed up the hill.

It might have quit at Longmire, but it was snowing again at Narada Falls. Huge, fluffy flakes drifted down almost faster than Jack's windshield wipers could swish them away. Maybe this was not such a good idea after all. But he was dipped if he'd turn around like a chicken. He kicked it into four-wheel drive and headed on up the hill.

Ev lost her angry, cloudy look for the wonder of watching the thick snowfall. She rolled down the window and held her hand out to catch the flakes as they whipped by. She didn't do that for long. She drew her hand back in. "It burns. I never thought it would burn."

Even with the four-wheeler, Jack fishtailed a little on

the tight turn above Narada Falls. Only two cars passed them coming downhill. Near the top of the Paradise ridge, the snowplow—the big grader blade—almost ran them off the road. Up in the cab, Len grinned cheerfully and waved.

Ev pointed out the right window to the jagged peaks obscured to a misty gray by the falling snow. "I forget. Is that the top?"

"No. That's the Tatoosh Range, across the valley. The peak is opposite, up that way, hidden in the clouds."

"That's right."

Michael Sanchez in a patrol car waved as he pulled out of the Paradise Visitor Center lot. His lights and siren leaped to life as he disappeared around the downhill bend.

Ev twisted to look behind. "He can't be after a speeder."

"The snowplow driver must have reported another car off the road, or an accident. All the snowplow vehicles have radios." Jack turned aside into the VC parking lot.

Only two other vehicles were left up here, and Jack's spirits, already low, sank into the deep, deep snow. He recognized Darryl Grade's dump truck sitting by the VC door.

He pulled in next to the other car, a snow-covered red sedan. Ev was out and headed for the steep snowbank before Jack could turn off the engine. He climbed out, suddenly wearied by the whole scene.

She tilted her face up, watching the flakes shoulder each other for space to come down. Jack was struck yet again by how beautiful her face was, with those huge brown eyes. She glowed. "This is amazing. I've never seen anything like this."

And then Darryl spoiled it all by coming out of the ranger bunker by the VC. He spotted them instantly and headed their way.

From out beyond the VC came a sound like a woman's moan. Jack's first thought was *mountain lion.* Up here? Could be. To see two within two days and three within two weeks? Phenomenal!

Darryl heard it too. He broke into a lumbering trot up the cement steps. He slipped and fell to one knee, hauled himself back up and continued.

A man's voice beyond the building called, "Help us!"

Ev frowned at Jack, perplexed, and jogged across to the steps and up them.

That moan again . . . no cat.

A woman.

A woman sat in the snow, her legs collapsed under her, up behind the VC. A man hovered over her, and Darryl knelt at her side.

Darryl stood up and fished out his key ring as Jack came running up. "Hang, am I glad you're here, Jack! Let me unlock the door. Help her, will you?"

Jack heard the keys and the glass door rattling as he turned to the woman.

She was fifteen months pregnant. Maybe twenty. This one wasn't a moan; it was a genuine cry. She bowed forward and murmured, "No. Not now," over and over.

Her husband looked at Jack wild-eyed.

Jack gave the guy a friendly smile. "If it makes you feel any better, this isn't the first baby to come knocking up here." He helped the woman to her feet. "I'm an EMT. Emergency medical technician. I've delivered two so far— I'd be pleased to help." *And one of them was my own son, and it was beautiful, and five years later he died.*

"And I was a paramedic for a couple years, before I entered the Park Service." Darryl appeared on the other side, and together they wafted the woman into the VC.

The building wasn't nearly as warm as Jack had hoped. They took her down to the patrol rangers' room, where there was a cot and radio. Being small, the room would be as easy to heat up as any. Ev cranked the thermostat as they stepped inside.

262

Jack introduced Darryl and Ev and reached for a handshake. "Jack Prester."

"Greg Maloney. This is my wife, Shirley." He looked around, distraught, his eyes flitting about like a bird trapped in a greenhouse. "Don't we boil water or something?"

Darryl grinned. "We'll let Ev make the coffee. You and I can go over to the ranger cache and get some blankets and things. They might even have an OB kit there." He tucked his anorak around Shirley's legs and more or less dragged Greg out the door.

Shirley curled up on her side on the cot. "I feel so terrible."

"At this stage of the game, you're supposed to." Jack took his jacket off and laid it over her until they got back with the blankets.

"I mean about this. Causing all this. It isn't due until late January, and I wanted to see Paradise one last time before the baby came. We only took a walk up the hill a little way. It was so pretty. And all of a sudden—" Another pain cut her narrative short. "I'm scared."

"Don't blame yourself for this. Blame Ev here. She dreams of having adventures. This is one of them. You just happened to get caught in the middle of her dream."

Ev stared at him and opened her mouth. Suddenly she smiled. A genuine smile at his goofiness? Miracles occur on Christmas.

Jack made some brief motions to Ev, and she nodded. She removed the woman's snowboots and pants. Since she was busy, Jack started the coffee.

Darryl and Greg returned with all manner of supplies. They bundled Shirley in blankets to keep her comfortable until the action started in earnest. Jack and Darryl scooted the cot out to the middle of the floor, accessible from all sides.

Jack paused a moment to marvel all over again at that mysterious sodality among women. Ev and Shirley instantly struck up a substantive conversation between birth pains, once comments about the bump on Ev's head were gotten out of the way. Ev was drawing more medical history from the woman per minute than Jack could hope to pry out of her per hour. First child. No prenatal problems. No complications expected. The mother-in-law was flying in next week in order to be present at the birth. That woman always was late.

Jack flopped down in the chair beside the radio and keyed the mike. The repeater barked. He and Darryl smiled at each other. At least they wouldn't be working this gig blind.

"Who's dispatch?"

Darryl reached over and adjusted the frequency. "Try Fire-com directly. Pierce County Emergency Medical Services. We ought to be able to pull in China from this high up."

"Fire-com, Paradise Ranger station." Jack didn't know the call numbers, but it didn't matter.

"Go ahead." Loud and clear.

Jack and Darryl high-fived. Shirley cried out. Her water gushed. It dripped off the cot loudly enough to be heard above the harsh, constant whisper of the heater duct.

"Jack?" Darryl looked grim. Show time.

Jack stuffed the mike into Ev's hand. "You talk to 'em."

"What do I say?!"

"Tell them what's going on." He listened to Ev's hesitant voice, but whatever she said didn't really register. He was ripping the sterile seal off the OB kit. It contained among its other accoutrements three pairs of thin rubber gloves. He put on a pair and distributed the other two to Darryl and Greg.

The head was presenting, wet and dark and curly. So far, so good.

Jack's Matthew looked like that when he was being born. It was a hospital setting, not the close confines of a cluttered ranger den, but the basics—the raw life—were the same. Jack's eyes burned, and he tightened the reins on his memories.

Greg paid all his attention to Shirley. Good. Keep the poor addled lad out of the way.

Darryl knew what he was doing, stretching the birth opening gently with his fingertips as the perineum bulged. Jack had the rubber suction syringe waiting when the head flopped free. He aspirated the miniature nose and mouth and remembered his son in spite of his best intentions.

Darryl muttered something about the cord. Not good. Deftly he slipped it over the tiny head. It had been looped tightly across the baby's throat.

They worked together so well, Jack and Darryl, in perfect synchronization. Ev's tremulous voice informed Firecom of the birth as the baby's tiny feet slipped free. Jack took over the baby, the less important medically of the two people here, and left Darryl, the more experienced, to attend to the mother.

Greg lay scrunched in an uncomfortable knot near Shirley's head, passed out cold.

The baby cried. The baby marshaled her forces and squalled, lustily, gorgeously.

"They're sending MAST out," Ev announced. "What does that mean?"

"Helicopter." Darryl answered before Jack had a chance.

Jack frowned. "How are they going to get up here in this soup? You can spit farther than you can see."

Darryl paused to clamp off the cord. "They'll fly into Longmire under the overcast and visually follow the road uphill. It's dangerous. They might have to just set down at Longmire or Kautz and wait, and we'll bring her down the hill to them."

That could be even more dangerous. In fact, if Sanchez had just responded to a road-blocking accident, it would be impossible. No good options, in other words, but Jack didn't say that out loud.

Greg was back, groggy and utterly ashamed.

Jack held the scissors out to him. "Here you go."

Psychologists with their inscrutable jargon will tell you that the father represents the first step in the baby's socialization and individuation, its separation from Mommy. He is of the family but not of that strange and wonderful duality, mother and child, that has already existed for nine months. Jack had been allowed to cut his own son's umbilical cord, accomplishing that initial and ultimate separation, and the feeling that washed over him as he did it cannot be described in any language less than that of angels.

With shaky hands and misty eyes, Greg became a father in fact, word, and deed. The baby was on its own.

Weeping joyously, Shirley held out her arms.

"It's pretty cool in here yet. Skin to skin," Jack suggested, "to keep her warm."

Instantly Shirley opened her parka and flannel shirt. She took her brand new daughter tightly against her, snuggling her in her own body warmth. Perhaps some of her joy was simple relief.

Darryl swathed mother and child in warm blankets.

"Be back in a couple minutes." Jack tried not to say it curtly. He brushed past Ev as she reached again for the mike. Fire-com was asking something; he didn't hear just what.

In shirtsleeves he pushed out the glass doors into the swirling snow. He ought to gauge visibility in case the chopper pilot should ask, mark a good landing spot for when they arrived, perhaps wait out here to wave them in.

All he could do was sob.

It passed quickly. These jags of sorrow didn't last long anymore. It left behind the dull, numbing void that had become so familiar. He jogged around and down to his truck, as much to give his body something to do as to retrieve a tissue. He dug into the Kleenex box under the seat and blew his nose. The void filled up then with anger, also a familiar feeling. He hated himself when he came apart this way.

The temperature was probably not less than thirty-five. The snow became a rain-and-snow mix, and Jack quietly rejoiced. It would not accumulate so quickly or so deeply now. It would not obscure a chopper pilot's vision.

His M-1 key opened the ranger bunker. Their snow shovel stood propped just inside the door. He walked out into the widest part of the parking area, where trees and low bushes and stone retaining walls would not interfere with the bird's rotors, and began shoveling a big X.

The snow and rain ceased.

He sensed her rather than heard her. He straightened and looked behind him. Ev grimaced uncomfortably and acted as if it were a smile. She was wearing her coat again.

He grimaced a smile back at her and resumed shoveling. "How's it going in there?"

"Fine. Greg and Shirley were going to name it Rebecca if it was a girl, but they just now changed their minds. They're naming her Angel instead."

Jack's brain was so slow it took him a moment to connect. "Of course. Born in Paradise on Christmas Eve."

"Why do babies cry right away?"

Jack went back over the leg of the X he'd done first, making it good and black. "You've just been squeezed through a tube that's smaller than you are, it's cold and noisy out here, you only scored 60 percent on your Apgar test, and already you owe the government almost seven thousand dollars. You'd cry too."

"I mean, why do you make it cry?"

"Help the baby inflate its lungs. Fill its lungs with air." Jack should have said that in the first place. She'd asked a legitimate question. He should have answered it right.

Undaunted, she pressed on. "When Shirley expelled the afterbirth—incidentally, it's intact, Darryl says—I didn't

267

think it was gross. That really surprises me. You know what they look like."

"Terrible."

"More than terrible. Really hideous. But I didn't turn off. I could help him, and it didn't even bother me. I can't believe the changes in me that I—"

"Hey, look. Let's talk about something else, all right?"

She froze. He couldn't bear to look at her. He already had a mental image of the hurt in her doe eyes. He shoveled snow with a vengeance, feeling the welter of ugly, churning, indescribable emotions bubbling up inside again.

The chopper's *bligga-bligga-bligga* rattled in the trees somewhere below them. The rumble became a loud, rapid *plakl-plak-plak-plak-plak* as the monster rose into line-of-sight view. The pilot left the road and arched directly up the hill to the Visitor Center. His deafening, inelegant bird settled itself cautiously onto Jack's giant X.

Ev the adventurer was the one who greeted the paramedic and nurse on board, eagerly watched them as they tossed their gurney out into the snow, led the way up into the VC. Ev the budget analyst, who once upon a time couldn't stand anything that wasn't urban in form and function, was enthusiastically bouncing around almost a hundred miles from the nearest golden arches and rotating red-and-white bucket in the sky.

Jack put the snow shovel away and went inside. Greg glowed as he carried his daughter, firmly swaddled in a receiving blanket. Shirley glowed as the nurse strapped her down in the gurney, and they maneuvered her out the door. Ev glowed from the thrill of it all. She handed Jack his sheepskin-lined denim jacket without comment. Even Darryl glowed as he locked up the VC.

The bird lifted off and tipped away down the hill. Its *plak*s melted into *bligga*s, which dissolved in the thickening sky.

Jack more than half expected Ev to invite herself into

Darryl's vehicle for the ride down the hill. Darryl was cheery. Darryl was ripening into serious boyfriend status. Darryl was a genuine hero flush with the thrill of not just one victory but two, both on the same day. Jack didn't quite understand why she climbed into his truck. He wasn't sure, either, whether he could muster the emotional strength to be decent toward her, let alone cheerful and friendly.

Darryl's dump truck disappeared down around the bend.

He torched it off and let it idle a few moments as he cranked the defroster up to high. The film of moisture on the windows disappeared into thin air.

Ev was looking out at the snow, rapt. "It's going to be dark before we get back to Longmire, isn't it?"

"Almost. I'll take you on down to your cabin so you don't have to drive in this."

"I don't have anything to drive."

"Mike was talking about loaning you one of the spare GSA vehicles stashed down at Tahoma Woods. You'll have wheels tomorrow, assuming you're not gunshy. It's OK if you don't want to drive in this stuff anymore."

"I don't know. It might be kind of fun. Certainly different."

Jack snorted. "Well, if you want to experiment, do it in a parking lot. An empty lot." He eased it out onto the main road and headed home.

Home? A rattletrap furnished apartment he'd been in two weeks.

He glanced at her. She was angry. Big deal. So was he, and he wasn't sure why. "When you and Darryl went to the Zoolights." He glanced at her again. "You two stayed in town overnight."

She looked at him sharply, glaring.

He asked then, because he had to know. "Together?"

"That's none of your business!" she exploded. "I'm surprised at you, Jack. Mr. Puritan turns into Mr. Nosy."

"Everything Darryl does or does not do is relevant to

269

the case. You know that. And you never know which data are relevant until you clear the case and look back."

"Not private stuff!" She sat under a silent black cloud a few moments. "As it happens, no. Not together. Are you satisfied, Mr. Nosy?"

"Just filing it with all the other information." Which was malarkey. He had asked, and her answer filled him with the most unexpected relief. Ridiculous. She was a grown-up. What she did or did not do was strictly her own business.

Darryl wasn't plowing. Apparently he figured Len's last pass there was good enough. His tire tracks, wide as sidewalks, drew parallel lines through maybe an inch of snow.

Ev's accident had more of a telling effect on her than she might admit. She had lost her bubbly enthusiasm for adventure. She sobered. Within a few miles she began acting a little worried. She gripped the dashboard, even though they were creeping along at less than twenty-five.

He was having trouble concentrating. His muddle of conflicting feelings kept distracting him. That was bad.

"Jack? What do deer eat when it's snow like this?"

"They browse low tree branches, or they'll migrate to lower elevations where the snow cover is thin enough they can paw down through it to the grass." There. He gave her a decent answer once, but not because he was a decent guy. He was too drained, too tired, to get clever.

"Do you suppose that one was migrating?"

"Which one? I didn't see it."

"On the bank above the road back there. I thought you did."

Boy, he really was operating low-octane. He'd better shape up. He turned his headlights on, although it wasn't quite dark enough even in this dense forest to make a difference.

Then the rear end let go suddenly and slid around to the left. He counter-steered. Front axle and back swapped

270

ends. He swung the wheel desperately to bring it back. The axles swapped again, and he was moving head-downhill as the rear end slid back and forth like a pendulum. It took him more than a hundred yards to really straighten out, and then they were in the curves below the falls, and he was losing it again.

A deer bolted out across the road ahead of them and down over the side, here and gone again, *blink blink*. Involuntarily, stupidly, Jack hit the brakes in the kind of knee-jerk reaction a total nincompoop would make.

All four tires unhooked, and the truck went into a graceful, slow-motion pirouette. Jack heard a back fender *thunk* against something, probably a tree trunk. His headlights swept across the downhill road and into the trees, then across the uphill road.

Ev screamed. The cab tipped up and backward violently, snapping his head back. Glass and metal crunched. The noise seemed far off somehow.

Darkness.

25

Gloria in Excelsis Deo

Near darkness. Silence. Cold. Lots of cold. Lots of dark and silence too. The sensations made no sense.

Jack was sitting at an extreme tilt, practically on his left side, and here was a tree in his lap. The driver's side door was caved in completely, its glass gone, and this stupid wet tree trunk was right in his stupid face. The windshield was in one piece yet, yet in a million pieces, as windshield glass will do. A major tree limb had popped the left side of the windshield free of its mount. A foot of space separated it from its frame.

He looked uphill—very sharply uphill—at Ev. Her seat belt kept her from sliding into him. She was still bracing against the dashboard, her face frozen in a shocked look of disbelief. The headlights had gone out. In fact, so had the motor.

Fear and fury welled up and boiled over as his senses finally came tiptoeing back to where he could manage them again. He was so angry at himself for this brainless blunder that he couldn't think. And he was angry at God. Mostly he was angry at God. He was angry about this predicament, and about his wrecked truck, and about the sorrow in his life, and about the injustice of all this.

"Jack?" Ev was thawing out, somewhat, but she still looked dazed.

"Are you all right?"

"I guess so. I'm sorry I wanted to come up here. Twice in one day. You'd think I'd learn."

The appropriate response was "Aw, that's OK." Jack couldn't bring himself to make it. "There seems to be a tree in the way over here. Can you get out your side?" He twisted the ignition key a couple times. Dead. The battery must have broken loose. In this Ram, that meant that the mount was ripped off.

"I think so." She twisted and struggled and finally shoved her door open. She hung both legs out the door to keep from sliding when she popped the seat belt.

He waited until she wiggled herself out before releasing his own belt. He crawled up the seats to climb out.

The truck was wedged at a sorry angle among the trees, right headlight now its highest part, a good six feet down off the road. The back end had collided with something big and unforgiving. The rear bumper was mashed in, the bed bent, Maxx's iron cage crushed and twisted.

Jack might have made a howlingly moronic mistake, and he might be livid toward God, but that didn't mean he was totally stupid. They needed Him now, and nothing less would do. He swallowed his pride almost literally—it stuck like a lump in his throat—and in silent prayer begged God's help. He pleaded for wisdom and resources to succor and protect both himself and Ev.

Slipping and staggering, Ev climbed up onto the road. "What will we do, Jack? Do you know where we are?"

"Not exactly, but I'm going to." He groped around under his seat and found the topo map.

Her feet slid out from under her, and she fell heavily as she tried to return to him. It took her two false starts before she got back up on her legs and made it down the steep roadside slope. She slammed into him and clung to his arm to right herself.

"We can't just stay in the truck, right, Jack?"

"Right. With the windows out it'll get too cold. And we can't run the heater with the electrical system gone."

"Darryl will come up and get us."

"That's assuming he knows we're not safe at home and that we're still up here and need help." Jack got the flashlight out of his glove box. He couldn't see the lines in this dim light.

"He'll call me and I won't be there, and he'll come looking."

"He'll call you and you won't be there, and he'll call me and I won't be there, and he'll assume we went out for dinner together on Christmas Eve."

"I know!" She brightened. "You said once you keep your camping gear behind the seat. We can make a sort of camp until someone realizes we're here. They'll open the road up tomorrow. Even if they don't for some reason, we can walk down after resting here tonight."

"My sleeping bag is on the bed in the apartment getting dog hair all over it now, because Maxx always sneaks up on my bed when I'm not there. And the camp stove and lantern are sitting on the counter." He traced with his finger where the road went exactly. They were right . . . there.

"Oh. That's right. You didn't put it back in the truck after the power outage." She said it like an accusation, as if he ought to attend to that sort of thing promptly.

Jack pointed out the distance on the map. "If we walk this far uphill, we can spend the night in the restrooms at Narada Falls. We're both probably too tired to make a walk like that in a reasonable time through this slick snow, and it'll be dark in half an hour. If we walk downhill, we have to go this far to find shelter. See?" He showed her.

"That's even farther."

"And just as hard walking because of the slipperiness, despite that it's downhill."

274

God! Wisdom, please? Resources. I beg you. Angry as I am, I know I need you.

"What's that?" She pointed to an inked-in X.

A ski-and-saddle hostel.

Of course!

He tipped his head up to check out the darkening sky. Neither of them was so weary, emotionally or physically, that they couldn't claw their way safely to that point before nightfall. "You know how to read one of these things?"

"Is it the same as navigational charts?"

"Sorta. We're here, see? We follow this faint line, going neither uphill nor downhill, till we come to this. Then we scramble straight up a couple hundred feet, and we should hit the new trail. See? And that will take us to the hostel in another hundred feet."

She studied the map a long moment, bobbed her head, and stepped back. She was game. And her sudden, solid courage surprised him.

Jack had no idea how well the hostel would be stocked, if at all. He pulled from behind his seat some freeze-dried trail meals, a grotesque package begging to be labeled "Unfit for human consumption." He found a few other things he thought they might use. The Kleenex box was one of them. He stuffed it all into a canvas shopping bag because his rucksack was down at the apartment. He penciled a note explaining what they were doing and stuck it under his windshield wiper, bemoaning all over again the lack of a windshield to wipe.

They headed off around the hill single file, slipping and sliding and tripping in the tangled ground cover.

Thanks to the heavy overcast, their light faded even before 4:00. An ominous tension hung in the air. It was gloomy, unsettling. Jack paused every few yards, listening. If he had hackles, they would have bristled.

The hostel stood away from the main trail on a side path, and the X was off by a hundred yards, so they almost

275

missed it. Jack swept the hillside with his flashlight every few steps, and a glint off a window showed them where it was. His left shoulder was getting stiff and sore where the tree had slammed it. Ev's head must really be hurting. Twice in one day. She followed him meekly back the hundred feet of side trail to the hostel.

"Kerri was right. It's a cute little place." Ev stepped up onto the broad full-front porch.

It had a built-in bench to one side of the door and half a cord of stovewood stacked on the other. The siding was of milled logs, but Jack wasn't sure it was a log cabin as such. The roof pitched steeply.

The door was locked, but his M-1 let them in. He stood a moment, surveying their facilities. A sink and counter took up the far wall. The place could sleep eight— four bunk beds on each side wall—but the table just out from the sink looked too small to feed eight at a sitting, and there were only four chairs. A little potbellied stove sat in the middle of the floor in a box of sand.

"What a cute little stove!"

"You obviously have never tried to keep a wood stove going all night. The firebox is so small we'll be feeding it every forty-five minutes."

Since the inside was just as cold as the outside, building a fire was the first order of business. The place was beautifully set up for that. Beside the stove, a cut-off carton of split kindling and small pieces sat ready. A box of matches was taped to the side of the carton, though Jack had his Bic lighter. Paper. Any paper?

Paper indeed. Here beside the door were stacked enough newspapers to keep a recycler happy for days, a pile more than two feet high. On the other side of the door sat an even higher pile of odd paper. Bags. Half the stack was kitty-litter and ten-pound dogfood and catfood bags, all neatly folded. The other half was grocery bags. Someone must have donated a lifetime's accumulation of paper grocery bags.

Jack pulled a handful of dogfood bags out from underneath. The rest of the stack slid gracelessly over on its side into a mess. Typical of the day.

"You always pick one off the bottom?" Ev asked.

"I want the waxed paper. It should catch instantly." He'd restack the mess later. Maybe never. He was drained. He cranked the damper open, laid the crumpled paper, stacked in some kindling, zapped it in a couple spots with his Bic. He watched the fire leap to life. He watched the smoke come boiling out. Blocked chimney. He let loose an expletive, and he never used expletives.

No blocked chimney. The stovepipe damper was closed. He twisted it open to vertical. Problem solved. He should have seen the second damper before he started. His world was coming apart even as it was coming together.

He stood up and ran his flashlight around the room and into the rafters.

"What are you looking for?"

"Kerosene lamp or Coleman lantern. Light." None.

Ev started going through the drawers under the counter. She pulled out a box of a dozen six-inch white kitchen candles. "No lantern, maybe, but there has to be a hundred boxes of these. You mentioned the hostels were stocked by private donors and merchants. I wish a merchant had remaindered some candlesticks."

Jack lit a candle and tipped it slightly to drip a tiny blob of wax on the table. He pressed the candle base into it. He emptied his canvas bag item by item onto the counter as Ev explored the rest of the drawers.

"Here's the candlesticks. Someone must have bought out a thrift shop." She set up another four or five candles. "Look. These are kind of cute." She held up two. "Don't you think so?"

"Yeah." He didn't really look. He shuffled through his little sealed plastic bags of freeze-dried entrées. Plastic food. "No Christmas goose or plum pudding. You want pork chops, beef stew, or stroganoff?"

277

She sounded dispirited, probably by the meager choices. "Pork chops, please."

Jack was getting really, really tired. He scooped snow into a pan and put it on the stove to melt. He stuffed in some heavy pieces of wood, now that the fire was going well and they were getting a nice bed of coals.

Why didn't Ev help with some of this? Because her idea of roughing it was Motel 6, that was why. She set the table, but until they got some water boiling, they weren't going to have any dinner. It was past seven before they could sit down to their reconstituted repast. Jack blessed it and felt hypocritical, even downright guilty, knowing he was still totally bent out of shape at God.

He could be eating roasted pig at a luau right now, maybe even right this minute. And fresh, really-really fresh pineapple. Then there were his mom and dad and cousins and aunts and uncles eating pig and pineapple too. The whole crowd was making merry out there in the middle of the Pacific Ocean, basking in warmth, laughing and acting silly.

Freeze-dried beef stew. The cabin still wasn't warmed up enough to take your coat off.

Jack didn't have any coffee with him, but they found some instant in a cupboard. No sugar. Ev drank hers black, but Jack wasn't quite to that point of desperation yet.

She watched him from across the table. The candle flames danced as a dozen points of light in her eyes. They glistened with tears held back. "I wanted a white Christmas." She sighed. "Here it is. I have snow on Christmas. But I didn't exactly want to spend Christmas Eve with Scrooge."

"The luck of the draw. I was kind of thinking of spending it with people who greet you with 'Aloha,' myself." His shoulder ached.

Her voice dripped bitterness. "Yes. It's too bad you don't constantly get your own way. Life would be so much more fun for all of us."

That did it. As tired as he was, he couldn't just sit here anymore. He left his dirty paper plate on the table, lurched to his feet, and headed for the door.

"Jack? Where are you going?"

"I'm taking my cloud of gloom for a walk so it won't blot out your happy little ray of sunshine."

"Don't forget your flashlight."

He would have, had she not mentioned it, and that fried him even worse. It was bad enough to be beholden to her in the investigation, and far worse to be in her debt regarding that nasty little scene in the Clearcut. It doesn't feel good to get rescued by a girl. Everything she said and everything she did somehow showed him up. He snatched his flashlight off the counter and breezed out the door.

The cold air did nothing to cool his frustration and fury. He followed the path out to the main trail and walked aimlessly southeast. Actual snowfall was minimal beneath these dark evergreens. Their branches caught most of the snow before it reached the ground. Their dripping compacted what little snow there was and iced it over. It crunched as he walked.

He didn't walk far. He was too weary of mind and body. When the flashlight's nervous beam flitted past an eighteen-inch-high fallen log beside the trail, he sat down on it. The snow that iced the log crunched too. He pocketed the flashlight and listened to the constant whisper of tumbling snow in the cold darkness, but what he really heard was God.

His mind roared out at God his own complaints and arguments—the sorry day gone all awry, his truck, their predicament, and, somewhere far, far away, palm trees and warm breezes and glissading steel guitars.

Mele Kalikimaka.

Scrooge had it right with his humbug. Good old Ebenezer never got to bask with his loved ones on a tropic beach either.

Jack sat and fed on his own misery so long and deliciously that he lost the taste for it. His angry soul quieted from a howl to a whimper.

And then God, no longer patient with such self-pity, planted a few harsh realities of His own in Jack's heart.

You haven't been paying attention to what's been going on here, Jack, son. You always bring your dog along. Always. You just happened to leave him home on this one occasion when his cage was crushed. He would have been in it. But do I get any thanks? Do you remember how bent out of shape you were a couple of days ago when Ev didn't thank you right away for bringing her a box of Kleenex? How do you think I feel?

Darryl and Greg and Shirley, not to mention My child Angel, needed you two up there this afternoon. You're constantly babbling, 'Thy will be done,' in your prayers. All right. So you were doing My will in the place where I put you, just as you're always asking, but do I get any thanks?

You found that hostel, didn't you, even though you couldn't see it and you didn't know where it was. You're essentially unhurt. So is Ev, which is exactly what you begged of Me this morning. But do I get any thanks?

Do you realize how much Ev learned about herself this day, and how much she grew? She's a grand sight more appreciative than you are, and she doesn't even know Me.

"You wrecked my truck! You trapped me here in these cold, creepy woods when everyone I love is in Hawaii celebrating the birth of Your Son!"

You need Hawaii to celebrate My Son? You could do that in Minnesota. So your truck is wrecked. It's a piece of metal.

"But why?!"

Why not? I send My rain on the just and the unjust without prejudice. Fortune and misfortune come to saint and sinner alike. You know that. Still, I spared you. Instead of making you two walk for miles through the snow when you're both dangerously fatigued, I set you up in a snug

280

and homey situation. You have food, drink, comfort, warmth. What else do you think you need? Why are you still at odds with Me? How much more shall I do for you before you wake up and realize that you are blessed?

He sat in the dank, dismal blackness while the wet log sucked the warmth out of him wherever he touched it and the snow soaked through his shoes. Misery and remorse plunged him into a blackness darker than the night.

Not only had he thrown a thankless tantrum when he didn't find exactly the gift he wanted under the Christmas tree, he callously damaged Ev's gift, the thing she had asked for and received. How ugly, petty, un-Christlike. Indefensible. Pick your favorite pejorative adjective—they all fit.

He gave up trying to pray in words. Words could not express his feelings and bitter insights now. No sentence, no matter how carefully crafted, could come near saying what poured out of his heart. He was so sorry. He begged forgiveness, knowing God was much quicker to forgive him than was he himself, knowing the cost to God was infinitely more than the cost to him.

Thanksgiving. His dog was safe and warm at home. His whole extended family was well-knit, warm, and happy, without the friction or strife that plagues so many families. He and Ev . . . their situation . . . Angel . . . the gift of a Savior . . . all of it . . . all of it and more. Look at the bounty! Thank God. The intensity of his feelings—remorse, thanksgiving, sorrow, relief—pressed him down mightily and lifted him up mightily. In the cold, wet darkness, light filled him, and peace.

He wasn't going to be able to make up for his spoiled asininity, but he could do a little something to mend Ev's life. His heart still aching from his own nastiness, Jack stood up and crunched through the snow, backtracking to the cabin.

Ev was sitting at the little table as he came clumping

in. He stomped the snow off his shoes. She watched him, frowning.

This pile of brown paper grocery bags to start fires with was no less a gift of God than the hostel itself. He fished through it and chose four dozen mid-size rectangular sacks, plain ones with no printing on them. He grabbed four one-dozen boxes of household candles and his butane lighter and headed back outside. He heard Ev's chair scrape as the door closed.

He needed dry dirt or sand—wet dirt would make the grocery bags wilt and melt. Not to worry. He pried loose some of the lath under the north side of the porch. Underneath it was all dry dirt, and so powdered that it wasn't frozen stiff. It smelled moldy under here and stale, like a long-abandoned barn.

Scoop three inches of the cold, powdery dirt into the bottom of each of two opened bags. Fold the cut upper edge of each outward and over into a two-inch cuff all around the top. Carry the bags out and position them one by one. Place half a dozen along the front of the porch and the rest of them in a line out the path toward the trail. Pay attention that the seam down the back of the bag faces away from the person who would look at it.

It took him two dozen trips.

As he came and went, he noticed Ev watching him soundlessly from the porch. She stood in complete shadow, silhouetted against the near blackness of snow and sky beyond the porch roof, dark against the darkness.

He stuck a candle into the dirt in each bag, the farthest ones from the cabin first and the ones on the porch last. Finally, he flicked the Bic and lit the candles, doing the ones on the porch first and lighting his way out along the path to the end of the row.

Silently, Ev followed behind him through the beaten snow.

Where the path met the trail, she stood pressed so close beside him he could feel the motion of her breathing. She was looking. Just looking. Perhaps *gazing* was a better word.

The golden glow of four dozen luminarias limned the pathway and porch. Forty-eight soft, gentle lights stood triumphant against the blackness of the cloudy, moonless night.

The people who walked in darkness have seen a great light.

I am the light of the world.

The Light of the World is come!

Gloria in excelsis Deo!

"Thank you, Jack," she whispered. "It's beautiful."

"Merry Christmas."

26

The First Noel

When an endangered species is the principal suspect in a murder, how vigorously do you prosecute the case? Do you lay off and let the creature live undisturbed? Or are you morally bound to clear the case and let the chips fall where they may? If you are a Bigfoot, does killing a human being constitute murder in your own eyes? Probably not. Were the situation reversed, a human being who killed a Bigfoot would hardly call it murder.

Jack mulled these imponderable questions as he sprawled in an overstuffed chair in Kerri Haskell's living room. And then he thought about the utter absurdity of even asking himself such questions. He was basing his assumption that Bigfoot actually exists on the testimony of an insane man and a trick of his own mind. For the more he thought about his own supposed sighting, the more he became convinced that it never happened. It was inconceivable that, with 238 square miles of national park for the creature to be roaming in, Jack would slide down a talus slope and land at its feet. That would be statistically absurd. Elk and deer were common. Squirrels very common. He didn't land near any of those.

No, the episode with the Bigfoot was a weird and wacky result of his tumble. Nothing more.

At his feet, Maxx snarfed, yawned, and rolled over. His hulking body slammed against Jack's foot. The mutt obviously didn't care. He smacked his lips, belched, and drifted back to sleep.

"You want to climb Everest? Or K-2? Or one of those biggies? You come practice on Mount Rainier. That's how challenging Mount Rainier is. It has fairly easy routes, and also some of the most dangerous in the world." Jeff Haskell, seated at Ev's right on the sofa, was showing her what pitons and carabiners and such are. He had quite a collection in his climbing box. His ice ax, another item of his show-and-tell, stood propped against the coffee table.

On Ev's left, Darryl Grade sat close to her, peering over her shoulder. Since Darryl was an ex-ranger, he knew climbing. The basic ranger intake training includes some technical climbing. Therefore, his real interest lay not in pitons and carabiners but in pressing close. The thought of it all depressed Jack.

Ev bobbed her head, wide-eyed. Her fine black hair floated. "This is the first time I've ever been around a mountain you'd climb. I mean, that you'd need special equipment to climb. What's it called?"

"Technical climbing." Jack had pitons and 'beeners in his own jump box, along with a coil of obsolete goldline he'd picked up at a surplus store. He didn't get into rock climbing seriously, thanks to a certain degree of acrophobia, but he could pull it off if he had to.

Ev looked at Jack. "I suppose you know how to use all this stuff. You climb, don't you?"

"Only when forced into it. I don't climb recreationally, like Jeff here does. Since the Park Service ranger training center is on the south rim of the Grand Canyon . . ."

Ev frowned. "Horace M. Albright Training Center? What about Harper's Ferry?" No doubt those were names of places she'd seen on accounting ledgers in the Washington office. Jack knew she'd never been to either of them.

"Horace M. specializes in ranger skills. Harper's Ferry is mostly for interpretation. Naturalists. At the Grand Canyon, you go out on the rim for the hands-on training. That's a vertical mile to practice in. Pretty spectacular." Jack had hated that part of the course. And Grand Canyon is such a nice park too.

Over in her rocker in the corner, Kerri smiled wistfully. "I'd love to be stationed at the Grand Canyon. Or maybe just spend a month there. Explore. Go where the crowds don't go."

Jeff dumped his loose gear back in the box a fistful at a time. "Kerri can handle herself in the woods like the last of the Mohicans. She's an excellent outdoorsman. Outdoorswoman? What would it be, Liz?" If he was taunting Elizabeth, he didn't let it show in his voice or demeanor.

Elizabeth Munro sat in the corner near the twinkling Christmas tree. "Two words, I'd think. She's a good outdoor sportsperson."

Outdoor sportsperson. Gender neutral. Whoop-de-doo. Five syllables to do the work of three or less. That sort of thing irritated him, but he kept his mouth shut. Of the six people in this room, Jeff and Kerri were married, Ev and Darryl were sort of going together, and that left Jack, unpaired in life, with Elizabeth Munro, also unpaired— which made the two of them into a pair by default, and that irritated him even more than did Elizabeth's weird terms for everything.

Christmas Day ought never be irritating, either. And yet, as Christmas Days go, this had been a gentle, happy one. Kerri and Jeff, in the best Park Service tradition, had invited in the strays—Elizabeth, Jack, and Ev. Apparently Darryl came over for Christmas every year since his wife was killed, so he counted as a stray. Perhaps what irritated most was that Jack had never before been a stray. Always in the past, his extended family were the gatherers-in of the less fortunate. His first Christmas as a stray. *Hmph.*

His mind, though, kept drifting back not to pairings

and strays but to the puzzle of John Getz. He thought he had the equally onerous puzzle of Bigfoot solved, but he couldn't be certain. His hallucination at the bottom of that talus slope kept nagging at him.

He turned the puzzle around and started looking at it from John Getz's probable perspective. Whom would Getz fear, if anyone? From which direction might he believe danger could come? Nothing in his journal suggested he feared anyone at all. It also suggested he ought to fear everyone. He was an equal opportunity pest, harassing everyone with whom he came into contact.

Jack tried putting a different face to the puzzle. Why would Jay Chambers want to murder Getz? Why would Elizabeth? Why would Eerie Elroy, for that matter? Or Darryl, or Jeff, or Kerri, or Mike Sanchez? Each of them had reason and opportunity, but none had sufficient reason to off a person. Neither, that Jack could see, would any of them have some personal reason to use an obsidian blade.

Kerri was practically shouting. "Jack! Earth to Jack! Come in, Jack."

"What?" He snapped back to the moment.

Ev complained, "He's been like this ever since he slid down that slope Sunday afternoon. I'm worried about him."

Kerri was perched on the edge of her chair, ready to stand up. She repeated what was apparently her original question. "Would you like more coffee?"

"Oh. No. No, thank you. I'm fine."

She nodded, gathered up Darryl's and Jeff's coffee mugs, and headed for the kitchen.

Jack sat up straight and kicked his dog. Time to go, before Ev started ragging on him again to see a doctor. "Jeff, I appreciate your hospitality immensely. Dinner was great, and the atmosphere. Neat celebration. Thank you."

"We enjoyed it. Glad you could come over."

Then Elizabeth actually said, "Do you want me to drive you down to your apartment?"

287

Jack couldn't believe she'd say that. "It's four hundred yards. Less."

"But it's dark out."

Kerri came in and handed Jeff and Darryl their coffee refills.

Jack smiled charitably at Elizabeth as he nudged Maxx to his feet. "I appreciate the offer, but Kerri's in here, and the gorilla's in the closet. Nothing scary out there tonight."

Kerri cackled.

"Oh, hey. Before you go." From his pocket Jeff fished a single key on a ring. He tossed it to Jack. "It's our beater Volkswagen—the green squareback out there. Use it until your truck gets out of the hospital."

Jack looked at the distinctive key. The shaft was twisted a bit. "Sure you don't need it?"

"We're sure. It's not in real good shape on the outside, but it runs good. It'll get you where you're going."

Jack, an old associate, if not friend, of various Volkswagens, smiled. "What they call a classic, right? How many horses?"

Jeff smiled too. "Depends how many cylinders are firing."

"OK. How many cylinders fire?"

"All of them, sooner or later. Just don't count on any regularity."

Kerri sat down again. "It has a few little quirks. The windshield defroster is the bath towel tucked under the seat. To get it into reverse, push down and sort of give it a hard shove. And the passenger-side door won't lock or unlock from the outside. There's a key broken off in it. You have to lock it from the inside by pushing on the button. And the heater only works when the outside temperature is above seventy degrees."

"Sounds normal to me. I really appreciate this. Thank you." Jack stood up. He thanked both of them again and excused himself. He left the unpaired Elizabeth Munro behind and walked out into the cold, wet night. He ought to put Maxx on leash, but he didn't bother. The dog ranged out beside him, eagerly exploring smells at the bases of trees and fire hydrants.

The one or two inches of snow here at Longmire from the fall last night had melted away, leaving the ground soggy. Jack paused beside the Haskells' green VW square-back and tried the left door. It was not locked. The dome light was either turned off or inoperative. A big dark rust patch spread out across the roof. He wasn't about to knock it, though. It was wheels. He closed the car door and continued down the hill. He'd come get it if and when he needed it.

He thought again about the walk from the hostel out to the road at sunrise this morning, and how cheerfully Ev took the inconvenience. To her it had been just another stage in a new and thrilling adventure. He remembered his curious sense of loss as the tow truck hauled his beloved Ram up out of woods and dragged it mutely off to town.

He thought too about Ev's initial uneasiness as they sat down with the Haskells to Christmas dinner. What was old hat to him was apparently brand new to her. Her first Christmas of togetherness. A whole new dimension—family closeness and the Park Service as family—was reshaping her life. Now that he was reminded of the changes in her, he saw more and more of them.

The hearse was parked in front of his apartment. Now what?

Eerie Elroy sat with his back against Jack's door, his knees drawn up. Maxx trotted over to him and licked him generously about the face.

Jack smiled and extended a hand. "I suppose I should fire a shot across your bow in greeting—but what the hey, it's Christmas. Come on in."

Eerie chuckled. "Take it from me and don't bother. It doesn't discourage anybody." He let Jack give him a yank to his feet. He followed Maxx and Jack inside.

Jack flicked on the lights and turned the stove on under his teakettle. "Coffee or tea?"

"Sure. Guess so." Eerie flopped into a chair unbidden. "You got connections with Washington, don'tcha?"

"Not as many as I'd like." Jack might be resigned to missing out on Hawaii, but that didn't absolve Hal of unfairness. "What's up? People trying to kill you again?"

"Not that I noticed. And Sanchez gave me my gun back—as a favor to you, he said. Thanks." Eerie rubbed his face. He looked even wearier than he had on the fifteenth, when Jack told him about his dog. "It's Washington who declares what's wilderness areas and endangered species, right?"

"In broadest terms, right." Jack swung the second kitchen chair around so as to nearly face Eerie and sat down.

"How do I go about getting Washington to set aside a Bigfoot preserve, as an endangered species?"

Jack whistled. "Declare Bigfoot an endangered species, and designate the Cascades and Sierras as a wilderness preserve? That'd sure be the ultimate spotted owl."

"So how do I do it?"

"I'm not certain the usual channels would work. Did you run this idea past Jay Chambers? He ought to know more about it."

Eerie's demeanor cooled noticeably. "He says it can't be done. That's 'cause he doesn't think there is such a thing, you know?"

Jack yearned to describe his hallucination. He refrained. "The park is already wilderness area, you know. Your efforts would be focused on national forest lands not included in the wilderness designation yet."

"Mm." Eerie eyed him suspiciously. "You think I'm nuts, don't you?"

"Yeah, but it's a wholesome kind of nuts. Crazy with a purpose."

Eerie watched him a long, long moment. He grinned

290

suddenly, with crooked yellow teeth. "Know what I appreciate about you? You're honest. You care. Like coming to tell me about my dog. You didn't have to do that. And now. I think people who yammer about Jesus Christ are nuts too. Fanatics."

"We're all crazy one way or another. Some just show it more. I wish Christians were really as fanatical about Jesus as you are about Bigfoot—and as focused."

The teakettle wasn't whistling. Actually, its whistle quit years ago. Now it sort of wheezed when it reached a boil. It wasn't quite wheezing yet either, but it was making enough sizzling noise that Jack could tell the water was hot. "Coffee or tea?"

"Coffee, black."

Jack got out the instant and built two mugs of coffee. He laced his generously with chemicals that kept it from staying black.

Eerie studied eternity out Jack's back window. "What kinds of monsters are in the Bible?"

"Depends which version."

"You mean there aren't any?"

"Behemoth and leviathan." Jack plunked Eerie's coffee down in front of him. "You see, the Hebrew Scriptures of two or three thousand years ago had some words for things that have since been lost. We can't tell anymore what some of them were. Besides, the environment then was a lot different. They had plants and animals then that aren't there anymore. Anyway, certain of those obscure words are translated in different ways in different versions. The people who put together the old King James Version gave it their best shot, but they just didn't know all the animals identified by ancient Hebrew names. They did remarkably well, actually, considering nobody in England knew about Holy Land animals. They came up with dragons, cockatrices, unicorns—which were real by hearsay to them then. No translation problems with stuff basic to the faith, though."

291

"What's a cockatrice?"

"It's half snake half rooster. If you look at it or if it breathes on you, you're supposed to die."

"Never heard of such a thing." Eerie cackled. "But my ex-brother-in-law had breath like that." Silence. "You said you begin and end with Jesus. Tell me about that."

The question caught Jack off guard. He didn't know quite how to respond. "You ever spend much time around cattle and sheep?"

"Not much." Eerie looked a bit non-plussed also.

"Sheep are stupid, especially compared to cows. Sheep'll nibble a pasture down to bare soil and then stand around starving. Cattle move on and find new pasture. Dogs attack sheep, and they'll mill in a tight flock. Shucks, even a blind dog can't help but catch one, they're all crowded together so much. Cattle scatter or counterattack. Sheep can't think independently. Cattle do. And on and on. Cowboys are an intrusion in range cattle's lives. The cows don't need men in order to survive. Sheep need a shepherd to get them out of scrapes, help them find food and water, everything. They can't function on their own and survive.

"We human beings like to think we're independent-minded cows and can get along just fine without help. We can't. We're sheep. We can't make it on our own. The Bible calls us the sheep of God's pasture. Jesus says He's the Good Shepherd. Not the Good Cowboy." Jack raised his hands. "When I blow it—when I'm not adequate, when I don't know what to do—the Good Shepherd steps in and takes care of me because I belong to Him. He's where my life starts and ends. I can't operate without Him."

"Where're you from?"

"Colorado when I was a kid, then New Mexico."

Eerie nodded. "Guess you do know cows. And you believe in a God."

"I believe God demands blood payment for wrong-doing. Life itself. I believe He let His own Son bleed and die for my evil acts and thoughts so that I won't have to. In other words, Jesus bought me with His own blood."

"Then you owe Him. He don't have to do a thing for you."

"Exactly. Fortunately, He loves me enough that He's willing to help me out."

"He's real." Eerie's eyes pierced into Jack's.

"He's real."

"Like Bigfoot."

"Realer than Bigfoot. And infinitely bigger."

Eerie's eyes were piercing the walls now, the mountain, the cosmos. He stared off into space. Jack let him have the time.

Eerie Elroy's voice purred low, thoughtfully, dreamily. "When you came and told me about my dog. Skidder was his name. Logging term. Don't mean much if you don't work in the woods. Skidder. You came and told me about Skidder, I was feeling low anyway. Couldn't say why. After you left I figured it out.

"Just before you came, I was talking to Jay about being druid, and what druids believe in. And his gods and like that, they're sort of like clouds—you think you see them, but you can't really point to anything solid."

"They're nebulous."

"That's the word exactly. Nebulous. I heard that word before, but I never would've thought of it. They're concepts. Whatever you happen to believe. And that don't make sense to me. I was frustrated 'cause I needed more than that, but I couldn't understand what was happening, you know?"

Jack didn't know, but he didn't think this was the time to say so. At least, not yet.

Eerie pursued his thought. "You're talking about someone solid."

"He's not physical. Was once, but He's not now."

"I don't mean that kind of solid. I mean definite. You know what you're dealing with. I want that."

293

Jack was going to respond, but he held his peace, because Eerie's mind seemed to have drifted off again. Jack reminded himself that this man didn't approach life the same way he did. He must adjust his speed and his desires to Eerie's pace.

Eerie seemed to snap back to the moment. "I was talking to that Barney you mentioned. Remember?"

"Uncle Barney with the Chevy Impala?"

"Yeah. Has that kid with him."

"Ernest."

"Yeah. They were over at Jay's a couple days ago working on the circle. Barney claims he wanted to get the kid a Christmas present, but he doesn't have any money because he has some deal and it hasn't gone through yet. Anyway, he talked about how he wasn't into these circles and stuff, he was a Christian. Baptized and everything. But I know better, Prester. The guy's the biggest crook in Pierce County. Know what his deal is? A hit. He's filling a contract. And with that he wants to get a kid a Christmas present. That's why I never trusted anybody before who says he's a Christian. They're all crazy, Christians. Hypocrites."

"Foof, Elroy. You're right. But non-Christians are every bit as hypocritical. They've got no reason to feel smug."

Eerie cackled. "Ain't it the truth!"

"Christmas presents are a part of celebrating Christmas. So here's Uncle Barney, you say, celebrating the birth of God's Son by committing murder so he can buy the present." Jack wagged his head. "You can't beat that with a stick!"

"He's a piece of work, all right."

"He sounds like a real fruitcake. He give you any hints who's the lucky target?"

"Naw. Something about the Getz murder, but he didn't say exactly. I think he's planning to do it with his bow. It's silent, and he's going to be doing it close to people's houses."

Jack's neck prickled. "His bow."

"You know, hunting bow. Compound bow. Lot of people go bow-hunting around here. Jay goes."

Jack forced a laugh and tried his best to make it sound spontaneous. "If he has to keep quiet, it's sure not you who's the target. Nobody'd notice gunfire at your place. He could use a howitzer, and nobody'd care."

Eerie cackled again, loud and long. "Wasn't me anyway. He has to go to Seattle for it."

It was time to pay a call on Uncle Barney. Way past time.

Eerie frowned suddenly. "What's 'Noel' mean, do you know? Something to do with Christmas, I know, but what exactly?"

"Exactly? It *is* Christmas. That's what it means. I think it also can mean songs about Christmas. Why?"

"That carol keeps running through my head. I can't shake it. You know: 'Thee-ee fir-irst No-oh-el, thee-ee angels did saaaaay . . .' All these people celebrating Christmas, but they don't even think about Jesus. Like Barney. He don't give it a thought. It's weird."

"It's sad."

"Yeah." Eerie studied Jack's face awhile. "What do I have to do to belong to Jesus, so He'll take care of me? This that born-again stuff?"

"Yep. But let me warn you—"

"I ain't going to go off the deep end with that stuff, am I? I don't want to go crazy fanatical."

"You're crazy anyway, everyone thinks. What've you got to lose?"

Eerie laughed uproariously.

Jack pressed on. "Let me warn you, though, that this is no guarantee that suddenly everything's going to go your way. He does what's best in the long run, not what you want right this moment." *Aloha, Hawaii.* "Know what I mean?"

"You can guarantee He does what's best though, right?"

295

"Right, because that's the way He is. But that's not why you commit yourself to Him. You believe in Him because He's the only one in the universe worthy of your devotion, whether He ever does anything for you or not."

"That's good enough for me."

An hour later, after Jack made a couple phone calls, they walked down to the Longmire Inn for coffee and doughnuts, to celebrate Eerie Elroy Washington's new life as a believer. His first real Christmas.

27

Lo, How a Rose
E'er Blooming

How far have we come?" Ev scrunched down in her seat and wadded herself into a tight little knot, shoulders hunched.

"About sixty miles, I'd guess. The odometer doesn't work." Jack exited 167 and tried to remember Jeff's directions exactly. Get off here, go left, then right, then left at the light up the Peasley Canyon hill to I-5.

"When Kerri warned us the heater doesn't work well, I thought she meant it worked a little. It doesn't work at all. I'm so cold I can't feel my toes."

"You're just sore because you had to be up and out at six this morning. You didn't have to come, you know." He pulled the VW into the left-turn lane. The gearshift trembled as the motor idled.

"If Elizabeth really is the target, I want to come."

"I'm guessing. Eerie said it was connected with the Getz case, and in Seattle. That's Elizabeth. Why it should be Elizabeth, I can't imagine."

"Why didn't he call the police when he found out about it?"

"He did. He said the way the girl on the phone sounded when she said they'd take care of it, he knew they didn't bother to believe him. He's pretty down on himself."

"I suppose he'd sound a little strange, not knowing any details. Vague."

"Vague. Yeah."

"But the police are there now, right?"

"They have her house under surveillance, right. If an Impala or that pickup shows up, we've got him. I talked to a lieutenant last night who seems to know what he's doing."

She lapsed into silence for long, long minutes. The Peasley Canyon road was a pleasant drive—traffic filled, but pretty. It dumped them out onto I-5, and they were on their way north toward Seattle. They and ten million other cars.

She stared absently straight ahead. "I sent you a Christmas present to your home. It's in Kansas waiting for you at the post office. I didn't realize we'd be together working on another case."

"I didn't know we would either. Didn't know you'd be here, I mean. I mailed yours from Hutchison as I left town." For a moment he pondered what had not been said, and what it might mean. "Darryl give you a Christmas gift?"

She nodded. "I haven't opened it yet, of course." She slipped back into silence. It felt almost like guilty silence. Then, "Jack? Did your dad ever get so mad he hauled off and struck your mom?"

He looked at her. "Never."

"Did he ever come close?"

"No."

"How about your mom? Did she ever haul off and belt your father?"

"No. She often claims she'd never consider divorce. Murder, yes, but not divorce. That's a standing joke though, not a threat. Why? Did yours?"

"No."

Jack waited for the next cue. There was none. She stared out the window at the near darkness. During the shortest days of the year the sun didn't come up until nearly

298

8:00, and today was overcast anyway. He reached out and tipped her face toward him. "Ev? Why?"

She glanced away. "I wondered, is all."

"So why did you wonder?"

"No particular reason. Forget it."

"No, I won't forget it. You don't ask a psychologist something like that and then dismiss it. You've been quiet as a mouse eating marshmallows, and it's not just because you're a Popsicle either. What's going on?"

She shook her head. Her hair lifted away in about six directions. "Maybe we'll talk about it later."

"Better, talk about it with Elizabeth. You and she seem to confide in each other comfortably." And Jack realized just then the reason she wanted to come this morning.

Her casual, offhand question troubled him. He might be able to force her into an explanation, but would that be appropriate? He wasn't sure. He'd get down deeper quicker if he let her open up on her own.

He patted his jacket pocket again, making sure it was there. Anne Somersby's recording gizmo. He'd been carrying it around, waiting for some time he'd be in Tacoma, or she'd come out to the park, and he could give it back to her. It was a nifty device. Voice activated, it came on and started recording whenever sound reached it. It recorded continuously. When it came to the end of its reel, it simply reversed and recorded back again. Jack calculated you could gather about an hour of material before it started re-recording over the front of the tape. You could turn it off at any time, to save what was on it.

"Lot of traffic," Ev commented.

A lot of traffic indeed. Merchants claim the day after Thanksgiving is their biggest single shopping day of the year. A zoo. Black Friday. And the day after Christmas, they say, is the next biggest. That surprised Jack—why then?—until he hit traffic in Seattle. Everyone in the city was out driving. More than that, they had to be importing cars from

Spokane to get this many vehicles. The little squareback crept at the pace of a millipede up toward the 45th Street exit and the U district.

Ev watched the twenty-mile-per-hour flow. "Are we going to park out in front of her house and wait?"

"Barney knows my pickup, but not this VW. He shouldn't recognize us easily in the car here. So we'll cruise the streets around her house first, looking for his Impala or red pickup."

"He's going to notice Maxx in back there, surely."

"Oh, yeah. Maybe we can disguise him as a Yorkshire terrier. A pair of Groucho glasses with a fake nose, moustache, and eyebrows. Something."

She shined his nonsense through with that little toss of the head she so often employed. "Jack? Why Elizabeth?"

"Maybe it isn't. This case is the worst muddle I've ever tackled. Nothing falls in line. Barney could have been boasting falsely to Eerie."

And then her pretty mouth opened, and her eyes widened out to Frisbee size. "When he was speeding through the park that night! That was when she was stabbed! He was coming away from the first attempt on her life!" Ev twisted to face him. "Jack? The contract's been out awhile. He was counting on Christmas money, but he got scared off from the first attack!"

Jack nodded. "Looks that way. He had the compound bow with him when he parked at the Clearcut, and I'm pretty sure he went directly there. We want to know who hired him. Who contracted the hit. We may have a finger on Getz's killer also, if we can demonstrate a connection between Elizabeth and Getz."

"She says she never met him."

"She wouldn't have to know him to form a connection. Let's say they're both involved in some crusade someone else wants to stop. Or both belong to some organization someone else is trying to harass or destroy. It's easily possible—they're both activists. Or both are friends with a

300

third party who will be the next target. Could be half a dozen ways."

Ev wagged her head. "Now I see why you think the case is such a muddle. Someone brings up a simple statement, and you come up with all these strange combinations. Barney killed John Getz. Another contract thing."

"Why with an obsidian blade, if his weapon of choice is bow and arrow?"

She threw up her hands, literally and figuratively, and transferred her attention to the world beyond the windshield.

Elizabeth's neighborhood, when they finally got there, seemed quiet and benign, with no hint whatever that death might lurk in some shadow. Jack tossed his Stetson in the backseat and told Maxx not to stomp on it. Maxx did anyway.

They drove up and down the surrounding back streets lined with cozy little dwellings and an occasional apartment complex or fourplex. They passed a small flower shop with roses in the window. Where did they get roses this time of year? They passed a tiny art theater. Twice.

No Impala. No red pickup with plywood bedsides.

Jack pulled into a narrow parking space on a corner —so narrow, in fact, that the front wheels lapped over into the red curb zone. From this spot he could just see the front porch of Elizabeth Munro's little brown house. It sat halfway down the block beyond the next cross-street downhill of the VW.

He leaned on the steering wheel to watch. "I didn't call Elizabeth last night. I told the Seattle police department about the situation and got a stakeout assigned. But Elizabeth doesn't know. We can't be certain her phone isn't tapped. You want to go pay her a call and tell her what's up?"

"Sure."

A florist's delivery truck momentarily obscured view of the house as it came out the side street below this one and turned left, south down the hill. The white truck had roses three feet high at least painted on its side. What if someone parked in the way between Jack and Elizabeth's while Ev was out there? He could be putting her in danger.

He brushed the thought aside. "It's the small brown house with yellow trim and the vertical front lawn down the way there."

"I see it." She unpopped her seat belt with difficulty—the latches were a little rusty—and paused. "Barney doesn't know me, does he?"

"I can't think why he would. Even if he does, he'd know you as Elizabeth's friend. You've been seen with her at the Clearcut and elsewhere. I don't foresee a problem."

"I don't either. But the way you twist things around, I was afraid you might."

"Want my revolver?"

"No. I'm fine." She hopped out and walked to the corner, looked both ways, and crossed. Jack watched her march down the street to the next corner, and beyond that to Elizabeth's house. He tried to pick out the cops' surveillance team, but he couldn't. Maybe they were in an upstairs window nearby. He saw nobody on the street, in vehicles or otherwise.

Maxx set up a deafening non-stop barrage of snarling and barking.

A voice behind Jack's driver's side door suggested, "Keep your hands on the wheel. Like to tell us what you're doing here?" It was not Barney's voice.

Ev was knocking at Elizabeth's door.

"Maxx, shut up! Quiet! I know they're here, both of them." Jack watched the police uniform approach in his sideview mirror. Out of the corner of his eye, he could see movement on the far side of the car—a second cop. "John Prester, law enforcement specialist with the National Park Service, working out of Mount Rainier National Park. I called a Lieutenant Hedegaard last night about putting surveillance on Elizabeth Munro's residence, that brown frame house down the street there. Now if you two are involved in that assignment, you've missed guessing the right vehicle by a mile. We're looking for an Impala or a red vintage pickup. This green VW ain't it, boys."

Ev stepped inside. The door closed.

The cop was using extra-polite speech in that maddening tone of voice that suggested you were pond scum unworthy of consideration, and therefore he was being sarcastic with his politeness. "ID, please. One hand."

Jack fumbled for his badge case as he watched the house. Anger was dancing cheek to cheek with fear. If Barney did a turn around the block before pausing at Elizabeth's—and any hit man worth his blood money ought to take at least that minimal amount of care—he would see these two cops and instantly and forever disappear into the mists of Bellevue.

On the other hand, Barney might be clear out of the state hitting some other target altogether, or maybe he was going to wait until tomorrow, or next week sometime, or maybe he had decided the contract wasn't worth the effort and reneged. Maybe Jack could sit here until the VW's tires rotted without ever seeing Barney again.

He cranked the window down—it took two hands, one to crank and one to shove on the top edge of the glass—and passed his ID out to the cop. It was fully light now, and half a dozen pedestrians were scurrying about, most of them college kids. Bicycles whipped by constantly.

"A little bit out of your jurisdiction, aren't you?" the cop asked, but at least his tone of voice wasn't quite so supercilious.

"Klondike National Historic Park is basically a storefront downtown near the regional office." From the periphery of his vision, Jack saw the officer handing his ID case back—but a foot away from that open window and the loud black Lab's toothy jaws. Jack chose to ignore it until the guy moved in closer. "I'm hoping and praying that if

303

our perp shows up, he'll run from here down to either Klondike or region where I can arrest him. Do you suppose he can find King Street while he's being pursued?"

"Probably not." The voice dripped acid. "Maybe you'd better go back to the park and wait for him to come to you."

"Maybe you ought to get out of the street so you don't scare him off if he does come by."

The floral delivery truck with the roses on it must have been trying to find an address the first time it rounded the block. Here it came again, westbound to the corner, turning left once more, heading down the hill.

It stopped in front of Elizabeth's house.

The deliveryman hopped out instantly, almost before the wheels quit rolling. Since when do delivery trucks carry both a driver and a legman? Since when does a delivery boy look and walk like Ernest, even from this distance?

"That's him!" Jack torched off the VW and pulled out around the corner as the cops yelled behind him.

The delivery boy rang the doorbell.

Jack slowed for the other cross-street.

The delivery boy, half buried in a huge floral arrangement, looked furtively, nervously, back toward the driver of the delivery truck. He glanced momentarily at Jack's VW and turned to face the door. It opened.

Their lights flashing, the cops were coming after Jack. Those bozos! The driver of the florist's truck didn't see them. He was obviously intent on other purposes, for the point of an arrow emerged from the side door of the truck. Ernest handed off the flowers as he stepped aside out of the doorway—way aside. Not only did whoever stood in the door present a clear target, they couldn't see the truck and the street because of the flowers.

Jack didn't waste time thinking. He plowed the VW into the back end of the florist's truck. The arrow, safely astray, zipped into the steeply sloped lawn and stuck there.

"Maxx! Take Ernest!" Jack leaped out of the car and

left the door open for the dog. Snarling and barking, Maxx boiled out so fast he almost knocked Jack down. Ernest took off like a catapult.

The florist's truck had hopped the curb and jammed into a tree. Barney Hall must have been knocked flat inside it, for the way he came tumbling out suggested he didn't leave the truck on his feet. Maxx tore up the grassy slope toward Ernest.

Barney was armed. He fired a fast wild one at Jack—it sounded like a .38—and ran down the hill toward the main drag, 45th. Jack would have liked to use the VW to go after him, but its nose end was mashed into the truck, metal into metal. It would take too long to free it up.

The cop car paused long enough for one of the officers to leap out. Siren howling, the vehicle lunged forward in hot pursuit of Barney. Jack was back in running shape after his two weeks of being out of condition. Was Barney? For the short haul, at least, it would seen so.

Barney ducked down an alley and clambered over a wooden fence. The cop car screeched to a halt and turned aside to go around. Jack went over the fence fifty feet behind the luckless archer.

Barney was staying away from places the cops' vehicle could reach. He zigzagged through Seattle's backyards. Jack was keeping up, but he couldn't close.

They popped out onto 45th from a narrow slot between two stores. Barney darted into the street, prompting a wild symphony of squealing tires and tooting horns. The Christmas spirit having been abandoned on December 26, drivers yelled epithets. Jack was amazed that the man made it across the street in one piece.

Jack was close enough behind that he could cross in the traffic pause Barney had created. Barney crossed another street exactly that same way. The desperate little man was courting disaster at every turn. Two more sirens howled upstreet. The cops had called for reinforcements.

Barney disappeared inside the big steel-and-glass

double doors of a store. The University of Washington bookstore. If there was any surroundings on earth where Barney Hall would look out of place, it was a university bookstore.

And then the chase turned ugly. A security guard, an older fellow, moved toward Barney. Barney fired at him. The man stopped, then dropped to his knees as the thunderous noise bounced and echoed off the ceiling like a cannon in a closet. A dozen women screamed.

Barney wheeled and sent three at Jack. Jack was already ducking down and aside behind a free-standing bookcase. He yanked his own weapon, but there wasn't a chance he could return fire. Not with all these people around.

Barney ran again, clattering down a staircase in the next room. Jack was a hundred feet behind now. He lost visual contact. The man could be waiting downstairs, his gun leveled on the staircase. Barney could pick him off with no trouble at all. Jack wheeled and sprinted back to the double doors.

Cops, one of them with a handy-talkie, entered as he was leaving. Even as they were telling him to freeze he managed to yell his own status as a cop. Did they believe him? They seemed to. At least they hesitated.

Jack snatched the handy-talkie out of the cop's hand. "This is John Prester, the officer pursuing Barney Hall. He ran downstairs in the U Dub bookstore. Blue jeans, black jacket, red baseball cap, .38 automatic. He's fired four so far."

Downstairs the gun went off. More screaming.

"Five." He handed the radio back and asked the guy, "What are the ways out?"

"I'm not sure." The fellow frowned at his partner.

The other shook his head. "This one and a service entrance. I think out back by the back parking lot."

Jack took off running again, out the doors and down the block.

There was no traffic moving, no pedestrians in sight,

and there went Barney at a run, angling across a street and down the hill. He was shooting to kill. He'd already taken out at least one security guard. Jack stopped long enough to do something he had never done before. He took aim at another human being. He must put Barney down before the fellow killed an innocent bystander.

Then a blonde girl appeared at the far end of the street beyond Barney, right in the line of fire. Jack swung his gun skyward and aborted the shot barely in time. He bolted forward. If he pressed Barney hard enough, maybe the man wouldn't be able to stop long enough to fire again.

Barney began to slow perceptibly as Jack got his second wind. Jack was running comfortably now. He was good for another five miles, and Barney would play out soon. Jack holstered his weapon and concentrated on running.

Barney made it across an intersection Jack had to pause at, as cars roared by too fast to duck between.

Jack caught the light right at the next one. At the bottom of this slope, the street crossed a broad stream or canal under an old iron bridge. He glimpsed the I-5 bridge to the right, arching high across the water, a hundred feet higher.

He heard sirens coming down the street behind him. Good! They could reach Barney faster than he could, even if they had to contend with the traffic.

Barney was headed straight for the bridge when he stopped suddenly in the midst of traffic. Cars screeched, swerved, smashed into one another. If that was intentional on Barney's part—and it certainly looked so—it was fiendishly clever. The pile-up froze in place every vehicle at this end of the bridge and effectively blocked all its lanes. The cop car wouldn't be coming after him now. Motorists approaching across the bridge from the other side slammed on brakes, and Jack heard a few bumpers meet violently.

Barney sprinted out onto the bridge and ran down

the vacant southbound lane. He was so winded now that he stumbled.

Jack could work his way around this stationary tangle of vehicles, or he could go up and over. He leaped onto the hood of a blue Toyota, jumped from there to the roof of a minivan, and bounced across the hoods of two other cars. He dropped down to the pavement and resumed running as Barney, almost halfway across the bridge, slowed to a rapid, staggering walk.

Barney turned suddenly and fired. The slug thunked into the metal of the stalled northbound car beside Jack. A couple of motorists screamed. Heads dropped below window level.

Jack bellied out on the pavement, propped low on his elbows, and took careful aim two-handed. The nerves in his hands vibrated, as much from the wild run as from tension. He had never tried to hurt another person, and he almost couldn't do it now. But Barney was past being a person of interest in an attempted murder by bow and arrow. Now he was a menace to any innocent citizen who chanced to be in the wrong place when he fired. He turned away just as Jack squeezed the trigger.

Jack's .38 bucked in his hands, and the roar deafened him. He missed with the first two, he was so nervous. With the third, Barney's right leg buckled, and he slammed sideways into a vertical support. His own gun went off twice but at nothing in particular. He twisted around and returned fire. Jack flattened out.

He heard cops yell and fire at both ends of the bridge. But they were far too far out of range to hit anything. Jack raised his head to aim again. Barney was squirming to his knees, gripping the pedestrian rail, hauling himself to his feet. He fired toward Jack again, but he was out of shells. And out of luck.

Jack yelled too late. Barney wormed up over the rail, paused a moment on his good leg as he gripped a turnbuckle, then disappeared over the side.

28
Away in a Manger

An iron bridge has got to be the noisiest piece of road in the world. It clanged and creaked and thundered overhead constantly as its traffic passed. Jack stood on a cement retaining wall almost directly underneath and watched skindivers drag Barney Hall's body ashore. A uniformed cop dropped a blue tarp over it. They wouldn't bag it, probably, until the medical examiner got there.

"Over there." Ev's familiar voice came from up on the bank by streetside. She worked her way down over the side with Maxx on leash. Beside her walked a middle-aged man with thinning hair and an authoritative air about him.

Jack hopped down off his vantage perch to join them.

"Jack Prester, Lt. Ron Hedegaard." Ev stopped, and Maxx sat down obediently at her knee.

Lieutenant Hedegaard accepted a handshake. "Evelyn says you're a criminal psychologist. I have a question. The young man named Ernest Mulrose wants very much to see his uncle. I don't know whether that's good or bad. Do you have any advice?"

Jack mulled it a moment. "I suggest you let him come down."

Hedegaard said, simply, "Yeah," into his handy-talkie.

Jack asked Ev, "How's Elizabeth doing?"

"All right."

"And you?"

"Fine. Here. Some policeman gave it to the lieutenant here, and he gave it to me." Ev handed Jack his badge case.

"Oh, yeah." But then Ernest captured Jack's attention. The boy's hands were cuffed behind him. Still, he managed to step and slide his way down the bank rather gracefully. Of course, he was used to cross-country in the mountains.

Jack excused himself and walked down to the blue tarp. He caught Ernest's eye and waited as the boy approached.

Ernest was trembling all over. "You killed him."

"I tried to, but I only got him in the leg. Bad aim. He jumped."

"Why did you try to? You bought him lunch."

"He tried to kill Miss Munro, he shot an unarmed security guard, and he—"

"Two guards," Hedegaard's voice behind him corrected.

"And he was firing indiscriminately. I wanted to stop him before he took out someone else."

Ernest studied him a moment with red, puffy eyes. He turned away and looked down at the blue tarp.

The cop in charge, watching Hedegaard for cues, apparently got the nod. He lifted the tarp away. Soaking in the Ship Canal for half an hour hadn't made Barney Hall the least bit prettier.

Jack hesitated, sifting options. How best could he reach this tortured young man?

Ev promptly stepped in where angels fear to tread. She murmured, "I'm so sorry, Ernest," and wrapped her arms around him in a strong, maternal hug.

The man in the man-child stood stalwart for a heartbeat or two. Then the child in the man-child broke loose in piteous sobbing as his fragile, insecure life fell apart. Ev gathered him close, sobbing herself, and they sat down on the bank together to vent the sorrow of the world. Maxx stood around at loose ends, appearing as uncomfortable as everyone else looked.

Like so many people, Lieutenant Hedegaard pictured the National Park Service and the United States Forest Service as being pretty much the same agency, all staffed with forest rangers whose patrols consisted mostly of weaving among large trees. Jack spent maybe five minutes explaining the difference between the Forest Service (Department of Agriculture) and the Park Service (Department of the Interior) and forest rangers (desk jockeys in ball caps) and park rangers (desk jockeys in flat hats). Complicating the picture was Smokey Bear, a Forest Service emblem dressed in a Park Service flat hat. It was all very complex.

Ernest Mulrose stood up, distraught and dejected, and stared at the uneven ground. Ev scrambled to her feet beside him.

"Ernest?" Jack asked. "Who hired your uncle for this job?"

"I don't know."

"There's no one to protect. You don't have to keep your mouth shut out of loyalty anymore."

"I don't know." His voice hung flat and listless on the clammy air. "He never said."

Jack watched Ev's puffy face a few moments and saw nothing helpful there. "Cheese? I know a guy in the sheriff's department who's a Christian. His name is Sargent Means. I'll ask him to try to find you a foster family so you won't have to live with Harry, all right? And let's see about getting you some training as an auto mechanic. You'd be a crackerjack mechanic."

Ernest looked Jack in the eye for the first time. "You remembered all that?"

Jack smiled. "Hey, I'm mostly doing it for myself. Good mechanics are hard to find."

The medical examiner arrived, so they led Ernest up

to the road. Jack gave Hedegaard Sgt. Sargent Means's number and suggested remanding Ernest to Remann Hall in Tacoma.

Jack and Ev took their time walking back to Elizabeth's. Ev was very quiet, and Jack couldn't help but draw a number of deductions. The only problem was, he couldn't prove anything. He couldn't build a solid chain of evidence. And he couldn't shake the sight of Barney Hall, once so swarthy, lying blue and pallid beneath that tarp.

The VW sat four inches closer to the ground than it had two hours before. Its front suspension would have to be completely rebuilt.

Elizabeth heard Jack mention a rental car and immediately insisted that they borrow hers. Ev tried to talk her out of offering a car to Jack, pointedly calling attention to his penchant for wrecking loaners. Elizabeth won. She promised to explore reasons why someone might want her dead, and Jack and Ev headed back to the park.

Halfway home, Jack let the Colonel fry chicken for their lunch while he made some phone calls. They were less than five minutes back on the road again when Ev turned on him. "Why are you so sullen? What's wrong?"

"You're not expecting an answer, are you? When I asked you that very question, you clammed up. Tit for tat."

"Tit for tat nothing. Why? Barney Hall? Or Ernest? They're attempted murderers, Jack. You couldn't have handled it any differently, and Elizabeth was right in the line of fire. You saved her."

"Tit for tat for sure. You tell me why you've been moping, and then maybe I'll tell you."

She cast a sideways glance at him and concentrated her attention out the windshield. "I'm afraid you'll get mad. I mean, really mad."

"Then you're probably right."

"Hal let slip why he's so anxious to clear this case, and why he was so antsy when we didn't have lots of goodies for him. I've known about it for a week."

312

Jack waited. "So?"

"Do you know a Doug Howell in the Washington office?"

"Casually. He heads up a special forces unit that moves in on big problems in parks. We're lower key than his outfit. We sort of deal with little problems, low profile. But they're similar."

"Right." Silence. She licked her lips. "I guess he and Hal have a wager with each other. A pretty serious one, although Hal downplayed it. He really got worried when you called in sick right at the beginning there. Apparently this Howell has his people working on some sort of murder-and-drug thing in Everglades, and Hal has us out here, and they have money riding on whose team scores first."

Jack gaped as fury boiled up so fiercely he could feel his neck turn hot. "You mean the only reason I missed out on Hawaii was to protect Hal's stupid side bet?"

Instantly the thought came to him *No, Doofus. You missed out on Hawaii so you could point Eerie Elroy Washington down the road to eternal life.* The thought did nothing, however, to bank the fire.

A bet. A lousy, stupid bet. Jack wanted to rip the wheel off and throw it out the window. A lousy bet.

Ev snapped, "Now it's your turn. You promised."

"I said maybe." He could feel her eyes boring into him. He could talk about never having opened fire on a human being before, and then his first time, and the horror of seeing the man die. But he didn't. He broached the other subject on his mind. "I think I may have the answer. Barney Hall worked for Jay Chambers."

"Jay . . ." She studied the windshield. "Why would he kill Getz?" Her face softened. "Of course. Your supplemental says he's worried about Getz causing a backlash. He might think Getz would make a better martyr than advocate."

"Exactly. Instead of hearing Getz's extremist message, everyone would feel sympathy for the cause. After all, someone died for it. Saving ancient trees is as much an obsession for Jay as Bigfoot is for Eerie. He's just less obvious about it."

"Like when that doctor in Florida was murdered by an antiabortionist, the abortion movement profited."

"Too, Jay wants increased access, and Getz wanted to restrict access. Jay might have considered Getz a dog in the manger that must be removed."

"What's a dog in the manger?"

"Old fable where a dog sits in a manger full of hay, barking and biting. He himself can't eat hay, and the manger is no use to him. Still, he chases away the cattle who can eat the hay and who need it."

"I see." She trotted off along the same line of argument. "If he found out Getz tried to hire someone to cut down those ancient trees, like the Grandfather Cedar, he could. Possibly. To save the trees. With Getz gone, no one would do it. Maybe even a druidic sacrifice, you think? I mean—he did kill Getz and spill the blood at the cedar."

"Maybe. I can't find anything on current druidic practices."

"He knows knives, so he'd use one that can't be traced. He knows anatomy, your report says, and the wounds were surgically placed. He had opportunity. Why, I bet he snitched Elizabeth's sunglasses, and when she missed them, used the excuse to go get Getz. He knew she wouldn't walk back up the mountain with him to find them, and that would leave him free to go kill. Means, motive, and opportunity." She bobbed her head. "That's all three."

"This isn't overt in the reports, though you can dig it out. Toward me, he behaved as if Bigfoot exists—talking about ley lines and Tsiatko, an Indian legend. For Elroy, he maintains a demeanor that he doesn't believe in such things. That proves nothing, but it's a curious inconsistency. At the very least, it demonstrates that he holds no regard for the truth."

"How are you going to approach it?"

"I'm not sure. Item one is a warrant to search his knife collection for an obsidian blade. It's one of the phone calls I made at the Colonel's."

"What was the other?"

"I left a message for Darryl. I want his help finding Jay's place. Apparently it's way out in the woods." And he stopped speaking because he could feel the glacier seated at his side. "Why did you just freeze up?"

"It was that obvious?" She shrugged. "Darryl and I haven't been seeing eye to eye. I wish you'd called Elroy or someone."

"Elroy is too close to Jay."

"Then why would someone try to kill Elroy that night when you got run over? And Elizabeth?"

"That bothers me. I don't know. In Elroy's case, it could simply be some drunken ex-friends going overboard. Drunks do things like that. But Elizabeth. Why would he put out a contract on Elizabeth?"

She twisted to face him. "I talked to Elizabeth the whole time you were chasing Barney. Maxx caught Ernest right away, incidentally. And I'm glad you didn't send Maxx after Barney. Not if Barney was shooting at everything in sight."

"Yeah. Maxx would've gotten a bullet in the chops for sure."

In the backseat, Maxx heard his name and thrust his head into the space between them. He belched delicately as Jack absently scratched his ears.

Ev reached out and scratched him too. "Anyway, she can't think of any reason anyone would try to do her in. I started with the most obvious: relatives, animosity in her home, legacies or wills, anything like that. Nothing. Then her circle of friends. Then business associates. Maybe someone angry because she was dunning them at work. Nothing. Certainly nothing she came up with about Jay or anyone in the park."

Jack nodded. "At best, Jay is a person of interest. We

315

have nothing solid enough to call him a suspect. How about, Darryl and I will go find him, and you get on the phone and fax. Send Hal what we have, get some search warrants, and we'll go over Eerie's place, Jay's, and Barney's apartment in Eatonville."

She nodded.

Now was the time for the other question. "Why did you ask whether my parents ever struck each other?"

She chewed on her lip a moment. "That's what the problem is, Darryl and me. We got into a minor argument, and he almost hit me."

"Darryl?"

"Right away he got all apologetic and promised it would never happen again, but it made me uneasy. Anyway, I've been backing off a little, you might say. Some breathing space."

Jack grimaced. "Good instincts, Ev. When you first start going together, you're both on your best behavior. If something like that happens during early courtship, you can bet the ranch it will be worse later."

"What do you mean, courting? We're not courting. It's not that serious."

"You know what I mean."

Darryl almost hit her? If anyone understood the pressures that plagued Darryl Grade, Jack did. They shared practically the same circumstances. Jack empathized with Darryl's loneliness, and sorrow, and alienation, especially during the holiday season. He could appreciate that Darryl might crack a little. He was immensely disappointed that Darryl would crack in that direction, toward an innocent woman.

And he still felt uneasy about implicating Jay Chambers. It was nice to have a possible suspect on the carpet, but too many questions remained unanswered.

29

O Come, All Ye Faithful

The collection of ruts leading to Eerie Elroy's house was a freeway compared to the track up to Jay Chambers's place. Jay's lane would give a goat pause. It sloshed through a swamp at the bottom of a hill, ground up a steep slope, squeezed between two massive Douglas firs, and stopped in a mudhole beside the back door.

Jack was going to be three days chipping the dirt off Elizabeth's car before he returned it to her. Fortunately, it hadn't snowed this low yet, or he might not have made it up the hill, even with his four-wheel drive.

"Now I know why Jay drives a Jeep." Jack turned off the motor and listened a moment to the dead silence. "You don't bring your hearse up here, do you?"

"Naw. It's too heavy to push when it gets bogged at the bottom of the hill. You should've seen his road before he improved it." Eerie Elroy climbed out and walked to the door of a two-story A-frame. He knocked loudly. "Doesn't look like anyone's home."

Jack crossed through the mud, Maxx at heel. He knocked again. "Sure glad you were around to help me find this place. I was going to ask Darryl, but he must be out of town."

"Happy to come." And indeed, Eerie seemed a much

317

happier man today. A merry twinkle had replaced the list-lessness in his watery eyes. He walked across the yard to a rusty old burn barrel, extracted a key from underneath it, and unlocked the door.

They stepped inside.

The place was much too neat and orderly for a bachelor pad. Jay was one of those "a place for everything and everything in its place" people. The living room extended floor to roof beams, two stories deep. The upstairs rooms, directly above the kitchen, opened onto a balustrade overlooking the living room. A picture window six feet wide ran up the center of the great A-shaped living room wall, from bottom to top. And on the walls to either side of the window hung Jay's weapons collection. Battle-axes, swords, lances, knives, and a couple of crossbows covered nearly every square foot.

Jack pointed. "One's missing. Blank space there."

"I didn't see that. You're right. One of his crossbows."

"Not his pride and joy."

"No. That's up there." Eerie pointed to one high on the wall. "A modern one's gone."

The message light was blinking on Jay's answering machine. Jack paused to figure out how to work it and punched a button.

"Cute message. This is Monica, Jay. Sue hasn't seen the minutes of the last Friends meeting. Will you send them to her? Thanks."

"Jay? This is Bobby and it's—uh—one P.M. Uh, Janet says you're up in the park with Darryl. Call me when you get back down. I have those stats you want for your presentation next Monday. Enjoy the mountain." *Beep*.

Eerie nodded. "That's where he is, then. You can prob'ly find the mountain if you grope around in the clouds long enough, suppose?"

"Sure. I'll just tell Maxx to sniff it out. 'Find that mountain.' He'll lead me right to it, I bet."

318

Eerie bobbed his head. "Good. You know what Boxing Day is?"

"Today. The day after Christmas."

"I was down at the store this morning and happened to bump into the girl who works at the coffee shop. She's from England. And she's a Christian. I didn't know that. She invited me to help them celebrate Boxing Day, so I figured, why not?"

"Sounds great. Wish I weren't working." Jack smiled on the inside, but he didn't let it show on the outside. So Eerie was making some new friends already, friends among the faithful. God works fast when He wants to.

They closed the door behind them, replaced the key, and negotiated that execrable lane back to a welcome dirt freeway and on to civilization. With thanks, Jack let Eerie out at his hearse in the Ashford coffee shop parking lot and drove up to the park.

This was a big mountain. And Jay Chambers could be anywhere on it. Jack really ought to simply stake out the entrance to Jay's road and wait for the man. Barring that, he could radio the patrol rangers and ask them to locate the Jeep for him. It'd take half an hour at most. Or he could just go home and start looking for Jay tomorrow. On impulse he drove through Longmire and up the hill to Reflection Lake. An impulse destination. Why was he driving around blind?

Because he needed time to think. Chugging up the hill at twenty miles per hour behind a motor home gave him plenty of time to think.

The brown Cherokee sat in eight inches of snow at the far end of the Reflection Lake lot, Jay's customary parking place. This time, Jack enjoyed an advantage. New snow provided perfect tracking. With ease, he picked out Jay's boot marks and Darryl's as they left the Cherokee. For extra insurance—belt and suspenders, if you will—Jack ordered, "Maxx. Find Jay."

Maxx, bless his heart, did his level best. Snuffling

and snorting, he hopped over the stone wall to the trail and headed up around the lake. As soon as they were out of sight of the parking lot, Jack pocketed the leash, letting the dog range free.

The perpetually cloudy weather seemed to be clearing, the milky sky getting lighter. Or was it just his imagination and his yearning for the clear blue winter days of New Mexico? The smell of fir trees brought back to vivid memory that hallucination.

The footprints angled northwest and disappeared beneath the trees. Thick branches overhead had captured the snowfall, leaving the ground beneath virtually bare. Jack was going to have to depend upon his dog's nose, never a dependable option.

Suddenly Maxx stopped, tipped his nose high, and sniffed. With an enthusiastic bark he left the trail and took off cross-country, northeast. Jack yelled at him. Max paid no attention. How come this mutt behaved so much better for Ev? For anyone else? Jack ran after him.

Up ahead, Jay Chambers's distinctive voice cried out, "No! Please!"

Jack burst out through a thicket into a small glade and skidded to a halt.

Maxx had stopped too. His bulky tail flailed a couple of times, uncertain, for he had just found Jay Chambers. The man's body twitched in its death throes at the feet of Darryl Grade.

Darryl swung up a stubby crossbow, aimed it right at Jack's gut. He had nocked a bolt—a short, blade-tipped arrow. A similar bolt protruded from Chambers's chest. "Jack. Sorry to see you."

"The feeling's mutual. Maxx. Heel." As he marshaled his thoughts, he watched the dog come trotting around to settle at his left knee. "I see Jay figured out who killed John Getz."

"Yeah. And so did you."

"Just now."

Darryl dipped his head toward the lifeless form at his feet. "He claimed he didn't move the body, but I know better. Jay had a bad habit of saying whatever he thought was convenient at the moment. You couldn't trust anything he said."

"I got that impression too. But I think he was telling the truth. He didn't."

"He and Elizabeth did, from the cedar out to the trail."

"No." Jack's mind raced from thought to thought seeking any way to get that crossbow pointed in some other direction. Nothing came to mind. "I've read Getz's journals. He used blackmail as one of his many tools, but he didn't limit it to fact. With Kerri Haskell, he threatened to spread false rumors about her. Her marriage is shaky anyway—it could have ruined her life. He apparently held things over Jay's head. But you—he had solid evidence against you. His blackmail to manipulate you was valid. You killed Margaret and set it up to look like an interrupted burglary."

"You're guessing."

How many rounds did Darryl have, anyway? Jack saw the fletches of two more bolts sticking out of the quiver permanently attached to the underside of the bow. One in the bow and two in reserve.

"No, I'm not. You had perpetrated the perfect murder, that of your own wife. Now here was Getz, threatening to send you to jail with his evidence. You planned carefully. Jay told you he was going to hike out and measure the Grandfather Cedar on Sunday the second. You devised an elaborate plan. You would lure Getz to the Grandfather Cedar and kill him there. Also, you would precipitate a rockslide that day, Sunday the second, that would place you up here on the Stevens Canyon Road. Jay would know about it because he monitored the park radio.

"Jay would go back to the tree, find Getz, and come out and notify the road crew, who would happen to be working conveniently nearby. But Elizabeth asked Jay to investigate an alternate trail that day, so he postponed his walk to the cedar until the next week. He went with her instead. How am I doing so far?"

Darryl smiled bitterly. "Right on. They must have seen me go back there with Getz. That's the only reason they'd know about him. They saw what I did. To let me know they knew, they brought the body out to the trail and claimed to find it there. It was their way of telling me they knew."

"So you followed us when Elizabeth and Jay were with me on the nineteenth, and tried to stab her when you thought you had the chance. Maxx scared you off, but you weren't worried—you had already hired Barney to kill her. He was planning to, Darryl—that same day, in fact. He went up there with his compound bow. Then he saw cop cars and beat it out of there."

"You don't know any of that."

Jack grimaced. "Sorry, Darryl, but I do. At the site where Elizabeth was attacked, the next morning when you and I returned there I asked Maxx to find. He kept coming back to you. He knew whom he was smelling, who had been there. But I was too dense to pick up on it. Why did you kill Margaret? Insurance? I know there was quite a bit, but not a fortune."

"I got mad. A little out of control. I really blew, Jack. She was unfaithful. She said she was going to leave me."

"She was tired of being slapped around."

Darryl's mouth dropped open. "How did you know? I never told anyone. I didn't think she did either. Or about her infidelity."

Ev gave me that without realizing it, when she told me about the rift between you two, but I'm not going to mention her name. We keep her out of this in case you kill me. "But you were true to your wife?"

"Well, actually, I wasn't faithful either. Before or after. Ev thinks she's my first real love since then. I kind of regret leading her on that way, but it looks better. You know?"

Jack pressed on. "Margaret was heat of the moment, but Getz was cold blood. You were a paramedic—you know anatomy. You used a weapon that would confuse everybody—an obsidian knife—and used it expertly. But why did you make that attempt on Eerie Elroy? And with Haskell's Silverado, for pete sake?"

"The Silverado's big, and it was handy. And easy to hotwire. I didn't think Elroy would come up into the park. That surprised me. You know why Getz wanted all the trails ripped out, don't you?"

"A Bigfoot preserve. He saw the beast, same as Elroy."

"That's right."

"And in his journals he referred to Bigfoot sightings as 'Barney.' 'Saw Barney today.'"

"You're sharp, Jack. Yeah. Mount Rainier's never been logged. It's almost all ancient, all old growth. Bigfoot prefers old growth." His voice softened. "Getz claimed he had my knife, the one I used on Margaret. I went over his office with a metal detector. It's not there. He didn't have a safe deposit box or anything. Apparently he was lying. Still, he claimed he found it down along the river, exactly at the spot where I threw it. And he described it exactly. I was sure he had it."

"And you erased his hard drive, in case he had mentioned its location."

"Yeah. Leave it to Ev to find the backups. She's one smart lady."

And Jack saw a way to turn that bow aside. "In one of his entries, Getz mentioned hard evidence against you as being at the feet of Old Grandpa. I'd guess that was his cryptic, poetic way of saying he buried the knife right around here close. Near the cedar. Bet we could find it if we dug for it."

"Later."

OK, so the ploy didn't work. "You still didn't say why you tried to get Elroy."

"He and Jay were close. Jay confided too much in him. Elroy was faithful to the cause, you might say. He was going to end up being a druid sooner or later. But then they started to drift apart. Elroy soured on the faith. He's vindictive. He was going to spill stuff. Somersby is sniffing around looking for just that kind of thing. And part of that stuff was my secrets. After I ran him off the road, and he didn't come after me, I began to think he didn't realize it was me. He's the kind of person who shows up on your doorstep to avenge wrongs in person, and he didn't show up on mine."

"Why didn't you take the Silverado out through the gate and escape down Skate Creek?" Jack laid a hand on Maxx's head. The dog was getting nervous.

"It would be too easy for you to radio Lewis County and have them waiting for me at the other end. Besides, having a key to the gate would give me away. It didn't occur to me Mike might arrest Haskell. I should've. Then they'd say it was Haskell for sure, since he has a key too."

"OK, Darryl, you killed your wife in the heat of an argument. Manslaughter. Had you left it at that and been found out, you'd do a few years. Killing Getz, killing Jay . . ." Jack wagged his head.

"He and Elizabeth should never have moved the body out to the trail. They were goading me. Taunting me."

"Then who moved Eerie's dog?"

"What?"

"The area right around here, the general vicinity of the Grandfather Cedar. Eerie's dog was killed near here —and moved. Getz was killed near here—and moved. But not by Elizabeth or Jay. I think Bigfoot really does exist. I think, for some reason, this is an area a Bigfoot doesn't want people to enter. Maybe a nursery, with young nearby. Something. And I think the thing's intelligent enough to know that if a body's found here, people will come swarming. What's your conclusion?"

Darryl stared at Jack a moment and began to glance about nervously. The bolt tip wavered. It wasn't the best of chances to take, but it would have to do. Jack dived to the ground, reaching for his gun as he moved.

The bolt swished. It cut in so cleanly it left behind almost no pain. Jack didn't realize he'd been hit until he tried to raise his right arm, gun in hand, and it got hung up in the bolt that protruded from his ribs.

Maxx roared as Jack tried to get his gun swung around in front for a clean shot. He was rapidly losing coordination. Grass and leaves and loose snow flew. Thirty feet away, the dog yelped in pain.

Jack managed to fill his hands with his gun. He twisted around and squeezed a couple off at the blur that was Darryl, moving swiftly into the trees. The gun clicked, empty. He hadn't reloaded it since the last time he shot at a fleeing man. He dropped the gun as he struggled to his feet. He'd spin out if he wasn't careful, but he couldn't just lie there and wait for Darryl to nock another bolt. Where was Maxx?

In the thicket ahead, brush rattled. Maxx snarled. Jack charged forward recklessly into the trees. For Maxx's sake as well as his own, he had to keep Darryl running, keep the man moving too fast to reload his crossbow, turn, and aim well. The forest crashed and crunched as Darryl made good his escape.

But he wasn't making a clean escape. Jack remembered just then, inanely, that Anne Somersby's voice-activated recorder was still in his pocket. Still recording every sound. He fumbled, getting it out, and turned off the switch to preserve the tape that was Darryl Grade's confession.

Up ahead, Darryl cried out. He screamed again, louder. Jack could hear the swish of a bolt. Darryl had shot Maxx! And now he was beating his way through the undergrowth, running down the mountainside.

But no. Here came Maxx, literally flying through the air straight at him. Jack ducked aside as the dog slammed heavily into the duff and thin, crusted snow, two feet behind him. Jack stepped on a stick. Not a stick. It was the crossbow at his feet. Why would Darryl drop the crossbow, and a bolt still available in the quiver?

He was losing blood by the gallon. He didn't dare pull the bolt in his side—he'd only bleed worse. On the verge of throwing up, he was too shocked and light-headed now to function well or think straight. Darryl could come up behind him, and he wouldn't know—wouldn't see.

Then the darkness directly ahead of him rose up, expanded, filled the forest. A familiar stench assaulted his nostrils. And he saw that he wasn't the only one bleeding. A bolt lodged in the chest of the Bigfoot ten feet in front of him. Shiny blood matted the reddish brown hair all the way down its breast.

Jack grabbed the crossbow and nocked the last remaining bolt as the monster snatched up a boulder the size of a washbasket. The brute stood wavering, the boulder poised high above its head. Fumbling, trying to hurry, Jack armed the crossbow, the bolt ready.

He held the tiny, crackling black eyes, and they held his. And in those glittering eyes he thought he saw mirrored his own feelings—intense fear, but not fury. An overriding instinct for self-preservation, but not vindictiveness. Or was his own weakness playing hideous tricks on him?

"No!" His voice burst forth so loud he surprised himself. "No. You're not the enemy. You never were."

Slowly, cautiously, he lowered the bow, eased it down, unnocked the bolt. He slung the weapon over his shoulder and with both hands held that last bolt high, between his eyes and the creature's. Deliberately he snapped it in two and dropped it. He watched a moment longer, waiting, looking into those anthracite eyes.

"Maxx. Heel." He turned away from the stinking creature, exposing the back of his skull to a blow from that rock if the creature really wanted to do him in.

Somewhat unsteadily, Maxx fell in beside. Together, Maxx and Jack began the long walk out to the trail, and down to the road, and off the mountain to civilization.